DORCHESTER TERRACE

Anne Perry

headline

First published in Great Britain in 2011 by
HEADLINE PUBLISHING GROUP

First published in paperback in Great Britain in 2012 by
HEADLINE PUBLISHING GROUP

6

Cataloguing in Publication Data is available from the British Library

ISBN 978 0 7553 8617 8 (B-format)
ISBN 978 0 7553 8623 9 (A-format)

Typeset in Plantin by Palimpsest Book Production Limited,
Falkirk, Stirlingshire

Printed and bound by CPI Group (UK) Ltd,
Croydon CR0 4YY

Headline's policy is to use papers that are natural, renewable and recyclable
products and made from wood grown in sustainable forests. The logging
and manufacturing processes are expected to conform to the environmental
regulations of the country of origin.

HEADLINE PUBLISHING GROUP
An Hachette UK Company
338 Euston Road
London NW1 3BH

www.headline.co.uk
www.hachette.co.uk

to Donald Maass
and Lisa Rector-Maass
for their friendship and help over the years

Chapter One

It was mid-February and growing dark outside. Pitt stood up from his desk and walked over to turn the gas up on the wall lamps one by one. He was becoming used to this office, even if he was not yet comfortable in it. In his mind it still belonged to Victor Narraway.

When he turned back to this desk he half expected to see the pencil drawings of bare trees that Narraway had had on the walls, instead of his own watercolours of sky and seascapes that Charlotte had given him. His books were not so different from Narraway's. There was less poetry, fewer classics perhaps, but similar books on history, politics and law.

Narraway had taken with him the silver-framed picture of his mother. Today Pitt had finally put in its place his favourite photograph of his wife, Charlotte, smiling. Beside her were thirteen-year-old Jemima, looking very grown up, and ten-year-old Daniel, who still had the soft face of a child.

After the fiasco in Ireland at the end of last year, 1895, Narraway had been exonerated, of course – he was guilty of nothing – but he had not been reinstated as Head of Special Branch. Instead, Pitt's temporary status had been confirmed.

Even though that had happened several months ago now, he found it hard to get used to. He knew very well that the men who had been his superiors, then his equals, and now his juniors, also found the new situation difficult at best. Rank, of itself, meant little. It commanded obedience, but not loyalty.

So far they had obeyed him without question. But he had had several months of very predictable events to deal with. There had been only the usual rumblings of discontent in the huge immigrant populations, particularly here in London, but no crises, none of the difficult decisions that endangered lives and tested the judgement. Then, he suspected, he might find the trust in him strained, even to breaking.

He remained at the window staring out at the pattern of rooftops opposite and the elegant wall of the nearby building. He could still discern their familiar outlines in the fading light. The bright gleam of streetlamps was increasing in all directions.

He could remember Narraway's grave face, tired, more deeply lined after his difficult escape from total disgrace, and perhaps from the emotional toll of his experiences in Ireland. Pitt knew also of Narraway's acceptance at last of his feelings for Charlotte, but as always, his coal-black eyes had given little away.

'You will make mistakes,' he had said to Pitt in the quietness of this room, with its view of sky and rooftops. 'You will hesitate to act when you know you will hurt people, even destroy them. Do not hesitate too long. You will misjudge people; you've always thought better of your social superiors than you should have. For God's sake, Pitt, rely on your instinct. Sometimes the results will be serious. Live with it. The measure of your worth is that you make few errors, and that from each one you learn something. You cannot opt out; that would be the worst mistake of all.' His face had been grim, shadowed with memories. 'It is not only the decision you make that counts, but that you make it at the right moment. Anything that threatens the peace and safety of Britain can come into your jurisdiction.'

Narraway had not added 'God help you', though he might as well have. Then a dry humour had softened his eyes for a moment, and a flicker of both compassion for the burden that lay ahead, and envy, regret for the excitement lost, the pounding of the blood and the fire of the mind that he had been forced to give up.

Of course, Pitt had seen him since then, but briefly. There had been social events here and there, conversations that were polite, but devoid of meaning beyond the courtesies. The questions as to how each of them was learning to bend, to adapt and to alter his stride to a new role remained unspoken.

Pitt sat down again at his desk and turned his attention to the papers in front of him.

There was a brief knock on the door, and when he answered, it opened and Stoker came in. Thanks to the Irish episode, he was the one man in the Branch that Pitt knew for certain he could trust.

'Yes?' he said as Stoker came to stand in front of Pitt's desk. He looked worried and uncomfortable, his lean face more expressive than usual.

'Got a report in from Hutchins in Dover, sir. Seen one or two unusual people coming over on the ferry. Troublemakers. Not the usual sort of political talkers – more like the ones that really do things. He's pretty sure at least one of them was involved in the murder of the French Prime Minister the year before last.'

Pitt felt a knot tighten in his stomach. No wonder Stoker was worried. 'Tell him to do all he can to be absolutely sure,'

3

he replied. 'Send Barker down as well. Watch the trains. We need to know if any of them come up to London, and who they contact.'

'May be nothing,' Stoker said without conviction. 'Hutchins is a bit jumpy.'

Pitt drew in his breath to say that it was Hutchins's job to be overcautious, then changed his mind. Stoker knew that as well as he did. He was explaining too much. 'Just keep a watch on him. We've enough men in Dover to do that, with Barker. Keep us informed.'

'Yes, sir.'

'Thank you.'

Stoker turned and left. Pitt sat without moving for a moment or two. If it really was one of the French Prime Minister's assassins, would the French police or secret service get in touch with him? Would they want his help, or prefer to deal with the man themselves? They might hope to get information about other anarchists from him. Or on the other hand, they might simply contrive for him to meet with an accident, and the whole matter never reach the public eye. In which case it would be better if the British Special Branch affected not to be aware either. It would be a decision to be made later whether they had a private word with Paris after the event, or not. It was the type of decision Narraway had referred to: a grey area, fraught with moral difficulties.

Pitt bent back to the papers he had been reading.

There was a reception that evening. A hundred or so people of social and political importance would be gathered, ostensibly to hear the latest violin prodigy playing a selection of chamber pieces. In truth it would be to manipulate and observe the shifts in power, and to exchange the subtler information that could not be shared in the more rigid settings of an office.

Pitt walked in through the front door of his house in Keppel Street just after seven o'clock. He found himself smiling at the immediate warmth, after the bitter wind outside. The familiar smells of baked bread and clean cotton drifted from the kitchen at the far end of the passage. Charlotte would be upstairs preparing for the occasion. She was not yet used to being back in the society to which she was born, with its glamour and rivalry. She had found it shallow then, until it was out of her reach. Now he knew, although she had never said so, that at times she had missed the colour and the wit, the breath of challenge, however superficial.

Minnie Maude was in the kitchen preparing Welsh rarebit for him, in case the refreshments at the event were meagre. Her hair was flying out of its pins as usual, her face flushed with exertion, and perhaps a certain excitement. She swung around from the big stove as soon as she heard his footsteps.

'Oh, Mr Pitt, sir, 'ave yer seen Mrs Pitt? She looks a proper treat, she does. I never seen anyone look so . . .' She was lost for words, and held out the plate of hot savoury cheese on toast in front of her. Then realising the need for haste, she put it on the kitchen table, and fetched him a knife and fork. 'I'll get yer a nice cup o' tea,' she added. 'Kettle's boiled.'

'Thank you,' he said, hiding at least part of his amusement. Minnie Maude Mudway had replaced Gracie Phipps, the maid who had been with the Pitts almost since they were married. He was still not entirely used to the change. But Gracie had her own home now, and he was happy for her. Minnie Maude had taken her place, on Gracie's recommendation. It was working out very satisfactorily, even if he missed Gracie's forthright comments on what she knew of his cases, and her loyal and highly independent support.

He ate in silence, and considerable appreciation. Minnie Maude was rapidly becoming a good cook. With a more generous budget at her disposal than Gracie had ever had, she was experimenting – on the whole with great success.

He noticed that she had made enough for herself also, although a much smaller portion. However, she seemed unwilling to eat it in front of him.

'Please don't wait,' he said, gesturing towards the saucepan on the stove. 'Have it while it's hot.'

She gave an uncertain smile and seemed about to argue, then changed her mind and served it. Almost at once something else took her attention and she started putting clean dishes away on the Welsh dresser, still without eating. Pitt decided to speak to Charlotte; suggest that she say something to make Minnie Maude feel more comfortable. It was absurd for her to feel she could not eat at the kitchen table just because he was there. Now that she had taken Gracie's place, this was her home.

When he had finished his tea he thanked her and went upstairs to wash, shave and change.

In the bedroom he found Jemima as well as Charlotte. The girl was regarding her mother with careful appreciation. Pitt was startled to see that Jemima had her long hair up in pins, as if she were grown up. He felt proud, and at the same time, a pang of loss.

'It's wonderful, Mama, but you are still a little pale,' Jemima said candidly, reaching forward to straighten the burgundy-coloured silk of Charlotte's gown. Then she gave Pitt a flashing smile. 'Hello, Papa. You're just in time to be fashionably late. You must do it. It's the thing, you know.'

'Yes, I do know,' he agreed, then turned to look at Charlotte. Minnie Maude was right, but he was still a little surprised at how lovely she was. It was more than the excitement in her face, or the warmth in her eyes. Maturity became her. She had an assurance now at almost forty that she had not found when she was younger. It gave her a grace that was deeper than the mere charm that colouring or feature lent.

'Your clothes are laid out for you,' she said in answer to his glance. 'Fashionably late is one thing; looking as if you mistook the arrangements, or got lost, is another.'

He smiled, and did not bother to answer. He understood her nervousness. He was trying to counter his own sense of suddenly being in a social position he was not born to. His new situation was in nature subtly quite different from being a senior policeman, who was still eventually answerable to others. Now he was the Head of Special Branch and, except in the most major of cases, his own master. There was no one with whom to share the power of his knowledge, or the responsibility.

Pitt was even more aware of the change in his circumstances as he alighted from the hansom and held out his arm for Charlotte, steadying her for an instant as she stepped down. The night air was bitterly cold, stinging her face. Ice gleamed on the road and he was careful not to slip as he guided Charlotte over to the pavement.

A coach with four horses pulled up a little ahead, a coat of arms painted on the door. A liveried footman stepped down off the box to open the door. The horses' breath was visible and the brass on their harnesses winked in the light as they shifted weight.

Another coach passed by, the sound of iron-shod hoofs sharp on the stones.

Charlotte gripped his arm tightly, though it was not in fear that she might slip. She wanted only a bit of reassurance, a moment of gathering strength before they ventured in. He smiled in the dark and reached over with his other hand to touch hers for an instant.

The large front doors opened before them. A liveried

footman took Pitt's card and conducted them to the main hall where the reception had already begun.

The room was magnificent. Columns and pilasters at the sides gave it an illusion of even greater height stretching up to the painted ceiling. It was lit by four massive, dazzling chandeliers hanging on chains that seemed to be gold, although of course they could not have been.

'Are you sure we're in the right place?' Pitt whispered to Charlotte.

She turned to him with a wide-eyed look of alarm, then saw that he was deliberately teasing her. He was nervous. But he was also proud that this time she was here because *he* was invited, not her sister, Emily, or her aunt, Lady Vespasia Cumming-Gould. It was a small thing to give her, after all the years of humble living, but it pleased him.

Charlotte smiled and held her head a little higher, before sailing down the small flight of steps to join the crowd. Within moments they were surrounded by a swirl of colour and voices, muted laughter, and the clink of glasses.

The conversation was polite and most of it meaningless, simply a way for the company to take stock of each other while not seeming to do so. Charlotte appeared perfectly at ease as they spoke to one group, then another. Pitt watched her with admiration as she smiled at everyone, affected interest, passed subtle compliments. There was an art to it he was not yet ready to emulate. He was afraid he would end up looking as if he were trying to copy those born to this social station, and they would not ever forget that.

Some junior minister in government spoke to him casually. He could not remember the man's name, but he listened as if he were interested. Someone else joined in and the discussion became more serious. He made the odd remark, but mostly he watched.

Pitt noticed a difference in how people behaved towards him from even a few months ago, although not everyone knew who he was yet. He was pleased to be quite casually drawn into another conversation, and saw Charlotte smile to herself, and then turn to a rather large lady in green and listen to her with charming attention.

'. . . Complete ass, if you ask me,' an elderly man said heartily. He looked at Pitt, raising an eyebrow in question. 'No idea why they promoted the fellow to the Home Office. Must be related to someone.' He laughed. 'Or know a few secrets, what?'

Pitt smiled back. He had no idea who they were referring to.

'I say, you're not in Parliament, are you?' the man went on. 'Didn't mean to insult you, you know.'

'No, I'm not,' Pitt answered him with a smile.

'Good job.' The man was clearly relieved. 'My name's Willoughby. Got a little land in Herefordshire. Couple of thousand acres.' He nodded.

Pitt introduced himself in turn, hesitated a moment, then decided against stating his occupation.

Another man joined them, slim and elegant with slightly protruding teeth and a white moustache. 'Evening,' he said companionably. 'Rotten business in Copenhagen, isn't it? Still, I dare say it'll blow over. Usually does.' He looked at Pitt more carefully. 'Suppose you know all about it?'

'I've heard a thing or two,' Pitt admitted.

'Connections?' Willoughby asked.

'He's Head of Special Branch!' the other man said tartly. 'Probably knows more about either of us than we know about ourselves!'

Willoughby paled. 'Oh, really?' He smiled but his voice rasped as if his throat were suddenly tight. 'Don't think there's much of any interest to know, ol' boy.'

9

Pitt's mind raced to think of the best way to reply. He could not afford to make enemies, but neither would it be wise to belittle his importance, or allow people to assume that he was not the same master of information that Narraway had been.

He made himself smile back at Willoughby. 'I would not say you are uninteresting, sir, but not of concern to us, which is an entirely different thing.'

Willoughby's eyes widened. 'Really?' He looked mollified, almost pleased. 'Really?'

The other man looked amused. 'Is that what you say to everyone?' he asked with the ghost of a smile.

'I like to be courteous.' Pitt looked him very directly in the eye. 'But some people are less interesting than others.'

This time Willoughby was very definitely pleased and made no attempt to hide it. Satisfaction radiated from him as he took another glass of champagne from a passing footman.

Pitt moved on. He was more careful now of his manner, watching but speaking little, learning to copy the polite words that meant nothing. It was not an art that came to him easily. Charlotte would have understood the nuances within what was said, or unsaid. Pitt would have found openness so much more comfortable. However, this was part of his world from now on, even if he felt an intruder. Beneath the smiles, he knew that the smooth, self-assured men around him were perfectly aware of it.

A few moments later he saw Charlotte again. He made his way towards her with a lift of spirits, even a pride he thought was perhaps a little silly after all these years, but it was nevertheless real. There were other women in the room with more classical beauty, and certainly more sumptuous gowns, but for him there was a warmth lacking in them. They had less passion, less of that certain indefinable grace that comes from within.

She was talking to her sister, Emily Radley, who was gowned in pale blue-green silk with gold embroidery. Emily's first marriage had been a match to make any mother proud. Lord George Ashworth had been the opposite of Pitt in every way: handsome, of excellent family, and possessed of a great deal of money. After his death it was held in trust for his and Emily's son, Edward. A suitable time later, Emily had married Jack Radley. He was another handsome man, even more charming, but with no money at all. His father had been a younger son, and something of an adventurer.

It was Emily who had persuaded Jack to enter politics and aspire to make something of himself. Perhaps some of her hunger to affect other people's lives had come from Emily's observation of Charlotte and her involvement in several of Pitt's earlier cases. To be fair, at times Emily herself had taken part also, with both flair and courage. The sisters had exasperated and embarrassed Pitt, driving him frantic with fear for their safety, but also very thoroughly earned his respect and his gratitude.

Looking at Emily now, with the light from the chandelier gleaming on her fair hair and the diamonds around her neck, he thought back with a little nostalgia to the adventure and the emotion of those times. He could no longer share information about his cases, even with Charlotte. So much was not merely confidential but secret. It was a loss he felt with surprising sadness, as the moment drew him back to the past.

Emily saw him and smiled brightly. He excused himself and walked over towards them.

'Good evening, Thomas. How are you?' Emily said cheerfully.

'Well, thank you. And I can see that you are,' he responded. She was naturally pretty, with fair hair and wide, dark blue eyes. More importantly, she knew exactly how to dress to

11

complement the best in herself, whatever the occasion. But it was his job to watch people and read the emotions behind the words, and he saw in her now an uncharacteristic tension. Was she also now wary of him? The thought chilled him so that he acknowledged Jack Radley almost automatically, before turning to be introduced to the man Jack had been speaking with.

'My lord, may I introduce my brother-in-law, Thomas Pitt,' Jack said very formally. 'Lord Tregarron.' Jack did not mention Tregarron's position. Presumably he considered it sufficiently important that Pitt should have been familiar with it. It was then that Pitt remembered Charlotte telling him of Jack's promotion to a position of responsibility within the government and finally some real power. Emily was very proud of it. It was defensiveness he could see in her quick eyes and the slight stiffness of her shoulders. She was not going to let Pitt's promotion overshadow Jack's.

Tregarron was a minister in the Foreign Office, close to the Foreign Secretary himself.

'How do you do, my lord?' Pitt replied, smiling. Then he glanced at Charlotte, and saw that she had understood the words and the slightest gestures perfectly.

'Lord Tregarron was telling us about some of the beautiful places he has visited,' Emily said brightly. 'Especially in the Balkans. His descriptions of the Adriatic Coast are breathtaking.'

Tregarron gave a slight shrug. He was a dark, stocky man with thick, curling hair and a highly expressive face. No one could have thought him comely, and yet the strength and the vitality in him commanded attention. Pitt noticed that several women in other groups kept glancing at him, then looking away, as if their interest were a little more than was discreet.

'For a Cornishman to admire anyone else's coast has impressed Mrs Radley greatly,' Tregarron said with a smile.

'As so it should. And we have had our share of troubles in the past, between shipwreck and smuggling, but I have no time for separatists. Life should be about inclusion, not everyone running off to his own small corner and pulling up the drawbridge. Half the wars in Europe have started out of fear, and the other half out of greed. Don't you agree?' He looked directly at Pitt.

'Liberally helped with misunderstanding,' Pitt replied. 'Intentional or not.'

'Well put, sir!' Tregarron commended him instantly. He turned to Jack. 'Right, Radley? A nice distinction, don't you think?'

Jack signalled his approval, smiling with the easy charm he had had all his life. He was a handsome man, and wore it with grace.

Emily shot Pitt a swift glance and he saw a distinct chill in it. He hoped Jack had not seen it. He would not like it if Charlotte were so defensive of him. You do not guard anyone so closely unless you fear they are in some way vulnerable. Did she still doubt that Jack had the steel in his nature, or perhaps the intelligence, to fill his new post well?

Had Tregarron chosen Jack, or had Emily used some connection of her own, from her days as Lady Ashworth, in order to obtain the position for him? Pitt could not think of anyone she knew who was powerful enough for that, but then the whole world of political debt and preferment was one he was unfamiliar with. Narraway would have known. It was an oversight he should remedy.

He felt a sudden, powerful empathy with Jack, who was swimming with sharks in unfamiliar seas. But Jack had lived on his charm and his instinctive reading of people for long enough, before marrying Emily. Perhaps he would survive very well.

The conversation moved from the Adriatic Coast to a discussion about the Austro-Hungarian Empire in general, and then on to Berlin, and finally to Paris, with its elegance and gaiety. Pitt was content to listen.

The musical interlude for the evening began. Much of its exquisite beauty was wasted on people who were not so much listening as waiting in polite silence until it was over and they could resume their own conversations.

Charlotte heard the haunting beauty of the pieces and wished the musicians could have played longer. However, she understood the rhythm of such gatherings, and the purposes they filled. This break was to allow a regrouping of forces: a time in which to weigh what one had observed and reconsider what to say next, whom to approach, and with which opening gambit.

She sat beside Pitt, her hand lightly on his arm. Her mind, though, was on Emily, who was seated in a gold-painted chair a couple of rows in front of her, beside Lord Tregarron. She knew this promotion was important to Jack, but she had not realised before quite how steep a climb it had been, or that underneath the charm and the light banter, Emily was afraid.

Did she know Jack too well, aware of a fundamental weakness in him that others did not see? Or not well enough, not now seeing the strength of will beneath his easy manner, his charm, which looked so effortless?

She thought the truth was that, after a decade of marriage, Emily was finally realising that she was not only in love with Jack, but that she cared about his feelings, his success, for himself, not for what it brought to her. Emily had been the youngest and the prettiest of the three Ellison sisters, and the most single-mindedly ambitious. Sarah, the eldest, had been dead for fifteen years. Her death now seemed a lifetime ago.

The fear and the pain of that time had receded into a distant nightmare, seldom revisited.

Their father had also died, about four years ago, and some time later their mother had remarried. This was another subject fraught with mixed emotions, but now largely accepted by Emily, and totally by Charlotte. Only their grandmother was still horrified. But Mariah Ellison made a profession of disapproving. An actor, Caroline's junior by many years and Jewish to boot, gave Grandmama more than ample opportunity to express all her pent-up prejudices. That Caroline was thoroughly happy only added insult to the injury.

At least now Emily was learning how to love in a different way. This was not for her own survival: it was something more protective, more mature.

Not that the ambition was gone! It was very much present, woven into the fibre of her character.

But Charlotte understood Emily at least as well as Emily understood herself. Charlotte felt the same tigress-like instinct to protect Pitt, but she also knew that in his new position there was little with which she could help. He was on far more unfamiliar ground than Jack was, whose family had had no money, but aristocratic connections in half the counties in England. Pitt was the son of a gamekeeper, a mere outdoor servant.

But if Charlotte were to protect him, she would not signal as clearly as Emily did that she felt he had need of it. He would hate that! She must make him think she had never considered it remotely necessary.

When the performance was over and the applause died down, the conversations resumed. Quite soon Charlotte found herself talking to a most unusual woman. She was probably in her late thirties, like Charlotte herself, but in all other ways quite different. She was dressed in a huge skirted gown the

15

colour of candlelight through brandy, and she was so slender as to look fragile. The bones of her neck and shoulders appeared as if they might break were you to bump her too roughly. There were blue veins just visible beneath the milk-white skin, and her hair was so dark as to be nearly black. Her eyes were dark-lashed and heavy-lidded above her high cheekbones, her mouth soft and generous. To Charlotte it was a face that was instantly likeable. She felt a great strength in her the moment their eyes met.

She introduced herself as Adriana Blantyre. Her voice was very low, just a trifle husky, and she spoke with an accent so slight that Charlotte listened harder to make certain she had really heard it.

Her husband was also tall and dark, and he too had a remarkable face. At a glance he was handsome, yet there was far more to him than a mere balance or regularity of feature. Once Charlotte had met his eyes, she kept looking back at him because of the intelligence in them, and the fierceness of the emotion. There was a grace in the way he stood, but nothing of ease. She felt Pitt watching her curiously as she looked at the man and yet she did not stop herself.

Evan Blantyre was an ex-diplomat, particularly interested in the eastern Mediterranean.

'A marvellous place, the Mediterranean,' he said, facing Charlotte, and yet speaking almost as if to himself. 'Europe, and yet at the gateway to a world far older, and civilisations that prefigure ours and from which we are sprung.'

'Such as Greece?' Charlotte asked, not having to feign interest. 'And maybe Egypt?'

'Byzantium, Macedonia and before that Troy,' he elaborated. 'The world of Homer, imagination and memory at the root of our thoughts, and the concepts from which they rise.'

Charlotte could not let him go unchallenged, not because

she disbelieved him but because there was an arrogance in him that she was compelled to probe.

'Really? I would have said it was Judea,' she argued.

He smiled widely, seizing on her interest. 'Judea certainly, of faith, the roots of faith, but not of thought or, if you prefer, philosophy, the love of wisdom rather than commanded belief. I chose the word with care, Mrs Pitt.'

Now she knew exactly what he meant, and that he was deliberately baiting her, but also that there was an intense conviction behind what he said. There was no pretence in the passion of his voice.

She smiled at him, meeting his eyes. 'I see. And which of us carry the torch of that philosophy now?' It was a challenge and she meant him to answer.

'Ah.' Now he was ignoring the others in their group. 'What an interesting question. Not Germany, all brightly polished and looking for something brave and brash to do. Not really France, although it has a uniquely piquant sophistication. Italy has sown the seeds of so much glory, yet now it is forever quarrelling within itself.' He made a rueful and elegant gesture.

'And us?' Charlotte asked him, her tone a little sharper than she had meant it to be. In spite of herself she had allowed him to reach her pride.

'Adventurers,' he replied without hesitation. 'And shopkeepers to the world.'

'No present-day heirs?' she said with sudden disappointment. She was annoyed that she had allowed him to draw her in so fully.

'Austro-Hungary,' he replied too quickly to conceal his own feelings. 'They have inherited the mantle of the old Holy Roman Empire that bound Europe into one Christian unity after the fall of Rome itself.'

Charlotte was startled. 'Austria? But it is ramshackle, all

17

but falling apart, isn't it? Is all we are told of it nonsense, then?'

Now he was amused and he allowed her to see it. There was warmth in his smile, but also an irony too bright and hard to be easy.

'I thought I was baiting you, Mrs Pitt, and I find instead you are baiting me.' He turned to Pitt. 'I underestimated your wife, sir. Someone mentioned that you are Head of Special Branch. If that is indeed true, then I should have known better than to imagine you would choose a wife purely for her looks, however charming.'

Pitt was smiling now too. 'I was not Head of Special Branch at the time,' he replied. 'But still ambitious, and hungry enough to reach for the best, with no idea of my own limitations.'

'Excellent!' Blantyre applauded him. 'Never allow your dreams to be limited. You should aim for the stars. Live and die with your arms outstretched and your eyes seeking the next goal.'

'Evan, you are talking nonsense,' Adriana said quietly, looking first at Charlotte, then at Pitt, judging their reactions. 'Aren't you ever afraid people will believe you?'

'Do you believe me, Mrs Pitt?' Blantyre enquired, his eyes wide, still challenging.

Charlotte looked at him directly. She was quite sure of her answer.

'I'm sorry, Mr Blantyre, because I don't think you mean me to, but yes, I do believe you.'

'Bravo!' he said quietly. 'I have found a sparring partner worth my efforts.' He turned to Pitt. 'Does your remit run to dealing with the Balkans, Mr Pitt?'

Pitt glanced at Jack and Emily – who had now moved further away and were engaged in conversation elsewhere – then back at Blantyre.

'With anyone whose activities might threaten the peace or the safety of Britain,' he replied, the levity vanished from his face.

Blantyre's eyebrows rose. 'Even if in northern Italy, or Croatia? In Vienna itself?'

'You know it doesn't,' Pitt told him, keeping his expression agreeable, as if they were playing a parlour game of no consequence. 'Only on British soil. Further afield would be Mr Radley's concern.'

'Of course.' Blantyre nodded. 'That must be challenging for you, to know at precisely which point you can act, and which you must leave to someone else. Or am I being unsophisticated? Is it actually a matter more of how you do a thing rather than what you do?'

Pitt smiled without answering.

'Does your search for information ever take you abroad?' Blantyre continued, completely unperturbed. 'You would love Vienna. The quickness of wit, the music. There is so much there that is new, innovative in concept, challenging the mind to hear differently. I dare say they are musicians you have never heard of, but you will. Above all, there is a breadth of thought in a score of subjects: philosophy, science, social mores, psychology, the very fundamentals of how the human mind works. There is an intellectual imagination there that will very soon lead the world in some areas.'

He gave a slight shrug, mocking himself as if to deny the heat of his feelings. 'And of course there is the traditional as well.' He turned to look at Adriana. 'Do you remember dancing all night to Mr Strauss's music? Our feet ached, the dawn was paling the sky and yet if the orchestra had played into the daylight hours, we could not have kept still.'

The memory was there in Adriana's eyes, but Charlotte was certain she saw a shadow also.

'Of course I do,' Adriana answered. 'No one who has waltzed in Vienna ever completely forgets it.'

Charlotte looked at her, fascinated by the romance of dancing to the music of the Waltz King. 'You actually danced when Mr Strauss conducted the orchestra?' she said with awe.

'Indeed,' Blantyre responded. 'No one else can give music quite the same magic, as if one must dance for ever. We watched the moon rise over the Danube, talked all night with the most amazing people: princes, philosophers, scientists and lovers.'

'Have you met the Emperor Franz Josef?' Charlotte pursued. 'They say he is very conservative. Is that true?' She told herself it was to keep the conversation innocuous, but she was caught up in the dream of Vienna, new inventions, new ideas of society. It was a world she herself would never see, but – as Blantyre had said – Vienna was the heart of Europe. It was the place of the genesis of new ideas that would spread throughout the whole continent one day, and beyond.

'Yes, I have, and it is true.' Blantyre was smiling but the emotion in his face was intense, far more than the vividness of memory would evoke. There was a passion in him that was urgent, firing the present and the future.

'A grim man, with a devil on his shoulder,' he went on, watching her face as closely as she was watching his. 'A contradiction of a man. More disciplined than anyone else I know. He sleeps on an army bed and rises at some ungodly hour long before dawn. And yet he fell madly in love with Elisabeth, seven years younger than himself, sister of the woman his father wished him to marry.'

'The Empress Elisabeth?' Charlotte said with even sharper interest. There was a vitality in Blantyre that intrigued her. She was unsure how much he spoke with such intensity in order to entertain, possibly to impress, and how much his own passion was so fierce he had no control over it.

'Precisely,' Blantyre agreed. 'He overrode all opposition. He would not be denied.' Now the admiration in his face was undisguised. 'They married, and by the time she was twenty-one she had given birth to her third child, her only son.'

'A strange mixture of rigidity and romance,' she said thoughtfully. 'Are they happy?'

She felt Pitt's hand touching her arm, but it was too late to withdraw the remark. She glanced at Adriana and saw in her eyes an emotion she could not read at all: a brilliance, a pain, and something she was trying very hard to conceal. Becoming aware of Charlotte's gaze on her, she looked away.

'No,' Blantyre said frankly. 'She is somewhat Bohemian in her tastes, and highly eccentric. She travels all over Europe wherever she can.'

Charlotte wanted to make some light remark that would ease the tension, escape from her misjudged question, but she thought now that such a thing would be obvious, and only make matters worse.

'Perhaps it was a case of falling in love with a dream that one did not really understand,' she said quietly.

'How very perceptive of you. You are rather alarming, Mrs Pitt.' But there was no anxiety in his voice; instead pleasure, and a distinct respect. 'And very honest!'

'I think you mean "indiscreet",' she said ruefully. 'Perhaps we had better go back to Mr Strauss and his music. I believe his father was a noted composer as well?'

'Ah, yes.' He drew a deep breath and his smile was a little wry. 'The "Radetzky March".'

At the further side of the room was Victor Narraway, newly elevated and a somewhat reluctant member of the House of Lords. He suddenly smiled as he saw Lady Vespasia Cumming-Gould. She was now of an age it would be indelicate to mention, but she still had the beauty that had made her famous. She walked with the grace of an empress, but without the arrogance. Her silver hair was her crown. As always, she was dressed in the height of fashion. She was tall enough to carry the huge, puffed upper sleeves that were current lately, and found her great sweeping skirt no encumbrance.

He was still watching her, with the pleasure of friendship, when she turned slightly and saw him. She did not move, but waited for him to come to her.

'Good evening, Lady Vespasia,' he said warmly. 'You have just made all the trivialities of attending such an event worthwhile.'

'Good evening, my lord,' she replied with laughter in her eyes.

'That is unnecessary!' Now he felt self-conscious, which was a very rare thing for him. He had held extraordinary power, discreetly, for most of his adult life, first as a member of Special Branch, then for the last decade and a half as its head. It was a new experience for him to be given such social deference.

'You will have to get used to it, Victor,' she said gently. 'Elevation to the peerage gains a different kind of influence.'

'Their lordships' deliberations are mostly a lot of pontificating,' he replied a trifle sourly. 'Very often for the sound of their own voices. No one is listening.'

She raised her eyebrows. 'Have you just discovered that?'

'No, of course not. But now that no one is obliged to listen to me, I miss the pretence of respect, but far more, I miss the knowledge of my own purpose.'

She caught the pain in his voice, even though he had tried to mask it with lightness. He knew she had heard it and was not sure if he wished he had been cleverer at concealing it, or that she knew him less well. But perhaps the comfort of friendship was of greater value than the privacy of not being understood.

'You will find a cause worth risking something for,' she assured him. 'Or if none presents itself, you will create one. There is enough stupidity and injustice in the world to last us both for the rest of our lives.'

'Is that supposed to comfort me?' he said with an answering smile.

She raised her silver eyebrows. 'Certainly! To be really without purpose is the same as being dead, only less peaceful.' She laughed very delicately. It was a mere whisper of amusement, but he knew she meant it passionately. He remembered her speaking only briefly of her participation in the revolutions against oppression that had fired Europe almost half a century ago. They had rocked the entire continent, except Britain. For a few short months, hope of a new democracy, freedom to speak and write as one chose, had flared wild and bright. People met together and talked all night, planning new laws, an equality that had never existed before, only to see it snuffed out again. In France, Germany, Austria and Italy all the old tyrannies were restored with barely any change. The barricades were swept away and the emperors and kings sat back on their thrones.

'I have grown used to being given my causes without the effort of looking for them,' he admitted. 'I accept the rebuke.'

'It was not meant as a rebuke, my dear,' she answered. 'I would welcome your assistance in finding something worthy of doing myself.'

'Nonsense,' he said very softly, looking across the room to where Pitt and Charlotte were speaking with Evan Blantyre. He saw Charlotte again with a sudden catching of his breath, a twist of his heart. The memories of their time in Ireland were still far from healing over. He had always known that it was his dream alone. She was there only to help him, and in so doing to help Pitt. It was Pitt whom she loved. It always would be. 'You are much occupied in worrying whether Pitt is going to be eaten by the lions,' he said, looking back at her.

'Oh dear! Am I so transparent?' Vespasia looked momentarily crestfallen.

'Only because I am worrying about the same thing,' he told her, pleased that she had not denied it. It said something for their friendship that she had owned the concern. Now she met his eyes, her anxiety undisguised.

'Are you afraid he will retain his respect for the upper classes, and defer to them even if he suspects them of treason?' he asked her.

'Certainly not!' she responded without hesitation. 'He has been a policeman far too long to do anything so idiotic! He is painfully aware of our weaknesses. Have you already forgotten that miserable affair at the Palace? I assure you, the Prince of Wales has not! Were it not for the Queen's own very personal gratitude to Pitt, he would not now have the position he does, nor, very likely, any position at all!'

Narraway pulled his mouth into a bitter line at the memory. He knew His Royal Highness was still carrying a deep grudge about the whole fiasco. It was not forgiveness that stayed his hand, it was his mother's iron will and strong personal loyalty to those who had served her, and done it with grace, and at risk of losing their own lives in the process. But Victoria was old, and the shadows around her were growing ever longer.

'Does the prince's anger concern you?' he asked Vespasia.

She gave a shrug so slight it hardly moved the deep lavender silk of her gown. 'Not immediately. By the time the throne is his, he might have more pressing issues to occupy him.'

He did not interrupt her brief silence. They stood side by

side, watching the swirl and shift, the courting and the snubbing of the glittering party in front of them.

'I am afraid that mercy will override the necessity for action,' Vespasia said at last. 'Thomas has never balked from looking at the truth, however harsh or tragic, or compromised by blame in many places. But he has not previously had to do more than present the evidence. Now he may have to be judge, jury and even executioner himself. Decisions are not always black and white, and yet they must still be made. To whom does he turn for advice, for someone who will reconsider, balance what might be a mistake, find a fact he had not seen, which may well change everything?'

'No one,' Narraway said simply. 'Do you think I don't know that? Do you imagine I have not lain awake all night staring at the ceiling and wondering if I had done the right thing myself, or perhaps sent to his death a man wholly or partially innocent, because I could not afford to hesitate?'

She studied him carefully: his eyes, his mouth, the deep-etched lines of his face, the grey in his thick shock of black hair.

'I'm sorry,' she said sincerely. 'You wear it with sufficient grace I had not seen it clearly enough.'

He found himself blushing. It was a compliment he had not expected from Vespasia. She had usually read him so very well. He was a little alarmed how much that pleased him. It made him vulnerable – something he was not used to – except with Charlotte Pitt, and that he must now force to the back of his mind again.

'You must have thought me inhuman,' he replied, then wished he had not been so open.

'Not inhuman,' Vespasia said ruefully. 'Just far more certain of yourself than I have ever been. I admired it in you, even if it left me in awe, and at some distance.'

Now he was really surprised. He had not imagined Vespasia in awe of anyone. She had been flattered by emperors, admired by the Tsar of all the Russias, and courted by half of Europe.

'Don't be so silly!' she said sharply, as if reading his thoughts. 'Privilege of birth is a duty, not an achievement! I admire those who have mastered themselves in order to be where they are, rather than been handed it by circumstance.'

'Like Pitt?' he asked.

'I was thinking of you,' she said drily. 'But yes, like Thomas.'

'And did you fear for me, when judgement lay in my hands?'

'No, my dear, because you have the steel in your soul. You will survive your mistakes.'

'And Pitt?'

'I hope so. But I fear it will be far harder for him. He is more of an idealist than you ever were, and perhaps more than I. He still has a certain innocence, and courage to believe in the best.'

'Was I wrong to recommend him?' Narraway asked.

She would have liked to answer him easily, reassure him, but if she lied now she would leave them isolated from each other when perhaps they might most need to be allied. And she had long ago given up telling the lies that mattered. She bothered now only with the trivial ones of courtesy, when the truth served no purpose.

'I don't know,' she said quietly. 'We shall see.'

Chapter Two

✦

Two days after that, Vespasia received news that a woman she had known and admired some time in the past was ill and confined to her bed. It is seldom easy to visit those who are not well, but it is far harder when both you and they know that recovery is not possible. What does one say that has any kind of honesty, and yet does not carry with it the breath of despair?

Vespasia had taken a bath perfumed with her favourite mixture of essences: lavender, rosemary and eucalyptus in bicarbonate of soda crystals, which always invigorated and lifted the spirits. Now she sat in her dressing room before the looking-glass while her maid arranged her hair before assisting her to fasten the tiny buttons of her dress. Today she had chosen a costume of dark indigo-shaded wool, which was both flattering and warm. She firmly believed that one should dress for the sick with as much care as for a party.

Still she had not made up her mind what to say; whether to speak of the present, which was now so different for Vespasia from how it was for Serafina Montserrat. Perhaps remembering the past – rich, turbulent, filled with both triumph and disaster – would be a happier choice.

It was also difficult to know what to take as a small gift. In February there were few flowers; those there were had been forced in artificial circumstances, and seldom lasted long. There was hardly any fruit at all. Vespasia had then remembered that Serafina liked good chocolate, so a box of carefully selected and beautifully wrapped Belgian chocolates with cream centres seemed a fortunate choice.

She had considered a book of memoirs, or foreign travels, but she did not know if Serafina were well enough to read. She still lived in her house in Dorchester Terrace, with her great-niece as a companion, but was there anyone who would read to her with spirit and charm, if she were not well enough to read for herself?

'Thank you, Gwen,' Vespasia said as her maid completed the dressing of her hair and she rose to put on her costume. Since kindness required that she make this visit generously and with good spirits, it were best she do it quickly. Turning over the possibilities of conversation in her mind achieved nothing. She would regret it profoundly and blame herself not only for selfishness but also for cowardice – that weakness she deplored more than any other – were she to leave it too late.

The morning was brisk and cold, but fortunately she had not very far to go. Her carriage was waiting at the door. She gave the footman the Dorchester Terrace address, and accepted his hand to step up. Seating herself as comfortably as possible in the chill, she arranged her skirts around her so as not to crush them more than necessary.

She watched the tall houses pass by, the few people out walking in the windy streets, heads bent against the first spattering of rain, and thought back nearly fifty years to her first meeting with Serafina Montserrat. The world had been in a turmoil of excitement then. The revolutions of '48 had filled them with hope and the willingness to sacrifice everything, even their lives, for the chance to overthrow the old tyrannies. It was illusory – perhaps it always had been – but for a brief space it was passionately alive, before the barricades were stormed, the rebels dispersed, imprisoned or killed, and everything was put back as before.

Vespasia had come home again, settled to an acceptable marriage, and had children, but never loved as she had then. Serafina had married also, more than once, but remained a fighter, both physically and politically.

Their paths had crossed since, many times. Vespasia had travelled all over Europe. She used her beauty and her intelligence to effect good where she was able to, but with a degree of discretion. Serafina had never been discreet.

They had chanced across each other in London, Paris, Rome, Berlin, occasionally in Madrid, Naples in the spring, Provence in the autumn. When they met they had spoken of laughter and grief, exchanged new hopes, old memories. This might be their last meeting. Vespasia found herself stiff. Her hands were clenched as if she were cold, and yet she was well supplied with rugs and the carriage was not uncomfortable.

They pulled up outside the entrance in Dorchester Terrace and her coachman opened the door for Vespasia to alight. She accepted his hand and took from him the ribboned box of chocolates. 'Thank you. Please wait for me,' she instructed him, then walked across the pavement and up the steps. It was early for a call, and she was very aware of it, but she wished to see Serafina alone, before any others might come at a more usual hour.

The door opened and she handed her card to the footman.

'Good morning, Lady Vespasia,' he said with only mild surprise. 'Please do come in.'

'Good morning,' she replied. 'Is Mrs Montserrat well

enough to receive visitors? If the hour is too early, I can return.'

'Not at all, my lady. She will be delighted to see you.' He smiled, closing the door behind her. She thought she detected in his voice something more than good manners, perhaps even a thread of gratitude.

She walked into the wide hall with its beautifully parqueted floor and sweeping staircase. She noticed there was a very handsome lamp built into the newel post at the bottom.

'I'm certain Mrs Montserrat will wish to see you, but of course I will take the precaution of going up to ask her maid,' he explained. 'If you would be good enough to wait in the withdrawing room, where the fire is lit, I shall return in a few moments. Would you care for a cup of tea?'

'Thank you, that would be most welcome. It is inclement weather.' She accepted because it would make him feel less uncomfortable about leaving her, if it should require several moments to make Serafina ready to receive anyone. She might require a little assistance first. Also it was possible she would find managing tea in bed embarrassing.

The withdrawing room was warm and elegant in a most unusual manner. The floor carpeting was pale, and the walls papered in the darkest possible green. The sombreness of it was brilliantly relieved by furnishings in Indian red and warm amber brocade, with cushions also in amber and green. Thrown carelessly across them were silk blankets with tasselled edges woven with the same beautiful colours.

The fire was low, but had clearly been lit since early morning, filling the air with the scent of applewood. There were paintings of northern Italian landscapes on the walls: one of Monte Bianco gleaming white in a clear evening sky; another of early morning light on Isola San Giulio, catching the roofs of the monastery, and making shadows in the clear water of Lago d'Orta, where half a dozen small boats lay motionless.

The décor was chaotically eclectic, and full of life, and Vespasia smiled at a score of memories that crowded her mind. She and Serafina had sat at a pavement café in Vienna and drunk hot chocolate while they made notes for a political pamphlet. All around them there had been excited chatter, laughter at bawdy jokes, voices sharp-edged, a little too loud with the awareness of danger and loss.

They had stood on the shore at Trieste, side by side, the magnificent Austrian buildings behind them and the sweeping Adriatic skies above, high-arched with clouds like mares' tails fanned out in the evening light. Serafina had cursed the whole Austrian Empire with a violence that twisted her face and made her voice rasp in her throat.

Vespasia returned to the present with a jolt when the tea was brought. She had nearly finished it by the time a young woman came in, closing the door softly behind her. She was in her mid-thirties, dark-haired, but with such unremarkable brows and lashes that the power of her colouring was lost. She was slender and soft-voiced.

'Lady Vespasia. How gracious of you to call,' she said quietly. 'My name is Nerissa Freemarsh. My aunt Serafina is so pleased that you have come. As soon as you have finished your tea I shall take you up to see her. I'm afraid you will find her much weaker than you may remember her, and somewhat more absent-minded.' She smiled apologetically. 'It is quite some time since you last met. Please be patient with her. She seems to be rather confused at times. I'm so sorry.'

'Please think nothing of it.' Vespasia rose to her feet, guilty that it had been so long since she had come to see her friend. 'I dare say I forget things myself at times.'

'But this is . . .' Nerissa started. Then she stopped, smiling

31

at her own mistake. 'Of course. I know you understand.' She turned and led the way out across the parqueted hall again and up the handsome staircase. The young woman walked a little stiffly, picking up the dark, plain fabric of her skirt in one hand so she did not trip.

Vespasia followed her up and across the landing, and – after a brief knock on the door – into the main bedroom. Inside it was warm and bright, even in the middle of this dark, winter day. The fire was excellent; the logs must be applewood also, from the sweet smell of them. The walls were painted light terracotta, and the curtains were patterned with flowers, as if Serafina could carry the summer with her, regardless of the iron rule of time and season.

Vespasia looked across at the bed and knew she did not keep the shock from her face.

Serafina was propped almost upright by the pillows at her back. Her hair was white and dressed a little carelessly. Her face was devoid of any artificial colour, although with her dark eyes and well-marked brows she did not look as ashen as a fairer woman might have. She had never been beautiful – not as Vespasia had been, and still was – but her features were good and her courage and intelligence had made her extraordinary. Beside her, other women had seemed leached of life, and predictable. Now all that burning energy was gone, leaving the shell behind, recognisable only with effort.

Serafina turned slowly and stared at the intruders in her room.

Vespasia felt her throat tighten until she could barely swallow.

'Lady Vespasia has come to see you, Aunt Serafina,' Nerissa said with forced cheerfulness. 'And brought you some Belgian chocolates.' She held up the box with its beautiful ribbons.

Slowly Serafina smiled, but it was only out of courtesy. Her eyes were blank.

'How kind,' she said without expression.

Vespasia moved forward, smiling back with an effort that she knew must mar any attempt at sincerity. This was a woman whose mind had been as sharp as her own, whose wit was nearly as quick, and she was no more than ten years older. She looked empty, as if the fire and the soul of her had already left.

'I hope you'll enjoy them,' Vespasia said, hearing the words hollow as they left her lips. For a moment she wished she had not come. Serafina appeared to have no idea who she was, as if all the past had been wiped out and they had not shared the kind of friendship that is never forgotten.

Serafina looked at her with only a slow dawning of light in her eyes, as if gradually shreds of some understanding returned to her.

'I am sure you would like to talk for a little while,' Nerissa said gently. 'Don't tire yourself, Aunt Serafina.' The instruction was aimed obliquely at Vespasia. 'I'll put another log on the fire before I leave. If you need anything, the bell is easy to reach and I'll come straight away.'

Serafina nodded very slightly, her eyes still fixed on Vespasia.

'Thank you,' Vespasia replied. There was no escape. It would be inexcusable to leave now, however much she wished to.

Nerissa went over to the fire, poked it a little, which sent up a shower of sparks, then carefully placed another log on top. She straightened her back and smiled at Vespasia.

'It is so kind of you to come,' she said again. 'I'll return in a little while.' She walked over to the door, opened it with a single movement, and went out.

Vespasia sat down in the chair next to the bed. What on earth could she say that made sense? To ask after her friend's health seemed almost a mockery.

It was Serafina who spoke first.

'Thank you for coming,' she said quietly. 'I was afraid that no one would tell you. I have bad days sometimes, and I don't remember things. I talk too much.'

Vespasia looked at her. Her eyes were not empty any more, but filled with a deep anxiety. She was desperately searching Vespasia's face for understanding. It was as if the woman Vespasia knew had returned for a moment.

'The purpose of visiting is to talk,' Vespasia said gently. 'When you lie alone thinking, perhaps not feeling well, the whole pleasure of seeing people is to be able to share ideas, to laugh a little, to recall all the things we have loved in the past. I shall be very disappointed if you don't talk to me.'

Serafina looked as if she were struggling to find words for some idea that eluded her.

Vespasia thought immediately that, without meaning to, she had placed a further pressure on her, as if she were hoping to be entertained. That was not what she had meant at all. But how could she retrace her steps now without sounding ridiculous?

'Is there something you would particularly care to talk about?' she invited.

'I forget things,' Serafina said very softly. 'Sometimes lots of things.'

'So do I,' Vespasia assured her gently. 'Most of them don't matter.'

'Sometimes I muddle the past and the present,' Serafina went on. Now she was watching Vespasia as if on the edge of the abyss in which some horror waited to consume her.

Vespasia tried to think of a reply but nothing that came easily was great enough for what was clearly, at least to Serafina, a matter of intense importance. She was frightened. This was no mere apology for being a little incoherent. Perhaps the terror of losing the grip of one's mind was deeper and far more real than most people took time or care to appreciate. Maybe they dared not!

Vespasia put her hand on Serafina's and felt the thin bones, the flesh far softer than it ever used to be. This was a woman who had ridden horses at a gallop few men dared equal; who had held a sword and fought with it, light flashing on steel as she moved with speed, lethally, and a grace that had a different kind of beauty. It was a hand so swiftly co-ordinated with her eye that she was a superb shot with both pistol and rifle.

Now it was slack in Vespasia's grip.

'We all forget,' Vespasia said softly. 'The young, less so, perhaps. They have so much less to remember, some of them barely anything at all.' She smiled fleetingly. 'You and I have seen incredible things: butchers, bakers and housewives manning the barricades; sunset flaming across the Alps till the snow looked like blood; we've danced with emperors and been kissed by princes. I, at least, have been sworn at by a cardinal . . .'

She saw Serafina smile and move her head in a slight nod of agreement.

'We have fought for what we believed in,' Vespasia went on. 'We have both won and lost more than the young today have dreamed of. But I dare say their turn will come.'

This time Serafina's eyes were clear for a moment. 'We have, haven't we? That's what I'm afraid of.'

'What frightens you, my dear?'

'I forget who is real and who is just memory,' Serafina replied. 'Sometimes the past seems so vivid I mistake the trivia of today for the great issues there used to be – and the people we knew.'

'Does that matter?' Vespasia asked her. 'Perhaps the past is more interesting?'

The smile touched Serafina's eyes again. 'Infinitely – at least to me.' Then the fear returned, huge and engulfing. Her voice shook. 'But I'm so afraid I might mistake some person now for someone else I knew and trusted, and let slip what I shouldn't! I know terrible things, dangerous things about murder and betrayal. Do you understand?'

Frankly, Vespasia did not. She was aware that Serafina had been an adventurer all her life. She had never let the causes die from her mind. She had married twice, but neither time had been particularly happy, and she had had no children. But then she could outride and outshoot so many men, she was not an easy woman with whom to be comfortable. She never learned to keep her own counsel about her political opinions, nor to temper the exercise of her more dangerous skills.

But this was the first time Vespasia had seen fear in her, and that was a shock. It touched her with a pity she could not have imagined feeling for such a proud and fierce woman.

'Are any of those secrets still dangerous now?' she asked doubtfully. She tried to find the balance between reassuring Serafina so she would be less frightened, and seeming to patronise her by implying that her knowledge was outdated and no one would still be interested. It was a judgement so easy to mishandle. Vespasia herself would hate to be relegated to the past as if currently not worth bothering about, even though one day assuredly it would be true. She refused to think of it.

'Of course they are!' Serafina told her, her voice husky with urgency. 'Why on earth do you ask? Have you lost all interest in politics? What's happened to you?' It was almost an accusation. Serafina's dark eyes were alive now with anger.

Vespasia felt a flash of her own temper, and crushed it immediately. This was not about her vanity.

'Not at all,' she replied. 'But I cannot think of anything current that might be affected by most of my knowledge of the past.'

'You used not to be a liar,' Serafina said softly, her mouth a little twisted with unhappiness. 'Or at least if you were, you were good enough at it that I did not know.'

Vespasia felt the heat burn up her face. The accusation was just. Of course some of the events she knew, the acutely personal ones, would still be dangerous, if she were to speak of them in the wrong places. She would never do so. But then she knew exactly where she was, and to whom she was speaking.

'Those sorts of secrets you would keep,' she said to Serafina. 'You would not mention them, even to the people involved. It would be such awfully bad taste.'

Suddenly Serafina laughed, a rich, throaty sound, taking Vespasia back forty years in the time of a single heartbeat. Vespasia found herself smiling too. She saw them both on the terrace of a villa in Capri. The summer night was heavy with the scent of jasmine. Across the water Vesuvius lifted its double peaks against the skyline. The wine was sweet. Someone had made a joke and laughter was swift and easy.

Then a log burned through and fell in the fireplace with a shower of sparks. Vespasia returned to the present: the warm bright room with its flowered curtains, and the old, frightened woman in the bed so close to her.

'Then you had better ask Miss Freemarsh to be sure that certain people do not call on you,' Vespasia said with absolute seriousness. 'There cannot be so many of them left now. Give her a list, tell her you do not wish to see them. You must have a lady's maid who would help you?'

'Oh, yes. I still have Tucker,' Serafina said with warmth. 'God bless her. She's almost as old as I am! But what reason shall I give?' She searched Vespasia's eyes for help.

'No reason at all,' Vespasia told her. 'It is not her concern whom you will see, or not see. Tell her so if she presses you. Invent something.'

'I shall forget what I said!'

'Then ask her. Say, "What did I tell you?" If she replies by repeating it, then you have your answer. If she says she couldn't recall, then you may start again too.'

Serafina lay back on her pillows, smiling, the look in her eyes far away. 'That is more like the Vespasia I remember. They were great days, weren't they?'

'Yes,' Vespasia answered her, firmly and honestly. 'They were marvellous. More of life than most people ever see.'

'But dangerous,' Serafina added.

'Oh, yes. And we survived them. You're here. I'm here.' She smiled at the old woman lying so still in the bed. 'We lived, and we can share the memories with each other.'

Serafina's hand slowly clenched on the sheets and her face became bleak with anxiety again. 'That's what I'm afraid of,' she whispered. 'What if I think it's you, but it's really someone else? What if my mind takes me back to the days in Vienna, Budapest or Italy, and I say something dangerous, something from which secrets could be unravelled and understood at last?'

Her frown deepened, her face now intensely troubled. 'I know terrible things, Vespasia, things that would have brought down some of the greatest families. I dare not name them, even here in my own bedroom. You see –' she bit her lip – 'I know who you are now, but in thirty minutes I might forget. I might think it is the past, and you are someone else entirely, who doesn't understand as you do. I might . . .' She swallowed. 'I might think I am back in one of the old plots, an old fight with everything to win or lose . . . and tell you something dangerous . . . secret. Do you see?'

Vespasia put her hand on Serafina's very gently, and felt

the bones and the thin, knotted tendons under her fingers. 'But, my dear, right now you are here in London, in late February of 1896, and you know exactly who I am. Those old secrets are past. Italy is united, except for the small part in the east still under Austrian rule. Hungary is still lesser in the empire, and getting more so with each year, and the whole Balkan peninsula is still ruled from Vienna. Most of the people we knew are dead. The battle has passed on from us. We don't even know who is involved any more.'

'You don't,' Serafina whispered. 'I still know secrets that matter – loves and hates from the past that count even now. It wasn't really so long ago. In politics, perhaps, but not in the memories of those who were betrayed.'

Vespasia struggled for something to say that would comfort this frightened woman, but it would have to make sense, or it would only leave her feeling more misunderstood, and ultimately abandoned.

'Perhaps Miss Freemarsh will see that you are not left alone with anyone, if you ask her?' she suggested. 'That would not be unnatural, in the circumstances.'

Serafina smiled bleakly. 'Nerissa? She thinks I am fantasising. She has no idea of the past. To her I am an old woman who enlarges her memories and paints them in brighter colours than they were, in order to draw attention to herself, and to make up for the greyness of today. She is far too polite to say so, but I see it in her eyes.' Serafina looked down at the coverlet. 'And she has other things on her mind. I believe she might be in love. I remember the excitement, the wondering if he was coming that day, the next, the torment if I thought he favoured someone else.' She looked up at Vespasia again, laughter and sadness in her eyes, and questioning.

'Of course,' Vespasia agreed. 'One does not forget. Perhaps one only pretends to now and again, because the sweetness of it comes so seldom as one gets older. We remember the pleasure and tend to forget the pain.' She drew her mind back to the present issue. 'Does Nerissa have any idea of who you are, and what you have accomplished?'

Serafina shook her head. 'No. How could she? The world was different then. I knew everybody who mattered in one empire, and you did in the other. We knew too many secrets, and I wonder if perhaps you still do?'

Vespasia was momentarily discomfited. She did know far more of the present world and its political and personal secrets than she would tell anyone, even Thomas Pitt. How had Serafina seen through her so easily, and in a mere quarter of an hour?

The answer was simple: because at heart they were alike, believers who cared too much, women who used their courage and their charm to influence the men who held power and could change nations.

'A few,' Vespasia admitted. 'But old ones too, embarrassing possibly, but I think not dangerous.'

Serafina laughed. 'Liar!' she said cheerfully. 'If that were true there would be sadness in your voice, and there isn't. I hear no regret.'

'I apologise,' Vespasia said sincerely. 'I underestimated you, and that was rude of me.'

'I forgive you. I expected it. One has to lie to survive. My fear is that as I get worse, I shall lose the judgement, and possibly even the ability, to lie any more.'

Vespasia felt another, even more painful wave of pity for her. She had been magnificent, a tigress of a woman, and now she lay wounded and alone, afraid of shadows from the past.

'I shall speak to Miss Freemarsh,' she said firmly. 'What about your Tucker? Is she still able to hold her authority with the other servants?'

'Oh, yes, God bless her. I wouldn't have anyone else. But she is seventy if she is a day, and I cannot expect her to be here all the time. Sometimes I see how tired she is.' She stopped; more explanation was not necessary.

'Perhaps it would be possible to get you a nurse who would be by your side all the time, at least all day, when people might call,' Vespasia suggested. 'Someone who understands sufficiently to interrupt any conversation that might veer towards the confidential.'

'Do such people exist?' Serafina asked dubiously.

'They must do,' Vespasia said, although she had only just thought of it. 'What happens to people who have been in high positions in government or the diplomatic service, or even the judiciary, and know things it would be disastrous if they spoke of to the wrong person? They also can become old and ill – or, for that matter, drink too much!'

Again Serafina laughed. It was a light happy sound, an echo of who she used to be.

'You make me feel so much better,' she said sincerely. 'I am growing old disgracefully, shabbily in a way, and becoming a liability to those I loved and who trusted me, but at least I am not alone. If you are not too busy doing great things, please come and see me again.'

'I shall come with pleasure,' Vespasia replied. 'Even if I should be fortunate enough to have some great thing to do – which I doubt.' She rose to her feet. 'Now I must see Miss Freemarsh, and Tucker, if I can. Then I will look for a nurse with intelligence and discretion.'

'Thank you,' Serafina replied, her voice for an instant husky from gratitude and perhaps relief.

Vespasia left the room and went further along the corridor, hoping to find Tucker. She could remember her as a young woman, just starting out in service when they were all in Italy, and Vespasia herself not yet twenty. She had seen her again briefly, maybe a dozen times over the years, but would she recognise her now? She must be greatly changed.

There was a young laundry maid carrying a pile of freshly ironed sheets coming towards her.

'Excuse me, will you tell me where I might find Miss Tucker?' Vespasia asked.

The maid dropped a half-curtsy. 'Yes, m'lady. She'll be downstairs. Can I fetch 'er for yer?'

'Yes, please. Tell her that Lady Vespasia Cumming-Gould would like to speak to her.'

Tucker appeared within a few moments, walking stiffly but with head held high along the passageway from some stairs at the further end. Vespasia knew her without hesitation. Her face was wrinkled and pale, her hair quite white, but she still had the same high cheekbones, and wide blue eyes, which were a little hollow around the sockets.

'Good morning, Tucker,' Vespasia said quietly. 'I am obliged you came so quickly. How are you?'

'I am quite well, thank you, m'lady,' Tucker replied. It was the only answer she had ever given to such a question, even when she had been ill, or injured. 'I hope you are well yourself, ma'am?'

'Yes, thank you.'

The ritual civilities observed, Vespasia moved on to the subject that concerned them both. 'I see that Mrs Montserrat is not well, and very anxious that she should not cause any ill feeling by her possible lapses of memory.' She saw instantly in Tucker's face that she understood precisely what Vespasia meant. They were two old women, an earl's daughter and a maid, standing in a silent corridor with more memory and understanding in common than either of them had with most other people in the world. And yet it was unthinkable, especially to Tucker, that the convention of rank should ever be broken between them.

'It might be advisable if you were to remain in the room as often as you may, whether Mrs Montserrat thinks to ask you, or if she forgets. Even if you do no more than assure her that she said nothing indiscreet, it would comfort her a great deal.'

Tucker inclined her head very slightly. 'Yes, m'lady. I'll do my best. Miss Freemarsh . . .' She changed her mind and did not say whatever it was she had been about to.

'Thank you,' Vespasia knew she had no need to add more. 'It is nice to see you again, Tucker. Good day.'

'Good day, m'lady.'

Vespasia turned and went to the main staircase.

'It was kind of you to call,' Nerissa said when she met Vespasia at the foot of the stairs by the lamp on the newel post.

'Nonsense,' Vespasia replied rather more briskly than she had intended to. The comfort of speaking to Tucker the moment before slipped away from her. She was deeply disturbed and it had taken her by surprise. Physical decline she was prepared for – to a degree it was inevitable – but the slipping away of mental grasp, even of identity, she had not considered. Perhaps because she did not want to. Could she one day be as isolated and afraid as Serafina was, dependent on people of a generation who neither knew nor understood anything of who she was? People like this cool young woman who imagined compassion was no more than a duty, an empty act performed for its own sake.

'I came because Serafina and I have been friends for more years than you are aware of,' Vespasia said, still tartly. 'I am gravely remiss in not having come before. I should have taken the care to know how ill she is.'

'She is not in pain,' Nerissa said gently. Something in the patience of her tone irritated Vespasia almost unbearably. It was as if in her perception Vespasia were also not quite able to grasp reality.

Vespasia bit back her response with a considerable effort, because she needed this young woman's co-operation. She could not afford to antagonise her.

'So she assured me,' she said. 'However, she is in distress. Maybe she has not told you so, but she is convinced that in her lapses of memory she may be indiscreet, and the thought of it troubles her profoundly.'

Nerissa smiled. 'Oh, yes, I'm afraid she is not always quite sure of where she is, or what year this is now. She rambles quite a bit, but it is harmless, I assure you. She speaks of people she knew years ago as if they were still alive, and frankly I think she romanticises the past rather a lot.' Her expression became even more patient. 'But that is quite understandable. When the past is so much more exciting than the present, who would not want to dwell in it a little? And we all remember things with perhaps more light and colour than they really possessed.'

Vespasia wanted to tell this young woman, with her indifferent face and healthy young body, that Serafina Montserrat had a past with more vivid colour than any other woman Nerissa was likely to meet in her lifetime. But her purpose was to safeguard Serafina, to remove the fear, whether founded or not, rather than put Nerissa Freemarsh in her place.

'The reality doesn't matter,' she said, ashamed of the evasion but knowing that it was necessary. She could not afford to tell Nerissa more than a suggestion of the truth. She clearly did not consider it important enough to guard with discretion.

'Serafina is anxious that she may unintentionally speak of someone else's private affairs,' she continued. 'Would it not be possible to see that her visitors are limited, and that someone is with her who would interrupt if Serafina seems to be wandering in her mind? The assurance that that would not happen might relieve her anxiety. Tucker is excellent, but she cannot be there all the time. I can look for someone suitable, and suggest a few possible names.'

Nerissa smiled, her lips oddly tight. 'You are very kind, but Aunt Serafina would dismiss such a person within a short while. She hates to be fussed over. Her fantasy that she knows all kinds of state secrets and terrible things about the private lives of archdukes and so on, is complete imagination, you know. The few people who call on her are quite aware of that. It pleases her to daydream in that way, and it does no harm. No one believes her, I promise you.'

Vespasia wondered if that were true. In the past, thirty or forty years ago, Serafina had certainly known all manner of things about the planned rebellions within the vast Austro-Hungarian Empire. She had been part of some of them. She had dined, danced and very possibly slept with minor royalty – even major, for all Vespasia knew. But that was all long ago. Most of them were dead now, and their scandals with them, along with their dreams.

Nerissa smiled. 'It is kind of you to care, but I cannot stop all Aunt Serafina's visitors. It would leave her terribly alone. To talk to people, to remember, and perhaps romance a little, is about the only real pleasure she has. It is generous of you to consider another servant, but that is not the answer. I don't wish to tell Aunt Serafina, but it is not economically wise at present.'

Vespasia could not argue with her. It would be both impertinent and pointless. She had no idea as to Serafina's financial situation. 'I see.'

'I hope you will come again, Lady Vespasia. You were always one of her favourites. She speaks of you often.'

Vespasia doubted it, but it would be ungracious to say so.

'We were always fond of each other,' she replied. 'Of course I shall come again. Thank you for being so patient.'

Nerissa walked with her across the parquet floor towards the front door, and the carriage waiting at the kerbside, horses fretting in the wind.

Victor Narraway was already extremely bored with his elevation to the House of Lords. After his dismissal from Special Branch and his adventure in Ireland – which had stretched him emotionally far more than he had foreseen – he had needed something to occupy his extraordinary intelligence, and to use at least some of his talents. For Narraway to interfere in Special Branch now that Thomas Pitt was Head would imply that he did not have confidence in Pitt's ability. Even such a suggestion would undermine anything Pitt was able to do, not only in Pitt's mind, but in those he commanded, and those in government to whom he reported. It would be the greatest disservice Narraway could do to him, and a betrayal of the loyalty Pitt himself had shown, who had believed in Narraway when no one else had. Pitt had trusted in his innocence in the O'Neil case when his guilt seemed clear – indeed, morally it was clear that he was partly at fault. Still Pitt had refrained from blaming him for anything.

So Narraway was left bored, and more acutely alone than he had expected to be; watching and unable to interfere.

Not that there was much to interfere with. In the months since Pitt had been in charge there seemed to have been little out of the routine, and nothing that challenged the imagination or the nerve.

Narraway had considered foreign travel, and indeed had made a late autumn trip to France. He had always enjoyed its rich countryside. He had walked around some of its older cities, reviving half-forgotten knowledge and adding new threads to it. However, after a while it became stale, because he had no one with whom to share it. There was no Charlotte this time, no one else's pleasure to mirror his own. That was a pain he still preferred not to think of.

He had had the time to attend more theatre. Drama he had always enjoyed. Comedy was, for him, profoundly the poorer without the presence of Oscar Wilde, who was now stigmatised for his private life and whose work was no longer performed on the stage. It was an absence he felt with peculiar sharpness.

There was always opera, and recitals of music such as that of Beethoven or Liszt – two of his favourites. But its passion only stirred in him the hunger for something to do, a cause in which to pour his own energy.

He sat in his book-lined study with its few small watercolour seascapes, the fire burning and the gaslamps throwing pools of light on the table and floor. He had eaten a light supper and was reading a report of some politician's visit to Berlin, reaching desperately and without success for a spark of intrigue or novelty. So he was delighted to be interrupted by his manservant announcing that Lady Vespasia Cumming-Gould had called.

He sat upright in his chair, suddenly wide awake.

'Ask her in,' he said immediately. 'Bring the best red wine . . .'

'White, sir, surely?' the manservant suggested.

'No, she prefers red,' Narraway replied with assurance. 'And something decent to eat. Thin brown toast, and a little pâté. Please.'

'Yes, my lord.' The man smiled, rolling the title around his tongue. He was inordinately proud of it. He did not say so,

47

but he thought his master was a great man, underappreciated by his government, for which he did not forgive them.

Narraway allowed him that indulgence. He had been in his service for many years, good times and bad. He deserved the pleasure.

Vespasia came in the moment after. She was wearing a deep shade that in the gaslight was neither blue nor purple but something in between – muted, like the night sky. He had never seen her in anything jarring or unsubtle. When she was in the room one looked at no other woman.

He walked over to her. He was taller than she, but not by much. He considered greeting her with the usual formalities, but they knew each other too well for that now, especially after the recent fiasco in Ireland, and then with the Queen at Osborne.

'Good evening, Victor,' she said with a slight smile. She had taken to using his Christian name recently, and he found it more pleasing than he would willingly have admitted. There was no one else who called him by his first name.

'Lady Vespasia.' He looked at her closely. There was anxiety in her eyes, in spite of her calm composure. 'Not Thomas, is it?' he asked with sudden anxiety.

She smiled. 'No. So far as I am aware, all is well with him. It is possibly nothing of importance, but I need to be certain.'

Narraway indicated the chair opposite his own. She sat in it with a single, graceful movement, her skirts seeming to arrange themselves as if without assistance.

'You would not have come unless it mattered to you,' he replied. 'I have not made my boredom so obvious that you have come simply to rescue me. At least, I hope not.'

She smiled in spite of herself. The humour lit her face, bringing back all the light of her beauty and the sharp memory of how radiant she could be.

'Oh dear,' she murmured. 'Is it dreadful?'

'Tedious beyond belief,' he answered, crossing his legs and leaning back in his chair comfortably. 'Most of the time. Nobody tells me anything of interest. Either they assume I already know it – and very possibly I do – or else they are afraid that they will be seen talking to me and people will assume they are passing me more dark secrets.'

The manservant reappeared with the wine and food. He served it with only the barest questions as to its acceptability, and then retreated.

Vespasia sipped the wine.

Narraway waited.

'Do you know Serafina Montserrat?' she asked quietly.

He searched his memory. 'Is she about our age?' he asked. That was something of a euphemism. Vespasia was several years older than he, but it was a detail of chronology, and of no importance.

She smiled. 'The manners of their lordships are rubbing off on you, Victor. It is not like you to be so . . . oblique towards the truth. She is somewhat older than I, and considerably older than you.'

'Then I have heard of her, but only in passing reference when speaking of certain European matters, mostly brief sputters of revolution in the Austro-Hungarian Empire, and Italian nationalism,' he replied.

'She would not like our efforts to be referred to as sputters,' Vespasia observed drily. There was amusement in her eyes, but an awareness of pain also.

'Why do you ask? Has something happened to her?' he asked.

'Time,' she replied ruefully. 'Rather more severely than it affects most of us.'

'She's ill? Vespasia, it is not like you to be so evasive.' He leaned forward, the ease in him gone. 'What is it that concerns you? We know each other well enough not to skirt around the truth like this.'

Some of the tension in her relaxed, as if she were no longer bearing it alone.

'She is becoming very severely forgetful,' she said at last. 'To the point of slipping back into the past and imagining she is young again, and in the midst of all manner of intrigues with people who are no longer alive – or, if they are, are long since sunk into decent retirement.'

He was still not sure why it troubled her so much. There was more than pity in her eyes: there was a shadow of fear.

He waited, watching the firelight on her face.

She took a second slice of toast and spread pâté on it, but did not eat.

'She is afraid that she will accidentally betray some secrets that still matter,' she told him. 'Do you think that is possible? Her niece, Nerissa Freemarsh, assures me that it is largely fancy. She did not say so in so many words, but she implied that Serafina was creating a daydream to make her essentially tedious life more exciting than it was, and therefore herself more interesting. She would not be the first person to embroider the truth in order to gain attention.'

She lowered her gaze, as if she were ashamed even of the suggestion, and yet had to acknowledge it. 'In her circumstances it would be easy enough to understand. If I were bound to my bedroom, alone and dependent upon the care of others for almost everything, especially those who are concerned in their own lives and ignorant of mine, I might well retreat into memories of the days when I had courage and strength, and could do what I wished and go where I pleased. No one wishes to be obliged, and to have to plead where they used to command.'

Narraway dreaded that too. He still had excellent physical health and his mind was as sharp as it had ever been, but already he was becalmed in a professional backwater. Perhaps a slow decline into complete obscurity awaited him, and eventually even the helplessness she spoke of now with such pity. Words of denial rose to his lips. He met her steady gaze with its total understanding, and they remained unsaid.

'What would you like me to do?' he asked.

She considered for only a moment. 'I know something about Serafina, but mostly to do with the revolutions of '48, and of course Italian unification and freedom from Austrian rule. But we have met seldom since then, and spoken without details. I know she fought hard, and was physically extraordinarily brave, far more so than I. But did she really know secrets of anything that could matter now? Those old revolutions are so long ago. Does anyone care any more who said or did what?'

Narraway thought about it for several minutes before answering her. The coals settled in the fire and he took a pair of delicate brass tongs to replace them with more.

'For the political outcome, I doubt it,' he said finally. 'But if she knew of some personal betrayal, memories for that sort of thing are long. Although, as you say, most of the people involved are dead, and it concerns Britain very little. But I will ask a few discreet questions, even if it is to set your mind at rest that there is no one left whose life she might jeopardise. Of course, I don't know how we persuade her that it is 1896, rather than whenever she believes it to be. I'm afraid that is the best I can think of, at present.'

Vespasia smiled at him, gratitude warming her face. 'Thank you. It will be a beginning, and perhaps all we can do.'

'Is she afraid for her own safety?' he asked.

She was startled. 'I don't think so. No. She's concerned that she might unintentionally betray someone else, not being fully aware of who she is talking to.'

He looked at her across the low table between them and the tray of food, and bottle of wine in its cradle, the firelight winking on the dusty glass.

'Are you sure?'

Her eyes widened. 'Perhaps not,' she said very softly. 'I thought it was the confusion of not knowing that frightened her most, the dread that she might betray all that she has been in the past by speaking too much now. But maybe you are right, and she is afraid of someone trying to ensure her silence, even at the cost of her life. But what can she possibly know that matters now, so many years later?'

'I don't know,' he admitted, picking up a slice of toast himself. 'Perhaps nothing. But it will give me something worthwhile to do to find out. I shall be in touch with you as soon as I learn anything beyond what you already know.'

'Thank you, Victor. I am grateful to you.'

He smiled. 'I can do nothing tonight. Have some more wine and let us finish the pâté.'

The following morning Narraway began to search for any reference he could find regarding Serafina Montserrat. In the past he would have had access to Special Branch files. Or – even more simply – he could have gone to his predecessor and asked him for whatever he could recall. But now he had no authority, no position from which to ask anything, and – perhaps more importantly – no ability to demand that whatever he said be kept private.

He could have gone to Pitt, but Pitt had enough to be concerned with in his new command. Moreover, he certainly would know nothing himself; he was far too young. He had been a child at the time of Serafina's activities, if it turned out they were more than peripheral anyway.

Narraway began at his club on the Strand, approaching one of the oldest members quite casually. He learned nothing at all. A second enquiry gained him exactly the same result.

By mid-afternoon he had exhausted the obvious avenues, which were certainly few enough. He did not want to raise interest, so he had kept his enquiries very general. He simply asked about the times and places, mentioning no individual people. The answers had included much that was interesting: memories of a year of brief hope for freedom, which remained elusive even now. Vespasia's name had come up briefly, but not Serafina's. If indeed she had known anything of danger or embarrassment to anyone, she had kept her own counsel quite remarkably.

By late afternoon, as it was dusk and growing colder, he was beginning to believe that Serafina's imagination was a great deal more colourful than the reality had been. Walking briskly across Russell Square under the bare, dripping trees, he accepted that he would have to go to a more direct source and ask openly.

He smiled at his own inadequacy. He should have more sympathy with Serafina Montserrat, especially if she had once been as dynamic as Vespasia had said. To lose power, he thought, is like watching yourself fade away, pieces of you slipping out of control and vanishing so that you grow ever smaller and more helpless, until there is nothing of you left except a tiny heart that knows its own existence, but can do little to affect anything else.

He should have more pity for the old especially, treat them with the same dignity he would have were they more powerful than he, instead of so very much less. He made the resolution, but would he keep it?

He came out in Woburn Place and hailed a passing hansom. Giving the driver his home address, he climbed in with some relief.

The next day he telephoned Lord Tregarron at the Foreign Office, with whom he had at least an acquaintance from his days at Special Branch. He arranged to call upon him that evening. Tregarron's father had been dead some years now, but he had been an expert on the Austro-Hungarian Empire. He had spoken both German and Hungarian, the predominant two of the eleven different languages among the mass of peoples and nationalities loosely joined in the empire that claimed to be the descendant of the Holy Roman Empire of medieval Europe, heirs of the might and the influence of Rome itself.

Narraway spent most of the day reading what was available in the library in the British Museum, reminding himself of the history of the empire in the last fifty to sixty years, and of the various rebellions of each of its constituent parts in their passion to gain more autonomy. It surprised him not at all to learn that Serafina was Italian. Venice and Trieste were swallowed up by Austria, losing their ancient culture and their ties to their own people. Venice had regained its freedom, but Trieste and its surrounds not yet.

He found little mention of Serafina's name, and then it was obliquely, as if of interest but no importance. Was she making up her knowledge of dangerous secrets, as Vespasia half feared, to colour in retrospect a life that was rapidly slipping away from her?

It was after dinner when Narraway reached Tregarron's house in Gloucester Place. He stepped out of his hansom into the first scattering of freezing rain on the stone-flagged pathway. The footman showed him immediately into the oak-panelled study with rows of bookcases filled with leather-bound volumes, and pictures of Cornish seascapes in the two panels free for such decoration. Tregarron himself came in a moment later.

'Evening, Narraway,' he said cheerfully. 'Can I offer you something? Brandy? A decent cigar? It's a miserable night. It must be important to bring you away from your own fireside at this hour.' He waved towards a large leather chair for Narraway to be seated.

'No, thank you,' Narraway declined the cigar, but sat down comfortably. 'I don't want to keep you longer than I need. It is gracious of you to spare me the time.'

'Old habits,' Tregarron said drily, sitting in the companion chair opposite him and leaning back, crossing his legs. 'How can I help you now? You said something about the Austro-Hungarian Empire. Pretty good shambles, especially after that awful business in Mayerling.' He pulled his face into an expression of regret and a certain unmistakable degree of disgust. 'Emperor's only son, heir to the throne, commits suicide with his mistress in a hunting lodge. If that's what it was, of course.' He let it hang in the air as a slight question. 'Maybe the best interpretation they could put on it, in the circumstances.'

'Rubbish,' Narraway said briefly. 'Unless he was insane. No royal prince takes his own life because he can't marry his mistress. His wife might have been any kind of a bore, or a harridan – you just live separately. Been done by more kings than I've had good dinners. The old Emperor himself has a mistress, in spite of having married for love, apparently.'

Tregarron smiled widely, showing strong teeth. 'My father spent years in Vienna. He said Franz Josef was supposed to marry the Empress's elder sister, but he fell madly in love with Sisi on sight and wouldn't have anyone else.'

'Yes, your father would probably know,' Narraway agreed. 'But that makes it even more unlikely that Rudolf would have shot his mistress and then himself simply because he couldn't possibly make her Empress, when the time comes.'

'Was it the Mayerling business you wanted to speak to me about?' Tregarron asked curiously. 'How does that concern our government, or Special Branch, for that matter?'

'No, it has nothing to do with Mayerling, or Rudolf,' Narraway said quickly. 'It goes back much further than that, possibly thirty years or more, forty, or even fifty.'

'Good heavens!' Tregarron looked startled, and amused. 'Before my time. However old do you think I am?'

Narraway smiled. 'I was thinking of your father. You said he spent years in Vienna . . .'

There was a brief tap on the door and, without waiting for a reply, Lady Tregarron came in. She was in her mid-forties but still extremely attractive in a quiet, comfortable way. Her features were unremarkable, her colouring quite ordinary mid-fair, but she carried with her a kind of serenity as if ill-temper were unimaginable.

'Good evening, Lord Narraway,' she said with a smile. 'How pleasant to see you. May we offer you something? Perhaps a fresh cup of tea? I assume you have dined already, but if not, I'm sure Cook would find you a good sandwich, at the very least.'

'A cup of tea would be excellent,' Narraway accepted. 'It's a miserable night.'

'Are you sure that's all?' she asked with concern.

'I don't want to disturb you for long. I can come to the point rather more quickly than I have been doing.' He turned to Tregarron. 'Have you heard of a woman named Serafina Montserrat? Perhaps in some connection with Austrian affairs?'

There was a slight flicker across Tregarron's face, but it was impossible to read. 'Montserrat?' he repeated. 'No, I don't think so. It's the kind of name one would remember. Italian? Or Spanish, perhaps?'

'Italian,' Narraway answered. 'From the north, Austrian-occupied territory.'

Tregarron shook his head. 'I'm sorry, I have no idea.'

Lady Tregarron looked from one to the other of them, then excused herself to ask the maid to bring tea.

Narraway knew Tregarron was lying. The expression in his eyes, the repetition of the name to give himself a moment to consider before denying, gave him away. But there was no point in asking again, because he had already taken a position he could not go back on without admitting he had lied. What explanation could there be for that? If Narraway had asked him with Lady Tregarron not present, would the answer have been different?

Was Tregarron's denial a desire to remain uninvolved in something? Surely anything Serafina knew was too old to affect anyone now, certainly any current government concern. Someone's reputation? A friend? Someone who would still be tarnished by connection with Serafina, or whatever it was she knew?

Or was it simply that Narraway was no longer in Special Branch at all, let alone head of it, and Tregarron did not trust him, but did not want to be abrupt enough to say so? That thought was peculiarly painful, which was ridiculous. It had been months now since his dismissal. Narraway should be over it and have found some new passion to consume his energy. There were years of spare time stretching without purpose ahead of him.

He forced his voice to sound light, free from emotional strain.

'I don't suppose it matters,' he said lightly. 'It was an enquiry for a friend. Apparently Mrs Montserrat is getting very frail.

It was something to do with informing those who might be concerned and wish to contact her before it's too late.'

Tregarron did not move at all, as if his body were stiff in his large, comfortable chair. 'Do I take it from your remark that Mrs Montserrat is dying?' he asked.

Narraway shrugged. 'That was what I gathered. I think she is of very advanced years.'

Tregarron blinked. 'Really? I suppose it was all a very long time ago. One forgets how the years pass.' He smiled ruefully, but the expression stopped far short of his eyes.

Narraway hesitated. Should he let Tregarron see that he had observed the slip, or might he learn more if he let it pass? He decided on the latter.

'Yes,' he agreed with a sigh. 'We were all a lot younger, and with dreams and energy that I, at least, no longer possess.'

Tregarron eased back in his chair, his body relaxing. 'Indeed. It's always more complicated than the young suppose. Perhaps that's just as well. If they grasped all the reasons why things won't happen, or can't be made to work, nothing would ever be tried. It's certainly a hell of a mess now. We don't need firebrands of any sort, especially in Austria. The poor devils have got little enough grip on their crumbling empire as it is, without hare-brained idealists running amok.'

He shifted a little and recrossed his legs before continuing. 'The Emperor's son died in one of the ugliest scandals of the century, and God knows, there have been other bad ones. We've had the odd few ourselves. Now his nephew, the only heir left, is wanting to marry a woman the old Emperor considers to be beneath the position that will be thrust upon her. The Hungarian situation is bad, and growing worse. Most of Europe recognises that the poor devils are second-class citizens in their own land. Italy and the Balkans are increasingly restless. And I'm afraid all of that is to say nothing of chaos in Russia, and the very considerable rising power of Germany, which is now united and tasting its own strength.'

He bit his lip and stared gravely at Narraway. 'We have more than enough to worry about. Let the past lie in whatever peace it can.'

'It wasn't important,' Narraway lied. 'A passing kindness I might have been able to do.' He smiled apologetically. 'I'm a trifle bored with listening to their lordships in the House. Perhaps I should find myself a country pursuit, except I am not a countryman, apart from the odd weekend.'

'Perhaps you should remain in London and listen more closely to their lordships. I'm sure you could find something to argue about, concentrate their minds now and then on a useful issue.' Tregarron frowned slightly. 'I . . . I hate to ask this, but are you confident in this fellow Pitt that they've put into your place in Special Branch? I know he was a good policeman, but this is not quite the same thing, is it! He'll need a judgement, a keenness of perception that police experience won't have taught him. He might be brilliant at solving mysteries and be able to unravel criminal activity and tell you exactly who's involved, but can he see the larger picture, the political ramifications? Has he actually mastered anything beyond the solving of crime? Does he understand anything deeper than that?'

Narraway knew exactly what Tregarron meant, but he affected a slight confusion to give himself time to think.

Tregarron leaned forward, filling the silence as if compelled to do so, in case he had offended Narraway. 'I know he's a good chap, and probably as honest as the day, and after that disaster with Gower, we'll destroy ourselves without honesty. But for God's sake, Narraway, we need a little sophistication as well! We require a man who can see ten jumps ahead, who can outwit the best against us, not just put a hand on the shoulder of the actual perpetrator of a crime, the fanatic with a stick of dynamite in his pocket.'

'I think one of Pitt's greatest assets will be that men who think they are clever will underestimate him,' Narraway replied.

Tregarron's eyebrows shot up and a faint humour lit his face. 'Should I consider myself suitably rebuked?' he enquired.

Narraway smiled, this time with genuine amusement. 'Not unless you wish to,' he said smoothly. 'I have every confidence in Pitt, and you may also.'

But as he went outside into the rain half an hour later, he was less certain than he had led Tregarron to suppose. Was Pitt's own innate honesty going to blind him to the degree of deviousness in others?

Pitt had been born a servant, spent his boyhood with a respect for the master of the estate: Sir Arthur Desmond, a man of unyielding honour and considerable kindness. Might Pitt, in some level below his awareness, expect others of wealth and position to be something similar?

How would he cope with the disillusion when he discovered that it was so often not the case?

Then Narraway remembered the affair at Buckingham Palace, and thought very possibly his anxieties were unnecessary. He lengthened his stride towards Baker Street where he would assuredly find a hansom to take him home.

Chapter Three

Pitt's office was warm and comfortable. The fire burned well, and every time it sank down he put more coal on it. Outside the rain beat against the windows, sharp with the occasional hail. Grey clouds chased across the sky, gathering and then shredding apart as the wind tore them. Down in the street passing vehicles sent sprays of water up from the gutters, drenching careless pedestrians walking too close to the kerb.

Pitt looked at the pile of papers on his desk. They were the same routine reports that greeted him every day, but if he did not read them he might miss one thread that was different, an omission or the cross-reference that indicated a change, a connection not made before. There were patterns that anything less than the minutest care would not disclose, and it might be the only warning of a betrayal or an attack to come.

He was disturbed in the rhythm of it by a sharp rap on the door. He turned the page down reluctantly.

'Come,' he answered.

The door opened and Stoker came in, closing it silently behind him. His face was as difficult to read as usual. Pitt had learned to see the agitation or excitement in him by

61

studying the way he moved, the ease or the stiffness in his body and the angle of his shoulders. Now he judged him to be alert and a trifle apprehensive.

'What is it?' he asked, gesturing towards the chair opposite the desk.

Stoker sat obediently. 'Maybe nothing,' he replied.

'If it was nothing you wouldn't be here,' Pitt pointed out. He trusted Stoker's instinct. He was the only one who had believed in Narraway when he was accused of treason in the O'Neil case. Everyone else believed the evidence. Stoker had had the courage to risk not only his career but his life to work secretly with Pitt against those who had corrupted and usurped the power. It was Stoker who had saved Pitt's life in the desperate struggle towards the end. He claimed not to believe in instinct, yet his mastery of small observations was acute. He heard the evasions that skirted around a lie, saw the smile that indicated nervousness, the tiny signs of vanity in a conspicuous watch chain, a folded silk handkerchief a shade too bright, the over-casual manner that concealed a far better acquaintance than that admitted to.

'What sort of questions?' Pitt insisted.

Stoker frowned. 'Down Dover way. Been a few questions about railway signals and points.'

'Railway points?' Pitt was puzzled. 'You mean where the tracks join, or branch? What does anyone want to know? Sure it's not just maintenance?'

Stoker's face was grim. 'Strangers asking about how they work, where they're controlled from. Can they be done by hand, that sort of thing. Thought it might be some fellow just wanting to explain it to his son, at first. But there have been a few questions about timetables, goods trains as well as the passenger trains from Dover to London, and branch lines as well, as if someone wanted to work out where they cross.'

Pitt thought for a moment or two. Some of the possibilities were ugly. 'Same man asking?'

'That's a bit hard to tell. Extremely ordinary-looking, except he had very pale, clear eyes. Man who asked about the goods trains had spectacles, couldn't see his eyes.'

'And the man who asked about the signals and points?' Pitt said, a tiny knot of anxiety beginning to tighten in his stomach.

'Different hair, as much as you could see under his hat. Doesn't mean anything. Anybody can put a wig on.'

'What's being moved in and out of Dover on the lines they asked about?' Pitt pressed.

'Looked into that. Heavy industrial stuff, mostly. Some coal. Fish. Nothing worth stealing, not with a rail crash anyway.'

Pitt thought for a moment. 'Passenger trains as well?'

'From Dover to London. Think it's some passenger they could be after?' Stoker asked.

'Lot of trouble for one passenger,' Pitt replied. 'More like anarchists thinking to create a major disaster, to show us they can.'

'What for?' Stoker was frowning, puzzled. 'That's not like anybody we know already. Couldn't even pretend there's any idealism or political motive in that.'

'That's what worries me,' Pitt admitted. 'It doesn't make sense. We haven't understood it yet. But you're right, there's something planned, even if this is just a distraction so we miss the real thing. But we daren't ignore it. If someone is prepared to cause a train crash to kill one person, then it has to be someone of overwhelming importance to them.'

He took a deep breath, and suddenly the room felt colder, even though the fire was still burning and the windows were still closed. The implication of what Stoker had said was inescapable.

'Who?' he said.

'Don't know.' Stoker moved his thin, strong hands in a very slight gesture of helplessness. 'Don't even know when, except it's soon. Nobody finds out timetables months ahead. Everything could change.'

'Who's coming from Dover to London in the next couple of months? Who would anarchists want to kill?'

'Nobody that matters, far as I can tell.' Stoker shook his head. 'Some Russian count is coming to stay on a private visit. Might be visiting some of our royal family at the same time, I suppose. One or two politicians, but no one important: a Frenchman and an American. Can't see why any of them would be worth killing, especially here. Probably far easier to do it at home, if you wanted to. Oh, one minor Austrian duke, but he doesn't hold any office, and he'd be easy enough to kill in Vienna. And whoever did it could escape there. Whole of Europe to go to. We're an island: a foreigner would stick out like a sore thumb, unless he hid in one of the immigrant communities in London. But why bother? It makes no sense.'

'Then this is to divert us from something else,' Pitt answered. 'Something bigger and a lot more important.'

Stoker nodded, his jaw tight. 'More important than a foreign prince or duke being assassinated right here in London, under our noses?'

'Well, if it's a diversion, that's the point,' Pitt said grimly. 'Can't hold our attention with something that doesn't matter. Keep looking. And tell me what you find.'

Stoker rose to his feet. 'Yes, sir. Maybe it's a dry run to see if we pick it up?'

'I thought of that,' Pitt agreed. 'Learn everything you can, but discreetly.'

When he was gone, Pitt sat back in his chair and

considered what Stoker had said. Many cases in the past had begun as whispers, a rumour that seemed trivial at first, a fact that didn't quite fit, an alliance that was outside the usual pattern. Narraway had years of experience in seeing the anomaly that was the first indication of a new plot or an attack on a new target.

Until his arrival at Special Branch, Pitt had been used to being called in only after a crime had been committed. He then worked backwards to unravel the history, the reasons, and find the proof of guilt that would stand up at trial. It was a new discipline for him to see the event before it occurred, and then prevent it.

Did those who had appointed him in Narraway's place really have any understanding of exactly the skills involved? Had they misjudged his abilities because they had seen Narraway's successes, and known that Pitt had contributed to most of the later ones? Could they be so naïve?

He had a gnawing fear in the pit of his stomach that they could.

His own judgement had sometimes been desperately flawed. He had been taken in completely in the whole O'Neil affair. He had been just as duped as the rest of them, until close to the end. He had believed Narraway innocent out of personal loyalty, which had nothing to do with reasoning.

He thought of Narraway's Irish past, the tragedies and compromises, the things Narraway had done that Pitt would not have – not through judgement but because his nature would have prevented it. Narraway was subtler, more experienced, and infinitely more devious than Pitt; a loose cannon where Pitt was predictable. And yet even Narraway had come within an inch of being ruined.

Was Special Branch itself on trial now? Was that the crux of it? The chance to proclaim them a failure and get rid of them altogether. Even within government, not everyone wanted them to succeed. And it would all be lost if there were one large, vital failure.

As he had told Stoker he would, Pitt made it his first priority to learn whatever he was able to regarding possible assassination targets. If the intended victim were indeed someone visiting a member of the royal family, then the minister in the Foreign Office responsible for Central and Eastern Europe was a good place to begin enquiring. If he knew nothing, Pitt would have to spread his search wider. Accordingly, he was at Lord Tregarron's office a little after half-past two.

He was still a trifle self-conscious announcing himself as Commander Pitt of Special Branch, but he had no doubts about doing so. If there was anything in the rumour, then foiling the plot was a matter of urgency. An assassination on British soil would be one of the most acute embarrassments imaginable, whoever the victim was.

He was received with courtesy by a smart young man, who was presumably a secretary of some sort, and who invited him to wait in a very comfortable room. The armchairs were of brown leather, and there were newspapers and quarterly magazines on the table before a briskly burning fire. He was even offered whisky, which he declined. The secretary made no move towards the tantalus on the sideboard, as if he had expected as much.

'Right, sir,' he said smoothly. 'We'll not keep you longer than we have to.'

Ten minutes later it was not the secretary who returned, nor Lord Tregarron himself, but Jack Radley. He came in and closed the door behind him. He was dressed in a black coat and striped trousers. He looked extraordinarily elegant, and slightly uncomfortable.

'Good afternoon, Thomas,' he said with a half-smile. 'I

assume this must be important for you to have come here in person. May I tell Lord Tregarron what it concerns?'

Pitt was a trifle taken aback. He had not expected to have to explain his errand to anyone else, but he had not called on Tregarron before. Maybe he should have foreseen it.

'I need some information urgently on possible visitors any of the royal family may be expecting from overseas within the next month or so,' he replied a little stiffly.

Jack's eyes widened, curious but unconcerned. 'Anyone in particular?'

'I don't know. That is what I have come to ask. It might be either official or private.'

'Is there some concern for Her Majesty?' Now Jack looked more anxious. 'Special Branch doesn't usually bother Lord Tregarron with this sort of thing.'

'Not so far as I know,' Pitt replied a little coolly. He heard the implied criticism that he was wasting their time. 'My information suggests the danger may be to the visitor, but it could be extremely unpleasant either way. I need to speak to Lord Tregarron as soon as possible.'

Jack nodded. 'I'll inform him.' He turned and left, closing the door behind him with a slight click of the latch.

Pitt waited, pacing back and forth across the dark red Turkish carpet, until Jack returned several minutes later, alone. Pitt started towards the door, but instead of opening it for them both to leave, Jack closed it again.

'This seems to be rather general,' he said unhappily. His finger was still on the handle, his body blocking the way out. 'What is it that makes you believe there is some threat? You made it sound as if it could come from almost any quarter. Whom do you suspect, and of precisely what? If I could take that to Lord Tregarron he might be able to help you.'

Pitt was not easily ruffled. Years in the police had taught

him the virtue of patience, and also that when people are shocked or frightened they often react aggressively. However, this faintly patronising tone from Jack, of all people, was as abrasive as vinegar on a cut in the skin.

'You make it sound as if I'm looking for some kind of personal favour to help me out of a predicament,' Pitt said tartly. 'It is Special Branch's duty to prevent any attempts at assassination on British soil, and to do so is as much in the interests of the Foreign Office as it is in our own. Neither of us wants some prince or duke shot while he's our guest.'

Jack paled and the skin across his cheekbones tightened. 'Is that likely?'

'I don't know! I don't know who's visiting, apart from the official government list.'

Jack stiffened. 'Exactly what do you know, Thomas? I'll see how it squares with the information we have. After the problems with Special Branch – Gower and Austwick and all that – you have to understand why Lord Tregarron is cautious.' There were high spots of colour in his cheeks, but his eyes did not waver.

'That is why I came in person,' Pitt said between his teeth. He was on the verge of adding that if Tregarron didn't trust him, then he had better ask the Prime Minister to have him replaced. Then he realised how childish that sounded, and how appallingly vulnerable. Had he heard someone else say such a thing he would immediately have seen their weakness, however much he might not have wished to.

He took a breath and spoke more levelly. 'I am aware of the delicacy of the situation, and one recent near failure,' he added. 'I would remind Lord Tregarron that in the end we succeeded – rather spectacularly.'

Jack stood motionless. 'I will remind him. He will still want to know the cause of your concern. What shall I tell him?'

Pitt was prepared. He had expected to answer to Tregarron personally, but he could see that it was going to have to be through Jack. He outlined what Stoker had told him and the slight anomalies he had observed.

'It doesn't seem like much,' Jack said gravely.

'By the time it does, it will be too late to deal with it discreetly,' Pitt pointed out. 'You might mention that also. Special Branch's job is not to stage spectacular rescues. It is, if possible, to avoid the danger and the embarrassment in the first place.'

Jack bit his lip. 'I'll go and tell him. Please wait.'

Again Pitt was too restless to sit in any of the chairs, comfortable as they were. He stood by the window, then paced, then stared out of the window again at the busy street below. The blustering wind whipped at coat-tails, caught umbrellas, and endangered hats. He could imagine the hiss and splash as the wheels of passing carriages sent arcs of muddy water up into the air behind them.

It was a quarter of an hour later when Jack reappeared. This time he looked distinctly embarrassed.

'I'm sorry, but we can offer no practical help. Lord Tregarron says that he has considered the information you passed to us, and it does not refer to any of the private visits of which we are aware, nor does it seem to tie into any of the anarchist groups in Europe that we know of. In his opinion it is no more than careless gossip, and there is no need for you to be anxious.'

He gave a bleak smile. 'He asked me to convey to you his thanks for passing on your concern, and for taking the trouble to come personally, especially in view of recent past events.' He seemed about to add something further, then changed his mind. Perhaps a glance at Pitt's face told him that he was already beyond the point of condescension.

Pitt felt again acutely like the policeman he had once been, whom well-trained butlers would send to the servants' entrance when he had been bold enough to knock on the front door. The gamekeeper's son was putting on the airs of a gentleman.

What would Narraway have done in this situation? The answer was obvious: he would not have been in this situation. Tregarron would have seen him, regardless of his estimate of the evidence.

Or would Narraway have been confident enough to judge the entire situation more accurately, and not needed Tregarron's opinion? Was that where Pitt had failed?

'Thank you for attempting to help,' Pitt said coolly. 'I shall have to acquire the information from some other source. This has been a waste of time, but it seems that neither you nor I have the power to avoid that. Good day.'

Jack started to say something, then changed his mind. He was pale, and there was a touch of high colour in his cheeks. He opened the door as Pitt went out and into the long corridor without looking back.

Jack watched Pitt until he was out of sight, then returned to Tregarron's office, knocking lightly. He was answered immediately.

Tregarron looked up from his desk, the question in his face.

Jack closed the door behind him. He found this embarrassing. Pitt was his brother-in-law, and he both liked and respected him. But he knew something of the circumstances of Pitt's promotion to Narraway's position, and how close the whole affair had come to disaster. He knew that Pitt must be nervous now, perhaps leaning too far towards caution, afraid of missing a clue, and consequently overreaching himself, and his authority. If he became officious he would make enemies.

'I think he was just being careful, sir,' he said to Tregarron.

Tregarron smiled, but it was tight-lipped. 'Don't let him be a nuisance over this, Radley. If people realise he's jumpy they may start to imagine there's something real behind it. We can't have Europe thinking we don't know what we're doing. Keep a tight rein on him, will you?'

Jack stood very straight. 'Yes, sir.' He considered adding something more, and then thought better of it. He was new to his position also and it was a major step up towards real power. Tregarron was one of the most dynamic figures in the Foreign Office. He had clearly taken a liking to Jack, much to Emily's delight. He hoped she had had no hand in his promotion. It was of intense importance to him to succeed on his own merit.

To begin with, he had been happy enough to live very comfortably on the wealth Emily had inherited from George Ashworth, but as time had gone by he had become less easy with it. Possibly that was due in part to the sense of purpose he saw in Pitt, and Charlotte's confidence in him. He wanted Emily to look at him with the same regard: one born of belief, not duty, or the customary deference women showed their husbands.

Tregarron was waiting for him to speak again.

Jack smiled. 'Yes, sir, I'll see that he doesn't embarrass himself, or us.'

'Thank you,' Tregarron acknowledged. 'You'd better look over those papers from the German ambassador.'

After dinner that evening, Pitt sat in the parlour in the big chair opposite Charlotte. The gaslight was bright, the heavy velvet curtains were closed. The fire burned well and the sound of the wind in the trees outside, mixed with the faint spatter of rain on the glass, was oddly comfortable. They were discussing moving house after Pitt's promotion, but seemed to be deciding against it – at least for the time being.

'Are you sure you don't want to?' he asked, looking at her. She was mending one of Jemima's dresses. The faint click of the needle against her thimble was the only sound from inside the room, except for the whisper of the flames. 'We could afford it,' he added.

'I know.' She smiled. 'The job is enough change for the moment.'

'You mean it might not last?' he interpreted, recalling Jack's figure stiff against the closed door, relaying Tregarron's dismissal. Could he tell her about it? Not being able to discuss things was the highest price of his promotion. It left him alone in a way he had not been used to in the fourteen years of their marriage. He tried to put the warmth back into his eyes, to take the sting – and perhaps the fear – out of his words. She was just as sharply aware as he was that if he failed he would not be able to go back into the ranks again, and there was nowhere else for him. He had no private means, unlike Narraway, or Jack Radley.

'No,' Charlotte said firmly, looking up and meeting his eyes. 'I mean that I like this house and I'm not ready to leave it yet – if I ever will be. We've had a lot of good times here, and bad – or they've looked bad for a while. Victor Narraway, Aunt Vespasia, Gracie and you and I have sat up all night in the kitchen, and fought some desperate battles.' She shook her head a little, ignoring her sewing. 'A new house would be empty in comparison. I expect there'll be more things happen, of course, but I'm not ready to let the old ones go. Are you?'

'No, perhaps I'm not.' He smiled, feeling the warmth blossom inside him. 'Every time I go down the corridor to the kitchen I see Gracie standing on tiptoe, and still a couple of inches short of reaching the plates on the top of the dresser.

I'm not used to seeing Minnie Maude, five inches taller. But she's a good girl. You're happy with her, aren't you?'

'I'll always miss Gracie, but yes I am,' she said with certainty. 'And Daniel and Jemima like her, which is almost as important.' Then she frowned, aware that something was wrong. She was uncertain if he was not telling her because it was confidential, or only because he did not want to spoil the evening. She could not ask, but could read the tension in him as easily as if he had spoken. For over fourteen years they had been friends, as well as man and wife. He kept all manner of secrets from the government, the police and the general population, but he kept only the details from her: not their existence, nor the importance he placed in any one of them.

He made the decision.

'I saw Jack today,' he said.

Charlotte waited, watching his face, reading the conflicting emotions.

'I had to see Tregarron about something, or at least to try to,' he went on. 'He sent Jack for me to report to, and relay his replies back.'

'Jack's new promotion,' she said with a little tightening of her lips. 'I think Emily's prouder of it than he is.'

'Did she push him into it?' he asked.

'Possibly.' A shadow across her face. 'Was he arrogant?'

Pitt relaxed at last, allowing his shoulders to ease and his body to sink into the familiar shape of the chair. 'Not really. I was annoyed because I was damned sure Tregarron wouldn't have dismissed Narraway like that, but I think I went to them with too little information. He didn't believe there was any cause for concern, and it may well be that they are right. I need to know a lot more. I should have waited. Narraway would have.'

'And you expect to walk in and be as good in your first year as he was after twenty?' she asked, her eyebrows raised.

'I need to be,' he said quietly. 'Or at least as near as makes no visible difference.'

'He failed sometimes as well, Thomas. He wasn't always right.'

'I know.' He did know, but that did not ease the anxiety, or the knowledge of what failure would cost.

Charlotte left home at nine o'clock the following morning, stepping out onto the pavement feeling a trifle self-conscious in her new riding habit. She looked extremely smart in it, which she was happily aware of, but it was a long time since she had worn such a flattering and rather rakish outfit. It had not been possible until lately. Money was reserved for essentials, which this most certainly was not when one had children who seemed to grow out of every piece of clothing within months.

A week ago she had agreed to meet Emily in Rotten Row in Hyde Park, to spend an hour or two on horseback. Accordingly she now walked briskly towards Russell Square where she was certain she could find a hansom cab. The wind had dropped and there was a very slight frost in the air. It was a perfect winter morning for a ride.

However, when she alighted in Hyde Park she felt far less enthusiastic than she had expected to when the arrangement had been made. She could not put from her mind Pitt's conversation about his meeting with Jack in Lord Tregarron's office.

The trees of the park were bare, a fretwork of black lace against the sky. The earth of the long bridle path was already churned up by hoofs, and the grass beyond was the strange, almost turquoise colour that the frost crystals lent it. In the distance there were at least twenty riders already out: women side-saddle, graceful in perfectly cut habits; men riding astride, some of them in military uniform.

The sound of laughter drifted on the slight breeze, the jingle of harnesses and then the thud of hoofs as someone broke into a canter.

Charlotte walked across the hard, frosty earth towards the group of horses still held by their grooms, and she wondered how much of the previous day's encounter Jack had relayed to Emily. Did he consider his work also to be bound by secrecy? More probably he imagined she would hear of it from Charlotte today, and would have prepared her, regardless of protocol.

She saw Emily standing at her horse's head. She was easily distinguishable from the other women there by her slenderness, and the gleam of winter light on her fair hair. A knot of it was visible beneath the brim of her exquisite riding hat, which was like a shallower version of a gentleman's top hat, its brim slightly curled. Charlotte estimated the cost of it, and felt a flicker of envy.

She walked onto the gravel, which crunched under her boots.

Emily turned. She saw Charlotte and immediately started towards her.

'Good morning,' she said with a tentative smile, her eyes searching Charlotte's. 'Are you ready to ride?'

'Very much,' Charlotte replied. 'I've been looking forward to it.' It was a strangely stilted conversation, nothing like the ease and good humour they usually had towards each other.

Side by side, without meeting glances, they walked back to the grooms standing with the animals. They mounted and moved out at a walk. They nodded to other riders they passed, but did not speak as there was no one with whom they were acquainted.

The longer the silence lasted, the more difficult it would be to break it. Charlotte knew she must say something, even if it was completely trivial. Words often meant little; it was the fact of speaking that mattered.

'We've been thinking about moving house,' she began, trying to avoid the subject of Jack and Pitt and Lord Tregarron without being obvious about it. 'Thomas asked me if I would like to, but I'm fond of the house in Keppel Street. A lot of important things have happened while we've been there, memories I like to live with, or at least I don't want to let go of yet.'

Emily looked sideways at her. 'Wouldn't you like somewhere slightly larger? Perhaps in one of the squares? Or do you think it's a little early to move?' She meant, was Charlotte certain that Pitt would measure up to the job.

For a moment Charlotte did not answer. She was the elder, but she would always be socially the junior because of Pitt's humble beginnings, and because Emily had a wealth Charlotte would never even dream of.

Emily coloured uncomfortably and looked away, as though she needed to guide her horse along this safe, flat, fine gravel and earthen path.

'It is always a good idea not to take success for granted,' Charlotte replied levelly. 'Then if one fails, one has so much less distance to fall.' She saw Emily's expression tighten. 'But actually I simply meant that I am not yet ready to leave a house so full of happy memories. I have no intention of entertaining, so we don't require the extra rooms.'

'Surely you'll have to entertain?' Emily asked. 'And anyway, it's such fun!' A smile flickered across her face, but it was one evoked by memory, not warmth of feeling.

'Only friends,' Charlotte said quickly, keeping her horse level with Emily's. 'And they are perfectly content with Keppel Street.'

'In Thomas's new position he will be expected to entertain

people you are not necessarily friends with.' Emily raised her fair eyebrows. 'There are certain social obligations with promotion, you know? Head of Special Branch is a great deal more than just a policeman, even a gifted one. You will have to get used to speaking easily to government ministers, ambassadors and all kinds of other ambitious and useful people.'

'I doubt we would ever be able to afford a house fit to entertain people like that,' Charlotte said drily. 'It's a promotion, not an inheritance.'

Emily winced. 'I didn't realise you felt so badly about it. I'm sorry.'

Charlotte reined in her horse. 'It?' she questioned.

Emily stopped also. 'Money. Isn't that what we're talking about?'

'It's what you're talking about,' Charlotte corrected her. 'I was talking about living in a house where I'm comfortable, rather than buying a bigger one that I don't need and that is a strange place to me, without familiarity or memories. I'm not you, Emily, and I don't want the same things.'

'Don't be so pompous!' Emily snapped back. 'This is really about Jack having to tell Thomas he couldn't see Lord Tregarron, isn't it?' Her tone was challenging, almost daring Charlotte to deny it.

'Did you say something about pompous?' Charlotte enquired.

'It was not—'

'Really?' Charlotte cut across her. 'It seems you know far more about it than I do. But then Thomas's work is secret. He can't tell anyone, even me.' She urged her horse on, moving ahead of Emily. She hated quarrelling, especially with someone she cared for so deeply. It left her unhappy and oddly alone, but she would not let Jack's sudden promotion go to his head, or to Emily's, and allow them thoughtlessly to make worse

Pitt's sense of being out of his depth. Perhaps she was being unnecessarily protective, but then so was Emily. She was doing this because she was afraid Jack was gaining political power he had very little idea how to use.

She reined in her horse again and waited until Emily caught up with her. Without meeting Emily's eyes she started again.

'I don't want to move yet. It's taking things for granted that haven't happened for certain. I would have thought you, of all people, would understand that. Your social position is assured, and your financial one, but you've a long way to go before you can say the same politically.'

'Is that Thomas's opinion?' Emily was not yet mollified.

Charlotte forced herself to laugh. 'I have no idea. He didn't mention it. Why? Do you think Jack has very little further to go? That would be a shame.'

Emily muttered under her breath, and Charlotte knew very well that what she said was distinctly impolite.

While Charlotte was riding in Hyde Park, Pitt was already in his office at Lisson Grove asking for all the recent information Special Branch had gathered about any dissident groups in Central or Eastern Europe, particularly within the vast Austro-Hungarian Empire. This stretched from Austria itself eastward to include Hungary; south into northern Italy and down the Balkan Peninsula to Serbia, Croatia, Slovenia, Romania; north to Bohemia, parts of Poland and the Ukraine. Within its borders, eleven different languages were spoken and several major religions were observed, including Roman Catholicism, Eastern Orthodoxy and Islam. Additionally, there were a large number of Jews in prominent and highly influential positions in Vienna, where anti-Semitic feeling was deep, ugly, and growing. Unrest of one sort or another was a way of life.

Vienna might be the cradle of all sorts of new thoughts in

politics and philosophy, medicine, music and literature, but it was also a city of sporadic violence, of light and shadow, of unease, as if there were some doom just beyond the horizon when all the gaiety would end. Were they afraid of revolution, like the French? Or war?

Pitt had requested to see Evan Blantyre, whom he had met at the musical evening recently. His knowledge of the Austro-Hungarian Empire was extensive and he might be able to offer the information and assistance Lord Tregarron had declined to. He was agreeably surprised when Blantyre agreed to see him almost immediately. Less than an hour later, he stood in a pleasant anteroom, which had paintings of the Austrian Tyrol on the walls. He was there only briefly before he was ushered into Blantyre's office. This was a large, comfortable room with a fire burning in the hearth, armchairs on either side of it. There were worn patches on the carpet and the colours were faded with age and sunlight. The desk was old, the wood gleaming like satin.

'Good morning, Commander,' Blantyre said with interest, holding out his hand.

'Good morning, sir,' Pitt replied, accepting the greeting. 'I appreciate your taking the time to see me so quickly. It may prove to be nothing of importance, but I can't let it go.'

'Quite right,' Blantyre agreed. 'Although I must say from the little you told my secretary, it all seemed rather coincidental, and no real reason to suspect that any foreign visitor is the focus of an attack, if indeed there is one.' He indicated the chair near the fire and they sat down opposite each other.

'It is probably nothing,' Pitt agreed. 'But a lot of issues start out as a whisper, one coincidence, and then another too soon after it, people showing an unexplained interest in something.'

Blantyre smiled ruefully, curiosity lighting his face. 'How

the devil do you know which ones matter? Is there an intel-lectual formula for it, or is it instinct, a particular skill?' His eyes were steady and bright. 'Or something only experience can teach you, and perhaps one or two very near misses?'

Pitt shrugged. 'I'm tempted sometimes to think there's a hell of a lot of luck in it, but I suppose that's an easy name for constant observation and running down everything that strikes a jarring note.' He smiled. 'And, as you say, one or two close shaves.'

Blantyre nodded. 'In other words paying attention to detail, and a lot of damned hard work. Tell me more of exactly what alarms you in these particular enquiries? Do you really think it is about intended violence? Against whom, for God's sake? If it really is Duke Alois, why here? It sounds unlikely to me, if only because of the difficulty of setting it up in what for the conspirators is a foreign country. And then, of course, of escaping where they won't have a network of friends or sympa-thisers. Every man's hand would be against them.'

'True,' Pitt conceded. 'But they would also be unknown to the general public. Few people here to recognise or betray them. And there is the other possibility.'

Blantyre frowned. 'What's that?'

'That they don't intend to escape. If they feel passionately enough about their cause, they may be prepared to sacrifice their own lives in the process.'

Blantyre looked down at the worn patterns of the carpet. 'I hadn't thought of that,' he said grimly. 'Of course, men do such things – and women too, I suppose. Patriots, misguided or not, come in all forms. Martyrs as well.' He looked up at Pitt again. 'I still don't find it very likely. That sort of great sacrifice isn't something you do in order to kill a nonentity. In sheer practical terms, the world doesn't take enough notice.' He pulled his mouth into a bitter smile, and then let it fade.

'Tell me exactly what you've found, and I'll do all I can to learn if it's part of a greater plot. God knows, the last thing we need is some Austro-Hungarian duke blown to bits on our front doorstep.'

Pitt told him the core of what he had gathered from Stoker's reports, and added the further information he had received since then. As he spoke he watched Blantyre's expression grow darker and more troubled.

'Yes, I see,' Blantyre said as soon as Pitt had stopped speaking. He sat pensively, with his strong hands held so the fingertips touched. 'If there were substance to it, it would be appalling. But how seriously have you considered that it is a wretched string of coincidences making a few unconnected enquiries look sinister, when in fact they are not at all? Or else – and this seems more likely to me – someone deliberately concocting this stuff to take your attention away from something else that *is* serious, and far more relevant?'

That was what Pitt himself had feared, and resisted putting into words. He smiled bleakly. 'Bluff?' he asked.

'Why not?' Blantyre raised his eyebrows.

'Or double bluff?' Pitt added.

Blantyre let out a sigh. 'Of course you are right. I really don't think there is any likelihood of an assassination here at the moment, but I will look into it, ask a few discreet questions, at least about the possibility.'

'Thank you.' Pitt rose to his feet. 'I can't afford to ignore it.'

Blantyre smiled and stood also. He held out his hand and Pitt took it, feeling the firm grip before he turned to go.

Pitt left the office feeling relieved, not of the anxiety that the danger was real, or the fear that it was a distraction from something far worse, but because Blantyre had taken him seriously. He had treated him as he would have treated Narraway.

Pitt smiled to himself as he went down the steps and out into the street and the heavy traffic. He was acutely aware of his vulnerability, not because of the weight of his new command, but the fact that he was so uncertain of himself in it.

Two days later, and now close to the end of February, Pitt was sitting alone in his office. The light was failing, and within the next quarter-hour he would have to stand up and turn on the gaslight. There was a knock on the door, and Stoker put his head around it.

'Mr Evan Blantyre here to see you, sir,' he said with surprise and a certain respect in his voice. 'Says it's pretty urgent.'

Pitt was surprised also. He had accepted that Blantyre, for all his courtesy, still thought the whole issue of a threat to any visiting Austrian dignitary to be largely a misreading of the information.

'Show him in,' he said immediately, rising to his feet.

A moment later Blantyre came in, closing the door behind him. He shook Pitt's hand briefly, and started to speak even before both of them were seated.

'I owe you an apology, Pitt,' he said gravely, hitching his trousers a little at the knees to preserve their shape as he crossed his legs. 'I admit, I didn't take this theory of yours very seriously. I thought you were jumping at shadows a bit. Understandable, after some of the recent tragedies.'

Pitt presumed he was referring to the Gower case and Narraway's dismissal, mistaken as that had been. He said nothing. It was ridiculous to have hoped that some of that wretched betrayal would have remained secret, but it still hurt him that so many people seemed to know of it. He waited for Blantyre to continue.

Blantyre's face was very grave. 'I looked into the information you gave me,' he continued. 'At first it seemed to be very superficial, a series of odd but basically harmless questions, unconnected to each other. But I examined them a little more deeply, one at a time, beginning with the tracing of the most likely route from Dover to London, which of course is by train.'

Pitt watched Blantyre's face and the intensity in it alarmed him. He waited without interrupting.

'It seemed to mean very little.' Blantyre gave a slight shrug. 'Hundreds of people must make such a journey. Enquiries would be natural enough, even several days in advance of travel. Then I found the signals that you mentioned, and the points at which such trains would pass a junction on the track. You are perfectly right, of course. Goods trains also travel there regularly, and a series of accidents – signals green when they should be red; points changed and a goods train diverted onto the wrong track – and you could have a disaster with enormous proportions. You would have far more than one man killed.'

He drew his breath in slowly, then let it out again.

'But I thought I had better see if the route tied in with any known person of importance. It did, rather more than I supposed. It turns out you are right, one of the minor Austrian dukes is coming. He is of no importance himself, but still a member of the Imperial family, and grand-nephew of our Queen, or something of the sort. He is making a private visit to a grandson of the Queen's. It is not a government matter at all, so they were not informed. But his coming, and the time that the enquiries concern, coincide precisely with the plans made for him to travel from Vienna to Paris, then to Calais, and across the Channel. From Dover he goes by train to London. He'll be staying at the Savoy.'

'Not the Palace?' Pitt said in surprise.

'It seems he wants to do a spot of entertaining himself,' Blantyre said with a tight little smile. 'But you see my point. When I made a few enquiries of certain friends in Europe, they made some slight investigation themselves, and found that questions had been asked about the entire route. It seems he will be bringing only a few servants: a secretary, a valet, that sort of thing.'

He hesitated only a moment. 'I'm sorry, Pitt, your instincts were correct. This is something you have to take seriously.'

Pitt was cold, in spite of the embers burning in the grate only a few feet from him. Until now he had felt as if he probably was imagining the danger, as Tregarron had said, but Blantyre's news made that impossible.

'Here,' Blantyre held out a small bundle of papers. They looked to be hastily scribbled notes, perhaps half a dozen sheets in all. 'You will need to follow up on it, of course, so I have given you the names of the people I spoke to, the facts and references I checked. I cannot oblige you to keep them secret, but I would ask that you tell as few people as possible, and only those you are certain you can trust absolutely, not only their honesty but even more their discretion. I would not have committed anything to paper, but I fear this is far too serious to allow care for individual reputation to override the necessity of preventing what is potentially, at least, a monstrous crime, which will kill not only a member of the Austrian royal family, but God knows how many innocent Britons.' He held the notes out in his hand for Pitt to take.

Pitt met Blantyre's gaze, then took the papers and looked down at them. They were exactly as Blantyre had said: names, places, dates, so that Pitt could check all the routes, the questions, above all, the names and descriptions of known anarchists involved in assassinations in Europe, and the methods they had used. Particular emphasis had been laid on those who were close to the physical appearance of the man who had enquired about signals and points on the railway.

He looked back up at Blantyre.

'I'm sorry,' Blantyre said gravely. 'I know you would rather have been wrong, but I'm afraid it would seem that you are not. Something is planned that could, at its worst, set us at war with Austria – God knows why! But we would find out far too late to save ourselves.'

Pitt's mind raced. He had not enough military or diplomatic knowledge to understand why anyone would want to do such a thing. With a British train wrecked, feelings would be high in both countries. Accusations would be made, things said it would be impossible to deny later. Grief and confusion would turn to anger. Each country could so easily blame the other.

'God knows what is behind it,' Blantyre said softly. 'It may be no more than yet another petty uprising of one of the Balkan nations wanting more independence, and resorting to their usual violence. It happens quite regularly. But it may also be a far deeper plan, intended to damage Britain. Otherwise why do it here?'

'You mean someone prompting them to do it?' Pitt said quietly. 'In order to accomplish . . . what?'

'I don't know,' Blantyre admitted. 'The possibilities are considerable. Maybe there is some treaty these people wish broken, or not entered into in the first place.'

'Thank you. I shall look into all these.' Pitt rose to his feet and offered his hand to Blantyre.

The following day Pitt sent for Stoker, who came into the office looking unusually cheerful. However, his lightness of mood disappeared as soon as he sat down obediently and waited for Pitt to speak.

'You'll remember Evan Blantyre came here yesterday afternoon,' Pitt said quietly. 'I'd given him the information we had. At first he thought it was all irrelevant, but he looked into it anyway . . .'

Stoker sat up a little more stiffly.

'And there are plans for Duke Alois Habsburg to visit London from March the sixteenth to the nineteenth. He is to travel first from Vienna to Paris, then Calais, to take the steamer to Dover, lastly the train to London. He won't stay at the Palace, but at the Savoy Hotel. There are plans to throw a party at Kensington Palace for his friends.' He grimaced as he saw Stoker's face. 'Exactly the route you have seen, and on the day for which enquiries were made.'

Stoker let out his breath with a sigh, his eyes wide. 'So it's real!'

'It could be,' Pitt answered. 'Or it could be something we have very subtly been allowed to know about in order to draw our attention away from something else. But either way, we can't afford to ignore it. This is the information Mr Blantyre gave me.' He passed it over. 'Read it, then lock it in the safe here. Check each of the details and each of the names.'

'Yes, sir. What are you planning to do?'

'Learn all I can about Duke Alois Habsburg, and check anyone who could have the slightest interest in assassinating him,' Pitt replied.

Stoker picked up Blantyre's papers, looked at them and made very brief notes from the top two. 'I'll come back and get more tomorrow,' he said, rising to his feet.

'Anything else?' Pitt asked.

'No, sir.' Stoker looked slightly surprised.

'You looked unusually cheerful,' Pitt answered, leaving the question in the uplift of his voice.

Stoker smiled. 'Yes, sir.' He hesitated, a faint colour in his cheeks. He realised Pitt was not going to let it go. 'Had to follow someone yesterday evening; he was a bit suspect.'

'And?' Pitt pursued. 'What did you catch him doing? Don't make me pull your teeth, Stoker!' He heard his own words, and how much he sounded like Narraway. Now the heat burned up his own face.

'Nothing, sir, actually. Turned out to be a blind alley.'

'And?' Pitt snapped.

'He went to a concert, sir. The music was rather good. I thought I'd hate it, but it was . . . sort of beautiful.' He looked embarrassed but happy, as if the memory still lingered with him.

'What was it?' Now Pitt was curious. Even after all this time, he knew nothing of Stoker beyond his professional skills and his indisputable courage. His personal tastes, his life apart from Special Branch, were a complete mystery.

'Beethoven, sir. All piano.'

Pitt masked his surprise. 'Yes, you're right,' he agreed. 'It must have been good.'

Stoker smiled, then he stood up, excused himself and went out.

Pitt bent to study the rest of Blantyre's notes. He added to them a large sheaf of papers he had borrowed from the Special Branch files, and began to study the history of the last ten years, quickly moving forward to the present, and the character and politics of the Duke Alois Habsburg.

Two hours later, his eyes stung and his head ached. He had read a mass of facts, opinions and fears. The Austrian Empire was geographically enormous and a single entity, as far as land was concerned. It was nothing like the British Empire, which was composed of countries, islands and – in the cases of India, Australia and Canada – near continents, half the earth away from each other. Austria was one large mass loosely held together by a dual monarchy: one in Austria, one in Hungary. It included the best part of a dozen other countries and territories, each with their own history, language and culture, and frequently their own religions as well.

It had always been uneasy. Its history was marked with plots, protests, uprisings, the occasional assassination attempts, and of course plenty of individual executions and general suppressions.

Franz Josef had been Emperor for nearly fifty years. In some ways he ruled with a light hand, allowing a considerable degree of individuality to remain, but in others he was rigid, conservative and autocratic. The very nature of the ramshackle empire meant that it was only a matter of time before it fell apart. The question was which of all the many divisive elements was going to be the catalyst.

Socialism and its reforms had raised its voice in Vienna in many ways. Pitt was startled to learn that the dead crown prince, the heir to the throne who had died at Mayerling, Rudolf, had believed in its principles so passionately that he had expressed his intent, upon his succession to the throne, to declare the Austrian Empire a republic and to rule as its president.

Pitt sat motionless with the papers in his hands and tried to imagine what old Franz Josef had thought of that. And what now of the new heir, Archduke Franz Ferdinand?

Blantyre had written a long note on him also. Apparently, for all his radical differences with the old Emperor, the new heir, Franz Ferdinand, had no sympathies of that nature. He abhorred socialism and its reforms just as heartily as his uncle.

Blantyre's conclusion was the only one likely from the evidence. There was a plot to assassinate Duke Alois Habsburg when he was on British soil, presumably in London, since there had been anonymous enquiries about arrangements as far as the Savoy and Kensington Palace.

It would be an appalling embarrassment for Britain. It would be a disaster for Special Branch, especially following only months after the O'Neil affair and the disgrace of that.

The next morning Pitt went again to see Lord Tregarron. He must have the Foreign Office minister at the very least made aware of the threat, and possibly have the trip altered in time, or place, or even route of travel, at the last minute. And Duke Alois himself must be made aware of the danger also.

As before, he was met first by Jack, who was again very smartly dressed in black coat and striped trousers. He looked uncomfortable when he came into the room where Pitt had been asked to wait. He closed the door behind him and took a deep breath.

'Good morning, Thomas. How are you?'

It was an obvious attempt at civility in a situation he already foresaw as being uncomfortable.

Pitt had anticipated a resistance, until Jack made Tregarron aware of the seriousness of the threat. He determined to keep his temper, not only for Charlotte's sake, but because the moment he lost control of himself, he lost it also of the situation.

'Well, thank you,' he replied. 'But concerned.' He tried to keep his expression neutral. 'I took the various pieces of evidence I have to Evan Blantyre, as the best expert I know on the Austro-Hungarian Empire, and asked him to evaluate the likelihood of serious trouble in Britain within the next couple of months.' He saw Jack's face darken and his jacket pull tight as his stiffened shoulders strained the fabric.

'Apparently Duke Alois Habsburg is visiting one of our royal family in a few weeks' time. He plans to travel from Vienna to Paris, and then to Calais, and by ferry to Dover, and lastly by train to London—'

'The obvious route,' Jack interrupted.

'I am aware of that,' Pitt replied. 'The exact timetable might be less obvious, but people are making enquiries about it, even so far as the Savoy Hotel, where it is known he will stay, and Kensington Palace where a party will be given for him.'

A flash of anxiety crossed Jack's face. 'Really? Austrian officials making sure the route is well planned and safe?'

'No, the people who are checking are known agitators and anarchists,' Pitt replied. 'One or two of them are implicated in bombings in Paris.'

'Arrest them,' Jack told him.

'For what? Checking railway timetables?'

'Exactly. Aren't you being a bit alarmist? Alois is a very minor figure, you know.' Jack gestured with his hands, as if appealing to reason. 'Or maybe you don't? If somebody planned an assassination, Alois wouldn't be worth their time, or the risk.'

'Are you certain?' Pitt said very seriously.

'Yes,' Jack responded immediately. However, his tone of irritation made Pitt wonder if he really was certain, or if he had not given the matter any thought until that moment. He would defend his superior instinctively, and ascertain the details later. That was what a loyal second-in-command did.

Pitt shook his head. 'I think there is quite a lot about the Austrian royal family and its difficulties that we do not know. Did you expect the suicide at Mayerling?'

Jack was angry, caught by surprise. 'No, of course not. No one did,' he said with considerable annoyance.

'But with hindsight we can see that they should have,' Pitt pointed out. 'It was a tragedy waiting to happen.'

'How do you know that?' Jack demanded, coming further forward into the room.

Pitt smiled. 'It's my job to know a certain amount of things. Unfortunately I didn't know it at the time, and I doubt Narraway did. Or if he did, then no one listened to him.'

Jack winced and his eyes became harder. 'I'll go and ask his lordship, but honestly, I think you are scaremongering, Thomas, and I believe he will think so too. There is no earthly reason to assassinate Alois Habsburg. He's a harmless, totally lightweight junior member of the Austrian royal family, of which there are hordes, just as there are of ours.' Without adding anything more, he turned and went out of the room, leaving Pitt to wait again.

This time it was no more than five minutes before he came back into the room looking tense, as if now he wanted to say far more than he dared.

'Lord Tregarron will see you, but he can only spare a few minutes.' He held the door open for Pitt to go through. 'He has a meeting with our ambassador to Poland in a very short while.'

'Thank you,' Pitt accepted, going out and following Jack down a wide elegant corridor. About thirty feet along, Jack stopped and tapped quietly on a large arched door.

Tregarron greeted them stiffly but with the necessary courtesy, then looked only at Pitt as Jack retired to the back of the room, making himself all but invisible.

'Radley informs me that Evan Blantyre seems to believe there is some assassination attempt planned against Duke Alois Habsburg when he visits London next month.' He spoke quickly, giving Pitt no chance to interrupt him. 'I imagine you have to take notice of these things, but someone is trying to distract you from your more urgent business. Duke Alois is, as Radley has told you, a charming, somewhat feckless young man of no importance whatever. It would be completely senseless for anyone to waste their time harming him, let alone to set up an elaborate plot to do it in a foreign country, and then have to escape.'

He shook his head with annoyance, as if bothered by something in his way. 'It is out of the question that we should admit to the Austrian government that we cannot look after him or guarantee his safety in the capital city of our own Empire. I imagine they would find it impossible to believe we were so incompetent, and see it as a rebuff. If you think Special Branch cannot deal with it, I will ask the Home Secretary to take care of the matter. He has the ordinary police at his beck and call.' He smiled bleakly. 'Ask Narraway's advice. I'm sure he would make himself available to you.'

Pitt was so angry he could think of no words he dared say. His hands were shaking. He could feel the colour burn up his skin. He knew Jack was looking down at the floor, too embarrassed to meet his eyes.

'Good day, Mr Pitt,' Tregarron said bluntly.

'Good day, sir,' Pitt replied, and swung on his heel to go out. He passed Jack without even glancing at him, nor was he aware of the rain in his face as he stepped into the street.

Walking into his own house that evening was like a warm embrace, even before Charlotte met him at the kitchen door. She took a long, careful look at his face, and guided him away from the savoury cooking smells and into the front parlour. The fire was burning and the gaslamps were lit but turned low. This enveloping comfort was new since his promotion, and the ability to afford so much coal.

'What is it?' she asked as soon as she had closed the door.

'What's wrong with the kitchen?' he countered, evading answering her.

'Thomas! Minnie Maude is not Gracie, but she's far from unobservant. You are the master of the house. She watches you to see if all is well, if the day is good or bad, what she might do to please you. This is her home now, and it matters to her very much.'

Pitt breathed out slowly, letting some of the anger ease from him. He realised with self-conscious displeasure how little he had appreciated the effect his mood had on others. He had been born in the servant class; he should have known better. Without any warning, he was whisked back to his childhood and saw his mother in the kitchen of the big house and remembered the look on her face, the sudden anxiety when Sir Arthur Desmond had been in one of his rare dark moods, or word had come down that he was not very well.

'I saw Lord Tregarron today,' he said to Charlotte. 'First Jack, of course, and he told me, obliquely, that I am fussing over nothing and if I can't manage my job to ask for Narraway's help.' He could not keep the bitterness out of his voice.

She considered it for a moment before replying. 'That is extremely rude,' she said at length. 'I wonder what is bothering him that he should descend to such ill manners.'

'Are you asking in a sideways fashion if I was rude to him?' he said with a tight smile, knowing he was driving a wedge between her and Emily, and yet not being able to stop himself. He felt horribly vulnerable. 'I wasn't. I told him my information came from Blantyre. He's as good a source as there could be.'

'Perhaps that is the problem,' she said thoughtfully. 'Are you sure you are right, Thomas?'

'No,' he admitted. 'I'm just sure of the price if I am right and we do nothing.'

Chapter Four

Vespasia returned to call again on Serafina Montserrat a week after her first visit. It was a bright, fresh day, but surprisingly cold. She was pleased to come inside the house, even though it had an air of emptiness about it. Pale flowers were arranged carefully in a vase on the hall table, but without flair, as if whoever had done it were afraid to be criticised for individuality. All the pictures were straight, the surfaces dust free, but it looked in some way as if the mistress of the establishment were not at home. There were no small articles of daily use visible: no gloves or scarves, no outdoor boots on the rack below the coat stand, no silver- or ebony-topped cane.

She was waiting in the cool, green morning room where the footman had left her when Nerissa came in. She closed the door so softly behind her that Vespasia was startled to see her there.

'Good morning, Lady Vespasia. It is so kind of you to call again,' Nerissa began. Her unremarkable face was marred at the moment by tiredness and lack of colour. Her plain, dark dress did nothing to help, in spite of a pale fichu at the neck.

Vespasia felt something vaguely patronising in the younger woman's tone, as if visiting an old lady were a thing one did out of charity rather than friendship. It left her with the feeling that one day she might be seen in the same light, which was like a sudden chill to the skin.

'It is not kind at all, Miss Freemarsh,' she said coolly. 'Mrs Montserrat and I are more than acquaintances. We have memories in common of times of marvellous hopes and dangers, and too few people with whom to share them, and others to recall of friends we will never see again.'

Nerissa smiled. 'I'm sure you have,' she replied. 'But I'm afraid you will find Aunt Serafina somewhat less lucid than even a week ago. She is failing very quickly.' She gave a brief, apologetic smile. 'Her memory has become even more disjointed, and she has longer lapses into complete fantasy. She cannot now appreciate the difference between what she has read or been told, and what has really happened in her own experience. You will have to be patient with her. I hope you understand?'

'Of course I do,' Vespasia assured her. 'And even if I do not, it hardly matters. I have come to visit a friend, not to cross-question a witness as to history.'

'I did not mean to offend you,' Nerissa said, lowering her eyes. 'I only wished to prepare you for the deterioration you will see in her, even in so short a time, in case it causes you distress. It really is rather serious. And I hardly know how to put this delicately, but . . .' She stopped, as if unable to find the right words.

'But what?' Now Vespasia was ashamed of herself for having been cool. The younger woman was clearly concerned. Perhaps other visitors had been tactless, or allowed their own embarrassment to show too plainly. 'What is it that disturbs you, Miss Freemarsh?' she asked more gently. 'Age and illness?

Forgetting things is something that happens to most of us who are fortunate enough to have long lives. It can be frightening to realise that we may all be affected one day, but it is not something to be ashamed of. There is no need for you to apologise.'

Nerissa looked up and met her eyes. 'It is more than forgetting, Lady Vespasia.' She lowered her voice to a mere murmur. 'Aunt Serafina creates fantasies, imaginings as to what she did in the past, and it is embarrassing, because her accounts are very colourful, and some of them involve real people and events.' She chewed her lip, biting it until it was pink. 'I wish I could protect her from anyone remembering her like this, when she has no control over her mind, and most of the time very little discretion over her tongue.' She turned away and lowered her gaze until she was staring at the floor. 'She has a great admiration for you, you know . . .'

Vespasia was startled. She and Serafina were not quite contemporaries, Serafina being a decade older, but even so, they were completely unalike. Vespasia had used wit, intelligence and her extraordinary beauty to learn information and persuade men of great power to act, as she believed, either wisely or generously. Serafina had been an adventurer in the most physical sense; brave, skilled and with an iron nerve. She had ridden with the insurgents in Croatia, manned the barricades, rifle in hand, in the streets of Vienna, before the ignominious collapse of the revolution and the Emperor's return to power in '48.

Vespasia had done that only once, in Rome, far back in her youth. Their paths had crossed perhaps half a dozen times since then. They had known of each other through allies in the common cause.

'Are you sure?' she said quietly. 'I think perhaps "respect" would be more accurate, as I have for her. And a friendship in later years, born possibly out of the understanding of what we fought for then; and the passion, the hope and the losses of those days.'

'You are very modest,' Nerissa replied, a very faint edge of bitterness in her voice. 'But admiration is what I meant. You actually did some of the things that Aunt Serafina now imagines she also did. You knew the people she would love even to have met.' She looked at Vespasia squarely, even defiantly. 'She will try to impress you. I'm sorry. It is humiliating to see. It might be better if you simply left a card. I will tell her you called when she was asleep, and you did not wish to disturb her.'

'She will not believe you,' Vespasia replied. 'She will know perfectly well that you are keeping people from visiting her because you are ashamed of her. I will not be party to that.'

The colour swept up Nerissa's pallid cheeks and her eyes were hot with anger. But she was not yet mistress of the house, and she dared not retaliate.

'I was merely trying to save your feelings,' she said very quietly. 'And to save Aunt Serafina from being remembered as she is now, rather than as the proud and discreet woman she used to be. I'm sorry if you do not see that.'

'I see it very well,' Vespasia told her, finding herself torn between pity and irritation. 'And I assure you my feelings are of no importance. I shall remember Serafina as I knew her in the past, regardless of what happens now. I am quite acquainted with the idea that as we grow older we change, and it is not always either easy or comfortable.'

'You have not changed,' Nerissa said with candour that bordered on resentment. 'You are still beautiful, and I doubt your mind ever wanders from the point, or that your memory creates things that did not happen.'

'Not yet.' Vespasia was now embarrassed herself, as if her

health and good fortune were blessings she had not deserved. 'But no one knows about the future. In another ten years I may be profoundly grateful if my friends still remember me at all, and call upon me even if I am tedious, and ramble a little, or lose myself in a past when I was more alive, more able, and still dreamed of great accomplishments.'

Nerissa did not reply but turned and led Vespasia up the wide stairway to the landing and across it to Serafina's bedroom door. As she did so, in the hallway the footman opened the front door and Vespasia heard his voice.

'Good morning, Mrs Blantyre. How pleasant to see you. Please do come inside; the weather is most inclement.'

Nerissa half turned and Vespasia caught sight of the amazement in her face. There was also an expression there that might have been resolve, and then a flash of emotion quite unreadable.

'I think Aunt Serafina has another visitor,' she said quickly. 'I must go down and welcome her.' She tapped sharply on the door in front of them. Then, without waiting for an answer, she pushed it open for Vespasia, and excused herself again to go downstairs.

'Of course,' Vespasia acknowledged her, and went into the room alone.

Tucker was standing near the door to the dressing room, a silver-backed hairbrush in her hand. The moment she saw Vespasia she smiled and her face filled with relief.

'Good morning, m'lady. How are you?'

'Good morning, Tucker,' Vespasia replied. 'I am very well. I am glad to see you with Mrs Montserrat. How are you?' It was a purely rhetorical question, a matter of good manners. She smiled at Tucker and nodded slightly, then turned towards the bed.

Serafina was sitting up, her hair dressed. She looked wide

awake, and as soon as she met Vespasia's eyes she smiled back. Only when Vespasia was closer did she see a vacancy in her look, an expectancy as if she had very little idea who her visitor was.

Vespasia sat down in the chair beside the bed, for a moment feeling exactly the embarrassment and distress she had told Nerissa was unimportant. Unexpectedly, it was overwhelming. She had no idea what to say to this person in front of her, helpless, a spirit trapped not only in an ageing body but in a mind that had betrayed her. What should she talk about that was not idiotic, an insult to what they had both been in the past, and that seemed so suddenly to have slipped from Serafina's grip while still remaining in hers?

Serafina was waiting, staring at her hopefully.

'How are you?' Vespasia asked. She felt it was completely inane, yet how else could she begin?

'My leg hurts,' Serafina replied with a rueful little shrug. 'But if you break bones, you can expect that to happen. I've broken enough I shouldn't be surprised.'

Vespasia felt a twinge of alarm. Was it possible Serafina really did have a broken bone? Could she have tripped and fallen? Old bones break easily.

'I'm sorry,' she said with sincerity. 'I hope the doctor has seen it? Has it been properly cared for?'

'Yes, of course it has,' Serafina answered her. 'It was in splints for weeks. What an incredible nuisance. I can't ride a horse with splints on, you know.'

Vespasia's heart sank. 'No, of course not,' she said, as if it had been a perfectly ordinary comment. 'And it still aches?'

Serafina looked blank. 'I beg your pardon?'

After glancing at Tucker, who shook her head almost imperceptibly, Vespasia looked back at Serafina and struggled for something to say that made any kind of sense. Surely Adriana

99

Blantyre had called to see Serafina and was even now on her way up? Or was it possible she'd come to see Nerissa? They were not so very different in age – six or seven years, perhaps. But socially they were worlds apart: Adriana the wife of a man of privilege, wealth and accomplishment; Nerissa a simple woman of no standing, and past the usual age of marriage. Vespasia found herself listening for another footfall on the landing beyond the door, expecting interruption any moment. Knowing how vague and distracted Serafina was today, surely Nerissa would thank Adriana for calling, but advise her to come again another day?

She turned to Tucker. 'I saw Mrs Blantyre arriving. Perhaps you might suggest to Miss Freemarsh that she call at a more fortunate time?'

Tucker was about to reply when there was a knock on the door. A moment later Adriana Blantyre came in. Clearly Nerissa had warned her that Vespasia was already here.

'Good morning, Lady Vespasia,' she said with a smile of pleasure. Then she turned to Serafina. 'How are you today? I brought you some lilies from the hothouse. I gave them to Nerissa to put in water.' She perched on the edge of the bed, far from where she would disturb Serafina's feet.

'I'm well, thank you,' Serafina replied, blinking and looking puzzled. 'In fact I can't think what I'm doing still in bed. What time is it? I should be up.' A look of alarm filled her face. 'Why are you here in my bedroom?'

'You've been unwell,' Adriana said quickly. 'You are recovering, but it's too soon to be out yet. And the weather is very cold.'

'Is it?' Serafina turned to face the window. 'Is it autumn? The tree is bare. Or winter?'

'Winter, but nearly spring,' Adriana told her. 'Rather raw outside. The sort of wind that bites through your clothes.'

'Then it was nice of you to come,' Serafina remarked. 'Do you know Lady Vespasia Cumming-Gould?'

'Yes, we have met,' Adriana assured her.

'Vespasia and I are old friends,' Serafina said, nodding a little. 'We fought together.'

Adriana looked confused.

'Oh!' Serafina gave a little laugh. 'Side by side, not against each other, my dear, never against each other.' She shot a glance at Vespasia, a secret, amused communication, full of intelligence.

Adriana looked at Vespasia for confirmation, or perhaps for help.

Vespasia tried to keep the surprise from her face.

There was no possible course but to agree. 'Certainly,' she said with as much enthusiasm as she could. 'Each in our own fashion.' She must steer the conversation away from further trouble. How much did Serafina remember? Was this now the truth, or was she about to start one of the rambling journeys of the imagination that Nerissa had referred to?

'It sounds exciting,' Adriana said with interest. 'And dangerous.'

'Oh, yes.' Serafina leaned back a little against her pillows, her dark eyes gazing far away in the distance of recollection. 'Very dangerous. There were deaths.'

'Deaths?' Adriana's voice was a whisper, the colour fading from her face.

Vespasia drew in her breath to interrupt. There had been, of course, but it was long ago, and there was no point in raking over tragedy now. But Serafina continued before she could break in.

'Brave people,' she said softly. 'Passions were very high. Men and women sacrificed their lives for the cause of freedom.' She frowned and studied Adriana closely for several moments.

'But you know that. You are Croatian. You know all these things.'

Adriana nodded. 'I've heard the stories.' Her voice choked and she coughed to clear her throat, and perhaps to give herself a moment to master her feelings again. 'I wasn't there myself.'

Now Serafina seemed lost. 'Weren't you? Why not? Don't you want freedom for your people? For your language, your music, your culture? Do you want to wear the Austrian yoke for ever?'

'No,' Adriana whispered. 'Of course I don't.'

This time Vespasia did interrupt, politely but firmly. 'That was all ages ago, my dear. Mrs Blantyre was hardly even born then. Those are old griefs. Much has happened since that time. Italy is united and independent, at least most of it is.'

Serafina looked at her as if momentarily she had forgotten her presence. 'Trieste?' she asked, hope flaring in her eyes.

Vespasia thought for an instant of lying, but it was such a condescension, such a denial of respect that she could not do it.

'Not yet, but it will come,' she assured her.

'What are you doing about it?' Serafina asked. She was puzzled, as if raking her memory, but there was challenge in her question.

'Do you not think it wiser to discuss other things just now?' Vespasia suggested. 'Fashion, perhaps, or the latest art exhibition, or even politics here at home?'

'Prince Albert is German, you know,' Serafina said. 'The Saxe-Coburgs are everywhere. Everybody who is anyone at all has at least one of them in the family.'

'Prince Albert is dead,' Vespasia assured her firmly.

'Is he? Oh dear.' Serafina blinked. 'Who killed him? And

for heaven's sake why? He was a good man. How terribly stupid. What is the world coming to?'

'Nobody killed him.' Vespasia glanced at Adriana and back again to Serafina. 'He died of typhoid fever. It was many years ago now. And yes, you are quite right, he was a good man. Perhaps next time I come I shall bring you the latest edition of the *London Illustrated News*, and you can look at the current gossip, such as there is, and some of the fashions for spring.'

Serafina turned her hands outward in a gesture of resignation. 'Perhaps. That would be kind of you.' She closed her eyes. Her face looked pale and strained, her brows a little wispy, her eye sockets hollow.

Vespasia rose to her feet, staring at Adriana. 'I think perhaps we should leave Mrs Montserrat to have a little rest. She seems tired.'

'Of course,' Adriana agreed reluctantly. She looked at Serafina. 'I'll come back and see you again soon.'

Serafina did not answer. It appeared she had drifted off to sleep.

Adriana led the way out. Vespasia was at the door when she turned one more time to look at Serafina. The older woman was staring wide-eyed, suddenly very much awake, her expression one of terror. The next moment the look was gone, and her face was completely blank again.

Vespasia closed the door and, leaving Adriana outside on the landing with Tucker, she went back to Serafina. Gently putting her hand over the stiff, blue-veined hands on the coverlet, she asked, 'What is it? What are you afraid of?'

The fear returned to Serafina's eyes. 'I know too much,' she whispered. 'Terrible things, plans of murder, the dead piled up . . .'

'About whom?' Vespasia asked, trying to keep the pain out of her voice. 'My dear, most of them are gone already. These are old quarrels you are remembering. They don't matter any more. It's 1896 now. There are new issues, and they don't involve us as they used to.'

'I know it's 1896,' Serafina said quickly. 'But some secrets never grow old, Vespasia. Betrayal always matters, deaths that there didn't have to be. Brothers, fathers and husbands sold to the executioner for the price of advancement. Blood money can never be repaid.'

Vespasia stared at her and saw the clear, sharp light of intelligence in her eyes. There was nothing blurred now, nothing uncertain. But she was afraid, and she could not hide it. Perhaps that was what shocked Vespasia the most. In all the times they had met – in London, Paris, Vienna, in the ballrooms or at the secret rendezvous in some hunting lodge or backstreet room – she had never seen Serafina white with terror.

'Who are you afraid of?' she whispered.

Serafina's eyes filled with tears and her hand closed over Vespasia's, her thin fingers desperate. 'I don't know. There were so many. I'm not even sure which ones matter any more. And half the time I don't know what I'm saying!' Tears filled her eyes. 'I'm not sure who is allied with whom these days, and if I make a mistake, they'll kill me. I know too much, Vespasia! I thought of writing it all down, and letting everyone know that I had, but what good would that do? Only the guilty would believe me. It's all so . . .'

Vespasia held Serafina's hand with both of hers. 'Are you certain there are still secrets that matter, my dear? So much has changed. Franz Josef is a relatively benign old man now, broken by tragedy . . .'

'I know. And I know what that tragedy was, more than you do, Vespasia.'

'Mayerling?' Vespasia asked with surprise. 'How do you

know that? They burned the place to the ground, and all the evidence with it.'

'Not all,' Serafina said softly. 'I know people. I've only lost my wits in the last year.' She searched Vespasia's eyes. 'But there are other secrets, older ones. I know who shot Esterhazy, and why. I know who Stefan's father really was, and how to prove it. I know who betrayed Lazar Dragovic.' The tears spilled down her tired cheeks. 'I'm so afraid I'll forget who I'm talking to, and say something to give it away.'

Vespasia realised that Serafina was frightened not only of letting slip the secrets, but that whoever was involved would fear the revelation enough to kill her before she could make it.

There was no use speaking to her and suggesting she discuss nothing more than the weather and other such trivia. Today she knew what year it was, and she knew Vespasia. But earlier, when Adriana Blantyre had been there, Vespasia was uncertain how much she had known, and how much she was deliberately pretending to be deeply sunk in fantasy and confusion. Remembering the look in Serafina's eyes, the blank helplessness, she feared it was the latter. Anyway, what purpose could there be in trying to mislead Adriana? If she had any connections in Croatia still, surely that was the last thing Serafina would wish to betray?

'Perhaps it would be a good idea to see fewer people for a little while?' she suggested. 'It might even be possible to make sure they are those who would know little of such things anyway, so even if you mistook who they were, what you said would be incomprehensible to them anyway. I know that could be terribly boring, but at least it would be safe.'

Serafina understood it, sadness filling her face. 'Perhaps it would,' she agreed. 'But will you come back again? I . . .' Embarrassment prevented her from finishing the request.

'Of course,' Vespasia assured her. 'We could talk of whatever you wish. I should enjoy it myself. There are too few of us left.'

Serafina nodded with a smile, and sank back in the pillows, her eyes closed. 'And Adriana,' she whispered. 'Take care of her for me. But . . .' She gulped and her voice choked. 'But perhaps I shouldn't see her again . . . in case I say something . . .' She stopped, unable to finish her thought.

Vespasia remained a few minutes longer, but Serafina seemed to have drifted into a light sleep. Vespasia moved the sheets a little to cover the thin hands – the old get chilled very easily – then she walked softly from the room.

She went down the stairs and asked the maid in the hallway to send for Nerissa so she might express her good wishes and take her leave.

Nerissa appeared within moments, her face shadowed with anxiety.

'Thank you for coming, Lady Vespasia,' she said a little stiffly. 'I'm sorry you had to see Aunt Serafina so . . . so unlike the person she used to be. It is distressing for all of us. You will know now that I was not being alarmist when I said she is sinking rapidly.'

'No, of course not,' Vespasia agreed. 'I'm afraid she is considerably worse, even in the few days since I last saw her. I think it might be wise, in view of her . . . imagination, if you were to restrict her visitors rather more. I suggested to her that it might be best to see only those who are young enough to know little or nothing of the affairs in which she used to be concerned. She was pleased with the idea. It will ease her fears. And of course, as you say, it would be very sad if people were to remember her as she is now, rather than as she used to be. I would much prefer not to have it so, were I in her position.'

She was uncertain exactly how to phrase Serafina's request regarding Adriana.

'You might gently turn aside Mrs Blantyre, if she calls again,' she began, and saw the puzzlement in Nerissa's face. 'She is of Croatian birth, which seems to awaken particular memories and ideas in your aunt,' she continued. 'You do not need to give explanations.'

Nerissa bit her lip. 'I can't ask Mrs Blantyre to call less often, or to leave earlier. She is an old friend. It would be . . . very discourteous. I couldn't explain it without causing offence and saying more than I know Aunt Serafina wishes. But of course I shall do my best to discourage anyone from staying very long. Tucker is already helping greatly with that. She very seldom leaves my aunt alone. Thank you for your understanding, and your help.' It was final. She was not going to accept any advice.

'If there is anything further, please call me.' Vespasia had no choice but to leave the matter.

'I will,' Nerissa promised.

Vespasia walked down the steps to her carriage with her feeling of unease in no way lifted. Serafina had seemed so sure she did not want to see Adriana again, but for whose sake? There had been a tenderness in her when she spoke the younger woman's name that was deeper than anything Vespasia had ever seen in her before. And Adriana, in turn, had seemed to care more than casually, more than a mere act of kindness, however genuine. Was it simply fellow exiles, with a love of country, or something closer?

Vespasia was in her carriage and more than halfway home when she suddenly changed her mind and rapped with her cane to draw the coachman's attention. He stopped and she asked him to take her instead to the home of Victor Narraway.

As she had expected, when she arrived Narraway was not in, but she left him a note asking that he might call her at his most immediate opportunity. The matter was of some urgency, and she required his advice, probably his assistance.

Narraway came home in the late afternoon, tired not with exertion, either mental or physical, but from the boredom of having sat most of the day in the House of Lords and listened to tedious and exhaustively repetitive arguments. He found Vespasia's note with a lift of excitement, as if at last something of interest might happen. Never in his life had Vespasia disappointed him. He put through a telephone call to her, even before taking off his coat.

Her invitation was simple and he accepted without hesitation. At last there was the possibility of something he could do that had meaning.

He found himself sitting forward a little in his seat in the hansom as he watched the familiar streets go by. His imagination raced as to what it might be that concerned her to the degree she would seek his advice with such a sense of impending danger. There had been a haste in her handwriting, as though she were consumed by a deep anxiety, and the tone of her voice on the telephone confirmed it. Vespasia did not exaggerate, nor was she easily alarmed. His mind went back over other tragedies and dangers they had been concerned in together, most of them involving Thomas Pitt. Some had come very close to ending in defeat; all had held crime and potential disaster.

As soon as he reached her house he alighted and paid the cabby, then went up the steps. The door opened before he had time to pull the bell. The maid welcomed him in, took his coat, and showed him to Vespasia's calm sitting room with its windows and french doors onto the garden.

'Thank you for coming so promptly,' she said, rising to her feet. It was an unusual practice for her. He noticed that she did not have quite her customary composure. There was something almost indefinably different in her manner. She was as exquisitely dressed as always, in a blue-grey gown with deep décolletage, with pearls at her ears and throat, and her hair coiled in a silver crown on her head.

'I presume you have not eaten? May I offer you supper?' she asked.

'After you have told me what it is that troubles you. Clearly it is urgent,' he replied.

She gestured to him to be seated, and resumed her own place beside the fire.

'I visited Serafina Montserrat again today,' she told him. 'I found her considerably worse, not in apparent physical health, but her mind has deteriorated a great deal – I think.' She hesitated. 'Victor, I really do not know at all quite how much she is losing her wits. When I first arrived she seemed lucid, but her eyes were filled with fear. Before I had the opportunity to speak with her for more than a few moments, Adriana Blantyre called.'

'Evan Blantyre's wife?' He was startled. Blantyre was a man of considerable substance and reputation. 'Courtesy, or friendship?' he asked quietly.

'Friendship,' she answered without hesitation.

He watched the deepening anxiety in Vespasia's eyes, and noted the presence of another emotion he could not read. 'Perhaps you had better tell me the heart of it,' he said quietly. 'What is it you fear?'

Vespasia spoke slowly. 'As soon as Adriana came into the room, Serafina seemed to begin rambling, as if she had no idea what year it was. Adriana was very patient with her, very gentle, but it was disturbing. Serafina spoke as if they had been allies in the fight to get rid of the Austrian rule from northern Italy. It was as if Serafina were not even aware of all the recent history of Italian unification – Garibaldi, Cavour, any of it.'

'What year does she imagine she is in?' Narraway was beginning to feel the same intense pity he knew disturbed Vespasia, even though, as far as he was aware, he had never met Serafina Montserrat.

'I don't know,' Vespasia replied. 'Possibly the fifties, or early sixties, not very long after the revolutions of '48.'

'And who does she believe Adriana to be?' he asked, puzzled. 'She cannot be more than forty, at the very outside. I would have thought less.'

'That's what makes so little sense,' Vespasia answered. 'Serafina took her for a Croatian patriot, which is not completely divorced from the truth. But she was rambling. Her eyes were far away, her hands clenched on the sheets. And then when Adriana left, I remained behind for a few moments, and suddenly Serafina was completely herself again, and the fear returned.' She took a deep breath. She was sitting upright, as always, and her hands did not move, but he saw an almost imperceptible change in her. 'Victor, she is afraid that someone may kill her in order to prevent her from revealing the truths she knows. She spoke of betrayals, old grudges and deaths that cannot be forgotten, but as if they were all current, and there were more violence to come. She mentioned Mayerling.'

'Mayerling?' He was incredulous. 'But Serafina was living here in London at the time, wasn't she?' he asked. 'And she must have been well into her seventies and surely not privy to anything of the Austrian court any more. Vespasia, are you sure she isn't . . . romanticising?'

'No, I'm not sure!' Her face was full of grief. 'But her fear is real, that I have absolutely no doubt of. She is terrified. Is it possible that there is something for her to fear?' Her voice dropped. 'Something apart from loneliness, old age and madness?'

He felt the pain strike him, to his shame, not for Serafina Montserrat, but for Vespasia, and for himself. Then the instant after, it became pity.

'Probably not,' he said quietly. 'But I promise that tomorrow I shall begin to look into it. I had better do it discreetly, otherwise, if by any wild chance this is true, I shall have given whoever she fears more to fear from her.'

'Yes, please be careful.' Vespasia hesitated. 'I am sorry if I am asking you to waste your time. She seemed so sure, and then the next moment completely lost, as though she were alone in a strange place, searching for anything familiar.'

Narraway brushed it aside. He did not want her to feel obliged to him. He told her the truth, startled at how simple it was for him.

'I'm glad of something to do that is a challenge to my mind rather than my patience,' he told her. 'Even if it should prove that Mrs Montserrat has nothing to fear, as I hope it will.'

Vespasia smiled, and there was amusement in it as well as gratitude. 'Thank you, Victor. I am grateful that you will do it so quickly. Now that that is decided, would you like some supper?'

He accepted with pleasure. It would be so very much more enjoyable to share the evening with her than to eat alone. Before the O'Neil business, and going to Ireland with Charlotte on that desperate mission, he would have considered dining at home a peaceful end to the day, and the idea of company would have been something of an intrusion. Solitude, a good book, the silence of the house, would all have been comfortable. Now there was an emptiness in it, a deep loneliness he was incapable of dismissing. No doubt it would pass, but for the moment, Vespasia's quiet sitting room held a peace not only of physical rest, but also an ease to the mind he enjoyed disturbingly well.

Narraway gave Vespasia's request a great deal of thought. It was clear that she had glimpsed in her own future the same fear of helplessness and terrible slow decay that she had seen in Serafina Montserrat, and perhaps she could guess that he had understood it too. Please God, he had not shown it! It was a nakedness of the soul he would infinitely prefer no one else ever saw.

The thoughts came to him as he sat quietly in his own chair by the hearth, after midnight, still not ready to go to bed. Was he afraid of sleep, of nightmares, wakening in the dark in confusion, for an instant not knowing where he was? Or perhaps for longer than just an instant? Would that time come? Would he be alone, pitied, no one remembering who he used to be?

And yet it was untrue. He did not pity Serafina Montserrat, and he did not even know her. Whatever happened, he would never pity Vespasia. In a way that would be the ultimate betrayal of all she was. Physical changes were temporary, part of the tests of life, and they included loss of the senses and the perception. It was not pathetic to lose some of one's awareness of the present and slip back to happier times.

He could recall his own youth with sharper detail than he expected: his early years in Special Branch, long before he was head of it; in fact when he was only learning, newer than Pitt ever was, because he had not had the decades of police experience. He had had authority, and travelled in some of the most exciting cities in Europe. He smiled now at the memories. They seemed happy and exciting, looking back, even though he knew he had at times been lonely then. And there had been failures, some of them harsh.

Now he thought of Paris only for its grace, the old quarters steeped in the history of revolution. In his youth he had been able to stand in the Cordeliers with his eyes closed and imagine if he opened them he would see the ghosts of Robespierre, the giant Danton, the raving Marat, and hear the rattle of tumbrils over the stones, smell the fear. The passion haunted the air as if it had been yesterday.

He had been gullible then, believed people he should not have done, one beautiful woman in particular, Mircille. That had been a mistake that had nearly cost him his life. He had felt a starry-eyed pity for her that had bordered on love. He had not been so stupid again.

Thinking of that brought back sharp recollections of what Herbert, his commander at the time, had said to him. And with his memory of Herbert, he knew the answer as to whom he should seek with Vespasia's questions.

He was at the railway station by half-past seven the following morning, and caught the train southwards into the bleak, rolling countryside of Kent before eight o'clock. At Bexley he alighted into a hard, driving wind and walked along the main platform to look for a carriage.

By nine o'clock he was knocking on the door of an old cottage just off the high street. The bare, twisted limbs of wisteria covered most of the front walls, but he imagined in the summer it would be covered with soft pale lilac flowers. Now he could smell rain in the wind, and the bitter, clean aroma of woodsmoke drifting from the chimney.

The door was opened by a middle-aged woman wearing an apron over her dark skirt. She looked startled to see him.

'Mornin', sir.' She seemed uncertain what to say next.

'Good morning,' Narraway saved her the trouble of finding the words. 'Is this the home of Geoffrey Herbert?'

'Yes, sir, it is. Mr Herbert is just eating his breakfast. May I tell him who is calling?' She did not add that it was an uncivil hour to visit, especially unannounced, but it was in her eyes.

'Victor Narraway,' he replied. 'He will remember me.'

'Mr Victor Narraway,' she repeated. 'Well, if you would come in out of the cold, sir, and take a seat in the sitting room, I'll tell him you're here.' She grudgingly pulled the door wider open.

He stepped inside. 'Actually . . . it's Lord Narraway.' He was not used to the title himself, but this was an occasion when the respect it might command would be of service.

She looked startled. 'Oh! Well . . . I'll tell him, I'm sure. Would you like a cup o' tea, sir, I mean, your lordship?'

Narraway smiled in spite of himself. 'That would be most appreciated,' he accepted.

The sitting room was architecturally typical of a cottage: low-ceilinged; deep window ledges; large, open fireplace with heavy chimney breast. But there the ordinariness ended. One entire wall was lined with bookshelves; the carpets were oriental in rich jewel-coloured designs; and there were Arabic brass bowls on several of the surfaces. It all brought back sharp memories of a man of vast knowledge and eclectic tastes.

Herbert himself came into the room only twenty minutes later, when Narraway had had his tea and was beginning to get restless. He had not seen Herbert in fifteen years and he was startled by the change in him. He remembered him as upright, a little gaunt, with receding white hair. Now he was bent forward over two sticks and moved with some difficulty. His clothes hung on him and his hands were blue-veined. His hair had receded no further, but it was thin. The pink of his scalp was visible through it.

'Lord Narraway, eh?' he said with a faint smile. His voice

was cracked, but his eyes were bright, and he manoeuvred himself to the chair without stumbling or reaching to feel his way. He sat down carefully, propping the two sticks against the wall. 'It must be important to bring you all the way down here. Dawson told me you are not in the Branch any more. That true?'

'Yes. Kicking my heels in the House of Lords,' Narraway replied. He heard the edge of bitterness in his tone and instantly regretted it. He hoped Herbert did not take it for self-pity. He wondered what to add to take the sting from it.

Herbert was watching him closely. 'Well, if you're not in the Branch, what the devil are you doing?' he asked. 'You aren't here looking up old friends; you don't have any. You were always a solitary creature. Just as well. Head of the Branch can't afford to be dependent on anyone. You were the best we had. Hate to admit it, but I'd be a liar not to.'

Narraway felt a surge of pleasure, which embarrassed him. Herbert was a man whose good opinion was worth a great deal and had never been easily won.

'So what do you want?' Herbert went on before Narraway could find any gracious way of acknowledging the compliment. 'No need to explain yourself. I wouldn't believe you anyway. If you could afford to tell me it would hardly be worth the bother.'

'Austria-Hungary,' Narraway replied.

Herbert's sparse eyebrows shot up. 'Good God! You're not still raking over Mayerling and Rudolf's death, are you? Thought you had more sense. Poor bastard shot the girl, then shot himself. He was always a melancholy creature, other than the occasional attack of social good cheer. Wine, laughter and a pretty face, and he was fine, until the music stopped, like his mother. He was always a disaster waiting to happen. Could have told you that years ago.'

'No,' Narraway said succinctly. 'It's not about Rudolf at all, so far as I know.'

'Then what? You said Austria-Hungary.'

'Going back thirty years, maybe, or more, uprisings, planned or actual,' Narraway said.

'Plenty of them.' Herbert nodded. 'Autocratic old sod, Franz Josef. Relaxed his hold a bit recently, I'm told, but back then he ruled with a rod of iron. He and Rudolf never saw eye to eye. Chalk and cheese. What about it?' He frowned, leaning forward a little and peering at Narraway. 'Why do you care? Why now?'

'Thought you weren't going to ask me,' Narraway said pointedly.

Herbert grunted. 'Of course there were uprisings. You know that as well as any of us. Stop beating around the bush and tell me what it is you're really asking.'

'A major revolt, drawing in other countries as well. Possibly a Hungarian uprising?'

A look of contempt flickered across Herbert's gaunt face. 'You can do better than that, Narraway. You know as well as I do – or you ought to – that the Hungarians are content to be a safe, second-rate power, ruled by Vienna and having a very comfortable life, if not quite cock of the walk. If they rose up against the Austrians they'd lose a great deal, and gain nothing. They are quite clever enough to know that.'

'The Croatians?' Narraway suggested.

'Different kettle of fish altogether,' Herbert agreed. 'Erratic, unstable. Always plots and counterplots, but nothing has ever come of them, at least not yet. That's not what all this is about, is it? Foreign Office thinks there's going to be another Croatian problem of some sort, do they?'

'Not so far as I know,' Narraway said truthfully.

'Blantyre's your chap,' Herbert observed. 'Evan Blantyre.

Knows the Croatians as well as anyone. Lived there for a while. Wife's Croatian. Beautiful woman, but unstable, so I hear. Delicate health, always sick as a child. Not surprising, family caught up in rebellions and things.'

Narraway leaned back in his chair. 'I'll ask him, if things look as if they're heading that way. What about the Italians? They still haven't got some of their northern cities back. Trieste and that region, for example.'

Herbert thought about it for a few moments. 'Italian nationalists,' he said thoughtfully. 'Could be trouble there. Disorganised, though, in spite of Cavour and Garibaldi and all the unification stuff. Still quarrel like cats in a bag. Thought they'd quietened down a bit.'

'Perhaps,' Narraway said dubiously. 'Do you remember in the past an Italian woman by the name of Montserrat?' He watched Herbert's face for even the slightest flicker of recognition.

Herbert smiled a long, slow curl of amusement, his eyes bright. 'Well, well,' he said with a sigh. 'Serafina Montserrat. Why on earth are you asking about her? She must be seventy-five at least, if she's still alive at all. I remember when she was thirty. Rode a horse better than any man I knew, and fought with a sword. Used to be quite good myself, but I was never in her class. Knew better than to try. Save making a fool of myself.'

'Italian nationalist,' Narraway made it more an answer than a question.

'Oh, yes.' Herbert was still smiling. 'But not averse to lending a hand to anyone who was against Austria, wherever they were from.'

'Openly?' Narraway asked.

Herbert looked shocked. 'Good God, no! Secretive as a priest, and devious as a Jesuit too.'

'You make her sound religious.'

Herbert laughed. It was a purely happy sound, bringing to his face for a moment the shadow of the young man he had once been. 'She was as far from a nun as a woman can get. Although I didn't know most of that at the time.'

'How did you learn?' Narraway asked. 'Perhaps more importantly to me, when did you learn and from whom?'

'From many people, and over several years,' Herbert replied. 'She worked very discreetly.'

'That's not what you implied,' Narraway pointed out.

Herbert laughed again, although this time it ended in a fit of coughing. 'Sometimes, Narraway, you are not nearly as clever as you imagine,' he said after several moments, still gasping for breath. 'You should have taken more notice of women. A little self-indulgence would have helped you a great deal, not only about women in general, but about yourself as well, and therefore about most men.' His eyes narrowed. 'Too much brain and not enough heart, that's your trouble. I think secretly you're an idealist! It's not pleasure you want – it's love! Good God, man, you're a total anachronism!'

'Serafina Montserrat,' Narraway reminded him sharply. 'Was she a wild woman, riding and fighting beside the men, and sleeping with a good few of them, or was she discreet? I'm not here simply because I have nothing to do and need somebody else's business to meddle in. This could be important.'

'Of course you need something to meddle in!' Herbert said without losing his smile. 'We all do. I'd have died of boredom if I didn't meddle in everything I can. The locals all loathe me, or pretend they do, but they all come to see me now and then because they think I know everybody's secrets.'

'And do you?' Narraway enquired.

'Yes, mostly.'

'Serafina,' he prompted.

'Yes, she was as tough and as skilled as most of the men, better than many,' Herbert responded. 'Not really a beauty, but she had so much vitality that you forgot that. She was . . .' He seemed to be staring back into memory. 'Elemental,' he finished.

Narraway could not help wondering how well Herbert had known her himself. That was a possibility he had not considered before. Was he asking for information about a past lover of Herbert's own? Or was that merely imagination, and a little wishful dreaming?

'You have not so far touched on anything remotely discreet,' he pointed out.

'No,' Herbert agreed. 'She seemed to be so obvious in her support of Italian fighters for freedom from Austria that most people assumed she was as open about everything else. She wasn't. I deduced, completely without proof, that she knew a great deal about Bulgarian and Croatian plans as well, and even had connections with early socialist movements in Austria itself. That last I am convinced of, but I couldn't produce an iota of evidence to support it.'

'A clever woman,' Narraway said ruefully. 'Bluff and double bluff.'

'Exactly,' Herbert agreed. He leaned forward in his chair, wrinkling his jacket even further. 'Narraway, tell me why you want to know. It's all water under the bridge now. You can't and shouldn't prosecute her for anything. And if you ask me officially, I shall deny it.'

Narraway smiled, meeting the other man's eyes. Herbert's thin cheeks coloured very slightly.

'She is ill and vulnerable,' Narraway answered, wondering, even as he said it, if he were wise in doing so. 'I want to make sure she is protected. To do that, I need to know from what directions attacks might come.'

Herbert's face lost all its good humour. 'Attacks?' he said sharply.

'The threat may be more imagined than real. That is why I need to know.'

Herbert sat still without answering for several moments, staring past Narraway into the view of the rain-swept garden with its sharply pruned roses and buds fattening on the trees. When at last he returned his gaze to the present, his eyes were clouded.

'I've realised how little I actually knew about her,' he said quietly. 'She was a creature of intense passion. Everything done with a whole heart. I assumed I knew why, and what her loyalties were, but since what you need now is far deeper than that, I have only observations and beliefs to offer you – for what they are worth.'

'More than the little I know now,' Narraway replied immediately. 'First, is she image or substance, in your belief?'

'At first, I thought image,' Herbert said with an honesty that clearly pained him. 'Then I came to believe there was substance. I am still of that opinion.'

'What changed your mind?'

'A betrayal,' Herbert said very quietly. 'There is no point in asking me the full story of it because I don't know. At the time I only knew of the execution, and that it was for plotting an assassination . . .'

Narraway felt a sudden chill. 'An assassination?'

Herbert looked at him sharply. 'For God's sake, man, it was thirty years ago, and it didn't happen anyway. The whole thing was abortive. The leader himself was captured, beaten and shot. Most of the others escaped.'

'But Serafina Montserrat was involved?' Narraway persisted. 'How? Are you skirting around saying that she was the one who betrayed the leader?'

Herbert was horrified. He glared at Narraway as if he had blasphemed. 'No! She was all kinds of things: wilful, reckless, arrogant at times – certainly promiscuous, if you want to call it that – but she would have died for the cause. It was only through a mixture of extreme skill and courage, and the loyalty of others, that she survived. And a degree of luck. "Fortune favours the bold" was never truer of anyone than it was of her.'

Again Narraway wondered exactly how well Herbert had known her. Not that it mattered, as long as what he was saying was the truth, as far as he knew it.

'So she could be in danger?' he concluded. It was barely a question any more.

'I don't know,' Herbert said honestly, but there was more emotion in his eyes than Narraway could recall ever having seen before. 'It was so long ago, and from the standpoint of anyone in London, far away. Who do you know that gives a damn about Croatian independence of Austria?'

'No one,' Narraway admitted. 'But betrayals always matter. The time and place of them are irrelevant.'

'They do,' Herbert agreed. 'Passionately. Far too passionately to wait thirty years for revenge.'

Narraway could not argue with that. Almost certainly all of the people concerned were dead, or too old to execute revenge any more, just as Serafina herself was.

'Thank you,' he acknowledged the point. 'Can you think of anyone else who might give me more light on the subject of why she is so afraid?'

'Andelko Kirasic,' Herbert suggested thoughtfully. 'And the current expert in that area of the Foreign Office is Tregarron. But you will know that. And, of course, for northern Italy, with which Serafina was most concerned, it is Ennio Ruggiero, and for Croatia, Pavao Altabas.'

Narraway got to his feet. 'I'm obliged.' He held out his hand. 'Thank you again.'

Herbert smiled. 'It's good to see you, Narraway. I always knew you'd do well.'

'You taught me well,' Narraway replied sincerely. 'I hope to hell I taught my successor as much.' He hesitated.

'Why do you say that?' Herbert asked.

'Did you worry about me?' Narraway asked him. 'That I would succeed, that I had the steel, and the judgement?'

Herbert smiled. 'Of course, but I had more sense than to let you know it at the time.'

'Thank you,' Narraway said wryly.

'Wouldn't have done you any good,' Herbert replied. 'But you caused me a few sleepless nights – unnecessarily, as it turned out.'

Narraway did not ask him about what.

Narraway went to see Ruggiero, as Herbert had suggested, and spent over an hour without learning anything more detailed than Herbert himself had already told him. Ruggiero was an old man and his memory was clouded by the emotions he remembered. Italy was now united, and he wanted to forget the frictions and griefs of the past. Especially he wanted to forget the losses, the sacrifices and the ugliness of fighting.

Narraway thanked him also. To have probed and argued, perhaps caught the old man in lies, not of intent but of wishful thinking, facts covered over by dreams, would have benefited no one.

Next he went to visit Pavao Altabas and found only his widow. He had died recently, and Herbert had been unaware of it.

The wife was much younger than her husband had been

and she knew nothing of the uprisings. The name of Serafina Montserrat meant nothing at all to her.

Lastly, he went to see Lord Tregarron, not at the Foreign Office but at the club where both were members. It was the end of the day and Tregarron was tired and unwilling to talk. However, short of getting up, very conspicuously, and leaving, Narraway gave him no civil alternative.

They sat opposite each other in armchairs on either side of one of the huge log fires. Narraway ordered brandy for both of them. The steward brought it with murmured words of apology for interrupting them, although they were not as yet in conversation.

'Leave us to talk, will you, Withers?' Narraway asked him. 'No interruptions, if you please!'

'Certainly, my lord,' Withers said calmly. 'Thank you.' He bowed and withdrew.

Tregarron looked grimly at Narraway, waiting for him to explain his intrusion.

'Damned long day, Narraway,' he said quietly. 'Is this really necessary? You're not in Special Branch any more.'

Narraway was surprised how deeply the reminder cut him, as if his position had defined his identity, and without it he was of no standing to those who had so recently treated him with something akin to awe. He hid his hurt with difficulty. If he had not needed Tregarron, he would have found a way to retaliate, even though, at the same moment, he realised how retaliation would betray his own vulnerability.

He forced himself to smile, very slightly. 'Which removes the duty from me, but does not take away the freedom to meddle, if I can do it to the good,' he replied.

Tregarron's dark face tightened a little. 'Am I supposed to deduce from your last remark that you are justifying some interference in foreign affairs that otherwise I might object to?'

Narraway's smile grew bleaker. 'I have no intention of interfering in foreign affairs, justifiably or not. I would also like it if foreigners did not interfere in ours. But my concern is with information about the past that may prevent an action I am uncertain of, and I need to know more.'

Tregarron's heavy eyebrows rose. 'From me? You must know that I cannot tell you anything. Do not keep obliging me to remind you that you are no longer Head of Special Branch. It is uncomfortable, and ill-mannered of you to put me in a position where I have no choice.'

Narraway kept his temper with difficulty. He needed Tregarron's information, and he no longer had any means of forcing it from him, as Tregarron knew. It was an aspect of having lost power he was finding it hard to accustom himself to.

'I am not seeking any current information,' he said levelly. He found himself suddenly reluctant to explain his reasons to Tregarron. 'It is the general climate of issues thirty or forty years ago.'

'Thirty or forty years ago? Narraway, what the devil are you playing with? Thirty or forty years ago where?' Tregarron leaned forward a little in his chair. 'What is this about? Is it something I should know?'

'If I should come to believe that it is, I shall certainly tell you,' Narraway answered. 'So far it is only rumours, most of which seem to me more like overheated imagination. I wish to prove, or disprove them, before I bother anyone else with them.'

Tregarron's attention sharpened. 'Regarding what, exactly?'

Now Narraway had no choice but either to tell the truth, or very deliberately to lie. 'Certain whispers about a woman called Serafina Montserrat,' he answered.

A shadow crossed Tregarron's face. 'She wasn't young at

that time, at least not in her twenties. How on earth could she matter now?'

Narraway changed his mind as to what he had been going to say.

'Memories, stories,' he said fairly casually. 'If I know the truth, or something close to it, I can put them to rest safely.'

Tregarron tensed. 'Who is talking about Mrs Montserrat?' he asked. 'The issues she fought for were won or lost years ago, decades even. It sounds very like gossip. But it could be dangerous, Narraway. You should never take anyone's name lightly. Damage can be done that is hard to reverse. You did the right thing in coming to me. She worked mostly in the Austro-Hungarian sphere. She knew a lot of people, and was regrettably free with her favours.'

'But all years ago,' Narraway pointed out. He was surprised how much he resented Tregarron's implication, even though he had never met Serafina himself. She was Vespasia's friend. He took a deep breath before he continued. 'I imagine most of the men concerned are also dead, and their wives, who might have cared, as well.'

'Would you like it said of your father?' Tregarron snapped.

Narraway could not imagine it. His father had been rather dry, highly intelligent but remote, not a man who would be even accessible to a woman such as he imagined Serafina Montserrat to have been. He smiled at the thought, and saw a flash of fury in Tregarron's face, which was gone again so rapidly he was not certain if it had been real, or his imagination.

'The thought amuses you?' Tregarron asked. 'You surprise me. Would it have amused your mother too?'

That was a sharp wound, a territory Narraway did not wish to explore. 'Of course not,' he said quietly, his voice tighter than he had meant it to be. 'It is so far from the truth of what I was enquiring into that it had an oblique humour. It was no one's reputation in that area that was in jeopardy, so far as I am aware.'

'To do with what?' Tregarron asked, his face now all but expressionless.

Narraway chose his words carefully, thinking of what exactly Vespasia had said. 'To do with political freedom, old plots and current ones regarding throwing off the Austrian yoke in Croatia and especially northern Italy. The possibility of attempted assassinations, even.'

'Perhaps you don't understand me,' Tregarron said, now allowing a faint smile onto his face as well. 'Serafina Montserrat must be in her mid-seventies, at least. According to what I have heard, she was reckless and something of a troublemaker. She created an unfortunate reputation for herself, although some of the stories about her are probably apocryphal. Even if half of them are true, she was a highly colourful character, and a passionate Italian nationalist. She would have been quite capable of planning an assassination, both practically and with the steel in her nature to carry it through. However, so far as I know, she never succeeded in actually doing so.'

He crossed his legs, easing back in his chair a little, his eyes never leaving Narraway's face.

'The only event anything like that,' he continued, 'I heard as a story. I'm not sure what truth there is in it.'

Narraway watched him intently.

Tregarron assumed the air of a raconteur. 'A group of dissidents plotted to assassinate one of the leading Austrian dukes who was particularly vehement in his grip on the local government in northern Italy. It would be fair to say he was oppressive, and at times unjust. The Emperor Franz Josef has always been excessively military, but he used to be less dictatorial than he is now. Nevertheless, this dissident group planned the assassination of some duke – I forget his name – and very nearly succeeded. The plot was clearly thought out and very simple in essence. No clever tricks to go wrong, nothing left to chance.'

'But it didn't succeed?' Narraway questioned him.

'Because they were betrayed by one of their own,' Tregarron answered. 'They were put to flight. Montserrat was among those who fought hardest to save them, but she couldn't. She was wounded in the struggle that followed, and the ringleader was taken, summarily tried and executed.'

It was the kind of bitter tale that Narraway had heard often enough, especially when he had been in Ireland. He winced at the memory of those he had caught or prevented himself. He thought of Kate O'Neil, and of the actions he had thought responsible for his own loss of office. And then, in spite of himself, he thought of Charlotte Pitt, of love, loyalty, and wounds that would ache lifelong.

Was this what it was about: a retreat into ancient sorrows, come back to haunt old age? Was Serafina going back in her mind to that time, or another like it? Could she have been the one who betrayed the would-be assassin, and now feared some final revenge? Or justice?

Tregarron interrupted his thoughts.

'What can this have to do with anything today, Narraway? I can't help you if I don't know what on earth you're really looking for. Or why.'

'From what you say, I rather think it has nothing to do with anything today,' Narraway lied. 'As you point out, she must be in her seventies, at least. That is, if she is still alive at all, of course.' He rose to his feet, smiling very slightly. 'Thank you for your time, and your candour.'

★   ★   ★

But that was far from what Narraway thought as he rode home in a hansom through the wet streets, glancing every now and then at the cobbles gleaming in the reflected lamplight.

Tregarron had lied to him, if not in words, then in intent. There was something he feared, but Narraway was not sure if it was an old danger resurfacing, some past error that would jeopardise his present reputation or relationships, or if it was some totally new issue that Narraway was unaware of. But then if it concerned the Austrian Empire, even had he still been in Special Branch, he might not have been informed. Regular diplomatic affairs were nothing to do with Special Branch.

What troubled him, as he rattled through the night, was the thought that Serafina's estimate of her own past was, if anything, understated. If she believed she had made lasting enemies, then it was certainly possible that she was right. The idea of such a once magnificent woman lying old and broken, now fearing for her life, deeply and painfully aware that, even in her mind, she could no longer protect herself, hurt him with a disturbing depth.

Was he becoming soft, no longer able to judge an act impartially? Yes, he did love Charlotte. It was time to admit that to himself. In fact after Ireland, it would be absurd to deny it. He had always despised self-delusion in others, and he had come so close to practising it himself. That she would never care for him more than as a friend was something he had to accept. If he did so with grace, then it was a closeness he could keep.

Had that devastating vulnerability changed him?

Yes, perhaps it had. For one thing, it had given him a tenderness towards Vespasia he had not felt before: a greater understanding of her as a woman, not merely her formidable courage and intelligence. She too could be hurt in ways she would never have allowed him to see, had he not also newly experienced personal pain, surprise and self-doubt.

It was a frightening change, but not entirely a loss.

He determined to learn a great deal more than the very general picture he had of Austro-Hungarian affairs, particularly in reference to the dictatorial Emperor Franz Josef, whose only son, the Crown Prince Rudolf, had died so tragically at Mayerling.

The old man's heir was now his nephew, Archduke Franz Ferdinand, of whom he did not approve. For one thing, he had chosen to love a woman inappropriate to become the wife of the heir to the Empire. The poor creature was merely some countess or other. That made Ferdinand, in the old man's opinion, of unsound judgement, and lacking in the dedication to duty necessary to succeed him. But he had no choice. The laws of heredity could not be argued with, or the legitimacy of the entire monarchy was destroyed.

Should Narraway tell Vespasia the little he had learned, so that she knew that Serafina was not a fantasist about the past? Perhaps so. It would be a courtesy to Serafina. At least one person would believe her. Next time he saw Vespasia he would do so. It would be a good reason to see her again.

And should he speak to Pitt?

Not unless anything he learned about present-day Austrian affairs indicated that there could be an assassination attempt on some visiting royalty. Pitt had more than enough to do without chasing the current danger of that, if any existed, as well as all the usual Special Branch fears of anarchist bombings, and the constant rebellions in Ireland. There were more Russian dissidents in London, fleeing from the ever-increasing oppression and grinding poverty at home. Additionally, there were British-grown socialists who believed the only way to improve life for the poor was to commit outrages against the Establishment.

Pitt did not need to hear rumours about a betrayal thirty years ago, and a thousand miles away. Narraway had done the job himself long enough to know the importance of leaving alone what did not matter. Telling Vespasia would be sufficient.

Chapter Five

It was the last day of February, bright, gusty and cold, very much winter still. Stoker came into Pitt's office looking grim.

Pitt waited for him to speak.

Stoker stood in front of the desk, his eyes steady. 'More bits of information keep coming in that look like they're about this assassination attempt coming up in a couple of weeks.' He was ill at ease, his shoulders stiff. 'We're fairly certain as to the identity of the man asking about train signals near Dover, and have at least a possible identification of one of the men asking about how points are changed. The other man could be the same person disguised a little, but we can't be sure.'

'Who are they?' Pitt asked.

'The man who asked about the signals we think was Bilinski. The French are pretty sure about it. They've been following him for a while, in connection with an assassination in Paris. He was seen at least once with Lansing—'

'Our Lansing?' Pitt said sharply.

Stoker's face tightened. 'Yes, sir. That's the worrying part. We thought Lansing was in prison in France, but they let him go.'

Pitt felt a sudden chill. Lansing was English: a cold, clever man with allegiance to no one, and – as far as they could tell – to no cause. Why the French had released him was irrelevant now, but Pitt would find out later. It could have been some technicality of the law. A good advocate could often find one, and Lansing would be both willing and able to employ such a man. Or, what was worse, someone else might have paid for his lawyer just to get him loose.

Pitt looked up at Stoker, and saw the understanding of all that in his eyes. 'And he was the one who asked about the points and the goods trains?'

'Yes, sir,' Stoker answered. 'Word is that he's an expert on transport, especially trains: signals, altering the switches on lines, diverting them, blowing the couplings, that sort of thing. Exactly what Mr Blantyre said.'

'Any others?'

'Not yet, but we're still working.'

'Anything else about Alois Habsburg?'

'Nothing. I can't see any reason at all why anyone should want to assassinate him,' Stoker admitted.

'Except to embarrass Britain, and Special Branch in particular,' Pitt replied. 'Which it most certainly would.'

Stoker nodded. 'That's what it looks like, at least from one or two of the whispers there are. The Queen thinks well enough of us after the business at Osborne House, but there are plenty who don't. Most people don't even know about that, and never will.'

'I know.' Pitt pushed his hands deeper into his pockets, his shoulders tense. 'There are quite a few who think our power is a threat to their freedom, and to their privacy. A few decades ago they thought that of the police.'

'Idiots,' Stoker said under his breath. 'They send for them fast enough if there's a burglary, a riot, or even a kidnapping or two. We're like the army: nothing's too good for us if there's a war, and then when it's over they want us to become invisible – until the next time.' The contempt in his face carried an uncharacteristic bitterness.

Pitt could not help but agree with him, sharing his emotion and his anger, even if he chose at this moment not to voice it.

'We'd better take it seriously,' he replied. 'Who is Duke Alois Habsburg, exactly? What sort of entourage is he bringing with him? I don't care if that's a breach of his privacy or not!'

Stoker pulled a sour face. 'Difficult to find out anything much about him, except the usual, superficial things: where he was born, his parents, where he is in reference to the succession – which is nowhere. He's not really a politician, more of a philosopher, and a dabbler in science. Very clever fellow, by all accounts, but a dreamer. He might invent something brilliant one day, but probably completely useless. Or maybe write a couple of books about existence, or identity, or something. At least that's what his own people say. He's never done anything that makes any difference.'

'Is he related to our Queen?' Pitt pursued.

'By marriage, yes. Distantly – so is half of Europe.' Stoker's face still reflected his exasperation. 'Alois may be a favourite of hers, but he doesn't sound the sort. He's nice enough, but she doesn't go in for a lot of heavy thinking.' He stopped abruptly, a faint pinkness in his cheeks, aware that he had expressed his opinion rather too freely.

'On the other hand, he could just be looking to impress, and feel like a trip to London,' Pitt replied with a faint smile. 'Or he may be pretending to be an academic dreamer, and really be a brave man doing an important job.'

'I suppose that's true,' Stoker conceded with obvious reluctance. 'I hadn't thought of that, but I shall now.'

'Who's coming with him?' Pitt repeated. 'How many of the entourage are actually guards of one sort or another?'

Stoker sighed. 'Can't tell. From what we're told, they're mainly domestic servants: valets and butlers – that sort of thing. Probably couldn't tell a stiletto from a fire iron.' He blinked. 'Doesn't the Palace supply servants for guests?'

Pitt found himself smiling. 'Butlers, of course; valets are different. Each gentleman wants to have his own. Knows his likes and dislikes, probably carries all the remedies he might need and is fully aware of his weaknesses, which clearly is less embarrassing than spreading the knowledge of them even wider.'

'It's another life, isn't it?' Stoker observed with a faint smile.

'As ours are to many of the people we meet,' Pitt added.

Stoker shook his head but he was still smiling. 'We've got to protect this man, sir, whatever he is. If he's killed anywhere in our territory it's going to get very ugly indeed. Some bastard's going to come out of the woodwork and blame us.' He winced. 'Not to mention however many of our own people get killed or crippled at the same time.'

'I know,' Pitt agreed, thinking of Blantyre's warning. 'That could even be the purpose of the whole thing. Poor Duke Alois might simply be the means.'

Stoker's face paled. He said something under his breath, but would not repeat it aloud when Pitt looked up at him.

Pitt returned to the Foreign Office unwillingly, but he had no possible alternative. As before, the first person he was directed to was Jack Radley. They stood facing each other in the luxurious but impersonal waiting room with its formal portraits of past ministers on the walls.

'I hope this is about something different?' Jack said. He shifted his weight very slightly from one foot to the other as though that might somehow alter his ability to deal with any unpleasantness.

'It is about new coincidences,' Pitt replied, equally unable to relax. Neither his professional responsibility nor their personal relationship allowed him any ease. He was aware as he began of how deeply it would affect Charlotte if this new situation divided her from Emily. All the past experiences they had shared, the family memories and the adventures since would be shadowed by the present tearing of loyalties.

Jack's face had tightened, turning the corners of his mouth down.

'I have much more information regarding the probability of an assassination attempt against visiting Austrian royalty,' Pitt began. 'The man is a minor relation of the Queen, but you don't have to be in the Foreign Office to imagine what it would do to Britain's reputation in Europe, and everywhere else, if the man was shot while he was here, visiting Her Majesty – do you?'

He was a little more sarcastic then he had intended, but his own fear of it happening left an edge to his voice.

'I imagine Lord Tregarron would not be indifferent to that happening, or to his own position in the matter if it should,' he added.

Jack stared at him in silence, but his face was distinctly paler. For several seconds he weighed the new situation.

'You're sure you are not being unnecessarily alarmed?' he asked.

'The job is about thinking ahead, Jack. If you mean am I jumping at shadows – no. I think there's enough evidence now to take the threat seriously. Am I certain I'm not being distracted by a fear deliberately manufactured in order to draw my attention away from something else more important? No, of course I'm not. Bluff? Double bluff? I don't know. Is

Tregarron prepared to take the chance that a member of the Austrian royal family gets killed in a train crash, along with a few score British? If he is, then we should replace him with somebody a little less free with our lives, and our reputation. Someone who can see the scandal, the outrage, even the reparations likely to be demanded if it happens. Not to mention someone prepared to explain it to Her Majesty, with full inclusion of the fact that Special Branch told you details of the possibility, and you decided it was not worth your trouble to listen.'

Jack took a deep breath, then clearly changed his mind.

Pitt smiled bleakly.

'I'll tell Lord Tregarron what you have said,' Jack answered. 'If you would wait here, I shall come back as quickly as I can.'

It proved to be a tedious full quarter of an hour before Jack returned. The minute Pitt saw his face he knew that this time Tregarron would see him, but under a degree of protest.

Pitt followed Jack out of the waiting room and along the corridor to the arched door. At the word of answer, he opened it.

'Commander Pitt, my lord,' he announced, and stepped back for Pitt to go inside. This time he left them alone.

Tregarron was standing behind his desk, silhouetted against the late winter sunlight in the window beyond. He turned to face Pitt. His expression was shadowed and therefore difficult to read.

'Radley tells me you have continued to pursue this idea of a potential assassination attempt on Duke Alois when he comes to visit Her Majesty. You seem to be sure there may be something in it.' He said it almost expressionlessly. 'He advised me that we should take it seriously, at least in so far as, if there were even a shred of reality behind it, then it could be disastrous in its effect on our reputation, as well as costing a great many British lives. Is this your view?'

'Yes, sir,' Pitt replied, grateful that Jack had apparently put the core of it so succinctly. 'It is a threat we cannot afford to ignore. Even if the attempt is completely abortive, we should look incompetent if we did not act, but – probably uglier than that – also as if we were indifferent to it, and at the very worst, even complicit.'

He was pleased to see the immediate concern in Tregarron's face, even though it was accompanied by considerable irritation.

'That seems to be rather more decisive than when you first mentioned it to Radley a few days ago,' he observed critically. 'Why on earth should any dissident faction in Austria wish to cause such a disaster in order to assassinate a relatively harmless and, I may say, powerless, young minor aristocrat, of no political interest at all? It makes no sense, Pitt. Have you consulted Narraway on this extraordinary idea of yours?'

Pitt felt his temper rise as if the blood were burning in his face. He hoped Tregarron would not see it. He made a supreme effort to keep his voice calm and level.

'No, I have not. Lord Narraway is no longer privy to the information gathered by Special Branch and it would be a breach of my oath of discretion to discuss with him such matters as he does not need to know. And as far as political knowledge and judgement of affairs in the Austro-Hungarian Empire are concerned, I am advised that you are the expert, and therefore the appropriate person for me to consult with, sir.'

Tregarron's mouth tightened. The irritation in his expression was visible as he turned slightly and walked over towards the fireplace. He sat down in the large, comfortable chair facing the door, still with his back to the light, and waved for Pitt to sit opposite him.

'Then I suppose you had better tell me the precise evidence that you believe leads you to this extraordinary conclusion,' he said, reaching to poke the fire. 'Duke Alois is a man of negligible importance in Austrian affairs, let alone European. He is coming here solely because he has a certain charm and Her Majesty apparently likes him – or, to be more precise, likes his mother, who is no longer able to travel. Who on earth would possibly benefit from assassinating him? And I would point out that if anyone did wish to, then they have had ample opportunity to do so in his own home, and without taking a trainload of innocent people with him. Why on earth do you believe that anybody would do such a thing?' He stared at Pitt, his heavy eyebrows raised, disbelief written in every line of his face.

Pitt swallowed. The thought came to his mind that Tregarron would not have spoken to Narraway in this tone, but he dismissed it, not as untrue but as hampering to his own ability to deal with Tregarron with confidence. He must not allow comparisons to cripple him. He had weaknesses Narraway had not, but he had strengths also.

He sat a little more comfortably in his chair and crossed his legs.

'If I had the answers to these questions, sir, I would not need to ask you for more than confirmation of this, and possibly merely as a courtesy. Duke Alois appears to be a pleasant young man with nothing to commend him except his royal connections. That doesn't mean he is of no importance at all. Sometimes such men are pawns for others.'

A shadow crossed Tregarron's face, but he did not interrupt.

'However, I think it seems likely that he would be a target not in a personal sense, but simply because he is available,' Pitt continued. 'If he were to be killed while here in England it would be extremely embarrassing to Her Majesty's government, and there are always those who would find that to their advantage—'

'In Austria?' Tregarron said with open disbelief.

'There is nothing to prove that the plan is specifically Austrian,' Pitt pointed out, seeing the surprise in Tregarron's eyes with sharp satisfaction. Clearly that thought had not occurred to him. 'It could be German, French, Italian, even Russian,' he added. 'Our power makes it inevitable that we have many enemies.'

Tregarron leaned a little forward, the whole attitude of his body altering. 'Details, Pitt. I am perfectly aware of our position in Europe, and in the world. Most of what you say has always been true. Why now? Why this particular young man? You had better tell me the precise facts and observations that have come to your notice, and leave the interpretation of them to me.'

Pitt remained silent. His mind was racing. The man's arrogance was breathtaking. He was treating Pitt like some junior policeman reporting a burglary, incapable of seeing it in the context of a larger plan. Narraway would have had the response to wither him so he never presumed to override him again in such a way.

The words, even the composure, the confidence to do so eluded Pitt, and he felt like the gamekeeper's son he used to be, called up before the master of the house again. Except that Sir Arthur Desmond had never treated him with such contempt.

If Pitt were to refuse such details now it would imply that he did not have them. It was on the edge of his tongue to offer sarcastically that all Special Branch junior staff should report, in writing, to Tregarron, but he dared not. He could not function if he made an open enemy of this man.

With the difficulty of it almost choking him, he replied, 'How much detail would you like, sir? There are regular sources up and down the country who give us information, and we have connections in France, Germany and Austria with relation to this in particular. We have our own people, and we also have limited relations with the equivalent to Special Branch in most of Europe.' He watched Tregarron's face and saw a flash of anxiety, which disappeared as soon as it was there. Perhaps it was a sudden realisation that Pitt was better informed than he had supposed, and not merely putting his own interpretation on a few pieces of gossip.

'Most of what we hear is merely observation of people we know altering their habits or movements,' he continued. 'People they talk to, places they frequent. Such changes can be indicative of an attitude in planning . . .'

'Don't treat me like some policeman in training, Pitt!' Tregarron snapped. 'I have neither the desire to become a detective, nor the time. For God's sake, man, do your job! You are supposed to be Commander of the Branch, not some young constable on the beat!'

Pitt clenched his teeth. 'I am giving you my opinion based on the evidence, Lord Tregarron. You asked me for the details. They are a collection of small observations made of changes in habit; of people asking unusual questions; new alliances between people who have no known past in common; people spending money for which there is no obvious reason; unusual patterns of travel; information about known dissidents meeting each other and dealing with new people; evidence of guns or dynamite being moved; people disappearing from their usual haunts and turning up elsewhere. Even, on occasion, people dying unexpectedly: accidents, murders. Do you want me to continue?'

Tregarron's face was slightly pink. 'I wish you to tell me why you think any of this points to the attempted murder of some wretched minor prince of the Austrian Empire while he is travelling on one of our trains on his way to visit our Queen. I can't understand why it is all so plain to you. You seem to expect me to put this man off without any other reason beyond the uncertainty, perhaps the jitters, of our very new Head of Special Branch.'

There was a slight curl of contempt on his lip, which he did not bother to hide.

'It looks to me as if you've lost your nerve, man!' he went on. 'Promoted beyond your ability. I told Narraway that at the time. You're an excellent second in command – the best. I'll give you your due. But you are not born or bred to lead! I'm sorry you pushed me into the position where I am obliged to tell you so to your face.' He did not sound sorry so much as simply angry.

'You may be right, sir,' Pitt said stiffly, struggling to get his breath. 'On the other hand, Lord Narraway may be. We had both better hope that his assessment of what abilities it requires to lead Special Branch is better than yours.' He rose to his feet. 'If not, then we can expect some extremely unpleasant consequences, beginning with an assassination in London, a serious embarrassment for Her Majesty and possibly an icy relationship with the Austro-Hungarian Empire, with a demand for reparations. Good day, sir.'

Tregarron shot to his feet. 'How dare you—' He stopped suddenly.

Pitt stood still, his eyes wide, waiting.

Tregarron took a deep breath. 'How dare you imply that I do not take this threat seriously?' He slammed his fist on the bell on his desk. A minute later there was a brief tap on the door, and Jack came in, closing it behind him and stopping just inside the room.

'Yes, sir?' he said unhappily, deliberately avoiding looking at Pitt.

'Come in,' Tregarron barked.

Jack walked a few steps closer and then stopped again. He still avoided Pitt's eyes. 'Yes, sir?'

Tregarron stared at him. 'Pitt seems to believe that Duke Alois Habsburg is the possible target for an assassination attempt, albeit an ignorant, messy and pointless one. He doesn't know who the would-be assassin is, nor the purpose of the exercise, only that the outcome would be very ugly indeed.'

'It would be, sir,' Jack agreed, 'and it would also give Austria an enormous weapon to use against us for years to come.'

'For God's sake, I can see that!' Tregarron snapped. 'The point is, we can't jump at every shadow. We have to exercise our critical judgement rather than be danced around like puppets on strings on the end of every fear, real or not, likely or not, even possible or not. What is your assessment of this one, Radley? Do you agree with Pitt, on the basis of this host of minor alterations in behaviour of informants, spies, general hangers-on? Or do you think they are part of the climate at large and we should hold steady and not lose our nerve?'

Pitt was seething. 'I did not recommend losing our nerve, sir,' he said hoarsely.

Tregarron's glance did not waver from Jack. 'You recommended telling Duke Alois not to come,' he retorted. 'That is losing our nerve, Pitt. That is telling the Emperor Franz Josef, and the rest of the world, that we cannot manage to protect visiting princelings from mass murder in a train wreck, so they had better stay in Vienna, or Budapest, or wherever the devil it is they come from – where they have the ability to keep their trains safe!'

'Where it is not Britain's responsibility if they are killed or not,' Pitt countered.

Jack's face went white. He still avoided Pitt's eyes.

'Then what do we do?' Tregarron demanded. 'Do we make him welcome then, or do we tell Her Majesty that we cannot protect her great-nephew, or whatever he is, and she had better tell him to stay at home?'

'We would be the laughing stock of Europe, my lord,' Jack replied very quietly. 'We should give Commander Pitt all the extra men he may need, regardless of the cost and the inconvenience, in order to protect Duke Alois.'

Tregarron looked at him with surprise and some disbelief, 'You think this whole thing could be real?'

'No, sir,' Jack answered. 'I think it is so unlikely as to be all but impossible, but we cannot afford to ignore it. Commander Pitt has twenty years' experience of intrigue and murder, and if we ignore his warnings we will be entirely to blame if something should happen. Our position then would be untenable.'

'But bloody unlikely!'

'Yes, my lord, unlikely, not impossible.'

'I'm obliged for your advice.' Tregarron turned round to Pitt, looking at him sourly. 'I suppose you have to come to me with what you judge to be some serious threats, but I can't be second-guessing you at every fit and turn. You're supposed to make your own judgements. As soon as you get a little more used to your position, I expect you to do so. Good day.'

Pitt was too furious to speak. He inclined his head very slightly, then turned on his heel and strode out.

Jack caught up with him in the corridor a dozen yards beyond Tregarron's door.

'I'm sorry,' he said in little more than a whisper. 'But he does know what he's talking about, and the evidence is pretty thin.'

'Of course it is,' Pitt said between his teeth. 'People don't leave a trail that leads back to them. If they did we wouldn't need police, let alone Special Branch. Any fool could do it.' He did not slacken his pace and Jack was obliged to lengthen his own stride in order to keep up with him.

'Come on, Thomas,' he said reasonably. 'You can't expect a man in Tregarron's position to accept a story as basically unlikely as this one, unless you have real evidence. He knows Austria, he gets regular reports from all the people we have there, and a few others as well. He's damned good at his job.'

Pitt stopped abruptly and swung around to face Jack. 'Would you have said this, in these words, if it had been Narraway who'd come to you with suspicions? Or might you have given him the courtesy of assuming that he also was good at his job?'

The colour flushed up Jack's face. 'I'm sorry. That was incredibly clumsy of me. I—'

Pitt smiled bleakly. 'No, it was regrettably honest. And that is not a quality you can afford to exercise if you hope to rise in the diplomatic corps. One day you may also be damned good at your job, but it isn't today.' He started to walk again.

'Thomas!' Jack grabbed him by the arm, hard, forcing him to stop. 'Listen. I think you are jumping at shadows, and after the business in St Malo, and then Ireland and what happened to Narraway, I don't entirely blame you. But you can't force Tregarron to go against his own knowledge of the people and the country. If you really believe there is something threatened, then I'll arrange for you to see Evan Blantyre at short notice. I'll tell him it's a matter of urgency, even that there could be very unpleasant consequences if we make a bad judgement.' He looked at Pitt expectantly, his eyes wide, his stare direct, an expression on his face stronger than embarrassment, or vanity.

Pitt felt churlish, and very aware of how it hurt that he had to be offered, as if he had never met Blantyre, a meeting that would have been instantly granted to Narraway. Was it his lack of experience in the job, and the fact that Narraway was indisputably a gentleman while he was not, or was it that Narraway had amassed a wealth of knowledge about so many people that no one dared defy him? None of this would have been Jack's fault, and Pitt knew he would be a fool to squander the few advantages he had: the strength of family and the bonds of friendship, which Narraway had never possessed.

He forced the resentment out of his mind.

'Thank you,' he accepted. 'That's an excellent suggestion.'

Jack went back into Tregarron's office with sharply conflicting emotions. He was certain he had done the right thing in promising to make it possible for Pitt to speak in depth to Evan Blantyre, yet at the same time, he believed that Tregarron would not approve it. He was not even sure why. To some extent Pitt was overreacting, but that was better than reacting too little, or too late. Belittling him and making him doubt his own judgement helped no one.

He reached Tregarron's door again and tapped lightly. On the command to enter, he went back in.

Tregarron was at his desk. Papers on a different subject were spread out in front of him. He looked up at Jack, his face still bearing the faint marks of his previous anger.

'I'd like you to look through this and give me your opinion,

Radley,' he said, pulling the papers together more neatly. 'I think Wishart is right, but I'm predisposed to that view anyway. Do you know Lord Wishart? Good chap. Very sound.'

'No, sir, I don't,' Jack replied, holding out his hand and taking the papers.

'Must introduce you some time.' Tregarron's smile lit his face, transforming it into an expression of unique charm. 'You'll like him.'

'Thank you, sir.' Jack was flattered. Many people wanted very much to meet Lord Wishart, and few did. Emily would be delighted. He could picture her face when he told her. Then he had a sudden, uncomfortable feeling that it was a sop for having been so abrasive towards Pitt. Tregarron was quite aware that Pitt was Jack's brother-in-law. It was a relationship it would have been unwise to hide. That might have appeared devious. He wanted to say something further, but he had no clear idea of what it would be.

He looked down at the papers Tregarron had given him. They were to do with a proposed British diplomatic mission to Trieste, one of the Italian cities still under Austrian rule. This matter was largely cultural, with some mention of Slovenia, in whose territory it lay. It was complicated, as was every issue with the Austrian Empire, especially towards its eastern regions.

He saw an opinion written in Tregarron's flowing hand and read the first two sentences. Then he went back and reread it, thinking he had made a mistake. It was in direct contradiction with information Tregarron had received only yesterday.

'By this afternoon, Radley,' Tregarron prompted.

Jack looked up. Should he question what he had read, or would it be seen as exceeding his duty, perhaps even criticising Tregarron himself? He decided to say nothing. There would be an explanation for it, some additional fact that he was not yet aware of. If he read the whole report it would explain the apparent anomaly.

'Yes, sir,' he replied, forcing himself to meet Tregarron's eyes and smile briefly. 'Thank you.'

Tregarron nodded and bent his attention to the papers on the desk again.

Word from Blantyre came much more rapidly than Pitt had expected. He had thought it would be the following day, at the earliest, but it was late that same afternoon. Pitt was to go immediately to Blantyre's office, where he could spare at least a quarter of an hour before the next appointment he was obliged to attend.

Pitt grasped his coat and, forgetting his hat, went out to catch the next passing hansom. He presented himself, a little breathlessly, at Blantyre's office door. He stopped, having run up the stairs two at a time. Uncharacteristically for him, he straightened his tie, eased his shoulders to help his jacket lie a little more gracefully, and then raised his hand to knock.

It was answered almost as soon as he had his hands at his side again. A secretary ushered him in and, without any waiting at all, he found himself in Blantyre's office. They shook hands, and then Blantyre motioned him to be seated.

'Sorry for the haste,' Blantyre apologised. 'Tell me as briefly as you can, and still make any sense of it, what else you know and what you deduce from it.'

Pitt had already prepared what he meant to say. He began without a preamble.

'We followed all the leads you gave us, and we are almost certain of the identities of the men asking questions about the timetables, signals and points. There are various pieces of

147

further information, observations of new and unlikely alliances, people we know as troublemakers, sympathisers with anarchy or violent change.'

Blantyre nodded, his expression intent on Pitt's words.

'Such evidence as we have indicates the intended target is Duke Alois Habsburg, as you said,' Pitt went on. 'We have searched, but all we can find out about him indicates that he is, as you told us, a very agreeable young man, but a thinker rather than an actor. Had he not been royal, no one would ever have heard of him.'

Blantyre stiffened, his eyes wide. He let out his breath slowly. 'I was hoping I was wrong. This is very serious, Pitt. The tragedy and the embarrassment would be appalling. The whole of Europe would condemn us, but of course you know that. What is the weight of the evidence now, in your judgement?'

'Too serious to ignore,' Pitt said without hesitation. 'It may be an extraordinary collection of coincidences, but surely that happens once in a hundred times, or less. I can't afford to ignore it.'

'Of course you can't,' Blantyre agreed. 'From my own experience of Austro-Hungarian affairs, which is considerable, I still think it's extremely unlikely. It all seems pointless to me. But "unlikely" isn't good enough; we must be sure it's impossible. Or at least, as close to impossible as is within our power to make it. I need more details, and I haven't time to get them now, or to give this appropriate thought. Regrettably, I have an appointment that I can't shelve.'

He stood up. 'Tomorrow I have one meeting after another. Can you come to dinner at my home tomorrow evening? You and your wife would be most welcome. We can allow the ladies to retire to the withdrawing room, and we can talk at length. Tell me all the further details you are free to discuss, bearing in mind I also serve the government, and Her Majesty. I know how to keep a secret. Between us we should be able to judge the gravity of the threat, so you may react appropriately.'

Pitt rose to his feet as if a great weight had been taken from him. He had found an ally: perhaps the one man in England able to help him assess the value of his information.

'Thank you, sir,' he said with profound feeling. 'We would be delighted.'

Blantyre held out his hand. 'No need to be particularly formal, but we'll make a pleasure of it all the same. Eight o'clock is a trifle early, but we will need the time. This matter may, after all, be grave.'

Pitt took his leave and walked down the corridor rapidly, smiling. It had been more than a professional success. A man of substance and high office had treated him with the same dignity as he would have treated Narraway. There had been no condescension in his manner. Pitt was still smiling as he went down the stairs and out into the bitter wind knifing along the street.

The same afternoon that Pitt was speaking with Evan Blantyre, Charlotte decided that she should telephone Emily, no matter how awkward she felt, or that the quarrel had been primarily Emily's fault. One of them had to make the first move towards reconciliation, before the rift became too deep and the original cause was slicked over with the ice of further offences and became a habit. Since Emily apparently was not going to do it, then she must. She was the elder anyway; perhaps it was her responsibility.

When she picked up the receiver to put the call through she half hoped it was too late and Emily would be out making calls. Then she could satisfy herself with the virtue of having made the attempt without actually having to negotiate some kind of peace.

But the footman at the other end brought Emily to the telephone within moments of Charlotte being connected.

'How are you?' Emily asked guardedly.

'Very well, thank you,' Charlotte replied. They could have been strangers speaking to each other. The planned conversation disappeared out of her head. 'And you?' she said, to fill the silence.

'Excellent,' Emily answered. 'We are going to the theatre this evening. It is a new play, supposed to be very interesting.'

'I hope you enjoy it. Have you heard from Mama and Joshua lately?' Joshua Fielding, their mother's second husband, was an actor. It seemed a reasonable thing to ask. At least it stopped the silence from returning.

'Not for a couple of weeks,' Emily replied. 'They are in Stratford. Had you forgotten?'

Charlotte had, but she did not wish to admit it. There was a touch of condescension in Emily's tone. 'No,' she lied. 'I imagine they have telephones even there.'

'Not in theatrical boarding houses,' Emily replied. 'I thought you would know that.'

'You have the advantage of me,' Charlotte said instantly. 'I have never had occasion to enquire for one.'

'Since your mother frequents them, and you seem to be concerned for her welfare, perhaps you should have,' Emily returned.

'For heaven's sake, Emily! It was a simple enquiry – something to say.'

'I've never known you at a loss for something to say.' Emily's tone was still critical. 'And more pertinent than that,' she added.

'There is a great deal you have never known,' Charlotte snapped back. 'I was hoping for an agreeable conversation. Clearly that isn't going to happen.'

'You were hoping I was going to say something to Jack about helping Thomas in his present predicament,' Emily corrected her.

Charlotte heard the defensiveness in Emily's voice, and hesitated for a moment whether she should say something gentle, even protective herself. Then temper and loyalty to Pitt got the better of her.

'You overestimate my opinion of Jack's abilities,' she said coldly. 'Thomas will get himself out of any difficulties there may be. I am sorry I disturbed you. This is obviously a conversation better held at another time, perhaps some distance in the future when you are less defensive.'

She heard Emily's voice calling her name sharply, but she had already put the receiver away from her ear. This was only going to hurt more the longer she continued talking. She replaced the instrument in its cradle and walked away with a tightness in her throat. It would be better to find something useful to do.

Charlotte was delighted when Pitt came home and told her of the invitation to dine with Blantyre and his wife. It was a social occasion that promised to be most enjoyable. However, of much more importance to her was the relief she saw in Pitt that at last he had someone who would listen to his concerns. He had not told her what they were. As Head of Special Branch, there was a great deal he could confide to no one, but she knew him far too well to be unaware of the burden he carried.

For years he had shared with her so much of what he had done. She had been of help to him in many cases, especially those concerning people of the class to which she was born, and he was not. To begin with he had considered it meddling, and been afraid for her safety. Gradually he had come to value her judgement, especially her observation of people, and her strength of character, even if he still feared for her in some of her wilder interventions.

Emily too had involved herself with both courage and intelligence. But that was in a past that now seemed distant, and a quick sense of regret for the present quarrel caused her surprising pain. They were so much further apart than they used to be. She did not blame Emily that she felt a greater loyalty to Jack than to her sister. She herself gave her first passionate and instinctive allegiance to her husband. But this still carried a sense of loss, a loneliness for the laughter and the trust, the ability to talk openly of all kinds of things, trivial or important, which had always been part of her life. There was no one else she would trust in the same way.

Now she forced it from her mind and smiled at Pitt, more for his ease than for her own anticipation of the evening. 'That will be excellent. It will be lovely, and the only decent excuse I have had to wear a new gown I have bought for myself, rather than one borrowed from Emily or Aunt Vespasia. I have a very fashionable one, of a curious shade of blue, and it will be more than equal to the occasion.'

She saw Pitt's amusement.

'Adriana Blantyre is very beautiful, Thomas. I shall have to do my best in order not to be constantly overshadowed!'

'Is she brave and clever as well?' he asked with sudden gentleness. 'Or funny, and kind?' He did not add the rest of what he implied. She knew it and felt the warmth of a little self-consciousness creep up her cheeks, but she did not lower her eyes from meeting his.

'I don't know. I liked her. I look forward to knowing her a

little better.' Then suddenly she was serious again. 'Thomas, does Blantyre matter to you? Is he going to help you in something?'

'I hope so,' he replied. 'Jack arranged it.'

A hurt inside her slipped away. 'Good. Good . . . I'm glad. We will make it a good evening.' She wished he were free to tell her what troubled him, apart from the burden of taking on Narraway's job with the weight of responsibility it carried. She wanted to assure him that he was equal to it, but it would be meaningless, because she had very little idea what it was. She did not know whether his skills matched Narraway's, or even if they ever could. They were very different from each other. Until their experience in Ireland she had thought of Narraway as intellectual, happy to be alone. Whether that was natural to him or he had learned it, it had become his habit. Only when he lost his position in Special Branch had she seen any vulnerability in him, any need at all for the emotional warmth of others. How blind she had been. It was something she thought of now with a dull ache of guilt. She preferred to put it from her mind. That would be easier for Narraway also. He would not wish to think she remembered every emotion in his face, every word, perhaps regretted now. Some things should remain guessed at, but unspoken.

Regardless of such moments, there was a professional ruthlessness in Narraway that she believed would never be natural to Pitt. Indeed, she hoped it would not.

That was part of the difficulty. Two of the things she loved most in Pitt were the very qualities of empathy and love of justice, perhaps above the law, which would make leadership and its terrible decisions more difficult for him.

She had not yet found any way in which she could help him. The secrecy he was bound to keep excluded her from all practical knowledge. Blind support was all she could offer, and it had a very limited value. It was in some ways like the love of a child, and in the dangerous and painful decisions it left him essentially alone.

She looked at him now, standing in the middle of the kitchen as Daniel came in with his homework, and she saw the deliberate change of attention in him as he turned to his son. She knew the effort it cost, and ached to be able to help. She saw his hands clenched in frustration, and turned away to leave them alone, unwatched as they spoke of history homework, and how best to answer a complicated question.

'But how is that the Holy Roman Empire?' Daniel said reasonably, pointing to the map in his schoolbook. 'Rome is way down there!' He put his finger on the middle of Italy. 'It isn't even in the same country. That's Austria. It says so. And why is it holier than anywhere else?'

Pitt took a deep breath. 'It isn't,' he said patiently. 'Have you got a map of where the old Roman Empire used to be? I'll show you where it became the Eastern and the Western Empires.'

'I know that, Papa! And it wasn't up there!' He put his finger on Austria again. 'Why is all that bit part of the Holy Empire?'

Charlotte smiled and left Pitt to do his best with conquest and Imperial politics. No one else had ever been able to give a morally satisfying answer, and she knew Daniel well enough to expect a long argument.

Charlotte dressed for the dinner as she had done in her early twenties, before her marriage, when her mother had been trying so desperately, and unsuccessfully, to find her a suitable husband. She had chosen a colour and style that flattered the warmth of her skin and the hints of auburn in her hair. The cut of her dress showed to best advantage the soft curves of her figure. It was fashionable enough to feel up to date, but not so much that in a few months it would be outmoded. She had Minnie Maude help her coil up her hair richly, and pin it so it had no chance of slipping undone. To have one's hair falling out of its coiffure would be classed as just as disastrous as having one's clothing fall off! And rather more difficult to put right again.

She was not sure if she observed one or two grey hairs, or if it was only a nervous imagination. Her mother, many years her senior, had only a few. And of course there was a remedy for it. Apparently iron nails steeped in strong tea for fifteen days make an excellent dye for darker hair! Rinsing the hair in tea was, she considered, good for it every so often anyway.

She wore very little jewellery. This was not only as a matter of style, but also because she owned very little, a fact she did not wish to make obvious. Earrings were sufficient. There was natural colour in her face, but she added a little, very, very discreetly, and put a tiny dab of powder on her nose to take away the shine. Once she was satisfied that it was the best she could do, she would forget it entirely and focus on whoever she was speaking to, listen with attention and answer with warmth, and if possible a little wit.

They had hired a carriage for the evening. To keep one all the time was an expense they could not afford, nor was it in any way justified. If that day were to come in the future, perhaps it would be after they had moved to a house with stables. It would be exciting to make such an upward climb in society, but it would also leave behind a familiarity in which they had known much happiness. Charlotte was perfectly at ease not to have such a burden at the moment. She sat back in her seat, smiling in the dark as they were driven through Russell Square, its bare trees thrashing in the heavy wind. They turned left up Woburn Place, past Tavistock Square, open and windy again, then along the shelter of Upper Woburn Place and then the flickering lamplight of Endsleigh Gardens.

The carriage stopped and they alighted at the Blantyres' house, where they were welcomed in by a liveried footman. He showed them immediately to a large withdrawing room where a blazing fire shed red and yellow light on leather-upholstered chairs and sofas, and a carpet rich in shades of amber, gold and peach. The gaslamps were turned low, so it was difficult to see the details of the many paintings that decorated the walls. In a quick glance all Charlotte noticed was their ornamental gold frames, and the fact that they seemed to be mostly land and seascapes.

Adriana Blantyre came forward to welcome them, a step ahead of her husband. She was dressed in burgundy velvet. Its glowing colour emphasised the pallor of her face and the amazing depth of her eyes. She looked both fragile and intensely alive.

Blantyre himself greeted Charlotte with a smile, but his glance returned to his wife before he offered his hand.

'I'm so pleased you could come. How are you, Mrs Pitt?'

'Very well, thank you, Mr Blantyre,' she replied. 'Good evening, Mrs Blantyre. It is such a pleasure to see you again.' That was not merely good manners. On the two brief occasions she had met Adriana before she had found her different from most of the society women she knew. Adriana was far more concerned in matters of international importance, and yet also possessed an energy and a dry sense of humour that lay more in what she did not say than in any quick ripostes. Several times Charlotte had glanced at her, after some potentially odd remark by someone, and seen the light in her eyes.

They sat and talked casually: light comments on the weather, the latest gossip, rumours that were of no serious consequence. Charlotte had time to look at the paintings on the walls, and the very beautiful ornaments that graced the mantelshelf and two or three small tables. One was a porcelain figurine of a woman dancing. It had such grace it seemed as if any moment it must move. One of the largest was a huge statue of a wild boar. It stood with head lowered, menacing, but yet there was a beauty in it that commanded admiration, even a certain warmth.

'He's rather fine, isn't he?' Blantyre remarked, seeing her gaze. 'We don't have them here any more but they still do in Austria.'

'When did we have them here?' Charlotte asked, not really because she wanted to know, but she was interested to draw him into conversation.

His eyes opened wide. 'An excellent question. I must find out. Have we progressed because we no longer do, or decayed? Or are we merely different? We could ask that question of a lot of things.' He smiled, as if the possibilities amused him.

'Have you hunted boar?' Charlotte asked.

'Oh, long in the past. I lived for several years in Vienna. The forests around there abound with them.'

Charlotte gave an involuntary little shiver.

'I imagine you would greatly prefer the music and the dancing,' he said with certainty. 'It is a marvellous city, one where almost anything you care to dream of seems possible.' He looked for a moment at Adriana, there was an intense tenderness in his face. 'We first met in Vienna.'

Adriana rolled her dark eyes and a flash of amusement lit her expression. 'We first *danced* in Vienna,' she corrected him. 'We met in Trieste.'

'I remember the moonlight on the Danube!' he protested.

'My dear,' she said, 'it was the Adriatic. We didn't speak, but we saw each other. I knew you were watching me.'

'Did you? I thought I was being so discreet.'

She laughed, then turned away.

For an instant Charlotte thought it was out of modesty, because the look on Blantyre's face was openly emotional. Then she caught something in the angle of Adriana's head, the momentary light of a tear in her eye, and felt there was something she had missed, far deeper than the obvious words.

A few minutes later they were called in to the dining room and its lush, old-fashioned beauty distracted all Charlotte's attention. It was not the least bit English, except as the fashion had at times taken its inspiration from the Italians. There was a simplicity to the proportion, which lent an extraordinary grace, and a warmth to the colouring.

'Do you like it?' Adriana asked, standing close behind her, just moments before they all moved to their respective seats around the long polished table. Then she apologised. 'I'm sorry. If I ask, how could you possibly say you did not?' She gave a rueful smile. 'I love England, but this is a memory of my home I keep because I want people here to like what I used to know and love as well.' Without waiting for an answer, she moved away to take her place at the foot of the table, while Blantyre took his at the head.

Charlotte and Pitt sat opposite each other at each side. The meal was served by footmen and a parlourmaid, silently and with a discretion born of long practice. First there was a clear soup, followed by a light fish, and then the main course of lamb in red wine sauce.

The conversation moved easily from one subject to another. Blantyre was a highly entertaining host, full of anecdotes of his travels, especially his time in the capitals of Europe. Watching his face, Charlotte saw an undisguised enthusiasm for the curious and individual in each place, but a love for Austria that superseded all the others.

He spoke of the gaiety and sophistication of Paris, of the

theatre and art and philosophy, but his voice changed to a new intensity when he described the Viennese operetta, the vitality of it, the music lyrical enough to make everyone wish to dance.

'They have to nail the chairs and tables to the floor,' he said, almost seriously. He was smiling, his eyes staring into the distance. 'Vienna's always in my dreams. One minute you cry, the next you laugh. Each makes the other more powerful. There is a unique richness in the blend of so many cultures.'

Adriana moved very slightly, and the change in the light on her face made Charlotte look towards her. In an instant she saw a vulnerability, a pain in her eyes, and the shadows around her mouth, which was still too young for lines or hollows. Then as soon as she was conscious of it, it was gone. For a second, she had seemed utterly lost. Her hand was on her fork, and then she set it down as if she would not eat any more.

Blantyre had seen it – Charlotte was quite certain of that – yet almost without drawing breath, he went on with his tale of music and colour, as if to ensure that neither Charlotte nor Pitt would notice it.

The next course was served. Blantyre changed the subject and became more serious. Now his attention appeared more directed towards Pitt.

'It has changed lately, of course,' he said with a little grimace. 'Since the death of the Crown Prince Rudolf.'

Adriana's eyes widened in surprise, probably that he should mention such a subject at the dinner table, and with people they hardly knew.

Instantly Charlotte wondered if Pitt's real reason for being here could possibly be connected with the tragedy at Mayerling. But what concern could that be to British Special Branch? She looked at Pitt and saw a slight frown on his face.

'The Emperor is a martinet,' Blantyre went on as if he had noticed no reaction. 'Sleeps in an old army bed and rises at half-past four in the morning to begin his work on the papers of state. He dresses in the uniform of a junior officer, and I wouldn't be surprised if he eats only bread and drinks only water.'

Charlotte looked at him closely to see if he were joking. His stories had been full of wit and light-hearted mockery, gentle, as one is amused by those one is fondest of. Now she saw no lightness in his face at all. His nostrils were slightly flared, his mouth pulled a little tight.

'Evan . . .' Adriana began anxiously.

'Mr Pitt is Head of Special Branch, my dear,' Blantyre said, very slightly criticising her. 'He has few illusions. We cannot afford that he should have, but certainly not that we should add to them.'

Adriana went very pale, but she did not argue.

Charlotte wondered where the conversation was leading. How much of it was information that Pitt was seeking, and why had they come to learn it this way? She turned to Blantyre, meeting his eyes while trying to give away as little of her own thoughts as possible.

'He sounds rather grim,' she observed. 'Was he always like that, or is it the effects of grieving for the death of his son?'

Blantyre replied, 'I'm afraid he was always pretty much of a bore. Poor Sisi escapes whenever she can. A trifle eccentric, but who could blame the poor woman.'

Charlotte looked from Blantyre to Pitt, but saw the mystification on his face also, before he could hide it.

'The Empress Elisabeth,' Blantyre explained, eyebrows arched a little. 'God knows why they call her Sisi, but they all do. A Bohemian at heart. Always taking off for somewhere or other, mostly Paris, or perhaps Rome.'

Charlotte plunged in, hoping to learn that she was judging correctly that in some fashion this had to do with Pitt's current case.

'Which comes first?' she asked innocently.

Blantyre turned to her with a bright stare. Was that a ghost of amusement in his eyes? 'First?' he enquired.

She looked straight across at him. 'Her desire to escape his being a bore, or his retreating into solitude because she was always emotionally off on some adventure?'

He nodded almost imperceptibly. 'Neither, so far as I know. But the Crown Prince Rudolf was caught up in a considerable conflict between his father's rigid military dictatorship and his mother's erratic flights of fancy, both metaphorical and literal. He was really rather clever, you know, given half a chance to escape the straitjacket of duty.' He turned to Pitt. 'He wrote excellent articles for radical newspapers, under a pseudonym, of course.'

Pitt straightened, his fork halfway to his mouth.

Blantyre smiled. 'You didn't know? It doesn't surprise me. Not many people do. He was of the opinion that an invasion of Croatia would be a cause for war with Russia, which Austria would start against a completely anti-Austrian Balkan peninsula from the Black Sea to the Adriatic. He said not only the present would be at stake, but the whole future, for which Austria was responsible to the coming generation.'

Pitt stared at him. There was complete silence at the table.

'Almost a direct quote,' Blantyre said. 'As closely as I can match the English to the German.'

'Evan, the poor man is dead,' Adriana interrupted him, even though it seemed as if he might have finished speaking and intended nothing further. 'We will never know what good he might have done had he lived.' There was intense sadness in her voice and her eyes were downcast.

Charlotte's mind raced. She could think of no way in which a suicide pact between a man and his mistress, however tragic, could concern British Special Branch. And yet it appeared that Blantyre had introduced the subject very deliberately, even though it was hardly polite dinner-table conversation among people who barely knew each other.

Now Blantyre was looking at Adriana. 'My dear, you mustn't grieve for him so much.' He reached out his hand towards hers, but the table was too long for them to touch. Still his fingers remained in the open gesture, resting lightly on the white cloth. 'It was his own choice, and I think perhaps all that was left to him. He was tired and ill, and desperately unhappy.'

'Ill?' she said quickly, meeting his gaze for the first time since Rudolf's death had been mentioned.

'That is why he will not have an heir,' he said very gently.

'But he has two daughters!' she insisted.

'There will be no sons.'

'How can you know?' she argued.

'Because now the Princess Stéphanie is also infected,' he replied.

The expression in Adriana's face was unreadable: surprise, pity, but – more complex than that – it seemed to Charlotte to include a kind of hope, as if a long-standing problem had at last been resolved.

'So it would have been the Archduke Franz Ferdinand anyway?' Adriana said after a couple of seconds.

'Yes,' Blantyre agreed. 'Did you think poor Rudolf's death could have had something to do with the succession? It wasn't political, at least in that sense. If Rudolf had become Emperor, he had planned to make the Empire a republic and be president of it, with far greater freedom for the individual nations within.'

'Would that have worked?' she said dubiously.

He smiled. 'Probably not. He was an idealist, very much a dreamer. But he might have had influence.'

Pitt looked from one to the other of them. 'Is there any doubt that it was suicide?'

Blantyre shook his head. 'None at all. I know there are all kinds of rumours flying around, but the truth is deeper, and far more powerful than is known to the public. But I believe that some griefs should remain the property of those who are the victims. That is about the only decency we can offer them. I am quite certain that his death and that of Marie Vetsera were by their own hands, and there were no others involved, at least at the end. Who has blame for the patterns of their lives is not an issue for us.'

Pitt seemed about to say something, then changed his mind, and made instead some remark about one of the many beautiful paintings on the wall.

Adriana's face lit with pleasure immediately. 'The Croatian coast,' she said eagerly. 'That's where I was born.' She went on to describe it from her own very obvious nostalgia.

Charlotte noted Blantyre's face. There was a lingering sadness in his eyes, the same gentleness as before in his features as he listened to his wife remembering her childhood, the changing seasons, the sounds and the touch of the past. She said nothing more of Vienna, as if it were another world.

After dinner Charlotte and Adriana returned to the withdrawing room for tea and delicate, prettily decorated sweets.

'Your country sounds very beautiful,' Charlotte said with interest.

Adriana responded immediately, her eyes still soft with memory. 'It's unique,' she said, smiling. 'At least it was. I haven't been back for several years now.'

'Surely you can go back, at least to visit?' Charlotte asked.

Suddenly Adriana was very still. The delicate colour of her skin became even paler, almost as if it were translucent.

'I don't think I would like to. Evan is very protective of my feelings. He keeps telling me that it would bring back old pain that is best left to heal, and perhaps he is right.'

Charlotte waited, believing the explanation would come. Even if it did not, it would be clumsy to ask.

Adriana snatched her attention back to the present. 'I'm sorry, I am making no sense. My father died a long time ago, and my mother had some time before. It is still something I find it hard to think of. Other people mean well. They loved him and grieved also, but not as I did.' For some minutes she had difficulty keeping her emotions in control. She looked at Charlotte with startling trust, as if clearly there were a friendship between them, but she did not say anything more.

Charlotte thought of her own elder sister's death: the grief, the fear, some of the terrible disillusion in so many things that had followed it. It was during the series of murders during which she had first met Pitt, and perhaps in which she had begun to grow up and look more honestly at the people she loved. She had tried to accept failure, her own, and theirs, not to blame them because they fell short of her idealistic and rather immature perceptions of them.

She had no idea how Adriana's father had died, but clearly it was something that caused her a more complicated pain than sudden illness or a tragic accident. Even now, she would not speak of it.

Charlotte looked around the withdrawing room and chose a lovely, very ornate piece of carving in wood to admire, and ask about.

The tension was broken, and Adriana responded with a flush of gratitude, giving an account of its history.

★　★　★

In the dining room, the butler brought in the port and cigars, and at Blantyre's request he left them alone. Then the serious conversation began. Blantyre offered no preamble.

'I have looked more closely at the information you gave me, Pitt. I have been obliged to change my mind. I admit, I thought you were being a little hasty and had jumped to conclusions, perhaps due to your very recent promotion to your position. I was mistaken. I now believe that you are right to consider the danger serious, possibly even as catastrophic as it looks.'

Pitt was stunned.

Blantyre leaned forward. 'Of course, the indications are slight: an enquiry about timetables, which seems natural enough; desire to know how the signals work, in more detail than the average person knows, or wishes to; a technical description of how the points work. They do not indicate to the Foreign Office that there is anything amiss.' He gave a rueful, self-deprecating smile. 'To me, knowing the names of the men concerned, it indicates that they plan something large and complicated enough to require the use of men who have killed before, and are willing to cause any number of civilian casualties in order to succeed.'

'Why the Duke Alois?' Pitt asked him. 'Does he actually have far more political significance than we know after all?'

Blantyre's eyes were steady, his face very grave.

'I am unaware that he has any significance at all, but it is a good thought. There may be a number of things that have changed since my last accurate information. But even if he does not, this is a far bigger issue than the death of any one man, whoever he is.' He spread his hands on the white cloth. They were lean and strong.

'The Austro-Hungarian Empire is pivotal to the future of Europe. I don't believe the government of Britain fully realises

165

that. Perhaps no other government does either, even in Vienna itself. Look at the map, Pitt. The Empire is enormous. It lies in the heart of Europe between the rising industrial strengths of the Protestant countries in the west, especially Germany, newly united and growing in power every year, and the old, subtle and fractured east, which includes all the quarrelsome Balkan states, and Greece, Macedonia, and Turkey – "the sick man of Europe".'

Pitt did not interrupt. The brandy was forgotten, the cigars unlit.

'And to the south is Italy,' Blantyre went on. 'Like Germany, it is newly united, but still with the open wound in the north of an Austrian-occupied territory containing some of its most valuable cities. Also, of course, Serbia, Croatia, Montenegro and the other Adriatic countries, where the real powder keg lies. Small as they are, if they explode, they could eventually take the whole of Europe with them.'

His hands tightened a little. 'But far more than this, to the north lies the vast, restless bear of Russia: Slavic in its loyalties, Orthodox in its faith. It's ruled by a Tsar in Moscow who hasn't the faintest idea what really lies in his own people's hearts, never mind anywhere else, nor does he have the wits to do anything about it if he did.'

Pitt felt cold. He began to catch a glimpse of what Blantyre was leading towards.

'And Austria lies in the heart of it.' Blantyre moved his hand very slightly, as if it lay on a map, not the white linen table-cloth. 'The Empire has eleven different languages, a multitude of faiths – Catholic, Orthodox, Muslim, Jewish. Although admittedly the anti-Semitism is ugly, and rising, still the general tolerance is there. The culture is old, deeply sophisticated, long practised at holding the reins of power strongly enough to govern, lightly enough to give individuality space to breathe.'

He looked at Pitt, judging his reaction.

'Teutonic Germany is impatient, champing at the bit of its own sleek power. Bismarck spoke of "chaining the trim seaworthy frigate of Prussia to the ancient worm-eaten galleon of Austria". We have not taken enough notice of that. The Germans are dangerous and growing increasingly restless. Their young lions are waiting to take down the old. But even that is only peripheral to the real danger. Austria is the heart where all the different interests meet, safely. Remove it, and there is no neutral core. Teutons and Slavs are face to face. Protestant, Catholic, Muslim and Jew have no forum in which to speak familiarly. There is no longer a single culture where all take part.'

Pitt could see the indisputable logic in what Blantyre was saying.

'But why kill a minor member of the Austrian royal family, and here in England? What does that serve?' he asked.

Blantyre smiled, his face tight, eyes bleak. 'It doesn't matter who it is; the victim is incidental. Anyone would have done as well. Assassinate him at home and the authorities might be able to cover it up, make it seem like some horrible accident. Do it in England, where they have no control, in the territory of one of the best secret services in Europe, and it cannot be hidden. Better still, no doubt when you catch whoever is responsible, they will prove unmistakably to be Croatian. Austria will have no choice whatsoever except to try him and execute him, then to find all his allies and do the same – do you see?'

Pitt began to see, and the vision was appalling.

Blantyre nodded slowly. 'It is in your face. Of course you see. Austria would then be at war with Croatia. Croatia is Slavic. It will appeal to its mighty Russian cousins, who will weigh in on their side, even if not invited to. Then Germany will come in on the side of German-speaking, German-cultural Austria, and before you can stop the landslide, you will have war, the like of which we have never seen before.'

'No sane man would . . .' Pitt began, and tailed off.

'No sane man,' Blantyre repeated softly. 'No sane man with the knowledge and understanding to see where it would lead. How many sane nationalist revolutionaries do you know? How many dynamiters and assassins who see more than a few days ahead of them, let alone half a year, or a decade?'

'None,' Pitt said almost under his breath. 'God, what a mess.'

'We must prevent it,' Blantyre answered. 'Special Branch may never have had a more important job to do. Any help I can give is at your service, day or night.'

Pitt stared down at the table, shoulders hunched, all the muscles of his face and neck aching.

'Thank you.'

Chapter Six

The early afternoon was bright and very cold when Vespasia set out to visit Serafina again. She was not looking forward to it with any pleasure. To see Serafina in such confusion was distressing, and the very obvious fear she felt was even more painful. But it was a poor friend who abandoned someone because their company was not as enjoyable in their time of need as it had been in past years.

The carriage passed through the long familiar streets. Vespasia noticed a woman almost knocked off balance when a gust of wind caught her skirts and she grasped the arm of the man walking beside her. A hundred yards further on a man in grey held his hands up to keep his hat from being blown off. The clip of horses' hoofs rang loudly on the iron-hard stones.

Then suddenly Vespasia realised she could not hear it. They were slowing down, but still moving. With a chill of horror she knew the familiar hush of sawdust in the road, and its meaning. They were passing the home of someone very recently dead. Except that they were not passing, they were stopped and the coachman was at the carriage door.

'My lady . . .' He sounded uncomfortable.

'Yes,' Vespasia answered the words he had been reluctant to say. 'I see what has happened. I will still go in. Please wait for me here. I do not imagine I shall be long.'

'Yes, my lady.' He held out his hand and assisted her to alight.

She walked over the sawdust to the footpath and across it to the steps up to the front door. The curtains were drawn. The dark blue dress she was wearing was no longer appropriate. It should have been black, but she had not known. She knocked on the door, and was about to knock again when it was finally answered by Nerissa Freemarsh herself. Her face, normally stressed and a little colourless, today looked bleached by shock, her eyes red-rimmed, lids puffy. She drew in breath to speak, and let it out again in a gasp. She looked on the point of collapse.

Vespasia mastered her own feelings and took Nerissa by the arm, gently propelling her inside, and then closed the door before turning to speak to her.

'I can see what has happened,' she said quietly. 'I'm very sorry. It is always a shock, no matter how well one imagines one is prepared. I admit, I had not thought it would be anything like so soon, or I would not have come so ill-prepared, and perhaps intrusively early.'

'No . . .' Nerissa gulped. 'No, you are not intrusive in the slightest. You were so kind . . . to come . . .' She gulped again.

Vespasia felt a rush of pity for her. She was an unattractive young woman, not so much plain of feature as lacking in charm. Now she had lost perhaps the only relative she had, and even if she had inherited the house, it would do little to give her entrée to desirable social circles. Certainly it would bring her no friends of true value. In her sudden new loneliness she would be even more vulnerable than before. Vespasia hoped the lover she believed her to have was indeed real, and in no way in pursuit of her expectations from Serafina.

'Perhaps a cup of tea?' Vespasia suggested. 'I am sure you would benefit from a chance to sit down for a few moments. It must be a heavy burden for you. Is there anyone who will assist you in whatever needs to be done? If not, I'm sure I can recommend a suitable person, and instruct them as to your wishes, and of course Serafina's.'

'Thank you . . . thank you.' Nerissa seemed to compose herself a little more. 'I have barely had time to think of it. But certainly tea. Tea would be excellent. I'm so sorry I did not think of it. My good manners seem to have evaporated . . .' She drew in a deep, shuddering breath.

'Not at all,' Vespasia assured her. 'I dare say the kitchen is in a bit of a state. Servants need a firm hand at such times, and something to do, or they tend to go to pieces. It is all very distressing. They will be worrying about their own positions, no doubt. The sooner you can reassure them, the better able they will be to assist you.'

'Yes . . . I hadn't even thought . . .' Nerissa very deliberately steadied herself and turned to lead the way into the morning room. It was bitterly cold, the fire not having been lit. She stopped in dismay.

'Perhaps the housekeeper's sitting room?' Vespasia suggested. 'That is very often comfortable even when all else is in disarray.'

Nerissa seemed grateful for the suggestion. Ten minutes later they were in the small but very cosy room in the servants' quarters from which Mrs Whiteside governed the domestic arrangements. She was a short, stout woman with a surprisingly handsome face. At the moment she was clearly very distressed, but grateful to have something useful to do, and to see that Vespasia was composed and aware of the priorities of what was required at such a time. Nerissa disappeared to address the servants and Mrs Whiteside brought Vespasia a pot of tea while she waited.

After she had left, Vespasia waited for Nerissa to return so she might inform her of exactly what had happened.

There was a brief knock on the door. Vespasia answered, expecting Mrs Whiteside back again, but it was Tucker who came in, closing the door behind her. She looked suddenly older, as if ten years had stricken her in one night, but she stood straight, head high. She was wearing black without a white apron and totally without adornment of any kind. Her white hair was neatly dressed as always, but her skin was so colourless it looked like wrinkled paper. The hollows of her eyes were the only easily discernible features.

Vespasia rose to her feet and went towards her. She took Tucker's hands in hers, something she would normally never have imagined doing to a servant of any sort.

'My dear Tucker, I am so sorry. For all the warning one has of such an event, one can never anticipate the sense of loss.'

Tucker stood rigid, overcome by her emotions. She had lost a lifetime's companionship, something more intimate than many marriages, and possibly closer. She wanted to speak, but she was painfully aware that she could not do so without losing her composure. She might have come intending to say something, but now was not the time.

'Would you care for tea?' Vespasia asked, gesturing towards the tray that had been prepared for her. There was still plenty left in the pot – all it required was another cup.

Tucker swallowed. 'No, thank you, my lady. I just came . . .' She was unable to complete the sentence.

'Then please return to your duties,' Vespasia said gently. 'No doubt we shall have other opportunities to speak.'

Tucker nodded, gulped and retreated to the door.

It was another five minutes before Nerissa came back.

'Thank you,' she said with intense feeling. 'It was kind of you to come.' She sat with her hands knotted in her lap, motionless, knuckles white. 'It . . . it seems much easier when there is something to do.'

'Indeed,' Vespasia agreed. 'I gather from what Mrs Whiteside said that Serafina died some time during the night, and it was you who found her this morning. It must have been extremely distressing for you, and unexpected so soon.'

'Yes. Yes, we were not expecting it . . . for weeks . . . even months,' Nerissa agreed.

'We? You mean her doctor?'

'Yes. He . . . I . . . we sent for him, of course. Mrs Whiteside and I. He came almost straight away. Of course there was nothing he could do. It seemed she . . . died . . . quite early in the night.' She was gasping for breath, her speech disjointed.

Vespasia looked at the young woman sitting opposite her, tense, desperately unhappy, perhaps even guilty because she had not been there. This was natural, if not very reasonable. There was nothing at all she could have done except possibly make it so Serafina had not died alone. But it was also true that Serafina may have gone in her sleep, and would not have known the difference.

Or was Nerissa's guilt now rooted in the fact that she was relieved of a responsibility that must have been draining her emotions and occupied a great deal of her time? Even if undertaken willingly, it would be a relief to let go of it now. What future lay ahead of her? If she were the heiress of a handsome amount, as well as this extremely comfortable house, then she would have no lack of suitors. Please heaven, she would not choose one who was more enamoured of her possessions than of her.

Nerissa was waiting for Vespasia to speak, perhaps to offer

some words of comfort. The silence between them had grown heavy.

Vespasia gave a bleak smile. 'The fact of death is always painful. It reminds us of things we are far better to keep out of our minds in daily life. You are not alone, nor should you feel so. I am sure the doctor assured you that there was nothing you could have done to alter things, or even to help.'

'Yes . . . yes, he did say that,' Nerissa agreed. 'But one feels so helpless, and as if one should have known.'

'It would not have comforted Serafina to have you sitting up with her day and night on the assumption that at any moment she might die,' Vespasia said drily.

Nerissa smiled, in spite of her better judgement. 'Would you care to go up to her room and say a last goodbye?'

Vespasia did not believe it was 'goodbye', only a last '*au revoir*' – and possibly not so very long. Also, it was too late for any communication except in the mind. There was nothing of Serafina left but a shell that the soul had left. However, Vespasia was certainly curious to see if there had been any struggle, any fighting for the last breath, the final sleep. It would be more of a relief than she had imagined if there were not.

'Thank you.' She rose to her feet and Nerissa stood also. Vespasia followed her out of the housekeeper's room back into the main hall, then up the stairs to the room where only a few days ago she had visited Serafina.

Nerissa waited outside, next to a huge blue and white Chinese urn, containing fronds of bamboo. She was ashen-faced, staring out of the landing window several paces from the door.

Vespasia went in and stood alone. She looked at the body of the woman with whom she had not been truly friends, and yet their lives had had so much more in common than most of their generation. The passion of their beliefs separated them from others they knew day by day, even from their own families – perhaps especially from them.

Now all the fear was ironed out of Serafina's features. The worst she could imagine had either already happened, or the danger of it had passed and she was beyond all earthly success or failure. Vespasia looked at her, and saw nothing but the shell. The spirit was gone.

What had she imagined she could learn? There was no one here. Whatever Serafina had been afraid of must be discovered in some other way. She turned and went back outside to thank Nerissa, and offer her condolences once again. Then with increasing urgency in her mind she gathered her cape and went outside. She mounted into her carriage and was driven away, determined to visit Thomas Pitt.

She was kept waiting at his office at Lisson Grove no more than twenty minutes. The young man named Stoker knew who she was and insisted that Pitt would wish to see her.

'Aunt Vespasia?' Pitt said with some alarm. He rose from his chair and came over to her as she closed the door behind her. She did little more than glance at the pictures on the wall, the books, and notice the difference from when Victor Narraway had occupied the room. She sat down in the chair opposite the desk and faced him.

'Good afternoon, Thomas. Thank you for seeing me immediately. I have just called at the home of Serafina Montserrat, and found that she died unexpectedly, some time last night.'

'I'm sorry,' he said gently. 'I know that you knew her.'

'Thank you. She was a remarkable woman, more than I used to believe. But it is not the loss of a friend that concerns me. We were not especially close. Last time I visited her, a few days ago, she was profoundly afraid – indeed, I would

175

say terrified – that her mind was affected to the point where she rambled in memory, and might have forgotten where and when she was, and to whom she was speaking. That is not a unique circumstance in old age.' She gave a small, sad smile. 'But in her case it was dangerous, or so she believed. She knew many secrets from her time as something of a revolutionary in the Austrian Empire many years ago. She was afraid there were people to whom she was still a danger.'

She saw the sudden, sharp attention in his face.

'I thought at best that she was romanticising,' she continued. 'But I took the precaution of asking Victor Narraway if perhaps it might be the truth. He enquired into it. At first it seemed she was deluding herself, but he did not give up easily, and it transpired that she might have been understating her importance, if anything.'

'How far in the past?' he interrupted.

'A generation ago, at least. But she felt that some of her knowledge concerned people still alive, or those whom they might have loved and wished to protect. I can give you no names because I don't know any. But she was very, very frightened, Thomas.'

He looked puzzled. 'Of betraying someone accidentally, even now? Who? Did she tell you?'

'No. To me, she was very discreet. I suppose part of what made me think she was romanticising was the fact that she gave no names. But Victor said that she was more even than she claimed. Thomas, I was not absolutely certain that she was mistaken in her fear. One moment she was as lucid as you or I, when we were alone, then when someone else came in she seemed to lurch into near insanity, as if she had no idea where she was.'

'What was she afraid of?' he asked. 'Please stop being so circumspect and tell me what you mean.'

She took a deep, rather shaky breath, and let it out with a sigh. 'That someone may have frightened her to the point where she took her own life, rather than continue with the risk of betraying a friend, an ally in the cause.' Pity overwhelmed her, and a sense of guilt because she had done nothing to prevent this. She had known about it, and Serafina had begged for her help. Now she was safe in Pitt's office talking about it, too late, and Serafina was dead.

'What could you have done?' Pitt's voice, gentle and urgent, intruded on her thoughts.

She looked at him. 'I don't know. Which is not a good enough excuse, is it!'

'You could have done nothing,' he told her. 'Unless you were able and prepared to move in and sleep in the room beside her. Or perhaps be certain that she saw no visitors without your being present.'

'I tried to have Nerissa Freemarsh do that, even to engage a nurse,' Vespasia said bleakly. 'I did not try hard enough.'

'And the other thought?' he prompted.

She stared at him, for long, level seconds. To evade the issue now would be deliberately to lie. She could not do that. 'There is the possibility that she was not afraid unnecessarily. There may have been someone she could still have betrayed, knowingly or not.' She saw the tension increase in Pitt, the tightness in his face, an almost imperceptible increase in the rigidity of his body. He knew what she was going to say. 'They could have killed her,' she finished in a whisper.

Pitt nodded slowly. 'Her address?'

'Fifteen, Dorchester Terrace,' she replied. 'Just off Blandford Square. It is only a few streets away. You may need to hurry, in case things are moved . . . or hidden . . .'

Pitt rose to his feet. 'I know.'

*   *   *

Pitt took Stoker with him, explaining as they went. It was, as Vespasia had said, no more than a quarter of a mile away, and they walked at a rapid pace. He had barely sufficient time to acquaint Stoker with a little of Serafina's history and the reason why her fears were realistic enough that Special Branch must make certain they were not founded in truth. Stoker did not question his reasoning; the mention of Austria was sufficient.

The door was opened by a parlour maid, who was grim-faced and clearly in mourning. She was drawing in breath to deny them entrance when Nerissa came across the hall behind her.

'Good afternoon, Miss Freemarsh,' Pitt said to Nerissa. 'I am Thomas Pitt, Commander of Special Branch. This is Sergeant Stoker. We are here regarding the very recent death of Mrs Montserrat. May we come in, please?' He said it in a manner that did not allow her to refuse, and he took the first step across the threshold before she replied.

Beneath the red blotches from weeping, her face was ashen white.

'Why? What . . . what has happened?' She was shaking so badly Pitt was anxious that she might faint.

'Please let us come in, Miss Freemarsh, where you can sit down. Perhaps your maid might bring us tea, or some other restorative. It is possible that we may not trouble you at all, but your aunt was a woman of great importance to her country, and there are aspects of her death that we need to assure ourselves are in order.'

'What do you mean?' Nerissa gulped. 'She was old and ill. Her mind was wandering and she imagined things.' She put her hands to her mouth. 'This is Lady Vespasia's doing, isn't it!' she said accusingly. 'She's . . . meddling . . .'

'Miss Freemarsh, is there something about your aunt's death that you wish to conceal from us?'

'No! Of course not! I want only decency and respect for her – not – not policemen tramping through the house and . . . and making a spectacle out of our family tragedy.'

'It is not a tragedy that the old should die, Miss Freemarsh,' he said more gently, 'unless there is something in their death that is not as it should be. And I am not a policeman, I am the Head of Special Branch. Unless you tell them so, no one needs to think me anything other than a government official come to pay my respects to a much-admired and valued woman.'

Stoker stepped in behind Pitt and closed the front door.

Nerissa backed a little further into the centre of the beautiful hallway with its pictures and its sweeping stair and newel lamp.

'There is nothing for you to do!' she protested again. 'Aunt Serafina died in her sleep some time last night. The doctor says it was probably early, because . . . because when I touched her this morning, she was cold.' She shivered as if the memory put its cold hand on her now. 'Why are you doing this? It's brutal!'

Stoker fidgeted behind Pitt, moving his weight from one foot to the other. Pitt did not know if his impatience was with Pitt or Nerissa Freemarsh, and he could not afford to care.

'In your place, Miss Freemarsh, I believe I would prefer to have my mind set at ease,' he said quietly. 'But I am afraid I must be certain, whether it is what you wish or not. I would like to see Mrs Montserrat, and then have the name and address of her doctor so I can see him, and perhaps of her man of affairs also. Special Branch will take care of the funeral arrangements, according to whatever her wishes were.'

Nerissa was aghast. 'Can you do that?'

'I can do whatever is necessary to safeguard the peace and welfare of the nation,' Pitt replied. 'But it can all be dignified and discreet, if you do not oppose it.'

179

Nerissa waved her hand in a useless gesture, sharp and at the same time helpless. 'The doctor is upstairs with her now.'

Pitt swivelled round and went up the stairs two at a time. He threw open the door of the first bedroom facing the front of the house, and saw a young, fair-haired man in black bending forward over the bed. There was a Gladstone bag on the floor beside him. He straightened up and turned as the sound of the door startled him.

'Who the devil are you, sir, barging into a lady's bedroom like this?' he demanded. His face was fair, but his features stronger than might have been suggested by the slenderness of his build.

Pitt closed the door behind him. 'Thomas Pitt, Head of Special Branch. You, I presume, are Mrs Montserrat's physician?'

'I am. Geoffrey Thurgood. The reason for my presence here is obvious. What is the reason for yours?'

'I think our reasons are the same,' Pitt replied, coming further into the room. The ashes were cold in the grate but the colours in the room still gave it a suggestion of warmth. 'To be certain as to the cause of Mrs Montserrat's death, although I may need to know more of the exact circumstances surrounding it than you do.'

'She was of advanced years and rapidly deteriorating health,' Thurgood said with barely concealed impatience. 'Her mind was wandering more with each day. Even at the most optimistic assessment her death could not have been very far away.'

'Days?' Pitt asked.

Thurgood hesitated. 'No . . . I would have expected her to have lived another several months, actually.'

'A year?'

'Possibly.'

'What was the cause of her death, exactly?'

'Heart failure.'

'Of course her heart failed,' Pitt retorted impatiently. 'Everybody's heart fails when they die. What caused it to fail?'

'Probably her age. She was an invalid.' Thurgood too was losing what was left of his patience. 'The woman was almost eighty!'

'Being eighty is not a cause of death. I have a grandmother-in-law who is well over eighty. Regrettably she is as strong as a horse.'

Thurgood smiled in spite of himself. 'Then your mother-in-law may well have another thirty years.'

'There is nothing wrong with my mother-in-law, except her own mother-in-law.' Pitt pulled his face into an expression of pity and resignation, thinking of Charlotte's grandmama. 'Mrs Montserrat was not a fantasist, Dr Thurgood. She had done some remarkable things in her earlier years, and known a great many secrets that might still be dangerous. It was not ghosts she was afraid of, but very real people.'

Thurgood looked startled, stared at Pitt for a moment, then went pale. 'You're serious?'

'Yes.'

'May I see proof that you are who you claim to be?'

'Of course.' Pitt fished in his untidy pockets and pulled out the proof of his identity and office, along with a ball of string, a knob of sealing wax and a handkerchief. He gave the identification to Thurgood.

Thurgood read it carefully and handed it back. 'I see. What do you want of me?'

'Complete professional discretion, then the exact cause, time, and any other details you can give me of Mrs Montserrat's death, and whether it is what you expected, or if there are any aspects of it that surprise you or are unexplained.'

'I can't tell you that without a post-mortem . . .'

'Of course not,' Pitt agreed.

'I doubt the family will agree.'

'The family consists only of Miss Freemarsh,' Pitt pointed out. 'But I'm afraid it is not within her right to prevent it if a crime is possible.'

'You'll have to have the necessary legal—' Thurgood began.

'No I won't,' Pitt contradicted him. 'I'm Special Branch, not police. I will have no trouble ensuring that the law does not stand in our way. This may turn out to be unnecessary, but it is too important to ignore it.'

Thurgood's lips tightened. 'If there was a crime of any sort, then it is too important to ignore, Mr Pitt. I shall begin the arrangements immediately. I leave it to you to inform the family solicitor, who is bound to object. Miss Freemarsh is sure to see to it that he does.'

Pitt nodded. He was beginning to like Thurgood. 'Thank you.'

As Thurgood had foretold, the lawyer, Mr Morton, was less obliging, when Pitt went to see him at his office. He spluttered and protested, talked about desecration of the body, but in the end he was obliged to yield, albeit somewhat ungraciously.

'This is monstrous! You overstep yourself, sir. I have always been of the opinion that the police force is a highly dubious blessing, and the body that calls itself Special Branch, even more so.' His chin quivered and his blue eyes sparked with outrage. 'I demand the name of your superior!'

'Lord Salisbury,' Pitt said with a smile. 'You will find him at Number Ten, Downing Street. But before you leave to appeal to him, I would like a very approximate figure as to Mrs Montserrat's estate, and information as to whom it is bequeathed.'

'Certainly not! You trespass too far.' The old man folded his arms across his ample chest and glared at Pitt defiantly.

'If I have to find out by asking questions outside the family it will be a great deal less discreet,' Pitt pointed out. 'I am trying to deal with this as delicately as possible; and to protect Mrs Montserrat's heirs from unpleasantness, and possibly danger.'

'Danger? What danger? Mrs Montserrat died in her sleep!'

'I hope so.'

'What do you mean, you "hope so"?'

'She was a woman of great distinction. She deserves the best attention we can give her. If there is something untoward in her death, or in the property and the papers she leaves, I wish to keep it private. Indeed, I intend to. Allow me to do it gently.'

The lawyer grunted. 'I suppose you have the power to force me if I refuse. And from the look on your face, and your taste for authority, you will do.'

Pitt forbore from retaliating.

'She left a nice bequest for her maid, Tucker,' the lawyer said reluctantly, 'for whom she had a considerable affection. It will care for her for the rest of her life. Apart from that, the house in Dorchester Terrace and the balance of her estate goes to her niece, Nerissa Freemarsh. It is several thousand pounds. If she is careful it will provide an income for her sufficient to live quite comfortably.'

'Thank you. Are there any papers other than the ordinary household and financial ones you would expect? Any diaries?'

The lawyer looked at Pitt with gleaming satisfaction. 'No there are not!'

Pitt had expected that answer, but it would have been remiss not to ask.

'Thank you, Mr Morton. I am obliged to you. Good day.'

Morton did not reply.

*   *   *

183

The following day Thurgood sent a message to Pitt to tell him that he had completed his examination and was prepared to offer his report. He was ready to give, at least, the exact cause of death, but the circumstances he would leave to Pitt to discern.

Pitt had been to morgues before. It had been a grim part of his duty for most of his adult life, although rather less often since joining Special Branch. The moment he stepped from the bright, windy street into the building with its uncanny silence, he could smell the odours of death and chemical preservation, and the dampness in the air. It was as if with the constant washing away of blood, nothing in the building was ever fully dry, or warm. To him the smells of carbolic, vinegar and formaldehyde were worse than the smells of nature.

'Well?' he asked when he was alone with Thurgood in his office and the door was closed. The building was still cold, as though it were frequented by nothing living or breathing.

'Simply, it was laudanum,' Thurgood replied unhappily. 'She took it regularly. She found sleep eluded her and often she would be awake all night, hearing every creak in the timbers of the house, imaginary footsteps.'

'You mean she finally took too much?' Pitt said with disbelief. 'Could that be simply accidental? Wasn't she given it by someone who knew what they were doing? Miss Freemarsh? Or the lady's maid? Tucker has been with her most of her life. She would never have made such a mistake.' The fear flashed to him that Tucker could have done it on purpose, as an act of mercy to a woman living in such terrible fear. She would only have been hastening something that was inevitable. Then he remembered how, when he had interviewed Miss Tucker briefly, before leaving for Mr Morton's office the previous afternoon, he had seen only grief in her face, and the idea melted away.

'No, this was too large a dose to have been a single accident,' Thurgood replied, his face betraying his unhappiness. 'It was at least five times as much as she would have taken for sleep. Laudanum is not easy to overdose because the solution is weak. One would have to take a second, or, in time, even a third dose within a short time to have such an effect. It is deliberately prepared that way, precisely to avoid such accidents. And I made sure that both Tucker and Miss Freemarsh kept the supply out of the main bedroom or bathroom, in a cupboard with a lock.'

Pitt was growing even colder. 'And the key?'

'On a ring in a cupboard, whose handle was higher than Mrs Montserrat could have reached.' Thurgood looked as if he were chilled also. He stood stiffly. His hands clenched together. The bloodless skin stretched over his knuckles. 'If Mrs Montserrat had taken the same dose she was normally given at night before settling down to sleep, even if she were awake, she would have been too drowsy to have got up, gone from her room across the landing to the chambermaid's room where the tea kettle is, and other such things, then climbed on a chair to open the key cupboard, and finally a second chair to the medicine cabinet. This was administered to her by someone else. What I cannot say is if it was an accident, although I find it hard to believe anyone could give so much accidentally.' He met Pitt's eyes. 'Or else it was on purpose. I'm relieved to say that it is not my responsibility to find out.'

'I see. Thank you.' Pitt was bitterly disappointed, although with any honesty he had to admit he also did not want to think Serafina was so far departed from reality as to have taken her own life in a haze of fear and confusion – or even deliberately, rather than face the mental disintegration she knew had already begun. It was a humiliating end for a brave woman.

Now this began to look like murder.

Was it a simple domestic tragedy of greed and impatience: Nerissa unwilling to play companion and dreamer-in-waiting another year, or two, or even three? Perhaps her lover was losing the will to wait for her, or she was afraid he might? Perhaps it was just another wretched story of family misery turning into hatred for an imprisonment in loveless tedium. How old would Nerissa be? Mid-thirties, perhaps. How many more child-bearing years did she have? Desperation was a strong force, all but overwhelming.

Perhaps it had nothing to do with Serafina's past, or Special Branch. He must be sure.

'Thank you,' he said.

Thurgood smiled without pleasure. 'I'll send you a written report: amounts, and so on. But there is no doubt as to what it is, and I can't tell you anything more.'

'No marks on the body?' Pitt asked. 'Scratches, bruises? Anything to indicate her being held? Wrists? A cut inside the mouth? Anything at all?'

'Several,' Thurgood said thinly. 'She was an old woman and she bruised easily. If she had been forced to take it against her will I would have expected to find bruises all around her wrists. It takes some strength to hold a person fighting for her life, even an old woman.'

'Would you know if you were drinking laudanum?' Pitt persisted. 'What does it taste like?'

'You'd know,' Thurgood assured him. 'If she took that much, believe me, either she took it intentionally, or under some kind of duress. The only other alternative, and I've been thinking about this, is that she took the normal dose. Then, when she was in a half-asleep state, the rest was given to her. If there were some spilled, whoever it was would mop it up, perhaps with a little water, and there'd be no discernible trace.'

He shrugged with an air of hopelessness. 'Even if there were, it would prove nothing. She might often spill things. She was old and shaky, sitting up in bed.'

'I see. Thank you.'

Thurgood shrugged and spread his hands.

Pitt arrived back at Dorchester Terrace later that afternoon. Already the light was fading from the sky. The footman admitted him, and had him wait in the cold morning room until Nerissa sent for him to come to the withdrawing room. The curtains were drawn closed, as they had been the previous day, but she was rather more composed this time, even if just as tense.

'What is it now, Mr Pitt? Have you not caused us sufficient distress?' she said coldly. 'The doctor tells me that you have obliged him to perform an autopsy on my aunt. I don't know what purpose you believe that will possibly serve. It is a horrible thing to do, a desecration of her body that I cannot protest against strongly enough – for all the good it will do now.'

'It was necessary to know how she died, Miss Freemarsh,' he replied, watching her face, the anger in her, the clenched hand by her side. 'And I regret to say that it was from an overdose of laudanum.' He stopped, afraid she was going to faint. She swayed and reached out her hand to grasp the back of the settee to steady herself.

'An . . . overdose?' she said, licking her lips as though they were so dry she feared they might crack. 'I thought . . . I thought laudanum was safe. How could she do that? It was not even kept in the same room with her. We were so careful. It was in the upstairs pantry, and Tucker has the key. Even if my aunt felt she was not sleeping well enough, she could not have got up to dose herself. That makes no sense!'

'What would make sense, Miss Freemarsh?' Pitt asked more gently.

'I beg your pardon?'

'What do you think happened?'

'I . . . I don't know. How could I? She must have . . .' She sat still, unable to finish.

'What?' He did not allow her to wait. 'You have just told me that she would not have been able to find the laudanum herself.'

'Then . . . then someone must have . . .' Her hand went to her throat. 'Someone must have . . . broken in . . . or . . .'

'Is that possible?'

'I would not have thought so.' She was beginning to regain a little of her composure. 'But I do not know the facts. If you are quite certain that she died of too much laudanum, then I don't see what other explanation there can be. I did not give it to her, and I cannot believe that Tucker did. She has been loyal to Aunt Serafina for years.' She was staring at Pitt defiantly now. She lowered her voice just a little. 'Aunt Serafina used to speak rather a lot about her past. I always believed she was making up most of it, but perhaps she wasn't. She was afraid someone would try to hurt her, to keep her from revealing secrets. If the doctor is right – and I have no idea if he is – then that may be the answer.'

Pitt waited, still watching her.

'I don't know what else you expect me to say.' She shook her head very slightly. 'Lady Vespasia came to see her several times. Perhaps she may know who would wish her harm. Aunt Serafina trusted her. She may have confided in her. I really cannot help, and I will not have you distressing the servants any more. We none of us know anything. I will ask them if they heard noises of any sort in the night. And of course you may ask them if anything was found, but I will not have you frightening them with the idea that we have had poisoners in the house. Do you understand me?' She shook herself a little and glared at him. 'I will hold you responsible that you do not have them walk out in terror and leave me alone here.'

It was not made with grace, but it was a reasonable request. If it was even remotely possible that someone had indeed broken in, then she had a right to be afraid.

'I will check the windows and doors myself, Miss Freemarsh,' he promised. 'There is no need for any of your servants to be aware that Mrs Montserrat's death was other than from old age, unless you choose to tell them.'

'Thank you.' She gulped. 'How am I supposed to explain your presence here?'

'Mrs Montserrat was a woman of great distinction, to whom the country owes a debt,' he replied. 'We are taking care of the arrangements for her funeral, and you will not argue with us over this. It will explain my continued presence perfectly satisfactorily.'

She let out her breath with a sigh. 'Yes. Yes, that will do. I am obliged. Now what is it you wish to look at? Will it wait until tomorrow?'

'No, it will not. I'm sure your housekeeping staff are excellent. They may unintentionally remove all trace of anyone having broken in, if indeed such a thing happened.'

'I . . . see. Then I suppose you had better look. Although it is more than possible they have removed such a thing already.'

Pitt gave a very tiny smile. 'Of course.' But if he waited until the following day, it would allow her time to create such evidence, and he had no intention of permitting that. 'Now, if you would be good enough to show me all the windows and doors, I will examine them myself.'

She obeyed without speaking again. They went around every door and window one by one, where anyone could possibly have gained entry. As he had expected, he found nothing that proved, or disproved, that someone might have broken in. He also looked at the cupboard where the laudanum was kept and the key to it. It was all exactly as he had been told.

He thanked Nerissa and left.

Outside in the lamplit street, wind-whipped and cold, he hailed the first hansom he could find, and gave the driver Narraway's address. He climbed in and sat sunk in thought as they bowled along, almost oblivious of where he was.

In spite of Vespasia's fears, he had not expected the doctor's findings. Suddenly the world that apparently Serafina had hinted at had become real, and he was not prepared for it. It had sounded so much like the ramblings of an old woman who was losing her grip on life and longed to be thought important and interesting for just a little longer. He had to admit he had assumed that Vespasia was seeing in her a ghost of what might happen to herself, and was exercising kindness rather than a critical judgement.

Now he needed Narraway's opinion, something a good deal more balanced than the thoughts that teemed in his own mind. Narraway, of all people, would not be swayed by fancy.

It did not occur to him until he was almost at Narraway's door that at this time in the early evening he might very well not be at home. He felt a sense of desperation rise inside himself and leaned forward as if travelling faster would somehow solve the problem. He realised the stupidity of it and leaned back again with a sigh.

The hansom pulled up and he asked the driver to wait. There was no purpose in staying here if Narraway were out. He could be gone all evening. He was free to do as he wished – even take a holiday, if he cared to.

But the manservant told him Narraway was at home. As soon as he had paid the hansom Pitt went in and was shown to the sparse, elegant sitting room with its book-lined walls. The fire sent warmth into every corner, and the heavy velvet curtains were drawn against the night.

Pitt did not bother with niceties. They knew each other too well, and had long ago dispensed with trivia. Now the balance was more even between them. Though Narraway was the elder, the command was Pitt's.

'Serafina Montserrat is dead,' Pitt said quietly. 'She died some time early in the night before last.'

'I know,' Narraway replied gravely. 'Vespasia told me. What is there about it that concerns you? Is it not better she go before her mind loses all its grasp, and fear and confusion take over? She was once a great woman. The cruelties of old age are . . . very harsh.' He waited, dark eyes steady on Pitt's, knowing that there had to be something else. Pitt would not have come simply to share grief. 'Did she say anything dangerous before she died?'

'I don't know,' Pitt answered. 'It seems possible, even more so than I thought. She died of an overdose of laudanum.' He saw Narraway flinch but he did not interrupt. 'According to the post-mortem, it was many times the medically correct amount,' Pitt continued. 'Miss Freemarsh says that the bottle is kept locked in a cupboard in the maid's pantry, and is higher than Mrs Montserrat could have reached, even had she had the key. I checked and she is right. I questioned the lady's maid, Tucker, and she agrees. I searched the house and it is not impossible that someone broke in, but there is nothing whatever to indicate it.'

Narraway bit his lip, his face troubled. 'I assume there is no possibility she could have been given an accidentally large dose? Or worse, taken it deliberately?'

'Not accidentally. She didn't handle the bottle herself. Which rules out deliberately also, unless Tucker helped her, and after having spoken to her I don't believe that.'

'Loyalty? A mercy killing to hasten what was inevitable, but before she betrayed all that she had valued?' Narraway asked. 'Not a pleasant thought, but imaginable, in extreme circumstances?' His lips tightened into a bitter line. 'I think I would be grateful if someone were to do that for me.'

Pitt considered it. He tried to picture the frail, elderly maid, after a lifetime of service, giving her desperate mistress the last service she could, the final act of loyalty to the past, as well as the future. It made perfect sense, and yet, thinking of Tucker's face, he did not believe it.

'No,' he said again.

'Not even to save her from having the same thing done by somebody else, perhaps more brutally? Not a quiet going to sleep from which she didn't waken, but perhaps strangling, suffocating with a quick, hard pillow over the face?' Narraway asked. 'This would have been gentle. Are you certain no one could have got to her? Or to the niece, Miss Freemarsh? She could have done it as easily.'

'I thought of that,' Pitt replied. 'I don't think the niece has any understanding of what Serafina accomplished in the past, or any profound loyalty to her either. The possibility that someone else coerced Tucker into it is more likely, but I don't believe that either.'

'Reason? Instinct?'

'Instinct,' Pitt replied. 'But they could have got to the niece. That's possible. I think she's lying, at least to some degree. I assumed it was because she didn't really care very much for her aunt. There is a certain amount of fairly natural resentment that she is spending her youth as a dependant, certainly with expectations, but as long as the old lady is alive, as a companion and housekeeper, while her child-bearing years slip away.'

Narraway winced. 'You make it sound pretty grim.'

'It is pretty grim. But it's better than not having a roof over your head,' Pitt pointed out. 'Which may well be her only alternative. I'll have it looked into, just in case it matters.'

'And the other reason?'

'I think she has a lover.'

Narraway smiled. 'So not so grim as it sounded?'

'Depends on who he is, and what he's after,' Pitt responded drily. The thought flickered through his head again that Narraway seemed to know comparatively little about women. It was a surprise to perceive how large was his own advantage in having a wife, and also children.

Narraway was watching him, his face grave, an intense sadness in his eyes.

'Poor Serafina,' he said softly. 'Murdered after all.' He rubbed the heel of his hand across his face. 'Damn! If someone killed her, it means she knew things that still matter. She had all sorts of connections on the whole Balkan area: Austria, Hungary, Serbia, Croatia, Macedonia, and of course most of all in northern Italy. She was part of all the nationalist uprisings from '48 onwards. If there's something brewing now, she might have known who was involved: connections, old debts.'

Pitt did not have to weigh whether he should tell Narraway of the current assassination threat or not. It was never a possibility in his mind that Narraway would betray anything. His loyalty to Special Branch was greater than theirs had been to him.

'We have word of an assassination attempt on Duke Alois Habsburg when he visits here in a couple of weeks,' he said very quietly. He did not yet want to tell Narraway what a bloody and violent plan it was.

'Alois Habsburg?' Narraway was stunned. 'For God's sake, why?' He took a deep breath. 'Is he far more important than we ever supposed? What does the Foreign Office say?'

'That I have a severe case of inflated imagination,' Pitt replied. 'Due, in all possibility, to having been promoted beyond my ability.'

Narraway swore, with a vocabulary Pitt had not known he possessed.

'But Evan Blantyre is taking it very seriously, and has already given me a great deal of help,' Pitt added.

'Blantyre?' Narraway said quickly. 'He knows as much about the Austrian Empire as anyone, probably more than the Foreign Secretary. If he thinks it's serious, then it is. God, what a mess! But I don't understand: why Duke Alois? As far as we know, he's of no importance at all. Except, of course, he's related to the Queen, and it would be damn embarrassing if he were murdered here, most particularly after we had had plenty of warning that it was likely.' He bit his lip, something he did not habitually do. 'Have you considered the possibility that Special Branch is actually the target, and Duke Alois is incidental?'

'Yes,' Pitt said softly. 'He may be simply a convenient pawn, the man in the right place. Perhaps it doesn't matter who's killed, as long as it's done here.'

'Could he be a troublemaker, like the Crown Prince Rudolf?' Narraway said doubtfully, searching for another answer. 'Socialist sympathies? Does he write articles for left-leaning papers, with dangerous philosophical ideas, or subversive elements of any sort?'

'Nothing,' Pitt replied. 'As far as we can find out, he's a totally harmless dabbler in science and philosophy. If he hadn't been distantly royal, and with money, he would probably have been a university professor.'

Narraway frowned. 'It would make sense if he were dangerous to the throne in some way and they needed to get rid of him, but couldn't afford to do it on their own territory.' He looked at Pitt unhappily. 'There's a hell of a lot we don't know about this, Pitt, and you need to find out damn quickly. How much help is Blantyre being? And why?'

Pitt smiled bitterly. 'I thought of that too, but the answer's fairly simple. He sees the pivotal position of Austria in Europe, and the increasingly fragile threads that hold the Empire together. A really good hole ripped in it, such as would be caused by a major scandal, something that forced the Austrians to react violently against one of the smaller member nations, like Croatia, and the whole fabric could unravel.'

Narraway looked sceptical. 'Croatia has caused trouble for years,' he pointed out. 'There's nothing new in this. And Blantyre, of all people, knows that.'

'There is something new in it,' Pitt argued. 'Blantyre pointed it out, but if I think about it, I knew it for myself. We now have a unified Germany, with the strong, energetic power of Prussia in the lead. If Slavic Croatia seems to be the victim of German-speaking Austria's aggression, Slavic Russia will very naturally come to its aid. Newly unified German-speaking, Teutonic Prussia will come to Vienna's aid, and we will have a European war in the making that we may well not know how to stop.'

'God Almighty!' Narraway said in horror as the enormity of it dawned on him. 'Then guard Alois with your life, if necessary. Use Blantyre, use everybody. I'll do all I can, starting with finding out what happened to poor Serafina Montserrat, particularly if she knew anything about this.' His face was ashen but there was a tension in his body as if every nerve in him had come alive, both to pain and to joy. His breathing was faster. There was a tiny muscle jumping in his temple and his slender hands were locked rigid together as he leaned forward. 'We have to succeed.'

'I know,' Pitt agreed quietly.

'And Serafina's death?' Narraway asked. Then, as Pitt did not answer immediately, he continued. 'I have nothing to do, at least nothing that matters. Let me look into that. It may be important, but even if it hasn't anything to do with politics and is merely some miserable domestic tragedy, she deserves better than that it should be ignored.'

Pitt stared at him for several seconds.

'I assure you, I have solved the occasional crime before now,' Narraway said, his eyes bright with amusement, however complicated and brief. 'You will be challenging me no more to step into your shoes than I have you stepping into mine.'

Pitt drew breath to apologise, then changed his mind and simply smiled.

'Of course. She does deserve better.'

Charlotte reasoned that just because Pitt could not tell her about his current case that did not mean that she could not use her own intelligence and considerable deductive powers to work out what she must do to be of use.

It was perfectly obvious that Evan Blantyre was important to Pitt. At dinner at the Blantyres' house, the men had spent the rest of the evening in the dining room with the door closed, and given instructions to the butler not to interrupt them unless sent for. When they had finally emerged, they had seemed in close agreement about something. Pitt had expressed a gratitude that was far deeper than simply the thanks one owed for a good dinner and a pleasant evening.

On the way home he had said nothing, but Charlotte had seen that a great deal of the tension in him had eased. Certainly that night he had slept better than for over a week.

Therefore she judged it a good idea to cultivate the acquaintance of Adriana Blantyre. This was not in the least difficult, since she had liked her instinctively, and found her unusually interesting. Having grown up in Croatia and then northern Italy, Adriana had a different perspective on many things, especially upon all that was cultural or political. And she was certainly a very agreeable person, in spite of the anxiety that was to be seen in her face in repose, and the sense Charlotte had that there were secrets within her that she shared with no one. Perhaps this was because those secrets were rooted in experiences an Englishwoman could not even imagine.

This afternoon, Charlotte had invited Adriana to visit an exhibition of watercolours with her. Adriana had accepted without hesitation.

They met at two o'clock on the steps of the gallery and went inside together. They laughed a little as they clutched at hats and felt the wind pick up even the heavy cloth of winter skirts, whose edges were dampened by rain.

Adriana was dressed in a warm wine colour, which lent a glow to her pale skin. It was a beautifully cut costume with a slightly rakish air, which made one think of hunting dress. Her hat was narrow-brimmed, tipped well forward, and with a towering crown. It looked vaguely Austrian. Charlotte saw at least a dozen other women glance at her and their faces fill with disapproval, and envy. They looked dull in comparison, and knew it.

Adriana saw, and seemed a little abashed.

'Too much?' she asked almost under her breath.

'Not at all,' Charlotte said with amusement. 'You may guarantee at least three of them will go straight to their milliners tomorrow morning and demand something like it. On some it will look wonderful, and on others absurd. Hats are the hardest things to get right, don't you think?'

197

Adriana hesitated a moment to ascertain that Charlotte was serious, then relaxed into a wide smile. 'Yes, I do. But with hair like yours it seems a shame to wear a hat at all. But I suppose you must, at least out in the street – oh, and in church, of course.' She laughed lightly. 'I wonder if God had the faintest idea how many hours we would spend in front of the glass rather than on our knees, fussing over what to wear to worship Him.'

'In what to be seen worshipping Him,' Charlotte corrected her. 'But if He is a man, as everyone says, then probably not.' She smiled, and walked side by side with Adriana across the wide entrance hall and into the first display room. 'But if He were a woman, or had a wife, then He would certainly know,' she continued softly, so as not to be overheard. 'Presumably He invented our hair. He must have at least some idea of how long it takes to pin it up!'

'Every picture I have seen of Eve, she has it long enough to sit on!' Adriana exclaimed. 'To cover her . . . necessities. I don't think mine would ever grow so long.'

'Of course, a number of gentlemen have very little hair at all, especially in their advancing years,' Charlotte replied. 'It may well be some time since we have been permitted to dress a trifle more suitably to our state, and the climate. You should feel free to have as wide a skirt and as large a hat as you please.'

Adriana shot her a glance of gratitude, as if the levity had allowed her a sense of release.

They went around the paintings slowly, looking at each one with care.

'Oh, look!' Adriana said in sudden excitement. 'That is just like a bridge I used to know near where I was born.' She stood transfixed in front of the picture to the right of Charlotte. It was a small, delicate pastoral scene where a rivulet rattled over its bed and disappeared beneath a stone bridge, the light shining briefly in the water beyond. The cows grazed nearby, so well drawn that it seemed as if at any moment they would move.

Charlotte looked at Adriana and saw a range of emotions in her face. It was very close to both laughter and tears. Perhaps memories crowded so close together they were impossible to separate.

'It's beautiful,' she said sincerely. 'You must find it very different here. I sometimes wish I had grown up in the country, but if I had, I think I would miss it so terribly now that I might not ever reconcile myself to paved streets and houses close to each other – not to mention noise, and smoke in the winter.'

'Oh, there's mud in the country,' Adriana assured her. 'And cold. And in the winter it can be unbearably tedious, believe me. And so much darkness everywhere! It closes in on you in every direction, almost without relief. You would miss the theatre, and parties, and gossip about famous people, rather than just your neighbours, who would talk of the same things all the time: Mrs This about her grandchildren; Mr That about his gout; Miss So-and-so about her aunt, and how bad the cook is.'

Charlotte looked at her more closely to see how much she meant what she was saying, and how much she was very lightly mocking. After several seconds, she was still uncertain. That was invigorating. It was a bore always to be able to read people.

'Perhaps one should have a city home for the winter to go to the theatre and operas and parties,' she said with an answering half-seriousness, 'and a country home for the summer, to go for rides and walks, to dine in the garden, and . . . whatever else one chose.'

'But you are English.' Adriana was close to laughter now.

'So you spend the summer in town and go to your country estate for winter, where you gallop around the fields behind a pack of dogs, and apparently enjoy yourself enormously.'

Charlotte laughed with her, and they moved to the next painting. Charlotte only barely noticed Adriana glance back once at the gentle bridge in the sun, with the cows grazing nearby. She wondered how much Adriana missed her own country, her own people. She must have loved Blantyre very much to have left everything behind and come to England, which was in ways so profoundly different.

'Do you know any other places as well?' she asked aloud. 'I have never been to Italy, for instance, but from the pictures I have seen, it is very beautiful indeed.'

'It is,' Adriana agreed. 'Everywhere has something. It isn't really places that matter; it all comes down to people in the end.' She turned to look at Charlotte. 'Doesn't it for you?' There was complete honesty in her eyes, almost a challenge.

'Yes. I suppose I like London because the best things that have happened to me have happened here,' Charlotte agreed. 'Yes, of course it is all to do with people, it has to be. In the end, it comes down to whom you love. Beauty is exciting, thrilling, you never entirely forget it, but you still need to share it with someone.'

Adriana blinked and turned away. 'I don't think I really want to go back to Croatia. It wouldn't ever be the same. My family is gone. My mother died young . . . and my father . . .' She stopped abruptly, as if she regretted having begun. She straightened her back and shoulders, and moved to another painting, this time of a girl of about sixteen sitting on the grass in the shade of a tree. She was wearing a pale, muslin dress and the dappled light made her seem extraordinarily fragile, as if not altogether real. She had dark hair, like Adriana. The resemblance was marked.

Adriana stared at her. 'It was another world, wasn't it?' she said at last.

'Yes,' Charlotte agreed, thinking back to being with Sarah and Emily in the garden at Cater Street every summer when they were young, and Sarah was still alive.

Adriana moved a little closer to her. It was an odd gesture, almost of alliance. 'She looks so delicate,' she said, facing the painting. 'She probably isn't. I was ill a lot as a child, but I have been well for years now. Evan doesn't always believe it. He treats me as if I need watching all the time: extra blankets, another scarf, gloves on, don't step in the puddles or you'll get your feet wet. You'll catch a cold.' She pulled her lips into a strange, rueful half-smile. 'Actually I hardly ever get colds. It must be your bracing climate here. I have become English, and tough.'

This time it was Charlotte who laughed, quickly and in genuine amusement. 'We get colds,' she admitted. 'Some people seem always to be coughing and sniffling. But I'm very glad to hear that you have outgrown your ill-health. If you are strong now, that's all that counts.'

Adriana turned away quickly, tears slipping down her cheeks.

'I'm sorry!' Charlotte said instantly, wondering what she had said. Had Adriana lost someone to a simple illness? Even a child? That thought was hideously sharp, a pain to fill the heart and block out everything else. What could she say that would be any use at all?

Adriana shook her head. 'Please don't be. One cannot go backwards. There are always losses. I don't think there is anyone in the world I ever loved as I cared for my father. I wish he could know that I am well and strong here, and that I . . .' She waved her hand impatiently. 'I apologise. I shouldn't even allow the memories to come to my mind. We all lose people.' She looked back at Charlotte. 'You are very patient, and gentle.'

'I had two sisters. I lost one of them,' Charlotte said quietly.

'Sometimes I think of her and wonder what it would be like if she were still alive. If we would be better friends than we were then.' She forced her memory back to those dreadful days when the family, the whole neighbourhood, looked at each other with fear. Suddenly they had realised how little they knew of what even the people closest to them really believed, loved or dreamed of.

She blushed now to wonder if Sarah ever knew that Charlotte had been in love with Dominic, Sarah's husband. That was something she preferred not to recall quite so vividly. How much of anyone's past was so terribly embarrassing? Were there pieces everyone would like to live again and do better this time?

She linked her arm in Adriana's. 'Come on, let's go and get a hot cup of tea, and maybe some cake, or crumpets. You mentioned where you first met Mr Blantyre the other evening. It sounded far more romantic than London. I first met Mr Pitt when he was investigating a fearful crime near where I lived, and we were all suspect, at least of having seen something, and lying in order to protect those we loved. It was all grim and awful. You have to have a better tale to tell than that.'

Adriana looked at her with interest, and then, as their eyes met for longer, with understanding. Charlotte was certain that there were memories in Adriana also that were full of pain. 'Certainly,' she said cheerfully. 'Tea and crumpets, then I'll tell you about some of the really wonderful places I've been to. The blue and green lakes in the mountains in Croatia. You've never even imagined such colours! They lie like a necklace dropped carelessly by some great goddess of the sky.

'I wish I could really describe for you the forests of Illyria,' she went on. 'They are all deciduous trees, and in the spring with the young leaves it is as if the whole world were newly made.'

Charlotte tried to imagine it. Perhaps it was something like a beech forest in England, but she did not want to put words to it, or try to compare.

'And we have the Dinaric Mountains,' Adriana went on. 'And caves, dozens of them, seven or eight hundred feet deep.'

'Really?' Charlotte was amazed, but mostly she was moved by the depth of emotion in Adriana's voice, the passion of her words. 'Have you been in some of them?'

Adriana shivered. 'Only once. My father took me, and held my hand. There is nothing on earth darker than a cave. It makes the night sky, even with clouds, seem full of light. But you should see Istria, and the islands. There are over a thousand of them strung all along the coast. Those in the furthest south are almost tropical, you know.'

'You must miss something so beautiful.' Charlotte knew there was pain in the memory as well, but it was better to pretend it did not matter.

'I do.' Adriana gave her a sudden smile of great warmth, as if she understood all that had not been said. She changed the subject abruptly, as if the memories of her own country were too painful to bear any longer. 'Vienna is marvellous,' she said cheerfully. 'You have never really danced till you have heard a Viennese orchestra play for Mr Strauss. And the clothes! Every woman should have a dress to waltz in, once in her life. Come!'

Charlotte obeyed, falling into step with her.

The following day Charlotte was in the parlour giving serious consideration to whether to buy new curtains, possibly of a different colour, when she heard Daniel shouting angrily as he came down the stairs. He must have turned at the bottom to go along the passage to the kitchen, because his feet were loud on the linoleum.

The next moment Jemima came after him.

'I told you you'd break it,' she shouted. 'Now look what you've done!'

'I wouldn't have if you hadn't left it there, stupid!' Daniel shouted back.

'How was I to know you'd go banging around like a cart-horse?' Jemima was at the bottom of the stairs now.

Charlotte came out of the parlour. 'Jemima!'

Jemima stopped in the passage and swung around, her face flushed with anger. 'He broke it!' she said, holding up the remnants of a delicate, ornamental box. She was close to tears with fury and disappointment.

Charlotte looked at it, and realised it was beyond mending. She met Jemima's eyes, so much like her own.

'I'm sorry. I don't think there's anything we can do with that. I don't suppose he meant to.'

'He didn't care!' Jemima retorted. 'I told him to be careful.'

Charlotte looked at her, and imagined how tactful that had been. 'Yes,' she said calmly. 'You'd better put it in the waste basket, under the lid so you don't keep looking at it. I'll go and speak to him.'

Jemima did not move.

'Go on,' Charlotte repeated. 'Do you want to make it better, or worse? If I tell him about it in front of you, it will definitely make it worse, that I can promise you.'

Reluctantly Jemima turned around and climbed slowly back up the stairs.

Charlotte watched her until she had disappeared up the next flight as well, to her own bedroom, then she went along to the kitchen.

Minnie Maude was peeling potatoes at the basin. Daniel was sitting on one of the chairs at the kitchen table, swinging his feet and looking miserable and angry. He glared at

Charlotte as she came in, ready to defend himself from Jemima if she were immediately behind.

'Did you break it?' Charlotte asked.

'It was her fault,' he responded. 'She left it in the way!'

'Did you mean to?'

'Course I didn't!'

'Daniel, are you sure?'

'Yes! That's not fair! I didn't see it.'

'That's what I thought. So what are you going to do about it?'

He looked at her resentfully. 'I can't put it together again,' he protested.

'No, I don't think anybody can,' she agreed. 'I think you'll have to find her another one.'

His eyes widened. 'I can't! Where would I get it?'

'You won't get one just like it, but if you save up your pocket money you might find one nearly as nice.'

'She shouldn't have left it there!' He drew in a deep breath. 'It'll be all my money for weeks! Maybe months!'

'What if she puts in half?' Charlotte suggested. 'Her half for leaving the box in the way, your half for breaking it, not looking what you were doing, and not caring?'

Reluctantly he agreed, watching to see if she was pleased.

'Good.' She smiled at him. 'Now Minnie Maude will get you a piece of cake, then you will go upstairs and tell Jemima you are sorry, and offer to share pocket money with her to find another box.'

'What if she says no?' he asked.

'If you ask nicely, and she refuses, then you are excused.'

He was happy. He turned to Minnie Maude and waited for the promised cake.

'I'm going out for a little while,' Charlotte told them both. 'I may be an hour or two, or even more. Minnie Maude, please tell Mr Pitt, if he comes home before I do, that I've gone to visit my sister.'

'Yes, ma'am,' Minnie Maude agreed, reaching for the cake.

Charlotte did not bother to change. She took her coat, hat and gloves and went immediately, before she could lose the conviction within herself that she must go to Emily and make peace with her. There was no difficulty between them large enough to spread out like this and spoil all the sharing in good times and bad, all the efforts in which they had been united.

She walked briskly along Keppel Street to Russell Square where she caught a hansom. All the way there she spent composing in her mind over and over what she would say, how she would vary her answers according to how Emily responded.

The weather was milder. She passed several carriages bowling along briskly with ladies out visiting, or simply taking the air. Another month and it would be a pleasure to go to the Botanical Gardens. Trees and shrubs would begin to show green leaves, even flower buds. There would be daffodils in bloom.

She arrived at Emily's wide, handsome house and alighted. She paid the driver, and then walked up to the front door and pulled the bell.

She waited only a few moments before the door was opened and a footman greeted her with apologies.

'I'm sorry, Mrs Pitt, but neither Mr nor Mrs Radley is at home. You are welcome to come in and take a little refreshment if you would care to? It is a very brisk day and somewhat chill.' He held the door wide and stepped back to allow her to pass.

Charlotte felt ridiculously disappointed. It had never occurred to her that Emily would be out at this hour, but of course it was perfectly reasonable. All her screwing up of courage, the swallowing of pride, were to no avail. There was no one with whom to make peace.

'Thank you,' she accepted, going into the warmth of the hallway. It was windy outside. Already the light was fading from the sky and a coolness of dusk was in the air. 'That would be very pleasant. Perhaps I may leave a message for Mrs Radley?'

'Certainly, ma'am. I shall bring you a pen and paper, unless you would prefer to use Mrs Radley's desk in the morning room?'

'That would be a very good idea. Thank you.'

'I'll have your tea served here when you return. Would you care for hot crumpets and butter as well?'

She smiled at him, liking his thoughtfulness. 'Yes, please.'

She found the paper in Emily's desk and wrote:

Dear Emily,

I came by on the spur of the moment, because I quite suddenly realised how little I wish to quarrel with you. There is nothing of such importance that I should allow it to make me unreasonable or ill-tempered.

She hesitated. Maybe she was taking rather too much of the blame for what had been, at the very least, quite as much Emily's fault? No, better to continue in this vein. She could always be a trifle sharper if Emily took advantage. And it was true: none of the differences mattered, in the end.

All that is good so far outweighs everything else, that small differences must not be allowed to matter.

Affectionately,
Charlotte

She folded the note and put it in her reticule, then put the top back on the ink and laid the pen down.

She returned to the morning room where her tea and crumpets were served a few moments later. Then she gave her note to the footman, thanked him, and sat down to enjoy her treat, before going back outside into the cold to look for a hansom to take her home again.

Chapter Seven

Breakfast in Keppel Street on March the fifth was as busy as usual. Daniel and Jemima had to get off to school, homework packed in satchels, boots on, coats buttoned, and with scarves and gloves that matched each other. No matter how much care was taken the evening before, there always seemed to be something to hunt for. It was a sharp, icy morning with a knife-edge to the wind. Scarves were tied tightly. A button was found hanging loose. Charlotte hastily fetched a needle and thread, thimble and scissors to attach it more securely before she bundled them both out of the front door. At least there was now a tentative peace between them and they went down the pavement side by side.

Pitt had been debating with himself whether to seek Charlotte's opinion about the next step he planned to take in the case of Duke Alois, or not to trouble her with it. If he were mistaken, either way, he would jeopardise his position, and therefore the future of all of them. Even Minnie Maude, standing at the sink washing the dishes, would be without a job, or a home.

Would asking Charlotte be a courtesy, or merely spreading

the blame unfairly if he should fail? Would he do it because she might actually help, or simply because it would be less lonely for him?

Charlotte took a small piece of cheese out of the cupboard near the door. 'Have we got any more of this in the back pantry?' she asked Minnie Maude.

Minnie Maude took her hands out of the water. 'I'll go an' look, ma'am,' she said quickly.

'No, it's all right. You're busy. I'll see myself,' Charlotte replied, turning to do so.

'No!' Minnie Maude dripped water on the floor in her haste, then wiped her hands on her apron. 'I'll go. I'm not sure where I put it.' She went almost at a run, her heels clattering on the floor. Archie and Angus, the two cats curled up together in the wood basket by the stove, opened their eyes. Archie spat with irritation.

Charlotte shook her head, glancing at Pitt. 'I don't know what it is with that girl,' she said with a sigh and a smile. 'I'd think she was keeping a lover in that pantry, if I didn't know better.'

Pitt was startled. He put his empty cup down and stared at her in alarm.

'Oh, don't be ridiculous!' she said with a laugh. 'There's nobody there, Thomas! It's just her own little bit of space. I think she goes out there just to sit and think sometimes. Coming here is a big change for her. She's very aware of trying to fill Gracie's shoes, you know.' As she passed him, moving to the cupboard over the sink, she touched him gently, just brushing her hand over his hair. 'You should understand that.'

So she had seen his apprehension about trying to fill Narraway's place, perhaps more keenly than he had wanted her to. But why should he have doubted it? She had known him longer and better than anyone else in his life. Hers was not a blind love, nor one that chose to believe only what was comfortable. It was open-eyed, which perhaps was the only type of love that was safe in the end, and therefore infinitely precious. There were not secrets so much as small matters of privacy. Certain intrusions were clumsy, without respect.

Was Minnie Maude struggling with the same thing?

'She's good, though, isn't she?' he asked.

'Yes, she's excellent,' Charlotte answered. 'But she's not Gracie, and I have to keep remembering that. By the way, Gracie called by the other day. She looks so happy I couldn't but be happy for her too.'

'You didn't mention it!' he said quickly.

'You were rather occupied with Jack and Lord Tregarron.'

'Oh. Well, I intend to see the Prime Minister today, so that will probably make it even worse. I'm sorry.'

She bit her lip. 'Don't be. Emily'll get over it. She's desperate for Jack to succeed. I hope he doesn't know how much.' For a moment a far deeper anxiety shadowed her face. 'I hope he has no idea how afraid she is that he might not. I can't imagine living with that.'

'I don't think she needs to worry—' he began.

'Thomas! I'm not worried for her!' she protested. 'For him! He would know she doubted him.'

He drew in a deep breath. 'Aren't you afraid for me . . . at least sometimes?' Then instantly he wished he had not asked, but it was too late.

'You've already succeeded at enough things that I can live with a failure or two,' she said perfectly steadily. 'Nobody wins all the time, unless what they're aiming at is pretty easy.'

For a moment emotion robbed him of any words at all. His chest was so tight he gulped in his breath. He grasped her hand and pulled her towards him and held her. Then the instant after he heard Minnie Maude's footsteps in the corridor, and she came in holding a large wedge of cheese.

Charlotte took it from her with a wide smile, thanking her.

Pitt stood up, said goodbye, and went into the hall for his coat.

Pitt sent his request through the right channels, but he was insistent, and he refused to explain himself to footmen or secretaries.

'I am Commander of Special Branch, and I require to advise the Prime Minister of an incident which, if we do not prevent it, could be disastrous to Great Britain.' He gave no more detail than that, except that the matter was urgent.

It was a little after midday when he was received in Downing Street, residence of the Prime Minister, the Marquess of Salisbury.

'Good afternoon, Commander,' Salisbury said grimly. He held out his hand, since it was the first time they had met in this present capacity. 'I trust this is as grave as you imply?' There was warning in his tone that if he had been misled, the consequences for Pitt would be unpleasant.

'If it takes place, yes, sir,' Pitt replied, sitting in the chair Salisbury indicated. 'I am hoping we can prevent it.'

'Then you had better tell me what it is, and quickly. I have a meeting with the Chancellor of the Exchequer in forty minutes.' Salisbury sat opposite him, but waiting for his reply and clearly not at ease.

Pitt had already decided, while walking here through the rising wind, trying to keep his hat on, that he would say nothing about the likelihood of the threat to European stability being made, except as he was asked, only its nature. His answer should be clear: no prevaricating or defending himself in advance.

'The assassination of Duke Alois Habsburg, grand-nephew of the Emperor Franz Josef of Austria, sir. He is due to visit one of our own Queen's great-nephews, here in London, in eleven days' time. It appears as if the murder itself may be committed by causing a major rail crash between Dover and London.' He forced himself to add no more. It was not difficult. Salisbury's expression of dismay told him that the Foreign Secretary had not relayed the earlier warning Pitt had given him.

'A rail crash? Good God!' Salisbury's long pale face went a shade paler. 'I suppose you are perfectly sure of what you're saying?' He squinted at Pitt, as if it were his eyesight he disbelieved rather than his hearing.

Pitt chose his words carefully. Not only the Prime Minister's reaction today depended on them, but all future confidence in Pitt's judgement.

'I am sure that such an attempt is being planned, sir. However, I do not know by whom, nor where it will take place. So far I am certain only that the duke's route from Vienna all the way to London is being checked by people we know as anarchists of already proven violence. We cannot afford to take the threat lightly.'

'Lightly? What sane man would?' Salisbury was irritated, he had been caught on the wrong foot because no one had prepared him.

Pitt tried to think what Narraway would do. Pitt would not treat the Marquess of Salisbury as an equal, as Narraway might have, but he should behave as if it were he himself who was knowledgeable in the subject of terror and violence, not the Prime Minister.

'Only someone who disbelieved it, sir,' he said quietly. 'And on the face of it there seems to be no reason to harm Duke Alois, so the attempt makes little sense.'

Salisbury nodded.

Pitt continued, 'I need to find out if in fact someone else is the intended target, or alternatively, the Duke Alois is far more important than he seems. All I can learn so far is that he is a quiet, rather academically inclined young man who spends his time in the study of philosophy and science, but at no one else's expense. He is quite well liked, has plenty of money of his own, is unmarried so far, and has no political affiliations that we can trace. In other words he is perfectly harmless.'

Salisbury's face was grim. 'Whose wife or daughter is he sleeping with?' he asked.

Pitt grimaced. 'That I don't know. But it seems an extreme way of dealing with it to plot such a violent assassination, and in a foreign country.'

'You are right,' Salisbury agreed. 'Quite likely he has political convictions we don't know about – and that's not impossible; the Crown Prince Rudolf certainly had. He was a walking disaster waiting to occur, according to my information, after the fact, of course.'

Pitt made no comment. That was a diplomatic issue, not Special Branch's.

'The alternative is that either Duke Alois is very much cleverer than he pretends to be,' Salisbury went on, 'or the target is someone in his retinue. Alternatively, the whole thing has another purpose, such as to embarrass Britain and put us at a serious disadvantage in some future negotiation. You must prevent it. Whatever help you need, get it. What is it you want from me?' He frowned. 'Why aren't you in the Foreign Secretary's office?'

'Lord Tregarron does not believe the threat is real, sir,' Pitt replied. 'Mr Evan Blantyre does.'

Salisbury sat without moving for several moments. 'I see,' he said finally. 'Well, we'll go with your judgement, Pitt. Take whatever steps you need to make absolutely certain that when the Duke Alois comes to England, he has a happy and safe visit, and leaves in peace. If he is killed, let it be in France, or Austria, not here. And, please God, not by an Englishman.' He bit his lip and stared at Pitt, his voice suddenly husky. 'You don't suppose that this rail crash is a diversion, and it is actually the Queen this lunatic is after, do you?'

That was a thought that had not even crossed Pitt's mind. 'No, sir, I don't,' he said, hoping to God he was right, but far from sure. 'Although it might be advisable for Her Majesty not to visit this young man in Kensington Palace. We have more than sufficient guard present to take care of her in Buckingham Palace.' He allowed himself the barest smile. 'I am sufficiently acquainted with Her Majesty to know that advice for her safety will be received well. Counsel as to where she should, or should not be, would be an entirely different matter.'

Salisbury grunted. 'So do I. And I have not forgotten your accomplishments at Osborne. That is principally why you are in the position you are, and why I listen to you.'

Pitt felt the heat burn up his face. He had not referred to it in order to remind the Prime Minister of his own success, and now he felt extraordinarily clumsy to have mentioned it at all.

Salisbury smiled. 'You are not in an enviable position, Commander. But it is my belief that you are the best man for the job. I would be deeply obliged if you would prove me right.'

Pitt stood up, his legs a little stiff. 'Yes, sir. Thank you.'

When Pitt returned to Lisson Grove he found a message from Blantyre waiting for him, asking Pitt to contact him as soon as possible. Pitt telephoned, and they met at Blantyre's club for late luncheon.

Pitt had never been in such a place before, except as a policeman with permission to speak to one of the members. Now he was conducted by a uniformed steward who treated him with the respect he'd show any other guest. They walked through the oak-panelled corridors, in which were hung hunting scenes and Stubbs's paintings of horses in the larger spaces. The men's feet were soundless on the carpet. Blantyre was waiting for Pitt. Together they went to the table and took their seats.

In the dining room, Pitt found he was watched by life-sized portraits of the Duke of Wellington, the Duke of Marlborough, and a rather fanciful portrait of Henry V at Agincourt.

'All a bit military, isn't it,' Blantyre said with an apologetic smile. 'But the food's excellent, and they'll leave us alone as long as we wish, which is rather what I need at the moment. I recommend the roast beef – it's really very good – with a decent Burgundy. A trifle heavy, I know, but well worth it.'

'Thank you,' Pitt accepted. His mind was too occupied with why Blantyre had called this meeting to be concerned with what he might eat.

The steward came. Blantyre ordered for both of them, including the wine. As soon as they were alone, he started to speak.

'This young man, Duke Alois,' he said, looking at Pitt, his dark brows puckered. 'Do you know anything further about him?'

'I can find nothing that would make him worth anybody's time or energy to assassinate,' Pitt replied. 'If he is indeed the target, then I have to assume that there is a completely different reason for killing him.'

'My thoughts precisely,' Blantyre agreed. 'I have called on friends in Austria, and in Germany also. All I can find is that he is a harmless young aristocrat who intends nothing more adventurous than to while away his life studying the subjects that interest him. He has given no indication whatever that it is more than for his own pleasure.'

'Are you certain?' Pitt pressed.

Blantyre indicated the food just served them. 'Please eat. You will enjoy it. And yes, I am certain. My informants tell me he was offered a very agreeable post in diplomacy, and declined it. At least he was honest enough to say he had no disposition to be restricted in such a way.'

Pitt was beginning to feel impatient with Duke Alois, but he did not show it.

'On the other hand,' Blantyre went on, also beginning to eat his meal, 'he also appears to listen with great attention to the music of Gustav Mahler, and even Schoenberg, this new young composer who creates such odd, dissonant sounds. Is he interested and looking for meaning, or merely for a new experience? I think the latter more likely.' There was a sadness in his voice and in his dark eyes. 'A typical Austrian: one eye laughing, the other weeping. But I think it is better to do a small thing well than nothing at all. However, I am not a royal duke, thank God. Nothing is expected of me, so I start on a clean page.'

Pitt looked at him with a new appreciation of his sympathy and imagination. He had raised, as if perfectly natural to him, issues that Pitt had not considered.

'It is peculiarly repugnant to kill someone so innocent of any harm, or use,' Blantyre said wryly. There was no malice in his tone, only a slight sadness. 'Is it a good thing or a bad thing not to be worth anyone's effort to kill you?' He said it with a gentle, wry humour, looking at Pitt very directly.

Pitt answered with hesitation. 'At times most comfortable, and unquestionably safer, but I think in the end I should regret it. It seems like an opportunity wasted, let slip through your fingers like dry sand.'

Blantyre sighed. 'Or the wine you didn't drink. I suppose you sleep better, for whatever that is worth? I'd rather not spend my entire life emotionally asleep, however intellectually absorbing my pursuits.'

Pitt watched silently as the steward poured more of the dark Burgundy into cut-crystal glasses and the light burned red through it.

'But that, of course, is not why I asked you to come,' Blantyre said quietly, his face emptying of all pleasure. 'Events seem to have taken a new turn. A man named Erich Staum has been seen in Dover, apparently working as a road sweeper.' He stopped, watching Pitt closely. 'He is known to certain political authorities in Vienna as a political assassin of unusual skill and imagination.'

To give himself time to think, Pitt took more wine also. It was extremely good, a quality he was totally unused to. Perhaps it would have been familiar to Narraway.

'I suppose you are sure about this?' he asked with a smile, looking at the wine in his glass.

'There is doubt,' Blantyre admitted. 'But very slight. He has a face that is not easy to forget, especially his eyes. Even dressed in ill-fitting and dirty clothes, and with a broom in his hands, if one imagines him upright and shorn of the submissiveness, he is too like Staum to ignore the probability. He has used the guise of a railway porter before, a hansom cab driver, and a postman.'

'I see,' Pitt said quietly. Dustmen pushed carts with their equipment, and collected rubbish. No one gave them a second glance. It was the perfect disguise to carry explosives. No one even sees a road sweeper, never mind examines his cart. 'Why Duke Alois?' he asked, looking up at Blantyre again. 'We still have not answered that.'

'Staum is for hire,' Blantyre shook his head very slightly,

218

barely a movement at all. 'Anarchists don't always select victims for any reason. But you know that better than I do.' He took a deep breath, as if making a decision, then let it out in a sigh. 'Perhaps Duke Alois is incidental, and the main reason is to embarrass Her Majesty's government, which his assassination would certainly do.'

His hands clenched on his knife and fork. 'Things are getting worse, Pitt, more dangerous every year. Violent socialism is rising, national borders are moving around like the tide. There seems to be unrest everywhere and wild ideas and philosophies multiplying like rabbits. I admit, I am afraid for the future.' There was no melodrama in his voice, just a foreboding and the darkness of real fear. It shadowed his face, making his features pinched, more ascetic.

Because Pitt respected him, he felt the brush of it also, and the weight of his own responsibility settled even more heavily on him.

'We'll protect Duke Alois, whoever's after him, and whatever the reason,' he said grimly.

Blantyre let out a sigh. 'I know. I know.' He reached out and poured the rest of the Burgundy into first Pitt's glass, then his own. He did not offer a toast.

Pitt had no difficulty whatever in reaching the Foreign Secretary. Clearly Salisbury had been as good as his word. However, as far as cancelling Duke Alois's visit, nothing had changed.

'I'm sorry,' the Foreign Secretary said grimly. 'It would be quite impossible to cancel the visit now. Such a thing would signal to all Europe that Britain cannot guarantee the safety of a member of a foreign royal family visiting our own monarch.' His voice became even sharper. 'It would be a flag of surrender to every predator in the world. Surely you see that it cannot even be considered?'

Reluctantly, Pitt had to agree. He could imagine with horrible clarity the results that would follow. His mind raced with the possibilities as to who might be behind such a plan. Perhaps Blantyre was right and the purpose of the assassination was not to get rid of Duke Alois, who was almost irrelevant, but to embarrass Britain.

'Yes, sir, I do see,' he said quietly. 'I would very much like to know who is behind this. I will not let it go until I do.'

It was late and Pitt was tired, but he felt he must speak with Narraway. To do so was a kind of yielding, an admission that he needed advice. He hesitated even now as he walked along the cold street, his breath making wispy trails in the cold air. Not to ask was to set his own vanity above the lives of the men and women who would be killed if there really were a train crash. Not to mention the all but crippling damage to the service he was sworn to should he fail in this, after the other disasters so recently.

He reached Narraway's door with no indecision left, and when the manservant let him in, he accepted the offer of supper and hot tea, no wine. Blantyre's wine at luncheon had been more than he was used to anyway.

'Any progress on Serafina Montserrat's death?' he asked Narraway as they sat by the fire, Pitt leaning towards it, warming his hands after the cold walk.

'Not yet,' Narraway answered. 'But you didn't come to ask me that.'

Pitt sighed and sat back in the chair. 'No,' he conceded. 'No, it is something rather bigger than that, although I have no conviction that there could be a connection. Serafina Montserrat was afraid of something very violent happening, and that she had knowledge which she might accidentally let slip in one of the times when her memory lapsed, and she imagined she was in the past, and with someone she trusted.'

'Pitt, stop beating around the bush,' Narraway ordered. 'I don't know yet who killed Serafina, or why. It's quite possible it was simply a domestic tragedy, Nerissa Freemarsh finding the waiting in quiet servitude unbearable.'

Briefly Pitt told him what he feared about a possible rail crash and what Blantyre had said that lunchtime about Duke Alois's visit.

'Staum,' Narraway said quietly. 'Then there's a lot of money involved. He has no loyalty to anyone, and he is expensive. If he has ever failed we don't know of it.' He thought for a few more moments in silence, staring at the fire.

Pitt waited.

'It isn't what Staum wants, it's whoever's paying him,' Narraway said at last. 'Staum has no loyalties, no interests. A rail crash, with all the civilian casualties, is very extreme. Even anarchists are not usually so indiscriminate, not on that side. This could kill scores of people.'

'I know.'

'Either the target is someone so well guarded they cannot reach him any other way, which role Duke Alois doesn't fit at all, or else it is a decoy, to draw our attention from their real purpose. The idea of a rail crash with a passenger train, with the losses that would cause, is so appalling you can't possibly ignore it. It would be suicide for Special Branch.'

'I've thought of that!' Pitt said more sharply than he had intended. It was not anger speaking but fear.

'Any rumour of something else, however slight?' Narraway asked. 'What else is vulnerable?'

Pitt told him what else, even the most trivial and seemingly irrelevant. They were all issues going back to Narraway's own time as Head of the Branch, so there could be no question of confidence broken.

'Who else is travelling with the duke?' Narraway said when he had considered them all, and come up with nothing.

'No one who seems important,' Pitt replied, feeling the sense of helplessness twist even more tightly inside him. 'And time is short. We have little more than a week before he comes.'

Narraway sighed. 'Then my best guess is the same as yours – the rail crash is a diversion, because the assassination will happen before they ever reach the train. Staum will get Duke Alois somewhere in the streets of Dover. He won't know that we have anyone who can recognise him.'

'If we don't know him, how does Blantyre?' Pitt asked.

'Austrian connection, I presume,' Narraway replied. 'He's committed a few assassinations in Europe, but never here before, so far as we know.'

'Blantyre could be wrong,' Pitt said.

'Of course he could. Are you willing to take that risk?'

'No. We haven't the men to guard all the streets in Dover, especially if it means drawing them back from the points and the signals.'

'Which they are counting on,' Narraway agreed.

'If they blow up the main street of Dover they'll kill scores of people, and they might still miss Duke Alois—'

'They won't,' Narraway cut across him. 'They'll cause a diversion at the last moment, an overflowing drain, an over-turned cart, anything to force him to go down a side street, or else stand around as a stationary target while they clear the way. In those situations you must keep moving. Have several alternative routes. People going ahead of you. Never allow yourself to be cut off and have to stop.' Narraway's face was deeply lined, almost haggard in the firelight. 'You haven't much time, Pitt.'

'Find out who killed Serafina, and why,' Pitt urged.

'You really think that what she was afraid of telling someone had to do with this? She was rambling . . .'

'Do you know of a better reason why someone is willing to go to this length to kill Duke Alois?' Pitt asked. 'Or someone else in his retinue?'

'I think he could be incidental, just the excuse,' Narraway reminded him, his voice gravelly with weariness and the tension of knowledge and fear. 'Special Branch is important, Pitt. It's our defence against all kinds of violence from slow treason to anarchy that kills in minutes. If I wanted to cripple England, I would try to get rid of Special Branch first. And if I can think of that, so can others.'

'I know.' Pitt stood up slowly, surprised how his muscles ached from clenching them. 'I'll start again tomorrow morning.'

Early the next day at Lisson Grove, Pitt and Stoker went over every detail of Alois's visit from the time he stepped aboard the steamer at Calais, until he boarded it again at Dover to leave.

The office was warm, the fire beginning to burn well in the clear air after the sluggishness of rain, but there was no ease in the room.

'He'll be bringing just four men with him,' Stoker said, pointing to Calais on the map spread across Pitt's desk.

'What do we know about them?' Pitt asked.

'All part of his family's regular household retainers,' Stoker replied. 'As far as we can tell. Nothing we can find that would make them vulnerable to betrayal. None of them gambles or has debts out of the ordinary, no love affairs with anyone of suspicious background or politics. No one drinks more than average, which is pretty high.' He pulled his face into an expression of distaste. Pitt had no idea whether it was for what he imagined these men in particular to be like, or for foreigners in general.

'They're just what you'd expect of hangers-on of a minor royal duke,' Stoker went on. 'Decent enough, in their own way, I expect.' He looked up from the map to meet Pitt's eyes, but his own were unreadable.

'Competent to guard him from an attack?' Pitt asked.

Stoker shrugged. 'Can't say, because they've never had to. Honestly, sir, he's not somebody anyone would be bothered to attack. Are we going to put someone in with them?'

'Yes. It'll need to be someone who speaks German, if possible.'

'He speaks good English,' Stoker replied.

'Good. But we need to understand what they say to each other as well,' Pitt pointed out.

'We've got Beck, sir, and Holbein. They're both pretty good.'

'We'll use them,' Pitt agreed.

Stoker raised his eyebrows. 'Both?'

'Yes, both. We can't afford to fail. If we let some Austrian duke get assassinated on British soil, after we've been warned about it, it'll be a signal to every enemy we have that we're a wounded animal, and the jackals will close in.'

Stoker winced as if Pitt had hit him, but the understanding was bleak in his face, and his body stiffened. 'Yes, sir. Whatever happens to him, it bloody well won't happen while he's in England!' He bent to the map again, intense concentration in his face. 'The ferry leaves Calais at nine in the morning, weather permitting. It should arrive in Dover at noon. He'll be the first to disembark. He has a special carriage set apart for his use.' He looked up at Pitt. 'What about this man Staum, sir?'

Pitt pulled his face into an expression of acute unhappiness. 'He's one of the leading assassins in Europe, according to French and German sources, as well as Blantyre. He's for hire to anyone who'll pay him, which is mostly anarchists, of course. But it could be anyone who has the money and wants someone killed. He's been seen in Dover, working as a road sweeper, with broom and cart.'

Stoker looked grim and there was the first touch of fear in his eyes that Pitt had seen.

'Are we sure it's him? How do we know it isn't just someone who looks a bit like him? He can't be that different to look at, or he'd have been caught by now.'

'No, we're not certain,' Pitt conceded without comfort. 'But using such a man makes more sense than a train crash that kills scores of people and injures even more.'

'Depends what they want,' Stoker said bitterly. 'Anarchists don't usually make that much sense. That's why they're so damn difficult to predict. Added to that, the worst of them don't even care if they get caught.'

'I know. People who don't care always have a kind of advantage over those who do. But I don't envy them. Who the hell wants to have nothing worth living for?'

'I can't imagine that,' Stoker shook his head, his expression puzzled and sad. 'I suppose that's why we find them so hard to catch, we just don't understand them. What about this duke, sir? Do you think he's going to do pretty much what we tell him? Or will he want to show everyone how brave he is, and behave like a fool?'

'I don't know,' Pitt admitted. 'I'm still trying to find out more about him, and the rest of his men.'

Stoker swore gently and colourfully, under his breath.

'Couldn't have put it better myself,' Pitt agreed, surprised at the width of Stoker's imagination.

Stoker coloured uncomfortably. 'Sorry, sir.'

'Don't be,' Pitt smiled briefly. 'I am thinking much the same, just less satisfactorily put. Your vocabulary makes me think you spent some time in the navy, but I didn't see it on your record, at least not the one they showed me.'

'No, sir.' Stoker was clearly uncomfortable. 'It was . . . not quite official . . .' He stopped, lost for an explanation, a faint colour marking his cheeks.

'Learn anything?' Pitt asked.

'Yes, sir, quite a lot.' He stood still, waiting for the rest of the interrogation.

'Then it wasn't wasted,' Pitt answered. He was determined to ask Narraway one day what had happened. It would be wise to know, but it did not matter now.

'Sir—' Stoker began.

'Doesn't matter,' Pitt cut him off.

'Sir . . . I was going to say that if you want me to go to Dover and travel on the train with Duke Alois, I'll do that.'

'You don't have to,' Pitt replied. 'It'll be dangerous.'

'Aren't you going?' Stoker challenged.

'Yes, I am. All the more reason I need you here.'

'Then I'm coming too, sir. Anyway, I could use the bit of extra pay.' He smiled, but there was no lightness in his eyes and they did not waver an instant.

'Really?' Pitt spoke as if it were really all about a few shillings. 'Saving for something?'

'Yes, sir.' Stoker straightened his shoulders a little. 'I want to buy a cello, sir.'

Pitt could think of no possible answer to that, but he felt inordinately pleased.

Chapter Eight

Narraway sat by the fire in his study, the gaslight turned low, and thought about Serafina Montserrat. Pitt said he had asked the doctor to keep his own counsel regarding the conclusion that her death could not have been accidental. He had given the man his word that it would not be investigated by the police, but by Special Branch, because of its possible connection with a current case.

The question of an attempted assassination would occupy all of Pitt's attention, and he could not afford to be distracted by anything else. Narraway was not certain if his own promise to investigate it was wise. Detection was not a skill he had refined to anything like Pitt's degree. However, he still believed it possible that there was a direct link between Serafina's fears and the proposed assassination of Duke Alois. If there was, it was imperative he find it before it was too late.

If Serafina's death was a political act by someone afraid she might reveal a long-dead scandal or personal indiscretion it surely must have ceased to be embarrassing to anyone but themselves?

He did not think from what Vespasia had said of her that Nerissa Freemarsh had the nature to contemplate killing her aunt as an act of compassion to free her from the mental suffering of knowing that her own mind was betraying her.

Tucker, the lady's maid? That was more likely. She was devoted to Serafina. Vespasia had told him of that, and he trusted her judgement without question. She had certainly had enough maids to know, and seen dozens of others.

But then Tucker would also lose her position at Serafina's death. And she must know that she would be regarded with suspicion, before anyone else, if an overdose were discovered. After the years of looking after Serafina, no one would believe her capable of so simple an error.

If it were not political, that left only the far uglier thought that Nerissa Freemarsh had killed her aunt for personal reasons: possibly the inheritance of the house and whatever money Serafina possessed, before it was too late for her to enjoy it – or perhaps before the money had been spent on Serafina's care.

He would have to interview the household staff. There was no one else who could answer the difficult, probing questions he needed to ask. He stared up at the firelight patterns on the ceiling and tried to think of facts, physical evidence, anything at all that would prove who had put the extra laudanum in Serafina's medicine or food. Nothing came into his mind. Whoever had done it would have cleared up after themselves. The house would be dusted and polished every day, the dishes washed, everything put back into the cupboard or onto the shelf where it was normally kept. All household staff would be likely to be everywhere, except Serafina's bedroom. Only Tucker and Nerissa would be in there, and probably one of the housemaids.

Had anyone else been there? Would they have been noticed?

And how could they have any reason to harm Serafina, unless paid to do so by someone? That thought was absurd.

By midnight the fire had burned down. He stood up and turned off the lights, then went upstairs to bed, not having thought of any solution to his quandary, except to investigate the personal motive until he could rule it out. He had little over a week before Duke Alois arrived in Dover.

In the morning he decided to ask Vespasia's opinion. He dressed smartly, as was suitable to visit a lady for whom he had not only a deep affection, but a certain awe.

'Victor! How pleasant to see you,' Vespasia said with some surprise when he was shown into the withdrawing room a little after ten o'clock. She wore a highly fashionable dress of a pale blue-green shade with white lace at the throat, large sleeves and her customary pearls. She was smiling. She knew, of course, that he had come for a specific reason, and he was not foolish enough to try to hide it.

'Well?' she enquired, when she had sent the maid for tea.

He told her briefly the thoughts he had entertained the previous evening. She listened to him in silence until he had finished, merely moving her head fractionally every now and then in agreement.

'There is one thing you have not apparently considered,' she observed. 'Nerissa is not a particularly charming young woman, and, judging from her present position as companion to her aunt, she has no great means of her own.'

'I know that,' he said. 'Maybe she decided not to risk Serafina spending all of what would be her inheritance.'

Vespasia smiled. 'My dear Victor, there is another consideration far more urgent in a woman's mind than mere money.' She noted his expression with amusement. 'Nerissa is not especially plain in appearance, but she does not have a pleasing manner. She is quite unaware of how to flatter or charm, to amuse, to make a man feel high-spirited or at ease. She is also rapidly coming towards the end of her child-bearing years. At the moment her prospects are good, because she has expectations, very real ones. But if Serafina were to live another five years, which she might have, then it would have been a different matter. Her present lover may not be willing to wait so long.'

Narraway froze. 'Her present lover! Are you certain?'

'Yes. But I am not certain if it is an affair that has any realistic hope of ending in marriage. If it has not, then privacy may be all that she desires and does not already have.'

'Surely Serafina Montserrat would be the last woman on earth to interfere in an affair, let alone disapprove of it?' he said reasonably.

'Perhaps. But Nerissa may not realise that. I am not sure whether she is fully aware of Serafina's earlier life, or if she is of the opinion that most of it is overheated imagination. These are things it might be profitable for you to discover.'

'Yes,' he agreed, ceasing the conversation while the maid brought in the tea and Vespasia poured it. 'I will turn my attention to it.'

Vespasia smiled at him. 'Tucker will know,' she remarked, taking one of the tiny, crisp biscuits off the plate. 'Treat her with respect, and you will learn all kinds of things.'

He thought for a moment. 'If this lover of Nerissa's is serious, might he have killed Serafina, to preserve the money Nerissa could inherit? With the house, it would make him very comfortable.'

'Possibly.' Vespasia's face expressed her pity for such a thought, and her contempt. 'Which is why it is important that you discover who he is.' Her eyes softened with a deeper kind of sadness. 'It is also possible that his reason was nothing to do with money, or with Nerissa at all, except in so far as she gave him access to Serafina, and her . . . disintegrating memory.'

He knew as she said the words how much it hurt her. 'I know,' he agreed. 'I will investigate that too.'

Narraway rode in the hansom to visit Serafina's doctor, consumed in thought. He had come to realise how much more difficult detection was than he had originally appreciated. He was guilty of having taken Pitt's skill very much for granted. He did not even notice the brilliant blue sky darken over, or the people on footpaths hastening their steps. He did not see the first heavy spots of rain. He was unaware of the swift change in the weather until one man lost grip of his umbrella and it whisked into the street, startling horses and causing a near-accident.

Dr Thurgood was unable to give any further assistance. There was nothing medical to add to the bare fact that Serafina had died of an overdose of laudanum so huge that it was impossible she had given it to herself accidentally. Even taking her usual amount three times over would not account for the level he had found in her body.

Narraway asked if it could have been cumulative over a degree of time. He was certain in his own mind what the answer would be, so unsurprised when Thurgood pointed out that the present amount was far more than sufficient to kill her, so an accumulation was impossible.

He caught a hansom to go to Dorchester Terrace. On the journey he turned over in his mind the practical facts that would severely limit the number of people able to administer such a dose. The most obvious person was Nerissa Freemarsh, for reasons of her own.

Not that he seriously thought it *was* Nerissa, unless her lover had built up the nerve, or the desperation, to force her into it. What could have caused that? A sudden, urgent financial need? The longing to marry before it was too late for children?'

Then why now, why not sooner? Was it really coincidental that Serafina's death had happened just before Duke Alois's visit? It was not easy to believe. Far more likely that it had to do with Serafina's past, the vast store of intimate and dangerous knowledge her failing memory was letting slip, piece by broken piece.

At any other time he would have handed the whole case over to the regular police; it was their area of skill and would concern Special Branch only as a debt of honour to Serafina herself.

He arrived at Dorchester Terrace, alighted and paid the cabby, then walked up the pathway to the door. He was admitted by the footman and gave him his card.

'Good morning,' he said quickly, before the man could protest that the house was in mourning and would receive no callers. 'I need to speak with Miss Freemarsh. I hope she is still at home?' He was certain she would be. She was very traditional in her manner and dress, and, so newly bereaved, he was certain she would not be out of the house for some time.

The man hesitated.

'Will you inform her that Lord Narraway is here, on business to do with the recent death of her aunt, Mrs Montserrat.' He did not pitch his voice to make a request so much as give an order. 'I shall also require to speak with Miss Tucker, then the cook, the housekeeper, the housemaid and yourself. I would prefer to see Miss Freemarsh first.'

The man paled. 'Yes . . . yes, sir. If you . . .' He gulped and cleared his throat. 'If you like to wait in the morning room, my lord.'

'Thank you, but I prefer to use the housekeeper's sitting room. It will make people more at ease.'

The man did not argue. Five minutes later Narraway was on the comfortable chair by the fire, facing the plump, pink-faced housekeeper, Mrs Whiteside. She looked angry and bristling.

'I don't know what you think I can tell you,' she began, refusing to sit, even though he had asked her to.

'You are in charge of the house, Mrs Whiteside. You can tell me about each of the servants employed here.'

'You can't imagine that any of them killed poor Mrs Montserrat!' she accused him. 'I'm not standing here while you say wicked things like that about innocent people, lordship or not, whoever you are.'

He smiled with amusement at her indignation, and a quite genuine pleasure at her loyalty. She looked like an angry hen ready to take on an intruder in the farmyard.

'Nothing would give me more pleasure than to prove that true, Mrs Whiteside,' he said gently. 'Perhaps with some detail, you can assist me in that. Then we widen the circle to include others who might have observed something of meaning, even if they did not realise it at the time. The one thing that seems impossible to deny is that someone did give Mrs Montserrat a very large dose of laudanum. If you have any idea as to who that might be, or even why, then I would be obliged to you if you would tell me.'

It was the last sort of response she had expected. For several seconds she could not find words to answer him.

He indicated the chair opposite him again. 'Please sit down, Mrs Whiteside. Tell me about the members of your staff, so that I can imagine what they do when they are off duty, what they like and dislike.'

She was thoroughly confused, but she did her best to oblige

him. A quarter of an hour into her description, she began to speak naturally, even with affection. For the first time in his life Narraway had a vivid picture of a group of people utterly unlike himself, all away from the homes and families in which they grew up, slowly forming a new kind of family, with friendships, jealousies, loyalty and understanding that gave comfort to their lives, and a certain kind of framework that was of intense importance. Mrs Whiteside was the matriarch, the cook almost as important. The footman was the only man, Serafina not requiring a butler, and therefore he had a place of unique privilege. But he was young, and not above bickering with the maids over trivia.

Miss Tucker, as lady's maid, was not really either upstairs or downstairs. Her position was senior to the others and oddly lonely. Narraway became suddenly aware of this as he listened to Mrs Whiteside's descriptions.

'I don't know what else you want,' she finished abruptly, looking confused again.

The more he listened to her, the more certain he became that none of them had anything to do with Serafina's death. Their own lives were disrupted by it. Now even their home was no longer assured. Sooner or later Nerissa might choose to sell the house, or might have to, and they would be separated from each other and without employment. Then again, if she suspected them of disloyalty in speaking out of turn to Narraway, she might dismiss them without a 'character', and that would be even worse. He became suddenly sensitive to the fact that he must phrase his questions with care.

'To speak to them one at a time,' he answered her question. 'And see if anyone has noticed anything out of the ordinary in the house. Something not in its usual place, moved, or accidentally destroyed perhaps.'

She understood immediately. 'You think somebody broke

in and killed poor Mrs Montserrat?' The idea filled her with horror.

'The more you describe the people here, the less likely I find it that one of them could have gone upstairs, found the laudanum and given Mrs Montserrat a fatal dose.' He watched her as she saw the two alternatives and both appalled her.

'I'm staying right in this room while you talk to the maids,' she warned him.

'Of course,' he agreed. 'I wish you to, but please do not interrupt.'

His questioning proved fruitless, as he had expected, except to confirm in his own mind that they were ordinary, artless domestic servants, capable of occasional idleness, gossip, petty squabbling, but nothing of sustained malice. For one thing, they seemed far too unsophisticated for deception of the degree required to be of use as a poisoner. For another, they confided in each other too freely to keep such a secret. Mrs Whiteside's estimate of them was reasonably accurate. He made a mental note that if ever he were involved in detective work again, he would pay more attention to the observation of housekeepers.

Miss Tucker was a different matter. She had been with Serafina for decades. She looked pathetically frail now, lost because her usefulness was over. She would be cared for, but not needed. She sat on the chair opposite Narraway and prepared to answer his questions.

He began gently, and was amused to find her observations of the other servants very similar to Mrs Whiteside's, if a trifle sharper. But then she did not have to work with them any more. She no longer had a position to guard.

She was not without humour, and he regretted having to move his line of enquiry to more sensitive areas.

'Miss Tucker, I have heard from Lady Vespasia

Cumming-Gould that Mrs Montserrat was losing her ability to remember exactly where she was, and to whom she was speaking. Did you know that she was afraid of letting slip secrets that might affect other people very adversely?'

She sighed and looked at him with careful patience. 'Of course I did, poor soul. If you had asked me five years ago, I'd never have thought such a thing could happen to a lady like Mrs Montserrat.' She had difficulty controlling her grief, and her eyes blazed at him through tears for making her acknowledge it now.

'Someone killed her, Miss Tucker. I am thinking it less and less likely that it was someone already in this house.'

She blinked and said nothing.

'Who visited Mrs Montserrat in the last three or four months?'

She looked down. 'Not many. People like to feel comfortable and be entertained or amused. If you are of a certain age yourself, seeing what can happen, what may yet happen to you, is unpleasant.'

Narraway winced inside himself. He had many years to go to catch up with Serafina Montserrat, but it would come soon enough. Would he bear it with grace? Would anyone come to see him, except out of duty, or perhaps to see if he let slip any of the hundreds of secrets he knew?

Then he realised with a chill like ice that perhaps he too would be terrified of what he might say, and might be murdered to ensure his silence. Suddenly Serafina became of intense importance to him, almost an image of himself in a future to come.

'Miss Tucker, someone killed her,' he said with a catch in his voice. 'I intend to find out who that was, and see to it that they answer to the law. The fact that Mrs Montserrat was old and had very little family is irrelevant. Even the fact that in the past she was a great woman is irrelevant also. Whoever she was, she had the right to be cared for, to be treated with dignity and allowed to live out the whole of her life.'

Miss Tucker let the tears roll down her thin cheeks, which were almost colourless in the late winter light.

'No one here would hurt her, my lord,' she said in barely more than a whisper. 'But there were others who came into the house, some to visit her, some to visit Miss Freemarsh.'

He nodded again. 'Of course. Who were they?'

She pursed her lips slightly in concentration. 'Well, there was Lady Burwood, who came twice, as I recall, but that was some time ago.'

'To visit whom?'

'Oh, Mrs Montserrat, although of course she was very civil to Miss Freemarsh.'

Narraway could imagine it: Lady Burwood, whoever she was, being polite and indefinably condescending; and Nerissa hungering for recognition, and receiving none, except second-hand through her relationship to Serafina.

'Who is Lady Burwood?' he asked.

Miss Tucker smiled. 'Middle-aged, married rather beneath her, but happily enough, I think. She has a sister with a title and more money, but fewer children. She found Mrs Montserrat more interesting than most of her other friends.'

Narraway nodded. 'You are very observant as to the details that matter, Miss Tucker,' he said sincerely. 'Why did she stop coming?' It was a cruel question, and he knew it, but the answer might be important.

Miss Tucker's face flushed with amusement. 'Not what you assume, my lord. She fell and broke her leg.'

'I stand corrected,' he said wryly. 'Who else?'

She mentioned two or three others, and a fourth and fifth who had come solely to visit Nerissa. None of them seemed to have the remotest connection with Austria or past intrigues anywhere at all.

'No gentlemen?' he enquired.

She looked at him very steadily. She had kept decades of secrets, probably many of them of a romantic or purely lustful nature. A good lady's maid was a mixture of servant, artist and priest, and Mariah Tucker had been superb. A maid to Serafina Montserrat would have had to be.

'Please?' he said gravely. 'Someone murdered her, Miss Tucker. I shall repeat nothing that is not relevant to that. I am good at secrets also. Until a few months ago, I was Head of Special Branch.' It was still painful to say that.

Perhaps she saw it in his face. 'I see,' she nodded very slightly. 'You are too young to retire.' She did not ask the question that lay between them.

'One of my own secrets came back and caught me,' he told her.

'Oh dear.' There was sympathy and the very faintest possible humour in her eyes.

'Who visited the house, Miss Tucker?' he repeated.

'Lord Tregarron came to see Mrs Montserrat, twice I think. He did not stay very long,' she replied. 'Mrs Montserrat was not very well on either occasion. I did not hear their conversation, but I believe it was not . . . not amicable.'

He was surprised. He had not been aware that Tregarron had known Serafina.

'How do you know that, Miss Tucker? Did Mrs Montserrat tell you? Or do you know for yourself, perhaps?'

'Mrs Montserrat knew the first Lord Tregarron, in Vienna, a long time ago.'

'His father?'

'Yes.'

'Do you know the circumstances?'

'I surmise them, I do not know. Nor will I imagine them for you.'

'Did he speak with Miss Freemarsh?'

'Yes, at some length, but it was downstairs in the with-drawing room, and I have no idea what was said. I know it was some time, only from the maid, Sissy.'

'I see. Anyone else?'

'Mr and Mrs Blantyre both came, separately. Several times.'

'To see Mrs Montserrat?'

'And Miss Freemarsh. I imagine to discuss Mrs Montserrat's health, and what might be done to make her happier, more comfortable. I think Mrs Blantyre was very fond of her. She seemed to be.'

'Mr Blantyre also?'

'He is very fond of his wife, and very concerned for her health. Apparently she is delicate, or at least he is of that opinion.'

'And you are not?' he said quickly.

She smiled. 'I think she is far stronger than he appreciates. He likes to think she is delicate. Some men are pleased to believe themselves protectors of the weak, caring for some beautiful woman like a tropical flower, that needs to be defended from every chill draught.'

Narraway had not thought of such a thing. Now that she described it so clearly, it became real.

'So you believe Blantyre came in order to see that Adriana was not distressed by her visits to Mrs Montserrat?'

'I think that is how he wished it to appear,' she said carefully.

He noted the difference. 'I see. And Miss Freemarsh?' he asked. 'Would she say the same?'

'Most certainly.' The tiny flicker of amusement touched her mouth again.

'Miss Tucker, I think there is something of importance that you are deliberately not telling me.'

'Observations,' she said quickly. 'Not facts, my lord. I think you do not know women very well.'

He was now realising this for himself.

'I am learning,' he said ruefully. 'A difficult question, Miss Tucker, and I ask you not from personal curiosity but because I need to know. Does Miss Freemarsh have an admirer?'

Tucker's face remained completely impassive. 'You mean a lover, my lord?'

Narraway watched her intently, and still could not read the emotion in her behind the words.

'Yes, I suppose I do.'

'Yes, she does. But I know that because I have been a lady's maid all my life, and I know when a woman is in love: how she walks, how she smiles, the tiny differences she will make in her appearance, even when she is forced to keep the matter secret.'

He nodded slowly. Why had he not known that? It made perfect sense. Tucker would know everything. To those who had grown up with servants in the house, they were like furniture: familiar, useful, to be looked after with care, and treated as if they had neither eyes nor ears.

'Who is it, Miss Tucker?'

She hesitated.

'Miss Tucker, whoever it is may, knowingly or not, be behind the death of Mrs Montserrat.'

Tucker winced.

'Please?'

'It is either Lord Tregarron, or Mr Blantyre,' she said in little above a whisper.

Narraway was stunned. His disbelief must have shown in his face, because Tucker looked at him with disappointment that verged on a kind of hurt. She started to speak again, then changed her mind.

'You surprise me,' he admitted. 'I considered both men to be very happily married, and I gather Miss Freemarsh is . . . not . . .'

'Attractive to men,' Tucker finished for him.

'Quite,' he agreed.

Tucker smiled patiently. 'I have known of perfectly respectable, middle-aged men who have been uncontrollably attracted to the strangest women,' she answered. 'Sometimes very rough women, labourers with their hands, not even clean, and most certainly ignorant. I have no idea what it is that appeals, but it is true. With Mrs Montserrat, men loved her courage, her passion and her hunger for adventure. And she could make them laugh.'

Narraway believed it. Briefly, for a swift, perfect moment, he thought of Charlotte, and knew why he found her so deep in his own thoughts far too often. It was her courage and passion also, she too made him laugh, but it was also her fierce loyalties, and the fact that she would never betray Pitt, never even wish to.

What was it in Vespasia? Curiously enough, it was not her beauty. Even in her youth it would not have been, dazzling though she was. He could remember her youth clearly; she was not so very much older than he. It was the fire in her, the intelligence and the spirit; more especially recently, a vulnerability he would never have perceived, even a year ago.

'Thank you, Miss Tucker. You have been extraordinarily helpful,' he said aloud. 'I promise you I will do everything I can to see that the truth of Mrs Montserrat's death is discovered, and whoever is responsible is dealt with justly.' He did not say 'according to the law', because he was not certain that in this case that would be the same thing.

*   *   *

When Narraway finally saw Nerissa it was over three hours since he had arrived at Dorchester Terrace. He had eaten a luncheon of cold game pie and pickles, with a dessert of suet pudding and hot treacle sauce, the same as had been eaten in the servants' dining room. He had eaten his in Mrs Whiteside's sitting room, and the crockery had been cleared away.

Nerissa came in and closed the door behind her. She was wearing black, with a brooch of jet. It did something to relieve the plainness of her dress bodice. A white collar or fichu would have helped, but possibly it was too soon for that.

Nerissa's face was bleached of even the faintest colour, and she looked tired. The skin around her eyes was shadowed. Narraway felt a moment of pity for her. He tried to imagine what her daily life had been like, and the picture he conjured up was monotonous, without light or laughter, without thoughts to provoke the mind or even a sense of purpose. Had she been desperate to escape that prison? Wouldn't anyone, but especially a woman in love?

'Please sit down, Miss Freemarsh. I am sorry to have to disturb you, but there is no alternative.'

She obeyed, but remained stiff-backed in the chair, her hands folded in her lap, clasped together.

'I assume you would not do so if you did not have to, my lord,' she sighed. 'I find it very difficult to believe that any of the staff here would have contributed to my aunt's death, even negligently. And I . . . I cannot think of anyone else who might have done so. But since you seem convinced that it was neither an accident of her own making, nor suicide, then there must be some other explanation. It is . . . distressing.'

'I have to ask you about visitors, Miss Freemarsh,' he began. 'Since the laudanum was given directly to your aunt and had an almost immediate effect, it has to have been given to her by someone who came back to the house that evening.' He saw her pale and the stiff hands in her lap grip each other so the knuckles were white. 'Who could that have been, Miss Freemarsh?'

Nerissa opened her mouth, gulped air, and said nothing. He could see in her eyes the frantic racing of her mind. If she denied that anyone came, then the only conclusion was that it was someone already in the house: either herself, or one of the servants. He knew from the servants themselves that after dinner had been eaten and cleared away, they had taken their own meal and retired for the day. Unless at least two of them were in collusion with each other, their time was accounted for.

Nerissa had been alone. He imagined the long, solitary evenings, one after the other, every week, every month, stretching ahead into every year, waiting for a lover who could come only rarely. If he had called, then Nerissa herself would have let him in, possibly at a prearranged time. It might well have been the intent of both of them that the servants did not know of it.

He looked across at her now, waiting, and forced himself to think of Serafina, also alone in her bedroom, even the memory of her life slipping from her grasp.

'Mrs Blantyre came,' Nerissa said softly. 'Aunt Serafina was fond of her, and she enjoyed her visits. But I can't . . .' She left the rest unsaid.

'And she was alone with Mrs Montserrat?'

'Yes. I had some domestic business to deal with . . . a slight problem with the menu for the following day. I'm . . . so sorry.'

Narraway could scarcely believe it. If Miss Tucker were not mistaken, and either Blantyre or Tregarron was Nerissa's lover, was it even conceivable that Adriana Blantyre knew this?

How could any man prefer Nerissa Freemarsh – plain, humourless, desperate Nerissa – over the beautiful, elegant Adriana? Perhaps Blantyre was weary of Adriana's delicate health, which might deny him the marital privileges he wished. Was that an excuse? He might feel that it was a reason. But why on earth a plain, respectable woman like Nerissa? Perhaps because she loved him, and love was what he craved. And perhaps, also, precisely because no one would imagine it. What could be safer?

How had Adriana learned of it? Was that some careless word from Serafina, not realising the meaning of it herself? Could Adriana really be jealous to the degree that she would murder an old woman in her bed? Why? So Blantyre would have no more excuse to come to Dorchester Terrace? That was absurd.

But Adriana was Croatian; and Serafina had lived and worked in Vienna, northern Italy and the Balkans, including Croatia. He must look more closely into the past before he leaped to any conclusions.

'Thank you, Miss Freemarsh,' he said quietly. 'I am grateful for your candour. I don't suppose you could offer any reason why Mrs Blantyre should wish your aunt any harm?'

Nerissa lowered her eyes. 'I know very little, except what Aunt Serafina said, and she was rambling a lot of the time. I am really not sure what was real and what was just her confused imagination. She was very . . . muddled.'

'What did she say, Miss Freemarsh? If you can remember any of it, it may help to explain what has happened, especially if she also mentioned it in someone else's hearing.'

Nerissa's eyes opened wide. 'Mrs Blantyre? Do you think so?'

'We don't know who else she may have spoken to.' He was trying to suggest a further person, someone Nerissa could blame more easily. He did not know what he was looking for, but he could not assume it was Adriana, whatever the reason, until he had exhausted the other possibilities, and learned whom Serafina herself had feared.

Nerissa sat silent for so long Narraway was beginning to think she was not going to speak. When finally she did, it was steadily and reluctantly.

'She mentioned many names, especially from thirty or forty years ago. Most of them were Austrian, I think, or Croatian, some Italian. I'm afraid I don't recall them all. It is difficult when they are not in your own language. She said Tregarron, but it made no sense, because Lord Tregarron cannot have been more than a child at the time she seemed to believe it was. It was all very muddled.'

'I understand. Who else?' he prompted.

Again she considered for several moments, digging into memories that clearly were painful.

Narraway felt guilty, but he had to explain all the other possibilities, above all, in case it tied into the proposed assassination of Alois, however obliquely. Even if Adriana had left Croatia as a young woman, the family ties must still exist.

'Miss Freemarsh?'

She looked up at him. 'She . . . she spoke of Mrs Blantyre's family, the name Dragovic. I don't know what she said, it was difficult to catch it all. I don't know if any of it was real. But Mrs Blantyre was . . . distressed. Perhaps it awoke old tragedies for her. I can't say. Naturally I did not speak of it to her. I asked Aunt Serafina, but she appeared to have forgotten it. It was obviously very powerful. I'm sorry, I can't tell you any more.'

'I see. Thank you very much.' He rose to his feet and allowed her to lead the way back to the hall and the front door. He left her standing on the exquisite floor of the house that was now hers, looking dwarfed, crushed by the beauty of it.

'See what you think of that, Radley,' Lord Tregarron said, handing Jack a sheaf of papers. They were in Tregarron's office and had been working on a delicate matter concerning a British business initiative in Germany. It was detailed, and the possibility for damage was high, as well as the chance for success.

'Yes, sir.' Jack accepted the papers with a sense of acute satisfaction. He knew that Tregarron meant him to read them immediately. Such documents were never allowed to be taken from the building. He left the room and went to his own, far smaller office. Sitting in the armchair in front of the fire, he began to read.

It was interesting. He was continually learning more about Europe in general, and the delicate balance between one nation and another, most particularly the old, ramshackle and crumbling power of the Austrian Empire and the new, rising Germany with its extraordinary energy. Its culture was as old as the land itself. It had produced some of the world's great thinkers, and most of the most brilliant composers of music to enrich the human spirit, but as a political entity it was in its infancy. All the strengths and weaknesses of youth were very evident in its behaviour.

The same could be said in many ways of Italy, on Austria's southern borders. The country had been unified only in language and heritage, but politically it remained the patchwork of warring city states that it had been since the fall of the Roman Empire.

The more he read of all of it, the more fascinated he became. He was more than halfway through when he came to a passage he did not fully understand. When he went back to reread it, it appeared that Vienna was aware of certain aspects of the proposed business with Berlin that would give them a considerable advantage. Could Tregarron not know this? Or had he forgotten?

Jack read the passage again, made a note, and then continued until he came to the end. He went back and reread the page that troubled him. Then he picked up the whole and took it back to Tregarron's office. He knocked on the door.

It was answered immediately and he went in.

'Ah, what do you think?' Tregarron asked. He was smiling, leaning back a little in his chair, his powerful face relaxed, eyes expectant. Then he saw Jack's expression and he frowned. 'A problem?' he asked without any anxiety, rather with a look of very slight amusement.

'Yes, sir.' Jack felt foolish, but the matter troubled him too much to accept the cowardice of not raising it. 'On page fourteen the phrasing of the second paragraph suggests that the Germans are aware of the Austrians' agreement with Hauser, and we know that they are not. I don't know how. But it means the Austrians would profit from this quite unfairly.'

Tregarron frowned and held out his hand.

Jack passed him the papers.

Tregarron read the entire page, then read it again. Finally he looked up at Jack, his heavy brows drawn together. 'You are quite right. We need to rephrase that. In fact I think it would be better if we omitted that paragraph altogether.'

'That would still mislead Berlin, sir,' Jack said unhappily. 'I don't know how Vienna knows about it, but it's quite clear from the dispatch we had yesterday that they do.'

'If Austrian intelligence has learned that, somehow, it is not our concern to inform Berlin of it,' Tregarron replied. His eyes hardened. 'But you are perfectly correct to bring that to my attention. We must not mislead Berlin. The reference must be taken out. Good work, Radley.' He smiled, showing strong, white teeth. 'You have saved us what could have been a very considerable embarrassment. Thank you.'

Later that evening, as Jack escorted Emily to a dinner party she very much wished to attend, his mind wandered from the dinner table conversation. He found his thoughts returning to Tregarron's explanation of the discrepancy in the document they were preparing. It seemed an uncharacteristic error to have made. Tregarron was not a careless man. Far from it: he was meticulous in detail. How had he not seen that himself?

Emily was across the table from him dressed in pink, an unusual colour for her. She had always said it was too obvious, better suited to someone darker. But this gown, with its huge sleeves emphasising her slender shoulders and neck, and the white lace inserts in the low bodice, was extraordinarily flattering. She was enjoying herself this evening, but he could tell by the carefully controlled pitch of her voice, and the slight stiffness in the way she had held her head, that she was still angry with Charlotte. The quarrel had upset her, but she was determined not to give in until she received some more specific form of apology. His attempts to persuade her to answer Charlotte's letter had only made matters worse. She had called him an appeaser in a tone of total contempt. Her anger was with Charlotte, not him, but he knew very well not to try again, at least not yet.

The chatter swirled around him. He joined in politely. His charm had always been effortless and he needed only half his attention to exercise more than mere good manners.

Tregarron was not at this particular function, but someone mentioned his name. Jack saw Emily's face light with respect.

She spoke warmly of Lady Tregarron. Jack's mind returned again to the omission in the papers. How had Vienna known this particular piece of information? If it was their own intelligence service, they were operating within the British Foreign Office, and that was something that should have caused far greater alarm than Tregarron had shown.

Surely that must mean that that was not the answer? He did not know what was, and he put it to the back of his mind and turned to the woman next to him, devoting his attention to her.

They did not call their carriage to take them home until well after midnight.

Emily stifled a yawn with elegance. 'I enjoyed that so much,' she said with a tired smile, leaning her head against his shoulder.

He put his arm around her. 'I'm glad. Some of them were really very entertaining.'

She turned towards him, although in the dimness inside the carriage, and the lights from streetlamps moving across their faces through the windows, she could not see him clearly.

'What were you worrying about? And don't tell me you weren't. I know when you are giving someone your whole mind and when you are not.'

He had never set the pattern of lying to her, but discretion was an entirely different thing.

'Political papers I saw today,' he said perfectly truthfully.

'You can manage it,' she responded without hesitation. 'Tomorrow it will be clear enough. I've long thought nothing much is ever well solved when you are tired.'

'You are quite right,' he agreed, and leaned his head back. But he did not forget it. He had already made up his mind that tomorrow he would ask Vespasia.

* * *

249

'Good morning, Jack,' she said without concealing her surprise when he was standing in her morning room as soon as she had finished her breakfast. 'This must be of concern to bring you so early.' She studied him more closely. He had always been an unusually handsome man, not in a dramatic way, but with the kind of charm it is churlish to resist. Now he looked restless, hiding unease with less than his usual skill.

'May I speak to you in complete confidence, Lady Vespasia?' he asked.

'Oh dear.' She sat down and gestured for him to do the same. 'This sounds very grave. Of course you may. What is it that concerns you?'

In as few words as possible he told her about the agreement with Berlin, omitting the substance of it except for the one matter that concerned Vienna. Then he explained the sentence that troubled him, and watched for her reply, never taking his eyes from hers.

She considered it with care, and increasing anxiety.

He saw it in her face, and his own expression grew more grave.

'I am afraid,' she said at length, 'that if you are correct, then someone in the Foreign Office is giving sensitive information to Vienna, which properly should be kept from them. I suppose you have read this particular document very carefully and you cannot be mistaken?'

'I asked Lord Tregarron if there had been an error,' he replied. 'He said that he would attend to it, and thanked me for my diligence.'

'But that does not satisfy you, or you would not be here telling me,' she pointed out.

He looked profoundly unhappy. 'No,' he said almost under his breath.

'Have you mentioned this to Emily?'

He looked startled. 'No, of course not!'

'Or Thomas?'

'No . . . I . . .'

'Then please do not. If you speak to Thomas he is now in a position where he will have no choice but to act. I shall deal with it.'

'How? I don't expect you to do anything except advise me. I suppose I was hoping you would say that I am starting at shadows, and to forget the matter.'

She smiled. 'My dear Jack, you know perfectly well that you are not starting at shadows. At the very least, there has been a mistake of the utmost carelessness.'

'And at worst?' he said softly.

She sighed. 'At worst, there is treason. Keep your own counsel. Behave as if you consider the matter closed.'

'And what will you do?'

'I shall speak to Victor Narraway.'

'Thank you.'

Narraway listened to Vespasia with increasing concern. When she had finished she had no doubt that he regarded the matter with even more gravity than she had.

'I see,' he said when she fell silent. 'Please don't speak of it to anyone, at this point, especially not Pitt. We must not take his attention from Duke Alois at the moment. We have only a little more than a week to go before he lands in Dover.'

'Is he really only a trivial person, Victor?' she asked.

'If he's more, I haven't been able to find out. At the moment it seems likely he is a victim of convenience. It is the crime that matters. Who is killed may be of little importance, as long as they will cause sufficient attention to embarrass Britain.'

'I see. And Serafina's death?'

'Another matter that is not yet concluded.'

'Then I had better leave you to pursue whichever you consider most urgent. I apologise for bringing you further concerns.' There was the faintest gleam of humour in her eyes. He understood it perfectly, just as he knew she understood him.

'Not at all,' he murmured, rising to bid her farewell. In other circumstances he would have asked her to stay, but he was already turning over in his mind how he would pursue this new investigation: which favour he would call in, which debts he might collect, upon whom to apply a certain type of pressure.

At the door she hesitated.

'Yes,' he said to her unasked question. 'I shall tell you.'

'Thank you, Victor. Good evening.'

Narraway lay awake a great deal of the night, turning over and over in his mind what Vespasia had told him, and how it might fit in with Serafina's death. He reviewed all the people he had known, in any context, who might be of help. Who would he even ask regarding such a subject as the betraying of confidential information regarding German interests? Was it a deliberate sabotaging of an Anglo-German agreement?

Why? Was it an intended deviousness, something the Foreign Office, specifically Tregarron, had not considered Jack Radley should know? He was new to his position, perhaps a trifle idealistic, so perhaps not yet to be trusted with less-than-honest dealings?

If that was Tregarron's judgement, then it was correct. Jack had been troubled, and he had not been able to turn a blind eye.

Perhaps the first thing Narraway should do was find out more about Tregarron. The Foreign Office was certainly not above deceit, as long as they were certain they could claim innocence afterwards if it became known. To get caught was grossly incompetent.

Where should he begin so that his enquiries would never be traced back to Tregarron himself? The answer came to him with extraordinary clarity. Tregarron had gone to Dorchester Terrace, probably to see Serafina, perhaps to see Nerissa Freemarsh. Had Serafina still been alive, and fully possessed of her wits and her memory, she would have been the ideal person to ask. But surely a great deal of anything she knew, the excellent and loyal Tucker might also know. In the past he had grossly underestimated servants, and he would not make that error now.

He debated whether to take her some gift as an appreciation of her time, and decided that would be clumsy. Perhaps afterwards he would. To begin with simple respect would be the subtlest and most important compliment.

When he arrived at Dorchester Terrace at mid-morning the following day, fortune played into his hands. Nerissa was out. Special Branch, thanks to Pitt, was paying for the funeral. They had, however, left it to Nerissa to deal with the actual arrangements, which had been somewhat delayed because of the necessity for an autopsy.

'I'm sorry,' the footman apologised.

'I came to see Miss Tucker,' Narraway informed him. 'It is extremely urgent, or I would not disturb you at such a time.'

The footman let him in and fifteen minutes later Narraway was again sitting before the fire in Mrs Whiteside's room. Miss Tucker was perched on the chair opposite him, a tray of tea and thinly sliced bread and butter between them.

'I am sorry to intrude on you again, Miss Tucker, but the matter cannot wait,' he said gravely.

She had poured the tea but it was too hot to drink yet. It sat gently wafting a fragrant steam into the air.

'How can I help you, Lord Narraway? I have told you all I know.'

'This is a completely different matter. At least I believe it is. I would have asked Mrs Montserrat, were she here to answer me. But as I was turning the matter over and over in my mind, when I should have been asleep, I realised that a great deal of what she knew, you might also know.'

She looked startled, then very distinctly pleased.

He smiled, only faintly. He did not wish her to think him either self-satisfied, or in any way taking the matter lightly.

'What is it you think I might know?' she enquired, picking up her cup and testing to see if it were cool enough to sip. It was not, and she took instead a slice of bread and butter.

He took one also, then began. 'This is of the utmost confidence. I must ask you to speak of it to no one at all, absolutely no one.'

'I shall not,' she promised.

'I shall ask you as I would have asked Mrs Montserrat. What can you tell me of Lord Tregarron? It is imperative to Britain's good name, to our honesty in dealing with other countries, most particularly Germany and Austria, that I know the truth.'

She sat very upright in her chair. A tired, proud old woman at the end of a lifetime of service, was now being asked by a man – a lord – to give her advice, and her memories, to help her country.

'The present Lord Tregarron, my lord, or his father?' she enquired.

Narraway stiffened, drew in his breath and then let it out slowly. 'Both, I think. But please begin with his father. You were acquainted with him?'

She smiled very slightly, as if at his innocence. 'Mrs Montserrat knew him intimately, my lord, at least for a while. He was married, you understand. Lady Tregarron was a nice woman, very respectable, at times a trifle –' she searched for the right word – 'tedious.'

'Oh dear.' Without realising it, he had exactly mimicked Vespasia's tone of voice. 'I see.' He did see. A vision of endless polite, even affectionate boredom sketched before him. 'Was it love?'

She made a slight move with her lips. 'Oh, no, just a romance, a straying to pick flowers that belonged to someone else. Vienna has a certain magic. One is away from home, people forget that it is just as real, just as good, or bad!'

'And did Mrs Montserrat and Lord Tregarron part with ill feeling, or not?' he asked.

'Enmity, not at all. Ill feeling?' She sipped her tea. 'I think Lord Tregarron was very afraid that Lady Tregarron might find out, and that would have troubled him greatly. He loved her. She was his safety, not just for his feelings, the mother of his children – they had one son and several daughters – but also she was socially very well connected. She was a good woman, just unimaginative, and – heaven help her – with little sense of humour.'

'Who else knew of the affair?'

'I don't know. People are sometimes more observant than one would wish, but if they also stray a trifle away from the path then one does not worry too much.'

'I see. And the present Lord Tregarron?'

'I know less of him. He thought well of his father, but even more of his mother. He is devoted to her.'

'And his father?' he asked.

'There was some estrangement between him and his father,' she answered.

'Did Mrs Montserrat know why?'

Tucker hesitated.

'Please, Miss Tucker. It may be of some importance,' he pleaded.

'I believe he learned of his father's affair with Mrs Montserrat, even though by that time it had been over for many years,' she said reluctantly.

'Thank you, I am very grateful to you.' He picked up his tea. It was at last cool enough to sip.

She frowned. 'Is it of use?'

'I'm not sure, I'm not sure at all.' But an idea, vague and ill-defined as yet, was beginning to form in his mind.

Chapter Nine

Pitt felt uncomfortable sitting in the big carved chair behind the desk that used to be Narraway's and looking at Narraway himself sitting opposite, as a visitor. It was only months since their positions had been reversed and this still felt unnatural to him.

Narraway was smartly dressed, as always: slim and elegant, his dark suit perfectly cut, his thick hair immaculate. But he was worried. The lines in his face were deep, his expression without even the shadow of a smile.

It was just a few days until Duke Alois should arrive at Dover.

'I've just come from Dorchester Terrace,' Narraway said without hesitation. 'It's not impossible Serafina's murder was domestic, but it's extremely unlikely. Why now? And would Nerissa Freemarsh really have had the nerve? She could so easily be caught.'

'Who was it?' Pitt was saddened by events in Dorchester Terrace, but not yet concerned. The infinitely deeper question of Duke Alois's possible assassination engaged all his attention.

'It seems most likely that it was Adriana Blantyre,' Narraway replied. His voice was low, his face pinched with regret.

Pitt was stunned. He looked very intently at Narraway and saw no suggestion of irony or sarcasm in his face.

'Adriana Blantyre?' Pitt repeated, as if saying it aloud would make Narraway correct him, explain that she was not really whom he had meant.

'I'm sorry,' Narraway said gravely. 'I know you have had great help from her husband, and that you like Adriana herself, but I can see no reasonable alternative.'

'There has to be,' Pitt protested. 'Why in God's name should Adriana Blantyre murder Mrs Montserrat? How well did they even know each other? It makes no sense!'

Narraway sighed. 'Pitt, you're thinking with your emotions. Use your brain. There are a dozen ways in which it might make sense. The most obvious is Blantyre himself. He is an expert on the Austrian Empire, against whose dominion in Italy Serafina spent most of her life fighting. They would have a hundred acquaintances in common, friend or enemy. There could have been a score of causes on which they were on opposite sides.'

'Does that still matter now?' Pitt said with an edge of disbelief. He did not want to accept it. Adriana was at least a generation younger than Serafina. She must have some loyalty to the country of her birth. He had seen her face light up at the mention of it, but she had been in England now for over ten years, at the very least, and there was nothing whatever to indicate any interest in politics. Indeed, there was nothing to show that she had ever been actively involved.

'It sounds to me like Nerissa Freemarsh trying to move the suspicion away from herself to the only other person she could think of,' he said.

'Possibly,' Narraway conceded. 'But Adriana was there at

Dorchester Terrace the night Serafina died, and she was alone with her. Tucker confirms that. We will probably never know what Serafina said that was the catalyst, but she was rambling, raking up all sorts of old memories, in bits and pieces that made little sense. We need to know a great deal more about Adriana Blantyre's past, and what Serafina might inadvertently have given away about it. I'm sorry.'

The reasoning was too clear to deny.

'I can't do it,' Narraway went on, a slight edge to his voice, a self-lacerating humour. 'You'll need to look at Special Branch records, such as we have, of old Austrian and Croatian plots, things Serafina might have been involved in, or known about. There isn't very much, and I can tell you where it's filed, but I don't have access to it any more.'

Pitt met Narraway's eyes and could not read anything in them but acute intelligence, and a perfect defence. He was pleased. He did not want to see regret, or a sense of exclusion.

'I'll look,' he said quietly. 'Are we sure no one else could have been in the house?'

'Not according to Tucker, but Blantyre himself and Tregarron went there that week.'

Pitt stiffened. 'Tregarron? Whatever for?'

'To see Serafina. They would hardly have gone to see Freemarsh, except as courtesy demanded. At least on the surface.'

'The surface?' Pitt raised his eyebrows.

'There is still the question of Nerissa's lover,' Narraway said drily.

'So Tregarron knew Serafina?' Pitt picked up the original thread. 'Or else he went because of the questions I asked him about Duke Alois.'

'Presumably.'

'Thank you.'

Narraway smiled obliquely, and rose to his feet. 'Don't sidestep it, Pitt,' he warned. 'You need to have the truth, whatever you decide to do about it.'

Pitt read all the files about the Austrian oppression and revolts of the last forty years. They were exactly where Narraway had said they would be. He learned very little of use, except where to find a certain elderly gentleman named Peter Ffitch, who had once served in Special Branch, and had an encyclopaedic memory. He had retired twenty years earlier and was a widower now, living quietly in a small village in Oxfordshire, his neighbours having no idea of the colourful life he had once led.

Pitt caught the next train and was in Banbury just after lunchtime. He took a small branch line, and then a stiff walk through the rain to Ffitch's steeply thatched house in a cobbled road off the main street.

When he knocked on the door it was answered by a dark-haired woman of uncertain years, a white apron tied over a plain brown skirt and blouse. She looked at him with suspicion.

Pitt introduced himself, with proof of his identity, and told her that it was extremely important that he speak with Mr Ffitch. After some persuasion she admitted him.

Ffitch must have been in his eighties, with the mild features of a child and still quite a lot of fairish hair gone almost white. Only when Pitt looked more closely into his eyes did he see the startling intelligence there, and a spark of humour, even pleasure at the prospect of being questioned.

At Ffitch's request the woman, mollified by his assurances, brought them tea and a generous portion of cake, and then left them alone.

'Well,' Ffitch said with satisfaction. 'It must be important to bring the new Head of Special Branch all the way out here.

Murder or high treason, at the least. How can I help?' He rubbed his hands together. They were surprisingly strong hands, not even touched by age or rheumatism. He reached forward and put several more pieces of coal on the fire, as if settling in for the full afternoon. 'What can I tell you?'

Pitt allowed himself to enjoy the cake and the tea. The cake was rich and full of fruit, and the tea was hot. He realised momentarily how long the train journey had seemed, and the carriage had been chilly. He decided to tell Ffitch the truth, at least as far as Serafina was concerned.

'Oh dear,' Ffitch said when he was finished. His seemingly bland face was filled with grief, altering it completely. 'What a sad way for such a marvellous woman to end. But perhaps whoever killed her did not do her such a great disservice.'

'Perhaps not,' Pitt agreed. 'But I still need to know who it was, and why.'

'For justice?' Ffitch said curiously.

'Because I need to know the players in this particular drama, and what it is they want,' Pitt corrected him. 'There is very much currently to win or lose.'

'Still? Well, well.' Ffitch smiled, his body relaxing. 'I'm relieved to hear that it is not to embarrass or disgrace Serafina. I am often reminded that not even the past is safe. Strange business we are in. More than most people, our old ghosts keep changing. I have learned to live comfortably with that particular one. I would like it preserved.' He frowned. 'But you speak of present danger. Have some more tea, and tell me what I can do.'

'Thank you,' Pitt accepted. He glanced around the room. Ffitch may have lived in many countries, but this was essentially English. There were Hogarth cartoon prints on the walls, and leather-bound books on the five shelves on the far wall. From what Pitt could see they were mostly history and some of the great works of literature and commentary. He saw the light flicker on the gold lettering of Gibbon's *Decline and Fall of the Roman Empire*, and Milton's *Paradise Lost*. There was no time to look at more.

Ffitch poured the tea and passed Pitt back his cup.

'Serafina,' he said thoughtfully. 'I knew a lot about her, but I only ever met her a few times.' He smiled. 'The first was at a ball in Berlin. I remember it very well. She was dressed in gold, very soft, like an evening sky. Still, she looked like a tigress, only temporarily made friendly by warmth and good food.'

The smile of memory left his face. 'The second was in the forest. She came on horseback, slim as a whip, and lithe. She dismounted easily and walked with such grace, wearing trousers, of course, and carrying a pistol. What is it you need to know? If you are looking for whoever murdered her, it could have been any of a hundred people, for any of a hundred reasons.'

'Now, in 1896?' Pitt said sceptically.

Ffitch bit his lip. 'Well taken, sir. No, not now. But some of those old victories and losses still matter, at least to those involved. It sounds as if you're looking for something that came to light only recently, but from some old story?'

'Looks like it,' Pitt replied. 'She can't have been doing anything now.'

Ffitch pursed his lips. 'So something she remembered, and let slip in her confusion of mind, affects someone alive today so deeply that the betrayal of it still matters.' He nodded slowly. 'Interesting. There were some bad things. Some treason against England in Vienna, but I never knew who was involved.

'I tried very hard to find out because it was important. Quite a lot of information went from the British Embassy to the Austrians and embarrassed us severely. That was one of my worst failures.' He could not hide the distress in his face.

Pitt hated embarrassing him, but he could not afford the kindness of letting it pass.

'Was it ever known?'

Ffitch looked at him bleakly. 'No, not when I retired. If they had learned I like to think someone would have told me. Perhaps I delude myself either as to my own importance, or to the regard they had for me.'

'I doubt that,' Pitt replied, hoping it was true. 'I think at least Victor Narraway would have spoken of it, because if he had known, he would not have had me come out here and trouble you now.'

'Ah . . . yes, Victor Narraway. Always thought he would do well. Clever man. Ruthless, in his own way. Wondered why he left. Would have thought he had many good years in him yet. But I don't imagine you'll tell me.' His eyes narrowed. He looked at Pitt closely, quite openly assessing his ability, and almost certainly also his nerve.

Pitt waited, taking another piece of cake.

Ffitch sighed at last. 'Serafina might have known,' he said thoughtfully. 'Perhaps that was what she was afraid of.' He shook his head, the firelight flushing his cheeks. 'In her prime she could keep a secret better than the grave. What a damn shame.'

'Adriana Blantyre,' Pitt said softly.

Ffitch blinked. 'Blantyre? Evan Blantyre was young then, but clever, very clever. Always at the edge of things, never in the middle – at least that's how it looked from the outside.'

'What things?' Pitt asked.

Ffitch looked surprised. 'Plots to gain greater freedom from the Austrian yoke, what else? Italian plots, Croatian plots, even the odd Hungarian, although most of them were willing enough to pay lip service to Vienna, and carry on with whatever they wanted to in Budapest.'

'Not Serafina?'

'Certainly not. You want to know of the ones that went badly wrong? Of course you do. They all went wrong one way or another. Most simply failed, fizzled out, or succeeded for a few months. One or two ended really badly, shot before they could succeed, tricked or trapped one way or another. Probably the best organised, the bravest of the fighters was Lazar Dragovic. Fine man. Handsome, funny, a dreamer with the intelligence and the courage to carry it through.'

'But he failed . . .' The conclusion was obvious.

Ffitch's eyes were steady and sad, as if it had happened yesterday.

'He was betrayed. Never knew by whom. But yes, he failed. The rest of them escaped, but Dragovic was summarily executed. They beat him right there on the spot, trying to get the names of the others, but he died without telling them anything. They put the gun to his head and shot him, kneeling on the ground.' Even so long after, the misery of it pinched Ffitch's face with remembered pain.

'Might Serafina have known who betrayed him?' Pitt asked quietly.

'Yes. I suppose so. But I've no idea why she wouldn't have done something about it – shot whoever it was herself. I would have. She cared for Dragovic, perhaps more than for any of her other lovers. If she knew and did nothing, she must have had the devil of a good reason.'

'What sort of reason?' Pitt asked.

Ffitch considered for a few moments. 'Hard to think of one. The lives of others, possibly several others? A better revenge? But Serafina wasn't one to wait, especially since circumstances could change, and she might lose the later chance. She'd take what she could get at the time.' He turned and looked into the flames of the fire. 'I did hear a story – I don't know if it's true – that Dragovic's eight-year-old daughter was there and saw her father executed. They say Serafina had to choose between going after the man who was behind Dragovic's betrayal, or saving the child. She did what she knew Dragovic would have wanted, which of course was to save the child.' He turned from the flames and looked at Pitt with eyes filled with sudden understanding. 'The child's name was Adriana – Adriana Dragovic.'

The room was so quiet Pitt heard the coals settle in the grate.

'What did she look like?' he asked.

'No idea, but she had delicate health. I don't even know if she lived.'

Pitt was already certain in his mind as to the answer. 'She did,' he said quietly.

Ffitch stared at him. 'Adriana Blantyre?'

'I believe so, but I will find out.'

Ffitch nodded, and reached to pour them both a third cup of tea.

Pitt looked through all the old records he could find dating back thirty years to the story of Lazar Dragovic, his attempted uprising, his betrayal and his death. There was very little, but it removed any doubt that Adriana Dragovic was his daughter, and that she had later married Evan Blantyre.

There was also little room for doubt that it was Serafina Montserrat who had taken the child Adriana from the scene of the execution, and looked after her until she could be left with her grandparents.

What was conspicuously missing was any fact or statement that indicated who had betrayed Dragovic to the Austrians, resulting in the failure of the uprising and Dragovic's own torture and execution.

Had Adriana found out who it was, after all those years? Or had she listened to Serafina's ramblings and imagined she had learned the truth?

To Charlotte she was a charming friend, someone she had grown genuinely fond of, but what damage had been done to her when she had seen her father killed? What trust had been warped forever? Pitt had spent his professional life tearing the surface from secrets so well hidden no one else had imagined them. He had found scorching pain concealed by façades of a dozen sorts: duty, obedience, faith, sacrifice. He had seen rage so silent it had been ignored, until the dam burst and everyone in its path was destroyed.

All sorts of emotions can become unbearable, and so mask themselves as something else. That could be as true of Adriana Dragovic as of anyone.

Pitt was too late home that evening to visit Blantyre, but he did the following morning. It was a week until Alois would land in Dover. He could not afford to allow any more time to slip through his fingers.

He arrived at Blantyre's house early, in case he had intended to go anywhere other than to his office.

'Another development?' Blantyre said with surprise when Pitt was shown into his study where he was busy answering correspondence. Headed notepaper and envelopes were stacked on the corner of the desk, the cap was off the inkwell, which was an elegant thing in the shape of a sleeping lion – and there was a pen in Blantyre's hand.

'I apologise for disturbing you,' Pitt began.

'I assume it must be necessary.' Blantyre put his pen down and recapped the ink. 'Something has happened? More word of Duke Alois? Please sit, and tell me.'

He indicated a comfortable, leather-padded captain's chair similar to the one he was sitting in.

Pitt obeyed.

'It is the death of Serafina Montserrat that concerns me today,' he answered. 'I don't know whether it's connected to Duke Alois or not, but I can't afford to assume that it isn't.' He hated having to tell Blantyre this, but there was no escape. 'I'm afraid there is no question that she was murdered. There is no other possible conclusion from the evidence.' He saw the surprise and dismay in Blantyre's face and dreaded the possibility that Narraway was right. Was that why Blantyre had seemed so protective of Adriana? He knew she was emotionally so fragile she could do such a thing? Pitt could barely imagine the fear that must have caused him. How does any man protect the woman he loves from the demons within herself?

Blantyre was waiting, his dark eyes searching Pitt's face.

'The amount of laudanum in her body was far more than an accidental second dose could explain,' Pitt went on, knowing it was irrelevant. 'I have to consider the possibility that she knew something that has bearing on the reasons for the attempt on Duke Alois. And the reasons might tell us who is behind it.'

Blantyre nodded slowly. 'Of course. Poor Serafina. What a sad ending for such a brave and colourful woman.' He lifted his shoulders very slightly. 'What can I tell you that would be useful? If I had the faintest idea who was behind the attempt to assassinate Duke Alois, I would already have told you. I am still learning whatever I can, but there are dozens of dissident groups of one sort or another within the Austrian Empire. All of them are capable of violence, but as far as I have been able to discern, none of them with any known connection with Alois. I still don't know if he is any more than he seems to be on the surface, or if he is merely a pawn to be sacrificed in some cause we haven't yet identified – at least not specifically.'

'And why in England?' Pitt added.

'Worldwide attention, probably,' Blantyre grimaced. 'If it happens here, the Austrians will not be able to cover it up, or pass it off as an accident.' His expressive face reflected a sharp, sad humour. 'Or suicide,' he added.

'Are you suggesting Mayerling was a concealed murder?' Pitt asked with surprise.

'No.' Blantyre did not hesitate. 'I think they did what they could to keep it private, perhaps mistakenly. Rudolf was always highly strung, veering between elation and melancholy, and his childhood was enough to turn anyone into a lunatic. God knows, his mother is eccentric enough, to put it as gently as possible. He grew up with literally dozens of tutors, and no friends, no parent in evidence.

'The Empress was always travelling somewhere or other: Ireland for fox-hunting; Corfu for sun and reading poetry; Paris for gaiety, wit and of course a degree of scandal. If one can't create scandal in Paris one really isn't trying.'

Pitt did not interrupt. He watched Blantyre's face with intense interest and could not help being moved himself by the emotion in it. Blantyre spoke softly, looking not at Pitt, but somewhere beyond him.

'Austrian politics are infinitely more complicated than ours. The Hungarians are afraid of both Germany overtaking Austria itself, to their west; and all the Slavic parts of the Empire, backed of course by Russia, to the east. The Ottoman Empire is falling apart, and Russia will surely take any parts of that which it can. Serbia and Croatia could be the gateway to a slow erosion eventually eating into the heart of Austria itself.'

He smiled bleakly, looking at Pitt now. 'And of course

Vienna itself is a hotbed of ideas, the same socialism that is raging all over Europe, and which Rudolf admired. There was nothing of the autocrat in him. He was a dreamer, a man in love with the idealism of the future as he wanted it to be.'

The ashes settled in the fire with a very slight sound, but Blantyre did not move to restoke it.

'He was friendly with our own Prince of Wales,' he went on. 'They were distantly related, as most European royalty is, but far more than that, they were in extraordinarily similar positions. Like Edward, he had everything expected of him, but seemed to be waiting for it indefinitely. Unlike Edward, he had a wife he couldn't abide: cold, critical, boring but eminently suitable for a Habsburg Emperor.'

'And he fell in love with Marie Vetsera,' Pitt concluded.

'No. I think he just came to the end of the road,' Blantyre said sadly. 'There was nothing left for him to hope for. He had syphilis, among other things. Not a pleasant disease, and of course incurable.'

Pitt tried to imagine it, and failed. He could not see in his mind, or any part of his own experience, the hectic façade masking the inner desolation. There must have been many moments when death seemed like no more than a long sleep, for which he was infinitely weary.

Pitt found his route back to Serafina Montserrat, who had loved life so intensely.

'I have learned a great deal more about Serafina Montserrat's past,' Pitt said quietly. 'Including her presence at the beating and death of Lazar Dragovic, and her rescue of his eight-year-old daughter, Adriana.' Even against the light he saw Blantyre's face lose its colour and his body stiffen. If any proof had been needed of Adriana's identity, that would have been sufficient. 'Apparently it is still not known who betrayed him to the Austrians,' he added. 'Unless, of course, Serafina knew.'

Blantyre breathed in and out, and swallowed. His eyes met Pitt's without wavering, but he did not speak.

'In her rambling, it is possible she told Adriana, either directly,' Pitt continued, 'or enough in bits and pieces that Adriana was able to put it together and deduce the truth.'

Blantyre swallowed again, with difficulty, as though his throat were dry.

'Are you saying that Adriana believed it was Serafina who betrayed her father?' he asked. 'Why, for God's sake? Serafina was an insurgent herself. Are you suggesting she was secretly on the side of the Austrians?' There was intense disbelief in his voice, almost an anger at the idea, not even the reality. Or was it fear that Pitt was right?

'I don't know why,' Pitt admitted. 'It makes no political sense, from what we know, but there may be other elements that we know nothing about.'

Blantyre thought for several seconds. 'Personal?' he said at last.

'Perhaps?' Pitt waited for him to say that Dragovic and Serafina had been lovers. Did he know that? If he had been involved himself in the uprisings, on either side, then he might know it. Or he might have deduced it from what others had said, even Adriana herself.

Blantyre's face twisted into a gesture of misery and contempt. 'Are you suggesting they were once lovers, and she took his rejection so bitterly she was prepared to betray him, and the cause, to have her revenge? I find that impossible to believe. Serafina had many lovers. I never knew of her taking revenge for anything. Life was too short and too sweet for that. She was only ever accidentally destructive, never on purpose.'

'And Dragovic was loyal to the cause?' Pitt explored the other obvious line of thought.

Blantyre's eyes widened. 'So far as I know. But if he wasn't, what has that to do with Serafina's death now? Are you saying that she admitted to killing him, and said it was because he was a traitor? That's nonsense. No one would believe her. Dragovic was a hero. Everyone knew that, and I think events proved it. He was willing to die rather than tell the Austrians who else was involved. There is no doubt about that, because no one else was ever arrested. I know that myself.'

'Could he have been betrayed by one of Serafina's other lovers, out of jealousy over her?' Pitt asked. He hoped that was true. It would remove suspicion from Adriana, and he wanted that very much, for her sake, for Charlotte's, and above all for Blantyre himself.

'Yes . . .' Blantyre said slowly. 'Yes . . . that makes more sense. Though God knows who!'

'Someone who is still alive, or at the least, has someone who cares about their reputation enough to kill Serafina to preserve it, and is not only still alive, but here in London, and would know that Serafina is rambling, and could betray the truth, accidentally, and to Adriana,' Pitt replied. 'And of course, who had access to the house in Dorchester Terrace and could poison Serafina with her own laudanum. Or possibly this person brought more with them to add to hers. That must restrict it to a very few indeed.'

Blantyre rubbed his hand across his face in a gesture of intense weariness. He sighed. 'Nerissa Freemarsh?'

'A relative?' Pitt said with surprise.

'A lover,' Blantyre corrected him. 'And I doubt very much you will get his name from her. She is a . . . a very desperate woman, no family except Serafina, no husband, no child. Such women can be very . . . unpredictable.' He frowned. 'Are you suggesting that all this has something to do with Duke Alois?'

'I don't know.' Pitt thought of Lord Tregarron, and what

Tucker had told Narraway about Tregarron's visiting Dorchester Terrace. He needed to know a great deal more about that, absurd as it seemed. What on earth could Nerissa Freemarsh offer a man in Tregarron's position? A hunger, a need for his attention that perhaps his wife no longer had, unquestioning praise, a willingness to do anything he wished, which again, perhaps his wife would not? Maybe it was no more than simply a safe escape from pressure, duty, fulfilling other people's expectations. The more he thought about it, the more answers there were.

Had Serafina somehow discovered that, and raised a fierce objection? Considering her own past it would surely not be on moral grounds? A concern for Nerissa's reputation and the damage such an affair would do to it? If known, it would ruin any chance for a respectable marriage, if there were such a thing.

Or was it some other reason, even a care for Nerissa's feelings? She would know far more of the disasters of others whose emotions were involved than Nerissa did.

And Nerissa might misinterpret whatever Serafina said as a moral judgement, even a condemnation. If she loved Tregarron she would see it as the ruin of her last chance for love.

He hoped that somehow that was the truth, and Adriana Dragovic had nothing to do with Serafina's death.

'Apparently Lord Tregarron called to see Mrs Montserrat.'

Blantyre stiffened. 'Tregarron? Are you sure?'

'Yes.' There was no avoiding it any longer. 'And Mrs Blantyre visited her often. But you know that.'

'They have known each other on and off since that time,' Blantyre said quietly, 'and the death of Adriana's father was never spoken of. I don't know how much Adriana remembers. I hope very little: just confusion and pain, and then of course the loss. Her mother also was dead. She lost touch with Serafina. Serafina had no time for a child, especially one with extremely delicate health. Adriana lived with her grandparents until I met her. Then she was nineteen, and the most beautiful girl I had ever seen.' His face reflected an inner light, and a turmoil Pitt felt it intrusive to witness.

'The shadow of tragedy gave her a haunting quality, a depth other women did not have,' Blantyre continued. 'I would be grateful to you if you did not mention that time to her, unless it is absolutely necessary for the safety of the country. I can promise you that if she knew anything whatever of Duke Alois, or of Tregarron, for that matter, she would already have told me, and I would have told you.'

'Of course I won't mention it,' Pitt promised, 'unless my hand is forced, and I can see no reason why that should be. But I may have to ask her about her visit to Dorchester Terrace on the night Mrs Montserrat died, in case she saw or heard anything that can shed light on her death.'

'Then you will do so when I am present.' It was said gently, without threat, but it was more than a request. The power in Blantyre's voice, the force of his emotion, filled the room.

'As long as you will not cause delays I cannot afford,' Pitt agreed. 'Of course I will.'

Blantyre smiled very slightly, but there was a warmth in it. 'Thank you. I am obliged.'

Charlotte had had a delightful day with Adriana. She was finding her increasingly more interesting company as she came to know her better and they both felt more at ease. It had begun with the most formal of engagements, polite exchanges of views on art, fashion, the latest books. But now it was much more fluid, moving easily to anecdotes, more individual opinions on matters of importance where feelings were deep, and often now to an easy laughter at the amusing and absurd.

Today they had been to an afternoon soirée. The singing

had been very pleasant, but agonisingly serious. They had looked at each other, and had to stifle giggles and pretend they had suddenly had a fit of sneezing. An elderly lady of a very sentimental nature had been concerned for Adriana, and she had been obliged then to pretend she had suffered an unfortunate reaction to the hothouse lilies.

Charlotte had come to her rescue with a long and totally fictitious story about lilies at a funeral affecting her the same way. She had added to the verisimilitude of it by weeping for someone she could not endure. Everyone had praised her good nature and gentleness of heart – qualities she was perfectly sure she did not possess, as she admitted to Adriana later.

She had accepted the elderly lady's admiration with a straight face, and she and Adriana had excused themselves hastily before they burst into laughter again.

Charlotte had arrived home still smiling. She found Minnie Maude in the kitchen clearing away tea after Daniel and Jemima. There was a pile of crusts on the plate. She put them away very quickly when she heard Charlotte's footsteps and swung around, hiding them with her body. Her eyes widened.

'You do look lovely, ma'am,' she said sincerely. 'You should get another dress that same colour of goldy brown. There's not many as can wear that.'

'Thank you,' Charlotte also meant what she said, but she wondered why Minnie Maude was not making the children eat their crusts. She would let it go today. It would seem so churlish to make an issue of it after such a sincere compliment. But next time she would have to say something.

'I shall be down for dinner, but I must change out of this gown. It is rather too much for the parlour, I think!' She laughed again, and turned to leave.

'Can I 'elp yer, ma'am?' Minnie Maude offered. 'Them back buttons, any rate.'

'Thank you. That would be a good idea.' Charlotte turned and allowed Minnie Maude to undo the top half dozen or so at the back of her neck. Then she started for the door again. She had reached the bottom of the stairs and looked back to ask Minnie Maude to set the table in the dining room, when she saw her whisk into the cellar with what looked like the dish of crusts in her hand.

She went up the stairs slowly. Was she not giving Minnie Maude enough to eat? The girl should not have to pick at crusts. There was plenty of food in the house, and she was more than welcome to have as much as she wished. She had settled in well, both for her duties and her generally agreeable nature. In fact, Charlotte could honestly say that if Gracie had to leave – and she did – then Minnie Maude was an excellent person to replace her. She should make time to look into the matter more carefully.

But when Pitt came home he was clearly worried, and for the first time since the present case began, he wished to talk to her about it. After supper they were in the parlour, and Minnie Maude in the kitchen. She had barely told him about the soirée when he interrupted her.

'You know Adriana quite well now. You must talk to each other about many things. Does she ever mention Serafina Montserrat?' he asked.

She saw the earnestness in his face. He was not being politely interested.

'Only briefly,' she replied, trying to read his expression. 'She was very saddened by her decline.'

'And her death?'

'Of course. But since she was so . . . so damaged, so frightened, it was not the tragedy it would have been were she all right. Why are you asking, Thomas?'

'I need to know.'

'That means it has something to do with Special Branch.' The deduction was obvious. 'Did she really know something that matters even now?'

She was so used to asking questions that old habit asserted itself over her present discretion. She realised it too late. 'I'm sorry . . .'

He smiled. 'I asked you. I need to understand Adriana a great deal more than I do. Who better to ask than you? And I cannot expect you to give me the answers I need if I don't tell you what the questions are.'

His eyes were gentle, and there was an oblique humour in his face. But she heard the emotion in his voice and saw how stiffly he sat. Adriana was somehow tied into the case, and he could not tell her about the issue that kept him up late in the evenings and stopped him from sleeping through the night, no matter how tired he was. She had woken and found him lying on his back, eyes wide open. She had pretended not to know, to believe the casual air he affected when he knew she was watching him.

'What do you need to know about her?' she asked. 'She talks quite freely now. I hate breaking confidences, but you wouldn't ask if it were not necessary.'

'Do you know when she first met Serafina Montserrat?'

Charlotte thought back to their conversations. 'No. She speaks as if she has known her as long as she can remember.'

'As a child?'

'Yes. Not well. I think their encounter was brief, and at a time very painful to Adriana. They met again after Adriana was married, but I don't think she ever knew her as well as she did in the last few months. Why?'

He ignored the question. 'What does she say of her father?'

Charlotte felt increasingly uneasy. 'Quite a lot. Not so much directly, but mentioning him to do with other things. She adored him, and she had already lost her mother. He seems to have been brave, funny, kind, very clever, and to have been devoted to her. He died when she was eight. She still misses him terribly. I suppose when you lose someone as young as that you tend to idealise them a little, but if even half of what she recalls is true, he was a fine man. Certainly they were very close.'

Pitt's face was bleak, his lips pressed close together for a moment. The sorrow in him worried her.

'He was,' he answered. 'His name was Lazar Dragovic. He was a fighter for Croatian freedom from Austrian rule. He was the leader of a spectacular plot, which failed because he was betrayed by one of the conspirators. Most of them escaped but he didn't. He was beaten and then shot because he would not give away the names of the others.'

Charlotte was stunned, even though she had known from the way Adriana had spoken of it that his death had been tragic.

'I'm sorry. That's terrible. But it was thirty years ago, and in Austria. Why does it matter to Special Branch now?'

'Serafina was there. She rescued Adriana from the scene,' he said simply.

'She saw it?' Charlotte's stomach lurched and knotted into a hard pain inside her. She thought of Jemima at eight, her face still soft as a child's, her neck slender, her body innocent of shape, her eyes unafraid. She ached to reach back in time and protect the child Adriana had been, and was wounded by the impossibility of it.

Pitt nodded. 'It was Serafina who took her away. But I suppose she could not stay with her. She left her with grandparents.'

Charlotte had known Pitt long enough to make the leap of deduction. 'Did Serafina know who betrayed Adriana's father? Is that what you are afraid of? She knew, and she told Adriana, whether she meant to or not?'

'I'm afraid Adriana thought that Serafina herself did,' he admitted.

Charlotte sat frozen in her seat. She could see now why Pitt had looked so wretched. 'You think Adriana killed her out of revenge?' she said softly. 'The poor old woman was dying anyway! She wouldn't do such a thing! That's horrible!'

'Her father's death was horrible, Charlotte,' he pointed out. 'He was betrayed by his own and – worse than that – from what my informant told me, Serafina and Dragovic were lovers. That's the worst kind of betrayal. He was beaten and then killed, in front of his child. I think that warrants revenge.'

She thought of her own father and could not imagine it. She knew him only as a rather stern man, affectionate but without the passion she believed of a revolutionary: a man prepared to suffer appallingly in order to change injustice. But then how well had she known Edward Ellison? Not very. As a father – yes, but as a human being? She had taken him for granted. He was always there, calm, at the head of the table in the evenings, walking to church on Sundays, sitting in the evenings by the fire with his legs crossed and a newspaper spread open. He represented safety: the comfortable, unchanging part of life; the things you miss only when suddenly they are not there any more. Then there is a kind of loneliness you don't imagine until it happens.

For Adriana it had happened when she was a child, and horribly; in blood and pain in front of her.

'It wouldn't help,' she said aloud. 'But I suppose I can imagine it easily enough.'

'Did Adriana know it was Serafina who betrayed him?' Pitt persisted. 'She can't have known until very recently. Revenge like that is not content to wait thirty years. Think back; was there a time when you could see a change in her? Did she speak of Serafina at all? Even a chance remark in passing, a change in attitude, a shock of any sort. She can hardly have learned something like that without it affecting her profoundly.'

They sat still for several moments. Pitt glanced at the fire and put more coal on it. There was no sound from the rest of the house.

Charlotte went over every meeting in her mind, and recalled nothing that could have been such a discovery. 'I'm sorry . . .' She meant it. She was torn in her affection for Adriana, the passion and the vulnerability she saw in her. But far beyond that, she wanted to help Pitt find the truth. 'She didn't speak of Serafina often, and she didn't show any intense reaction at all, except pity. Honestly, Thomas, I don't think she remembers Serafina as part of her father's death.'

Pitt did not immediately reply.

'Are you certain she would remember any details after this length of time, even if she knew them then?' she said softly. 'Wouldn't she have seen the fear in Serafina, the knowledge that she was helpless and slowly losing her mind, as a far better revenge than a quick way out, falling asleep in her own bed, and just not waking up?'

'Yes,' Pitt admitted. 'But I'm not Adriana. Do you know her well enough to be sure of it?'

Charlotte thought for several moments, recalling every time she had seen Adriana: from the first welcome in their home, through the afternoons they had spent together, talking, laughing, admiring beauty, witnessing tragedy on the stage, each sharing with the other memories of things that had mattered to them. She did not believe Adriana could have murdered an old woman, whatever she believed her guilty of in the past.

But what would have made her believe she had? Uncontrollable temper? Bitterness? Weeping? The awareness of a terrible hatred? The last, perhaps, but would anyone show such things if they intended to murder? She had seen anger in Adriana, and consuming grief. Had that been what it was about?

She looked up at Pitt. 'I don't know. I'm sorry. I don't believe it, but that's because I like her, and I don't want to believe it. People who plan murder don't wear it in their faces, before or after. If they did, we wouldn't need detectives. You wouldn't be special, we could all do it.'

'I seem to remember you were rather good at it,' he observed.

'Out of practice,' she replied ruefully. 'I don't want to spy on Adriana, but I'll try.'

'Thank you.' He reached forward and held out his hand, palm open.

She placed her hand in his, and closed it gently.

Charlotte was in the kitchen a couple of hours later when the telephone rang in the hall. She went to answer it. Emily was put through.

'Charlotte?' Her voice was a little tentative. 'How are you?'

It was unquestionably time to accept peace, even if she had no idea what had prompted it. Had Jack said something to her? She would not ask; it did not matter at all.

'I'm very well, if a little tired of the cold,' Charlotte replied. 'How are you?'

'Oh . . . well. I went to the theatre yesterday evening and saw a new play. It was very entertaining. I think you might enjoy it . . . that is, if you and Thomas have time?' There was a note of uncertainty in her voice that was out of character for her.

'I'm sure we can make time,' Charlotte answered. 'It is very good to take one's mind from anxieties for a while. Quite often when you return to them, they appear less formidable. I imagine it will run for another few weeks, at the very least.'

'Oh . . .' The disappointment was sharp in Emily's voice

now. Clearly she had hoped for a meeting sooner and now she feared this was a rebuff. 'Yes, I'm sure it will.'

The silence was heavy. How much dare Charlotte say without breaking the trust Pitt had in her discretion? It was so easy to be led into saying what one knew, in order to mend a breach in a relationship, and then realise too late one had broken a confidence.

'But if Thomas cannot come, I would like to,' she said quickly. 'It may be one of those plays that are worth seeing more than once.'

She heard Emily breathe in quickly. 'Yes . . . yes, it is.'

It did not matter whether she went or not: the bridge had been created. 'Good,' she went on aloud. 'Because Thomas is so busy at the moment, he is often away from home late into the evening. Thank goodness Minnie Maude is working out so well.'

'Don't you miss Gracie?' Emily asked.

'Yes, of course. But I'm also happy for her.'

They talked for a few moments about trivial things: the latest word of Gracie in her new home, china she had bought and been proud to show Charlotte. None of it mattered in the slightest, it was the tone of voice, not the words, and they both understood that. But as they spoke, Charlotte became more certain all the time that Emily was afraid. Their new-found peace was still far too delicate to ask her why, so she ended the conversation cheerfully with a silly story about a mutual acquaintance. She had Emily laughing before she replaced the receiver on its hook.

After dinner, when Daniel and Jemima had gone to bed, Charlotte told Pitt of her anxiety.

'It was Emily who telephoned me earlier, while you were in your study,' she began. 'She was very agreeable. We didn't mention our differences at all.'

He was waiting for her to finish. He knew this was only the beginning of what she had to say.

'She didn't mention Jack,' she went on. 'Not that she does always . . . but . . . Don't look at me with that patient expression! I think she's worried, even frightened. Thomas, does this thing you are investigating really have anything to do with Jack? Is he making some kind of a mistake?'

'I don't know,' he said quietly. 'I'm not being oblique, I really don't.'

'Would you tell me if you did?' she asked, uncertain what answer she wanted to hear.

He smiled. He knew her so very well. 'No. Then you would feel guilty if you couldn't warn Emily. Better she blame me.'

'Thomas . . . ?'

'I don't know,' he repeated. 'I really don't. Perhaps I am the one who is mistaken, and I'm not even sure what about. You can tell Emily nothing with a clear conscience.' She wanted to ask him if he was going to be all right, but there was nothing sensible to say. She was no help to him if she behaved like a child, as if she had a right to be comforted, no matter who had to carry the burden of it. She made herself smile, and saw the relief in his eyes – and then, the moment after, the knowledge that she had understood it.

They laughed together, but it was a little shaky. They were too much aware of what could not be said.

Chapter Ten

❧

Stoker was pacing back and forth in Pitt's office, his hands pushed hard into his pockets and his outdoor scarf still wound around his neck. The windowsill behind him was white with a dusting of snow, and flakes were drifting past, almost invisible against a flat, leaden sky. There was less than a week to go before Duke Alois landed in Dover.

'It's Staum all right,' he said, stopping and facing Pitt. 'I've seen a photograph of him now.'

'What happened to the previous man?' Pitt asked.

'Took a holiday,' Stoker replied. 'Came in and told the office he'd come into a little money from some relative who'd died, and he was going away for a while. Staum was the first person to apply for the job, and no one else showed up within a day or two, so they gave it to him. Don't know what money changed hands.' He pulled his face into an expression of disgust. 'Might not have taken much.' He winced. 'On the other hand, I suppose, from what I know of Staum, he wouldn't shrink from killing the man, if it was necessary.'

Pitt felt the heaviness settle inside him. 'Then we can expect an attack in Dover itself. But I daren't take men away from the signals and points, just in case.' He was leaning back in his chair but there was no ease in him. 'The dust cart is a good idea. He can wheel the thing anywhere, and no one'll be surprised, or suspicious. Wear dirty clothes, a cap, keep his face down, and he's practically invisible.'

'Are we going to tell the local police?' Stoker asked.

'Not yet. Once they know it'll be public in hours. They won't be able to hide it. Everyone's behaviour will be different. And a man of Staum's skill will be watching to see that. They'll change their plans, and we won't know what they'll be. Of course they could do that anyway.'

Stoker's face tightened. A small muscle in his jaw flickered.

'I know,' Pitt said quietly. 'I can't find out anything more useful about Duke Alois. At least anything that seems remotely relevant to why anyone would want to kill him. He seems to be quiet, studious, well-liked . . . They say he has a nice, very dry sense of humour, and he's very fond of music, especially the heavier sort of German stuff, Beethoven's last works.'

'Doesn't make any sense.' Stoker was unhappy. 'We've missed something.'

'Perhaps that's the point,' Pitt replied thoughtfully.

'No sense?'

'Exactly. That makes it unpredictable. You can't guard against what you can't understand or foresee.'

'Are they that clever?' Stoker said doubtfully.

'Are we sure they aren't?' Pitt countered.

Stoker said nothing.

'I'm still looking into the four others who are coming with him,' Pitt went on. 'But they all seem just what you'd expect: friends, men who come from aristocratic backgrounds of a more minor sort, some army service, useful but not wanting to have a military career. Aides, a couple of servants, that sort of thing.'

'I feel like a sitting target,' Stoker said miserably, his voice edged with anger. 'I want to arrest Staum, any reason at all, but I know we need to have him where we can see him in case he leads us to other conspirators.'

'Yes we do,' Pitt agreed sharply, sitting up straight suddenly. 'Watch him. He's probably too clever to give anything away, but if he doesn't know we're onto him he may slip up, contact someone.'

'And then on the other hand, he may know very well that we're watching him, and keep our attention from what's really happening,' Stoker hunched his shoulders. 'I want to get this man.'

Pitt smiled bleakly. 'So do I, but it's second place to getting Alois in and out of Britain safely.'

'Yes, sir.'

This time Pitt was granted fifteen minutes with the Prime Minister without any difficulty. He did not waste any of it.

'Anything further?' Salisbury asked, standing with his back to the fire, his long face grave, his fluff of white hair standing on end as if he had run his fingers through it.

'Yes, my lord,' Pitt replied. 'We know who is in place in Dover, and at the vulnerable places on the railway line. We don't know where they intend to strike. Some of them may be decoys, because we know them, and I'd expect any attack would actually be done by people we don't know.'

Salisbury sighed. 'What a bloody mess. Anything good in it at all? Such as who is behind it, and why? Why Duke Alois, and why here in England?'

'The more I learn about Duke Alois the less sure I am

whether he is of any tactical value himself, or if he's just convenient.'

Salisbury's eyebrows rose but he smiled. 'Really . . .' His expression was without comment, but the amusement in his eyes conveyed his opinion of many minor royal dukes. Europe was teeming with distant relatives of Queen Victoria, and at one time or another he had had dealings with most of them. 'So he would be an incidental victim, killed to make a point,' he said.

'Yes, sir. Most anarchists' victims are. Wealthy, privileged, titled, any of that is an offence in itself. Doesn't matter what you do after that, as far as they are concerned. One person's blood is as good as another's to protest with.'

'As long as it isn't your own,' Salisbury added a little acidly.

'For some,' Pitt agreed. 'For others that's all part of it. Die for the cause.'

'God Almighty! What on earth do we do about them? How do you fight a madman?'

'Carefully,' Pitt shrugged. 'With knowledge, observation, and keeping in mind that he is mad, so don't look for sanity in what he does, only display, and passion.'

'What do they actually want? Do you know?'

'I'm not sure that they do,' Pitt answered. 'Except change. They all want change.'

'So they can be the ones with power, money and privilege.' It was a conclusion rather than a question.

'Probably, yes. But they are not looking that far ahead. If they were, they'd know that sporadic assassination like this hasn't ever achieved social change. It frightens people, and they get angry. If they kill Duke Alois they'll make him a martyr.'

'And us incompetent fools!' Salisbury said bitterly. 'Which

is probably what they are really after. They are Britain's enemies. Duke Alois is just the means to an end, poor devil.'

'Yes, sir. As they see it, to the greater good.'

'Stop them, Pitt. If they win, not just Britain but all civilised mankind is the loser. We can't be held ransom to fear like this.'

Pitt had known what Salisbury would say, but he still had to try.

'Are you sure there is no point in letting him know how serious the threat is, and asking him to come at another time?'

'Yes, I'm quite sure,' Salisbury replied.

Pitt drew in his breath to argue, and decided against it.

Salisbury looked at him wearily. 'I'm sure because I have already tried. He insists he will be perfectly safe in your hands.'

'Yes, sir,' Pitt replied, his mind using many different and far less civil words.

Salisbury smiled. 'Quite,' he said grimly.

Charlotte was in the hall about to pick up the telephone when she saw Minnie Maude come out of the cellar door and catch sight of her. Minnie Maude coloured unhappily, brushed something off her arms, gave a brief smile, which was a little shaky, and turned away.

Charlotte ignored the telephone. Something was troubling the girl and it was time Charlotte learned what it was. She followed Minnie Maude into the kitchen. She was standing at the sink with a string of onions on the bench and a knife in her hand. She had cut into the first onion and the pungency of it was in the air already.

The table was completely cleared away, the dishes washed and dried and back on the dresser. An uneaten slice of toast had disappeared. Was that why Minnie Maude had been in the cellar, to eat it herself? Had she grown up in such poverty that food was still so treasured that she felt compelled to take scraps in secret?

'Minnie Maude,' Charlotte spoke gently.

Minnie Maude turned around. Her eyes were red, perhaps from the onion, but she looked afraid.

Charlotte felt a tug of pity, and of guilt. The girl was only four or five years older than Jemima, and could look forward to possibly the rest of her life as a servant in someone else's home, with only one room she could call her own. In this house she was the only resident servant so there was not even anyone else to befriend. She knew she was replacing Gracie, who had been so loved. The loneliness, the constant effort to be good enough, must be a burden at times too heavy, and yet she had nowhere to escape it, except the cellar.

'Minnie Maude,' Charlotte said again, this time smiling, 'I think it would be a good idea if you toasted some teacakes. I know we have some. Let's have them hot-buttered, with a cup of tea. Perhaps in half an hour? You work hard. Elevenses would be nice for both of us.'

Minnie Maude's shoulders relaxed. 'Yes, ma'am. I'll toast 'em then.' Clearly she had been expecting Charlotte to say something else, something she feared.

'Are you getting enough to eat, Minnie Maude?' Charlotte asked. 'You may have as much as you wish, you know? If necessary, please cook more. We have no need to restrain ourselves. Just don't waste it.' She smiled. 'We have had our difficult times in the past when it mattered very much, and it is good not to forget them. But now there is more than enough for you to eat as you like.'

'I'm . . . I'm fine, ma'am.' Minnie Maude's face coloured pink with embarrassment, but she said nothing more. Very slowly, uncertain if she had permission to or not, she turned back to continue cutting the onions.

Charlotte knew she had not arrived at the truth. Were the trips to the cellar nothing to do with food, but perhaps simply to be alone? That made no sense. The cellar was cold. Minnie Maude had a perfectly good bedroom upstairs, which was properly furnished and warm. The problem was something else. Temporarily defeated, she went back to the hall.

She was almost beside the telephone when it rang. She picked it off its hook and answered. Adriana Blantyre was put through. Her voice was a little altered by the machine, but still perfectly recognisable with its huskiness, and very slight accent.

'How are you?' Adriana asked. 'I am sorry to call you so hastily. This is all most improper, but there is an exhibition on in a private gallery which I am very eager to see, and I thought you might enjoy it too. Have you ever heard of Heinrich Schliemann?'

'Of course!' Charlotte said quickly. 'He discovered the ruins of Troy, through his love of Homer. He died a few years ago. Is there something of his work on display?' It was not difficult to fill her voice with enthusiasm. It was the perfect opening for her to see Adriana again, and perhaps learn something of the evidence Pitt needed. She hoped fervently that it would prove Adriana innocent.

'Today,' Adriana replied instantly, excitement lifting her voice. 'I only just heard of it. I've cancelled my other engagements and I'm going. But it would be so much more fun if you were to come with me. Please don't feel obliged . . . but if you can . . .'

Charlotte needed no time to consider. 'I can. It has waited for thousands of years. That is more than long enough. We shall make a journey through time, and for a few hours today will disappear. Where is it, and where shall we meet?'

'I shall come for you in my carriage in an hour. Is that too early?'

'No, not at all. I assure you, I have nothing more exciting than that to do, and anything else that arises can wait.'

'Then I shall see you in an hour. Goodbye.'

Charlotte said goodbye also, and replaced the receiver. She would tell Minnie Maude where she was going, and then change into the smartest morning dress she had and prepare to be charming, friendly, intelligent, and – if there were no escape – to betray as well.

She sat in front of her bedroom dressing mirror. She stared at her reflection, and found it difficult to face. She despised what she was about to do, and yet she could see no alternative, except refusing to help Pitt. And he was doing what he had to. Someone had murdered Serafina, lying old, frightened and alone in her bed, terrified of the darkness that was closing in on her mind, robbing her of everything she had been, betraying her in a way against which there was no defence.

Charlotte had no choice, except cowardice. All she could hope was that her discoveries would prove Adriana innocent, not guilty.

They arrived at the exhibition in the late morning. As soon as they entered the doors, the past closed around them. It was as much about Schliemann himself as the things he had discovered. He had died in Naples, the day after Christmas in 1890, but his energy and the power of his dreams filled the gallery. A large portrait of him hung in the entrance: a balding man with spectacles, wearing a neat formal suit with a high-buttoned waistcoat. He looked to be in his late fifties, or early sixties.

'That's not how I imagined him,' Adriana said with a little shrug. 'He should be fierce, and magnificent, a man who would have fitted into Troy itself.'

Charlotte smiled. 'Just don't tell me that Helen of Troy was really quite plain. I couldn't bear it.'

Adriana laughed. 'They burned the topless towers of Ilium for her, so the poets tell us.' Her eye caught another portrait on the wall a few yards away. It showed a dark-haired woman, quite young, wearing a magnificent headdress with long, trailing pieces at the ears, and also a heavy necklace comprised of fifteen or more strands of gold.

Charlotte walked over to it, Adriana immediately behind her.

'She's rather beautiful,' Charlotte said, regarding her closely. She read the inscription below: 'Sophie Schliemann, wearing the treasures discovered at Hisarlik, said to be the jewels of Helen of Troy.' She turned to Adriana. 'I wonder what Helen was really like. I can't imagine anyone being so beautiful that a whole city and all its people were ruined for love of her. Not to mention an eleven-year war, with all the death and mutilation that must have cost. Is any love worth that?'

'No,' Adriana said without hesitation. 'It was nothing to do with love. But I have often wondered about love and beauty. To marry a woman because of the way she looks, when you do not care about who she is inside the shell of appearance, is no more than acquiring a work of art for the pleasure it gives you to look at it, or to exhibit it to others. If she is not a companion to you, one with whom you share your dreams, your laughter and pain, with whom you are not alone, is that not like buying food you cannot eat?'

Adriana's face was quite calm, the skin unblemished across its perfect bones, her eyes fathomless.

Charlotte had a sudden vision of the most terrible emptiness, a void she had never imagined before. Was that how Blantyre felt about Adriana: a fragile, exquisite possession? What would he feel when the first lines appeared, when the bloom faded from her cheeks, when her hair thinned and turned grey, when she no longer moved with such grace?

Charlotte had always secretly wanted to be beautiful: not merely handsome, as she was, but possessed of the kind of beauty that dazzles, as Vespasia had been. Now she was dizzy with gratitude that she was not. Pitt was not only her husband, he was the dearest, most intimate friend she had ever had, closer than Emily, or anyone else. She found she was smiling widely, with an inner light, as she replied, 'Poor Helen. Do you suppose that is all it was: a squabble over possessions that a whole nation paid for?'

'No,' Adriana shook her head. 'The classical Greek idea of beauty was as much of the mind as of the face. She must have been wise and honest and brave as well.'

'And gentle?' Charlotte continued. 'Do you think she had a wild and vivid sense of humour as well? And that she was quick to forgive, and generous of spirit?'

Adriana laughed. 'Yes! And no wonder they burned Troy for her! I'm surprised it wasn't the whole of Asia Minor! Let's look at the rest of this.' She touched Charlotte's arm and they moved forward together, marvelling at the ornaments, the golden masks, the photographs of the ruins, and the walls that must once have kept out the armies of Agamemnon and the heroes of legend.

'How much of it do you think is true?' Charlotte said after several minutes of silence. She must not waste this time when she could speak obliquely, and perhaps learn answers. 'Do you think they felt all the same things we do: envy, fear, the hunger for revenge for wrongs we can't forget?' Was she being too obvious now?

Adriana turned from the photographs she was looking at and faced her. 'Of course. Don't you?' A flicker of fear crossed her face. 'Those things never change.'

Charlotte fought to bring back schoolroom memories. 'Agamemnon killed his daughter, didn't he? A sacrifice to the gods to make the winds turn and carry his armies to Troy. And when he came home again eleven years later, his wife killed him for it.'

'Yes,' Adriana agreed. 'I can understand that. Mind, she had married his brother in the meantime, so there were a lot of different emotions mixed up in it. And then her son killed her, and on and on. It was a pretty nasty mess.'

'Revenge often is,' Charlotte said with a sudden change of tone, as if they were speaking of something present.

Adriana looked at her curiously. 'You say that as if they were people you knew.'

'Aren't all good stories really about people we know?'

Adriana thought for a moment. 'I suppose they are.' She gave a sudden, brilliant smile. 'I knew coming here with you would be more fun than with anyone else! Can you spare time to have luncheon as well? There is a most excellent place near here where the chef is Croatian. I would like you to taste a little of the food from my country. It is not so very different. You will not find it too strong, or too heavy.'

'I would be delighted,' Charlotte said sincerely. 'I know very little about Croatia. Please tell me more.'

'That is a dangerous request,' Adriana said happily. 'You may wish you had never asked. Stop me when it gets dark and you have to go home.'

Charlotte felt the guilt well up inside her, but it was too late now to turn back. 'I will,' she promised. 'Let us see the end of what Mr Schliemann found in Troy, and Mycenae.'

'Did you know he spoke thirteen different languages?' Adriana asked. 'He wrote in his diary in the language of whatever country he was in. English, French, Dutch, Spanish, Portuguese, Swedish, Italian, Greek, Latin, Russian, Arabic, and Turkish. And German, of course. He was German.' Her face was animated with excitement and admiration.

'He actually wrote a paper on Troy in Ancient Greek,' she went on. 'He was an extraordinary man. He made and spent at least two fortunes. He named his children Andromache and Agamemnon. He allowed them to be baptised, but placed a copy of *The Iliad* on their heads at the time, and recited a hundred hexameters of it. Wouldn't life be so much emptier without the world's eccentrics?' She was laughing as she said it, but there was a ring of passion in her voice and a vividness in her face that gave her the sort of beauty that made others in the room turn to look at her, as if she might, for an instant, have been Helen herself.

Charlotte thought back to the intensity of emotion she had seen in Blantyre's face when he looked at her: the protection; the pride; something that could have been lingering amazement that she should have chosen him, when perhaps she had had a dozen suitors, a score. How much did her beauty matter to him? Would he still have loved her had she been ordinary to look at, but with the same consuming emotions? How much was her vulnerability also a part of it, his need to protect her? Was that even more necessary to him than it was to her?

Charlotte knew as that thought filled her mind that she had to learn more about Croatia, about the past there, about Adriana's father's death, and above all about Serafina Montserrat.

They finished the tour of the exhibits, still talking about them with interest. Adriana's carriage took them to luncheon at the restaurant she had spoken of. She was eager to share everything about her country and the culture in which she had grown up. She had had too few people with whom she could bring back memories and describe for them what she had seen and loved.

'You'll enjoy this,' she said as each new dish was brought. 'I used to like this when I was a child. My grandmother showed me how it was made. And this was always one of my favourites. It is mostly rice with tiny little shellfish, and very delicate herbs. The art is all in cooking it to just the right tenderness, and being careful with the seasoning. Too strong and it is horrible.'

'Do the Croatians eat a lot of fish?' Charlotte asked.

'Yes. I don't know why, except that it's easy, and not very expensive.'

'And like us, you have a long coastline,' Charlotte added.

Adriana gazed at some vision inside her own mind, perhaps at times in the past. 'Ah,' she let out a sigh. 'Beautiful as England is, you've never seen a shore like ours. The air is warm, and the sky seems so high, with tiny drifting clouds in wonderful shapes, delicate, like feathers, and bright. The sand is pale, no shingle, and the water is colours you wouldn't believe. There are a thousand islands, and the southernmost are nearly tropical.'

Charlotte tried to see it in her mind. She pictured blue water bright in the sun, warmth that seeped through the skin to the bones. She found she was smiling.

The first course came and it was as delicious as Adriana had said.

'Croatia is very old,' Adriana went on. 'Not older than England, but nearer to the middle of things. We became part of the Roman Empire in AD 9, and of course we had Greek colonies before that. In AD 305 the Roman Emperor Diocletian built a palace in Split. The very last Emperor, Julius Nepos, ruled from there, until he was killed in AD 408. You see, we too have great Roman ruins.' She said it with pride, as if it were a link between them.

'Our first king, Tomislav, was crowned in AD 925.' She

stopped and pulled her face into an expression of resignation. 'In 1102 we entered a union with Hungary; that would be just after you were conquered by William of Normandy. Then in 1526 we chose a Habsburg king, and I suppose that was the beginning of the end. At least that is what my father used to say.' The pain shot through her voice and was completely unguarded in her eyes. She looked down quickly. 'That was about the time of your Queen Elizabeth, wasn't it?'

'Yes, yes, it was,' Charlotte said quickly, struggling to remember. Elizabeth had died around 1600, so it must be close. She felt brutal, but she had no better chance than this. She might betray Adriana's guilt, but on the other hand she might prove her innocence. That would be infinitely worth all her efforts. The discomfort she felt now was nothing.

The second course came, a white fish baked in vine leaves with vegetables Charlotte was unfamiliar with. She tried them, tentatively at first, then, aware that Adriana was watching her, with more relish. Their time was slipping away. She must introduce the subject of Serafina, or she would have lost the opportunity. How could she do it without being appallingly clumsy or, on the other hand, so devious as to make that obvious as well, and perhaps even more offensive?

'I wish I could travel,' she said, not knowing where that subject might lead. 'You must miss your home. I mean the one where you grew up.'

Adriana smiled with an edge of sadness. 'Sometimes,' she admitted.

'Do you know other people who have lived there, beside Mr Blantyre, of course?'

'Not many, I'm afraid. Perhaps I should seek a little harder, but it seems so . . . forced.'

Charlotte took a deep breath. 'Did you know Mrs

Montserrat, who died recently? She lived in Croatia once, I believe.'

Adriana looked surprised. 'Did you know her? You never mentioned it before.' Her voice dropped. 'Poor Serafina. That was a terrible way to die.'

Charlotte struggled to keep from contradicting herself and letting too much of the truth into her questions.

'Was it?' She affected ignorance. 'I know very little. I'm sorry if I gave the impression I knew her myself. She was a great friend of my aunt Vespasia – Lady Vespasia Cumming-Gould.'

'Lady Vespasia is your aunt?' Adriana said with delight.

Charlotte had said it too easily and now she was embarrassed, as if she had pretended to a relationship that did not exist. 'Actually she is my sister's great-aunt, by marriage to her first husband. But we hold her in higher regard and affection than any other relative we have.'

'So would I,' Adriana agreed. 'She is quite marvellous.'

Charlotte could not afford to let the conversation slide away from Serafina. 'I'm so sorry about Mrs Montserrat. Aunt Vespasia said she died quite peacefully. At least I thought that was what she said. Was I not listening properly? Or was she . . . ? No, Aunt Vespasia would never circle around the truth to make it meaningless.'

Adriana looked down at the table. 'No. She wouldn't. She was a fighter for freedom too, I believe.'

'Like Mrs Montserrat,' Charlotte agreed. 'They knew each other long ago. Aunt Vespasia said Mrs Montserrat was very brave – and outspoken in her beliefs.'

Adriana smiled. 'Yes, she was. My father told me about her . . .' She struggled for a moment, trying to catch her breath and steady her voice before going on. 'He used to say she was the bravest of all of them. Sometimes she succeeded just because no one expected a woman to ride all night through the forest, and then be able to think clearly by daylight, and even hold a gun steady and shoot.' She ignored the tears filling her eyes. 'I remember her laughter. And her singing. She had a lovely voice. I'm sorry.' She lowered her eyes and the tears ran down her cheeks. Blindly she fumbled in her reticule for a handkerchief, finally finding it and blowing her nose gently.

'There is no need to apologise,' Charlotte assured her. 'The loss of your father must have been terrible, and I know from what you say that you still miss him very much. Did you say that Serafina was there?'

Adriana was surprised. 'Yes. I . . . I must have. I don't talk about it because it always makes me lose my composure. I apologise. This is ridiculous. Everyone must be looking at me.'

'Lots of people were looking at you anyway,' Charlotte responded with a smile. 'Men look at beautiful women with pleasure, women with envy, and if they are stylish as well, to see what they might copy. Or the worst of them, to see if they can see a flaw.'

'Then I will have satisfied them,' Adriana said wryly.

'Nonsense. There is nothing wrong with a tender heart,' Charlotte assured her. She was losing her grip on the conversation. It was slipping away into the general again. 'Did Mrs Montserrat talk to you about your father? That must have been sweet as well as painful for you, because there would be no one else who knew him for you to remember with, or hear stories of his courage, or just the little things he liked and disliked.'

Adriana's eyes softened. 'Yes. She told me about his love of history, and how he could tell all the old tales of the medieval heroes: Porga who went to the Byzantine Emperor Heraclius, and he had the Pope send Christian missionaries in AD 640. And of Duke Branimir, and on and on. She knew the names of them all, and what they did, even though she was Italian. She enabled me to recall the stories he told me, when I had only bits of them in my mind.'

Charlotte tried to imagine Adriana sitting beside Serafina's bed waiting patiently as the old woman salvaged fragments from her wandering mind and recreated them for her, bringing back for a brief while the presence of her beloved father.

Did she remember that she had seen him beaten, covered in his own blood, and then bent to his knees and shot in the back of the head? The sight of faces distorted with rage, the gleam of light on gun barrels, the cries of terror and pain, then the stillness and the smell of gun smoke and blood, her father's blood. And then Serafina coming, grasping her, holding her, hurrying her away, perhaps on horseback, on the saddle in front of her as she rode like a wild thing to escape, to protect the child. But nothing anyone could do would protect her from her own nightmares for the rest of her life.

Looking at Adriana now, so exquisitely dressed, her skin paper white, Charlotte could see the demons were still in her eyes. If Serafina had let something slip, been careless even in a couple of words, had she let Adriana know that it was she who had betrayed Lazar Dragovic?

Or was it the name of someone else who had?

It was rude, an intrusion, to stare at her now, but Charlotte would never have another chance to see the truth. She could not afford to pass it by, however indelicate it was.

'I'm so sorry she's gone,' she said to Adriana. 'But Aunt Vespasia told me it was peaceful. As if she had taken too much laudanum, and simply gone to sleep.' Was that enough? It was a lie, of course. It was Pitt who had told her, but it was unimportant.

Adriana stared at her. 'Would a double dose of laudanum kill you?'

Charlotte hesitated. What should she say? Evade the truth, or tell it and see how Adriana reacted? She had to know. Pitt's case might rest on it, and other people's lives.

'No,' she answered levelly. 'I believe it takes far more than that, several times a single dose.'

Everyone else in the restaurant seemed as if they were moving slowly, asleep, fumbling their way.

Adriana stared at her. She started to speak but her mouth was so dry her voice faltered. She tried again. 'Several times?'

Charlotte could not stop now, or retreat. 'Apparently.'

'Then . . .' Adriana did not finish the sentence, but it was not necessary. They both knew what the end had to be.

'I'm sorry,' Charlotte said softly. 'Perhaps I should not have told you. Would a lie, or at least an evasion, have been better?'

'No.' Adriana sat motionless for a few more moments. 'I'm sorry, I can't eat any more. I think I need to go home. Do you know who gave it to her? Was it Nerissa Freemarsh, do you think? Serafina was so distressed by her failing memory . . . her mind . . .' She did not complete the train of thought.

'I don't know,' Charlotte said honestly. 'It might be considered an act of mercy by some, but the law would regard it as murder, all the same.'

'Perhaps she took it herself?' Adriana said desperately.

Charlotte knew that was not possible. Care had been taken that it should not be, knowing Serafina's own fear. Perhaps this was not the time to say so.

'Perhaps,' she agreed. 'She was terribly afraid of being indiscreet and letting slip old secrets that might damage someone who is still alive and vulnerable. I have no idea who that could be, or indeed if there is such a person. Do you know?'

'No . . . she said nothing to me.' Adriana spoke hesitantly, as if she were raking her memory for anything Serafina might have said.

'No one at all?' Charlotte pressed. 'That would explain it, if she took it herself.' Was she being deliberately and pointlessly cruel?

'Serafina knew Lord Tregarron,' Adriana said tentatively. 'Quite well, from what she said.'

Charlotte was puzzled. There had been the faintest flicker of amusement in Adriana's eyes, gone again the next instant. Tregarron was at least twenty-five years younger than Serafina, if not more. Thirty-five years ago that might have mattered less, but then he would have been very young, no more than a boy, and she in her late thirties. That was ridiculous. Adriana must be mistaken.

'Could it have been someone else, whose name sounded like his?' she suggested. 'Someone Austrian, or Hungarian, for example?'

'No, it was Tregarron,' Adriana insisted. 'He visited her in Dorchester Terrace.'

'Then she could not have known him far in the past.'

'No. I must have misunderstood that.' Adriana looked at Charlotte's plate and the unfinished dessert.

'Oh, I've had sufficient,' Charlotte said quickly. 'Let us go. It was a delicious meal. I shall have to eat Croatian food again. I had no idea it was so very good. Thank you for all you've shown me, and for the pleasure of your company.'

Adriana smiled, her composure almost returned. 'Didn't your Lord Byron say that happiness was born a twin? Pleasures tasted alone lose half their savour. Let us go and find the carriage.'

Charlotte arrived home in the middle of the afternoon, a trifle earlier than she had expected. She had much more

301

information to give Pitt but no conclusions, other than the growing certainty in her own mind that Serafina had known who had betrayed Lazar Dragovic, but for some reason had never spoken of it to anyone. Was that the secret she had been so afraid of letting slip? It made sense. At least to Adriana Dragovic, it still mattered passionately. Serafina had always tried to protect her, whether out of love or loyalty to Lazar, or simply human decency. She would have known what that knowledge would do to Adriana now.

Charlotte walked down the hall to the kitchen. It was too early for Daniel and Jemima to be home from school, but she was surprised to find the kitchen empty. Minnie Maude was not in the scullery either, nor was she in the dining room or the parlour. Could she be out shopping? Most of the household goods they required were delivered, and such as needed to be bought in person were gone for in the morning.

Charlotte went up the stairs and looked for Minnie Maude without finding her. Now she was worried. She even looked in the back garden to see if she could have tripped and hurt herself too badly to get up, or even to crawl back inside. She knew even as she did it that that was absurd. Unless she was unconscious, she would have made her way.

She must be in the cellar; it was the only place left. But Charlotte had been home a quarter of an hour! Why on earth would Minnie Maude be in the cellar for that length of time? There was nothing down there that could take so long to collect, and it would be perishing cold.

She opened the door. The light was on – she could see its dim glow from the top step. Had Minnie Maude slipped and fallen here? She went down quickly now, holding on to the handrail. Minnie Maude was sitting on a cushion in the corner, a blanket wrapped around her, and in her arms a small, dirty and extremely scruffy little dog, with a red ribbon around its neck. Minnie Maude looked up at her with wide, frightened eyes.

Charlotte took a deep breath.

'For goodness' sake bring it upstairs into the kitchen,' she said, trying to keep the overwhelming emotion inside her in some kind of control. Relief, pity, a drowning comprehension of Minnie Maude's loneliness, and all the conflicting feelings for Adriana, and for Serafina, everything to do with need and loss churned in her mind. 'And wash it!' she went on. 'It's filthy! I suppose it will be, with living in the coal cellar.'

Minnie Maude climbed to her feet slowly, still holding the dog.

'You'd better give it some dinner,' Charlotte added. 'Something warm. It's only very young, by the look of it.'

'Are you going to put it out?' Minnie Maude's face was white with fear and she held the animal so tightly it cried.

'I dare say the cats won't like it,' Charlotte replied obliquely. 'But they'll just have to get used to it. We'll find it a basket. Wash it in the scullery sink, or you'll have coal dust all over the place.'

Minnie Maude took a long, shuddering breath and her face filled with hope.

Charlotte turned away to go up the stairs. She did not want Minnie Maude to think she could get away with absolutely anything. 'Has it a name?' she said huskily.

'Uffie,' Minnie Maude said. 'But you can change it if you want to.'

'Uffie seems perfectly good to me,' Charlotte replied. 'Bring her, or is it him, upstairs, and don't put her down until you get to the scullery, or you'll spend the rest of the day getting coal dust out of the carpets, and we'll all have no dinner.'

'I'll carry 'er ter the kitchen,' Minnie Maude promised

fervently. 'An' I'll see she don't make a mess anywhere, I promise. She's ever so good.'

She won't be, Charlotte thought, not when she's warm enough and properly fed, and realises she can stay. But maybe that is better. 'She's your responsibility,' she warned as she held the cellar door open. Minnie Maude walked through into the hall, still holding the dog close to her, her face shining with happiness.

When Pitt returned home, late and tired, Charlotte told him very briefly about the dog, not as a question but simply so he would not be taken by surprise when he found the little animal in the scullery. Daniel and Jemima had both fallen instantly in love with it, and there was no further decision to be made.

In the evening, alone with the parlour fire dying down and the embers settling in the hearth, Charlotte told Pitt what she had learned from Adriana.

'Are you sure she said Tregarron?' he asked, sitting a little forward in his chair.

'Yes. But of course I'm not sure that is what Serafina said, or if it was, that it was what she meant. But I believe Serafina knew who betrayed Lazar Dragovic, and that whether she meant to tell her or not, somehow Adriana realised who it was.'

'Well it won't have been Tregarron,' Pitt said reasonably. 'He was too young to have been involved at all, and was here in England at boarding school anyway. He would have been about fourteen at the time. Why would Adriana have killed Serafina if she knew? Who would she be protecting? That doesn't make any sense.'

'Yes it does,' Charlotte said so quickly her voice was almost lost in the crackle from the fire as another log fell apart in a shower of sparks. 'If it was Serafina herself who betrayed Dragovic.'

'Serafina?' He was startled. 'But she was on the same side. And she rescued Adriana. My sources say she and Dragovic were lovers, at least for a while.'

'Thomas, don't be so naïve,' she said exasperatedly. 'The most passionate lovers also make the bitterest enemies, at times. And who knows now, or even then, if they were really lovers? Perhaps either one of them was only using the other?'

He started to argue. 'But they were both fighting for the same . . .' He tailed off.

'Balkan politics are not so simple,' she said. 'At least that is what I hear from those who know. And love affairs hardly ever are.'

He smiled with a flicker of ironic humour. 'At least that is what you hear from those who know?'

She blushed very slightly. 'Yes.'

'Do you think Adriana believed that Serafina betrayed her father?' he said, all humour vanished.

'I think it's more likely than that Nerissa Freemarsh had the nerve to murder her aunt out of frustration because she didn't die quickly enough,' she said quietly.

'And Tregarron?' he asked. 'What was he doing at Dorchester Terrace?'

'I don't know,' she admitted. 'Perhaps trying to make sure that Serafina didn't tell any more secrets in her confused state. Ones we don't even know about. They would be old, but perhaps still embarrassing. He's responsible for a lot of the British relations with the Austrian Empire, and the countries around its borders. Maybe Poland, the Ukraine, the Ottoman Empire? Even if the people concerned are dead, or out of office, the matters might still be better left alone.'

'Who could she tell?' he said thoughtfully. 'Not many people came to see her.'

'Would he leave it to chance? Would you?'

'No.' He sighed and leaned back again. 'Tomorrow I had better go and speak to Nerissa Freemarsh, and to Tucker again. I don't think it can have anything to do with . . . present cases . . . but I need to be certain. Thank you.'

She was puzzled.

'For questioning Adriana,' he explained. 'I know you didn't wish to.'

'Oh. No. Thomas, you don't mind about Uffie, do you?'

'What?'

'The dog.'

He laughed quietly, very aware of all the lingering pain there was. 'No, of course I don't.'

In the morning Pitt went to see Narraway and told him of Charlotte's conversation with Adriana Blantyre, and the conclusions he was forced to draw from it.

'I was hoping the answer would be different,' Narraway said quietly. 'I was sure it had to do with this wretched Duke Alois threat, but it seems the timing is coincidental after all. I'm sorry. What are you going to do?'

'Go back to Dorchester Terrace and check the amount of laudanum there was in the house,' Pitt replied. 'Exactly who had access to it, if anyone from outside could have had.'

'You think she learned the truth from Serafina, went away and thought about it, then came back with laudanum? That's cold-blooded.'

'If Serafina betrayed her father to his death, perhaps the blood for that never goes cold. I wish I were wrong.'

Narraway spread his hands in a small, rueful gesture, filled with a surprising gentleness. He said nothing, for which Pitt was grateful. Empty words would only hurt now.

At Dorchester Terrace he spoke first with Miss Tucker and then with Nerissa Freemarsh. He checked the laudanum as he had told Narraway he would. The conclusion was inescapable. Whoever had given her the extra dosage had brought it with them. Killing her had been carefully planned.

Tucker could add little, merely confirm what she had already said. Yes, Mrs Blantyre had called several times, bringing flowers and once a box of candied fruit. She was always kind. Yes, she had seemed distressed the last time she had called on the evening of Mrs Montserrat's death. Pale-faced, Tucker agreed that she had spent some time alone in the bedroom. It had seemed to be what Mrs Montserrat had wanted.

With Nerissa it was a different matter. She was tense as she came into the housekeeper's sitting room, and closed the door behind her with a sharp snap. She was still in black, but today she had several rows of very fine jet beads around her neck, and excellent quality jet earrings, which added a fashionable touch to her appearance.

'I don't know what else there is that I can tell you, Mr Pitt,' she said with a certain briskness. Being mistress of the house at last gave her a new air of confidence. The slightly nervous demeanour was gone. She stood straighter and somehow she looked taller. Perhaps she had new boots with a higher heel. Under the swirl of her black bombazine skirt it was not possible to tell. Unquestionably there was a touch of colour in her skin.

Pitt had decided to be totally discreet. The time left before Duke Alois's visit was very short and he could spare none of it in softening his approach.

'Did Lord Tregarron visit here often?' he asked.

'Lord Tregarron?' she repeated.

She was playing for time. It was a question she had not expected and she needed to think what to say.

'Is that something you find difficult to answer, Miss Freemarsh?' He met her eyes challengingly. 'Why would that be? Surely he did not ask anyone to keep that fact hidden?'

Now there was an angry flush in her cheeks. 'Of course not! That is absurd. I was trying to recollect how often he did come.'

'And have you succeeded?'

'Succeeded? In what? I don't know what you mean. It had nothing to do with me. He came to visit my aunt because he had heard she was ill, and he knew how much she had done for England in her youth, particularly with regard to the Austrian Empire, and our relationship with Vienna.'

'How very generous of him,' Pitt said with only the slightest asperity in his voice. 'Since as far as I can learn, Mrs Montserrat was passionately on the side of the rebels against the Habsburg throne. Was that not so? Was she a spy for them, perhaps, planted there to betray the fighters for more freedom?'

Now she was really angry. 'That is a dreadful thing to say! And completely irresponsible. But—' Suddenly she stopped as if a new and terrible thought had filled her mind. 'I . . . I had not even . . .' She blinked. 'I don't know, Mr Pitt. She always said . . .' Again she stopped. 'Now I don't know. Perhaps that was what it was all about. It would explain Mrs Blantyre . . .' Her hand had flown to her mouth as if to stop herself from crying out. Now it fell to her side again. 'I think perhaps I had better say no more. I would not wish to be unjust to anyone.'

He felt cold, as though the fire had died, instead of burning up hot and red in the hearth so the whole chimney breast was warm.

'Mrs Blantyre visited your aunt quite often, including the evening she died?' His voice sounded hollow.

'Yes . . . but . . . yes, she did.'

'Alone?'

'Yes. Mr Blantyre remained downstairs. He thought it would be less of a strain on Mrs Montserrat. She did not find it easy to speak to several people at a time. And sometimes they would converse in Italian, which he does not speak – at least not fluently.'

'I see. Does he speak Croatian?'

'I have no idea.' Her face was very pale. She sat rigidly, as if her bodice were suddenly constrictingly tight. 'Perhaps. He speaks German, I know. He spent quite a lot of time in Vienna.'

'I see. Thank you.' It left him no choice. He must go and question Adriana Blantyre. There was nothing to be gained by delaying it, not as he wished to. If he went now, Blantyre himself might still be at home. That would make it more difficult, more embarrassing and emotionally wrenching, but it was the right way to do it.

He thanked Nerissa again and left Dorchester Terrace to walk the short distance to Blantyre's house. It was no more than half a mile.

He was admitted by the butler and Blantyre himself met him in the hall.

'Has something happened?' he asked, searching Pitt's face. 'Some word of Duke Alois?'

'No. It concerns Serafina Montserrat's death.'

'Oh?' Blantyre looked tired and his face was deeply lined. He waved the butler away and the man disappeared obediently, leaving them standing alone in the middle of the beautiful hall. 'Have you learned something further?'

'I am not certain, but it begins to look like it,' Pitt replied. It was the worst part of his position as Head of Special Branch, and he could pass it to no one else. Blantyre had been more than a friend; he had gone out of his way, even taken professional risks, in order to help Pitt learn the reality of the threat to Duke Alois and persuade the Prime Minister to take the issue seriously. It made this investigation acutely painful, but it did not relieve him of the necessity of pursuing it.

Blantyre frowned. When he spoke his voice was level and perfectly under control. 'There's something I can do? I know nothing about her death at all. Until you told me otherwise, I assumed it was natural. Then when you mentioned the laudanum, I thought perhaps she had dreaded the losing of her mind to the point where suicide had seemed preferable. Is that not the case?'

'Is it possible that Serafina was working for the Austrian monarchy all the time, and that it was she who betrayed Lazar Dragovic to his death?' Pitt asked.

'Dear God!' Blantyre gasped and swayed a little on his feet. Then he turned and strode across the floor to the foot of the stairs. He grasped the banister, hesitated a moment, then started up.

Pitt followed after him, seized by a shadow of the same fear without any idea why. Could Charlotte have let something slip, without realising it?

Blantyre increased his speed, taking the steps two at a time. He reached the landing and went to the second door. He knocked, then stood with his hand still raised. He turned to Pitt a couple of yards behind him. There was a terrible silence.

Blantyre lowered his hand and turned the knob. He pushed the door open and walked into the room.

The curtains were still closed but there was sufficient daylight through them to find the way across to the big bed, and to see Adriana's black hair fanned across the pillow.

'Adriana!' Blantyre choked on the word.

Pitt waited, his heart pounding.

'Adriana!' Blantyre cried out loudly. He lurched forward and grasped her arm where it lay on the coverlet. She did not move.

Pitt looked and saw the empty glass on the bedside table, and the small piece of folded paper, such as holds a medicinal powder. He would not need to taste it to know what it was.

He walked silently over to Blantyre and put his hand on his shoulder.

Blantyre buckled at the knees and collapsed onto the floor, his body racked with pain, his sobs hollow, making barely a sound.

Chapter Eleven

~❦~

Pitt was in his office looking yet again through the plans for Duke Alois's visit, when Stoker knocked on the door.

Pitt looked up as he came in.

Stoker's expression was anxious and he was clearly uncomfortable.

'Mr Blantyre's here, sir. He looks pretty bad, like he hasn't ate or slept for a while, but he wants to see you. Sorry, but I couldn't put him off. I think it's about Staum.'

'Ask him in,' Pitt replied. There was no way to avoid it. Assassins do not stop for private grief. It might solve at least part of the problem if Staum were connected to Adriana, but there was nothing to suggest it. Adriana had killed Serafina in revenge for her father, and then apparently in remorse or despair, taken her own life. There was no reason to think she had even heard of Duke Alois, who would have been a child, even younger than herself, at the time of the uprising and the betrayal.

'Fetch brandy and a couple of glasses,' he added, then, seeing the look on Stoker's face: 'I know it's early, but he may well have been awake all night. It's civil to make the offer. Poor man.'

'I don't know how he can bear it,' Stoker said grimly. 'Wife killing an old lady who was dying anyway, then taking her own life. Mind, he looks as if he'd be better off dead himself, right now.'

'Ask him in, and don't be long with the brandy,' Pitt told him.

'Yes, sir.'

Blantyre came in a moment later. As Stoker had said, he looked like a man stumbling blindly through a nightmare.

Pitt stood to greet him. It was impossible to know what to say. Nothing could meet the horror of his bereavement. Pitt remembered Charlotte's grief when he had told her about Adriana. She had been stunned, as if at first the words made no sense. Then as understanding filled her, and horror at the torment she imagined in Adriana, the darkness of utter loss, she had wept in Pitt's arms for what seemed like a long time. Even when they had finally gone to bed, she had lain in the dark. When he touched her, her face was wet with tears.

She and Adriana had been friends for a few weeks. What Blantyre must be feeling was a devastation imaginable only to those who had experienced it.

Blantyre eased himself into the chair like an old man, as if his bones would bruise at a careless nudge. Stoker came in almost on his heels with the brandy, and he accepted it. Blantyre held the glass in both his hands as if they would warm the bowl and send the aroma up, but they were white as though bloodless.

'Stoker said you had some news,' Pitt prompted him after a few moments of silence.

Blantyre looked up. 'Staum is no longer alone in Dover,' he said quietly. 'There is another man called Reibnitz. Elegant, ineffectual-looking fellow, very tidy, humourless. He looks like a ledger-clerk, and you half expect his fingers to be stained with ink. Until he speaks; then he sounds like a gentleman, and you take him for some third son of a decent family, the sort in England who would go into the Church, for the lack of something better to do.'

'Reibnitz,' Pitt repeated.

Blantyre's face tightened. 'Johann Reibnitz, so ordinary as to be almost invisible. Average height, slender build, light brown hair, grey eyes, pale complexion. Could be any one of a million men in Austria or any of the rest of Europe. Speaks English without an accent, so for that matter he could be any one of just as many over here.'

'Nothing to distinguish him?' Pitt asked with growing alarm.

'Nothing at all. No moles, no scars, no limp or twitch or stutter. As I said, an invisible man.' There was no expression in Blantyre's eyes, as if everything he was doing were mechanical and there was no one inside his body.

'So Staum might be a decoy, as we feared?' Pitt said.

'I think so. He would be if I were planning it.'

'How do you know this?'

The ghost of a smile crossed Blantyre's face and vanished so completely it could have been an illusion. 'I still have contacts in Vienna. Reibnitz has killed several times before. They know, but they cannot prove it.'

It was Pitt's turn to smile. 'And you expect me to believe that that prevents them from removing him? Is Vienna so . . . squeamish?'

Blantyre sighed. 'Of course not. You are quite right. They use him also, as it suits them. He was one of their own originally. They believe that he has become a rogue, when the price is right.' He looked at Pitt with sudden intensity, as if something alive had stirred within him again. 'Would you order one of your own shot, if you believed he had become

314

unreliable? Would you not want him tried, given a chance to defend himself? How could you be sure the evidence was good? Should he not face his accuser? And would you detail one of your men to do it – give him orders to kill? Or would you feel that as head of the service it was your burden to do it yourself?'

Pitt was startled. It was a question he had avoided asking himself since the O'Neil affair. It was one thing to defend yourself in the heat of the moment; it was very different to order an execution: a judicial murder, in cold blood.

'You don't know, do you?' Blantyre said, then at last sipped his brandy. 'At least you are honest. You are a detective, a brilliant one.' There was sincerity in his voice, even admiration. 'You uncover truths most men would never find. You make certain. You weigh evidence, you refine understanding until you have as much of the whole picture as anyone ever will. You have intense emotions. You empathise with pain; injustice outrages you. But you hardly ever lose your self-control.' He made a slight gesture with his strong, graceful hands. 'You think before you act. These are the qualities that make you a great leader in the service of your country. Perhaps one day you will even be better than Victor Narraway, because you know people better.'

Pitt stared at him, embarrassed. He understood that there was a caveat coming and he did not want to hear it.

Blantyre twisted his mouth in a grimace. 'But could you execute one of your men, without trial?'

'I don't know,' Pitt admitted. It was difficult to say. The expression in Blantyre's face gave him no indication as to whether he respected that, or would despise it.

'I know you don't,' Blantyre relaxed at last. 'Perhaps your opposite member in Vienna hasn't decided yet either. Or perhaps Reibnitz is a double agent, working for the head of the Austrian Secret Service, and betraying his other masters to them, as the occasion arises.'

'Well, if he attempts to murder Duke Alois, perhaps we can relieve them of the decision,' Pitt said grimly. 'Is there anything more you can tell me about Reibnitz? Where he has been seen? Habits, dress, any way we can recognise him? Anything known of his likes and dislikes? Any associates?'

'Of course. I have written down all I have.' Blantyre pulled a folded piece of paper out of his inside pocket and handed it to Pitt. 'The name of my informant is there separately. I would be obliged if you would note it somewhere absolutely safe, and show it to no one else, except possibly Stoker. I know you trust him.'

Pitt took it. 'Thank you,' he said sincerely. 'Duke Alois will owe you his life, and we will all owe you for saving us from a national embarrassment, which could have cost us very dearly indeed.'

Blantyre finished his brandy. 'Thank you.' He put the glass down on the desk and stood up. He hesitated a moment as if to say something, then changed his mind and walked unsteadily to the door.

As soon as he was gone, Pitt sent for Stoker and told him all that Blantyre had said, including the name of the informant regarding Reibnitz. It took them all the rest of that day and the next to follow it up, but every fact that Blantyre had offered was verifiable, and proved to be true.

Leaving Stoker and the others under his command to check and double check all the arrangements from the moment the ferry landed in Dover, Pitt went to see Narraway. He had already arranged to do so and ascertained that Narraway would be at home. Neither pride nor chains of command were relevant now.

It was the middle of the afternoon with rain sweeping in

from the west. Pitt was soaked and put his hat, gloves and scarf on the leather-padded brass railing in front of the fire.

Narraway put more coal and wood on the embers and settled in his chair, gazing at Pitt.

'You are certain about Reibnitz?' he said gravely.

'I'm certain that what Blantyre told me is true,' Pitt replied. 'I've checked on the few Austrian political murders we know about. It's difficult to pin them down. Too many are anarchists striking at anyone at all, just as they are here, or else they're unsolved. Reibnitz fits the description for a murder in Berlin, and one in Paris. As Blantyre said, there's no proof.'

'But he's here in Dover?' Narraway pressed.

Pitt nodded. 'There is an ordinary-seeming man answering his description, and with a passport calling himself John Rainer, just arrived back from Bordeaux, after apparently having been away on business for several months. He has no friends or family who can confirm it.'

Narraway pursed his lips. 'He doesn't sound like an anarchist, more like a deliberate and very careful assassin.'

'He could still be paid by anarchists,' Pitt reasoned. He was cold, even in the warmth of the room. The rain beating on the windows sounded threatening, as if it were trying to come in. 'Many of them are chaotic, but they might have stolen money, or collected enough from supporters to pay someone professional like Reibnitz.'

Narraway looked at him steadily, the shadows from the firelight playing across his face.

'Why would anyone want to kill Duke Alois, and with such care? Or is it as we feared, and he's simply a means to an end?'

'Well, it would certainly embarrass us if he were shot while in England, visiting our royal family,' Pitt said bitterly.

Narraway nodded. 'Or we are being misdirected, and all our attention will be on Duke Alois, while actually something else is going to happen, and we will only realise it when it is too late?'

'I thought of that too,' Pitt admitted. 'I have only four men on the Duke Alois case, until he actually gets here. Everyone else is on the usual things, and watching for any movement, any change that stands out. We've got a socialist rally in Kilburn, but the regular police can deal with anything there. An exhibition of rather explicit paintings in one of the galleries in Piccadilly, and expect some protests, nothing else that I know of.'

'Then you'd better prepare for the worst.' Narraway's eyes were bleak, his mouth pulled into a thin line. 'You need all the allies you can find. It might be the time to exert a little pressure, even call in a few favours. This information from Blantyre needs further checking. It doesn't smell like casual anarchist violence.'

It was what Pitt had thought, and feared.

'I don't have any favours to call in,' he said grimly. 'Only to ask. And Blantyre is crippled by his wife's death. I still have no idea if any of it had to do with Duke Alois or not, but I can't see any connection. The duke is Austrian and has no visible ties with Italy or Croatia. He has no interest we can find in any of the other smaller parts of the Austrian Empire.'

'Prussia? Poland?' Narraway asked.

'Nothing.'

Narraway frowned. 'I don't like coincidences, but I can't think of any way in which Serafina's rambling mind, or the secrets she might have known forty years ago, have anything to do with anarchists today, or Duke Alois at any time. Tragically, the connection with Adriana and Lazar Dragovic is all too obvious. Although it surprises me. I would never have thought of Serafina Montserrat as a betrayer of anyone. I never met her myself and I suppose I knew her only through other people's eyes.'

'Vespasia's?' Pitt asked.

'I suppose so. You have no doubt that it was Adriana who killed her?'

'I wish I had, but I can't see any. She was there that night. She listened to Serafina many times, and we know that Serafina was afraid of letting secrets slip, forgetting where she was, and with whom.' A deep, painful heaviness settled inside him. 'We know that Serafina was one of Dragovic's allies, and that she was there when he was executed. She took Adriana away and looked after her. It was an appalling piece of duplicity, whatever she did it for, whoever's power or freedom was bought that way. No wonder she was afraid when she knew Adriana, as a grown woman, was coming to see her. It explains the terror in her that Vespasia saw.'

'And when she realised you knew, Adriana killed herself,' Narraway added. He watched Pitt steadily, as if to read his ability to deal with that burden, and how harshly he felt the guilt.

Pitt smiled at his understanding, but there was no pleasure in it at all. 'There is someone else to find,' he said, not as an evasion, but a step onward from where they were.

Again Narraway nodded, lips drawn tight. 'Be careful, Pitt. Don't create enemies you can't afford. If you're going to use people, be damned careful how you do it. People understand favours and repayment, but no one likes to be used.'

He leaned forward and picked up the poker from the hearth. He pushed it gently into the coals, letting in the air. The flames gushed up.

'There are a few people you can set at each other's throats,' if you need to shake things up a little. See what falls out,' he added.

Pitt watched him closely, waiting for the next words, dreading them.

'Tregarron,' Narraway went on, replacing the poker gently. 'He is devoted to his mother, and there was a certain ill-feeling towards his father.'

'Wasn't his father a diplomat in Vienna?'

'Yes. You might see if he knew anything about Dragovic, or Serafina, for that matter.'

'Is it important now? How could it affect Duke Alois?'

'No idea. Just a point of leverage. There are one or two others, people I could –' he looked for the right word – 'persuade to be more forthcoming. But they're heavy debts, ones I can call in only once.' He looked up at Pitt, his face tense, uncertain in the flickering light. 'I'll only do it if it matters. Does it?'

Pitt could not answer. Was the whole tragedy of Serafina, Dragovic and Adriana in the past now, and irrelevant to Duke Alois anyway? Or was his presence coincidental? A chaotic anarchist plan seemed less and less likely. There was nothing impulsive about this. It was weeks since they had heard the first rumour of an assassination.

He wanted to ask someone's advice – perhaps Vespasia's – but he knew that it was his decision. He was Head of Special Branch. In his place, Narraway would have listened, but never looked for guidance.

'I want to know if the betrayal of Dragovic was the only secret Serafina was afraid of revealing,' he said aloud. 'And who was Nerissa Freemarsh's lover, if he exists at all.'

'Freemarsh's lover?' Narraway's head jerked up. 'Yes, find that out. Find out if it was Tregarron. Find out what Tregarron really went to that house for.'

'I intend to.'

Pitt went to one of the sources that Narraway had mentioned. He took the train on the Great Eastern Line to just beyond Hackney Wick. From there he walked three-quarters of a mile through sporadic sunshine to Plover Road. It overlooked Hackney Marsh, which was flat as a table, and crossed by narrow, winding waterways.

There he found the man whose name Narraway had given him: an Italian who had fought with the Croatian nationalists at the time Dragovic was one of their leaders. He was well into his eighties now, but still sharp-witted in spite of failing physical health. When Pitt had identified himself and proved to his satisfaction that he knew Victor Narraway, he was willing to recall those earlier years.

They sat in a small room with a window overlooking the marsh. Beyond the glass, flights of birds raced across the wide sky, chasing sunlight and shadows, and wind combed the grasses in ever-changing patterns.

'Yes, of course I remember Serafina Montserrat,' the old man said with a smile. He had lost most of his hair, but he still had beautiful teeth. 'What man would forget her?'

'What about Lazar Dragovic?' Pitt continued. They were sitting almost knee to knee in the tiny room.

The old man's face filled with sadness. 'Killed,' he said briefly. 'The Austrians shot him.'

'Executed,' Pitt put in.

'Murdered,' the old man corrected him.

'Wasn't he planning to assassinate someone?'

The old man's seamed face twisted with contempt. 'A butcher of the people he was put there to rule. No damned business to be set over them anyway. Foreigner. Barely even spoke their language. But he was brutal. That would have been an execution.'

'Was Dragovic betrayed by one of his own?' Pitt asked.

'Yes.' The old man's eyes burned with the memory. 'Of course he was. Never would have been caught otherwise.'

'Do you know who?'

'What does it matter now?' There was weariness and a sudden overwhelming defeat in his voice. He stared at the wind and cloud patterns across the marsh. 'They're all dead.'

'Are they?' Pitt asked. 'Are you sure?'

'Must be. It was a long time ago. People like that are passionate, vivid. They live with courage and hope, and they burn out.'

'Serafina died only a few weeks ago,' Pitt told him.

He smiled. 'Ah . . . Serafina. God rest her.' For an instant, as memory lit in him, the young man he had been was visible.

'She was murdered,' Pitt said, hearing the grief in the old man's voice and feeling brutal.

'Is that why you came?' That was an accusation. 'English policeman, with a murder to solve?'

'With a murder to solve – two, if you count Lazar Dragovic – and, more urgently, the threat of more murder to prevent,' Pitt corrected him. 'Who betrayed Lazar Dragovic?'

'Who else is dead?'

'Adriana Dragovic.'

Tears filled the old man's eyes and slipped down his withered cheeks. 'She was a lovely child,' he whispered.

Pitt thought of Adriana, picturing her vividly in his mind: beautiful, delicate, and yet perhaps far stronger than Blantyre had imagined. Or was she? Had she killed Serafina, after all those years? Or not? Why did he still question it? He had all the evidence. It was only the reluctance of his emotions that prevented his acceptance of it.

The old man blinked. 'When did it happen? When?'

'A few days ago.'

'How? Was she ill? She was delicate as a child. Lung diseases, I think. But . . .' he sighed. 'I thought she was better. It's so easy to wish. But you said only a few days ago? Was it her lungs still?'

'No. She killed herself. Why is what I need to know now.'

The old man blinked. 'What can I tell you all this time later that can help? It was all long ago. Dragovic is dead, so are those who fought with him. And now you say Serafina and Adriana are dead too. What could I know that matters any more?'

'Who betrayed Dragovic?' Pitt answered.

'Do you think if I knew he'd still be alive?' The old man's voice shook with anger, his face was crumpled, his eyes wet.

'Did Serafina know?' Pitt insisted. There was a chance, a small chance that it mattered.

Seconds ticked by and the silence in the room remained unbroken. More cloud shadows chased each other over the marsh. They were thickening to the west. There would be rain before sunset.

Pitt waited.

'I'm not sure,' the old man said at last. 'I didn't think so, at first. Later I began to wonder.'

'Weren't she and Dragovic lovers?'

'Yes. That's why I was sure at first that she didn't know. She'd have killed him for sure, if she had. She grieved for him, inside. Few people saw it, but it was there. I'm not sure it ever really healed.'

'You are certain of that?' Pitt had to pursue it, but the more he heard, the uglier it became in his mind, the sharper the fear of what he would finally be unable to avoid.

'Of course I am. I knew Serafina.' Now there was anger in the old man's voice, a challenge in return.

Pitt wondered how well he had known her. Had he been her lover too? Might Dragovic's betrayal have been nothing political at all, but an old-fashioned triangle of love and jealousy?

'Did you know her well?' he asked.

The old man smiled, showing the beautiful teeth again. 'Yes, very well. And before you ask, yes, we were lovers, before Dragovic. You dishonour me if you think I would betray the cause out of personal jealousy. The cause came first, always.'

'For everyone?'

'Yes! For everyone!' Anger flared in his eyes against Pitt because he was young and knew nothing of their passion and their loss.

'Then whoever betrayed Dragovic was secretly for a different cause.' Pitt stated the only conclusion.

The old man nodded slowly. 'Yes, that must be so.'

'But if Serafina knew, why would she not expose him?'

'She would. She cannot have known. I was wrong.'

'When did you think she might have learned?'

'Oh . . . ten, maybe fifteen years after that.'

'How would she find out then, so long after?'

'I've thought about that too, and I don't know.'

'Are you certain it could not be she herself?' Pitt loathed asking, but it was no longer avoidable.

'Serafina?' The old man was shocked, and angry again, sitting more upright in his chair. 'Never!'

'Then it was someone she loved.' It was the most obvious conclusion.

'No. Men came and went. There was none whom she would have forgiven for that!' His voice was filled with cutting contempt. Pitt could imagine the young man he must have been: slight-built but wiry; handsome; filled with passion.

'Are you certain?' he probed.

'Yes. The only person she always loved was Dragovic's child, Adriana.'

Adriana had been only eight when her father was killed. She couldn't have betrayed him. Could she have let slip something by accident? The thought was so powerful, the guilt so consuming, he found even the words too brutal to say. Was that first, terrible realisation what Blantyre had been trying to protect her from? If Serafina had let that slip in one of her ramblings, little wonder Adriana had gone home and killed herself.

Except that the timing made no sense. She would have done that the day she discovered it, not several days later. And why would she kill Serafina?

The old man was studying his face. 'What is it?' he asked anxiously. 'Do you know something?'

'No, I don't,' Pitt replied. 'What I was thinking would make no sense of either Serafina's death or Adriana's. Serafina knew. That's why she was killed: to prevent her telling anyone else.'

'Then why would the child – the woman – kill herself now?' the old man asked. 'Unless she killed Serafina to silence her? And why would she do that? Except to protect whoever it was – and that makes no sense either!'

'Unless it were to protect her husband,' Pitt had spoken the words before he realised the full impact of what he was saying.

'Her husband?' the old man was aghast. 'Evan Blantyre?'

Pitt looked at him, studying the fragile skin, the deep lines, the strength in the bones. In its own way it was a beautiful face. 'Yes – Evan Blantyre.'

The old man crossed himself. 'Yes . . . God forgive us all, that would make sense. That would be why Serafina never told. She didn't know it until later, when Blantyre returned, and courted Adriana. He must have let something slip, and Serafina put it together. He pretended he could see the value of peace in the Austrian Empire: it held Europe together, now that Italy was united and independent, and Germany. But perhaps he always thought that. Then Serafina knew what he had done.'

'And she let Adriana marry him?' Pitt asked incredulously.

'How was she going to stop it? They were in love, passionately and completely. Adriana was beautiful, but she had nothing: no money, no status. She was the orphan daughter of a traitor to the Empire, an executed criminal. Serafina would have no proof, only her own inner certainty.' He shrugged his thin shoulders. 'Not that proof would have made a difference. He would have been regarded as a hero by the Viennese Emperor. No, she would have kept her silence and let Adriana be happy. She was delicate, needing someone to look after her, to help her regain her health. In poverty, she would have been left to die young, and alone. Serafina never had a child of her own. Adriana was the only thing left of the man she loved.'

Pitt tried to imagine it: Serafina watching the marriage of Adriana to the man who had betrayed her father, the man Serafina had loved so profoundly. And perhaps that was it: the depth of real love, greater than revenge, and deeper, infinitely more selfless than any kind of hate, or even hunger for justice. He felt a pain in his chest, a tightness in his throat that mirrored the tears in the old man's eyes.

The first drops of rain spattered against the windows.

If Blantyre had betrayed Lazar Dragovic, and Serafina knew it, then she might well have let something slip that told Adriana the truth too. Would Adriana have faced Blantyre with it, and had he killed her? He would have had no choice, if he were to survive.

No, the timings were wrong. Serafina was terrified that she would say something that sooner or later would lead to the truth. That made perfect sense. But it must have been Blantyre himself who feared it would happen, and he had killed her to prevent it. Then when Adriana knew Serafina had been murdered, and she was about to be blamed for it by Pitt, in despair, not guilt, she had killed herself!

Or knowing that she would at last put together all the different things Serafina had said, and the love she knew Serafina had always felt for her, she would deduce the truth. So Blantyre, with terrible, agonising regret, had killed her, to protect himself. That was the truth.

As it all fell into place it made sense of everything, even the passion, the detail with which Blantyre had explained to Pitt and Charlotte the crucial place of the Austrian Empire in European politics.

Was he right? Was Austrian survival as a united force necessary to the continued peace of Europe?

Perhaps it was.

It did not excuse the murder of Serafina Montserrat. Even less did it excuse the murder of Adriana.

Pitt rose to his feet. 'Thank you, sir,' he said gravely. 'You have saved the good name of two women who were murdered and defamed. I will do all I can to see that that injustice is corrected, but I may not be able to do it quickly. Believe me, I will not forget or abandon it.'

The old man nodded slowly. 'Good,' he said with conviction. 'Good.'

In the train on the journey back Pitt sat next to the window and stared out of it, even though it was streaked with rain and there was little he could see. He ignored the other two men sitting in the carriage reading newspapers.

If Blantyre had been with Serafina for long enough to hear her rambling, and the many lucid patches, then he had spent quite an amount of time with her. Even if he were

327

fortunate in what he heard during her meanderings, he had to have been there a matter of hours, not minutes. How often had he visited her? Why had neither Adriana nor Nerissa mentioned it?

The answer to the first was simple: Adriana might not have known.

The answer to the second was more complex. Nerissa could not escape knowing, unless he had visited when she was out of the house, possibly in an afternoon. The more probable answer was that she did know, and had chosen deliberately not to tell Pitt. Had that been to protect herself from having allowed him in to see Serafina alone? Or – more likely – to protect him from suspicion, perhaps because he had asked her to? Or – most likely of all – because Blantyre was her lover.

Except what, in heaven's name, would the brilliant, charming Evan Blantyre see in a woman like Nerissa Freemarsh? But then, who knew what anyone saw in another person? The outer appearance was trivial, if one understood the mind or the heart. Perhaps she was generous, easy to please, uncritical. Maybe she listened to him with genuine interest, laughed at his jokes, never contradicted him or compared him with others. It could be as simple as that she loved him unconditionally, and asked nothing in return, except a little time, a little kindness, or the semblance of it. Perhaps it was a defiance of the beautiful and maybe demanding Adriana?

The rain was harder on the carriage window now, and it was growing dark outside. The rattle of the train was rhythmic, soothing.

The most likely explanation of all was that he had visited Dorchester Terrace once with Adriana, realised how dangerously Serafina was rambling, and had secured for himself an ostensible reason for returning again and again so he could make sure just how great the danger might be.

Then a new and colder thought occurred to Pitt: Blantyre could learn from Serafina's disintegrating mind any other secret she might know about anyone or anything else. He might now have stored in his own knowledge all the secrets Serafina was so afraid she would let slip: names of men and women in old indiscretions of all sorts, over half of Europe for the last forty years.

Most of them were probably trivial: affairs, illegitimate children, romantic betrayals as opposed to political, and possibly thefts or embezzlements, purchases of office, blackmails or coercions. The list was almost endless, and more than half the people would be dead by now, and the office, the love, the money no longer of urgent importance, only memories that still tarnished and wounded.

What would Blantyre do with them? That was a troubling thought, but it might have to wait until after Duke Alois had been, and safely gone again.

Was that where Blantyre had gained his knowledge about the assassination plot? It did not seem possible. Serafina had been ill and confined to her bed for half a year. It was far longer than that since she had been involved in any affairs of state in England or Austria. Most of the people she had known were retired, or dead.

Was it even conceivable that Duke Alois was connected with someone else from that time? That seemed fanciful in the extreme. Pitt was sceptical of coincidences. Ordinary police work had taught him that, even before Special Branch. But on the other hand, it was equally foolish to imagine that everything was connected, or to see cause and effect in what was no more than things happening close to each other in time.

He sat back and let the rhythm and movement of the train lull him into near sleep. It was still at least half an hour before he would reach the station in London, and then as long again before he was home.

Pitt found Charlotte waiting for him, with the kettle on the hob and the fire still burning in the parlour. He stood by the scrubbed table as she made tea and cut him a sandwich of cold beef and pickles. He glanced at the basket beside the stove and saw the little dog, Uffie, half asleep, her nose twitching as she smelled the meat.

He smiled, took a tiny piece from where Charlotte had sliced it, and offered it to the dog. She ate it immediately.

'Thomas, I've already fed her!' Charlotte was smiling, even though the anxiety was still sharp in her eyes.

He picked up the tray and carried it through to the parlour. He had not realised how hungry he was, or how cold. He set it down and watched while she poured tea for both of them. It smelled fragrant. The room was warm and silent except for the slight whickering of the flames in the hearth, and now and then the sound of wind and rain on the windowpanes beyond the closed curtains. He glanced at the familiar pictures on the walls: the Dutch water scene he was so used to, with its soft colours, blues and greys, calm as a still morning. On the other wall was a drawing of cows grazing. There was something very beautiful about cows, a kind of certainty that always pleased him. Perhaps at least some of it was memory from childhood.

Charlotte was watching him, waiting.

How much could he tell her? What were the risks of failing to see something important, and her having the missing piece: something Adriana had told her, that she had not previously understood the relevance of?

On the other hand there were the promises of secrecy he had made regarding his office in Special Branch. If he could not be trusted to keep them, he was no use to anyone, and no protection to Charlotte herself. He must choose his words carefully.

'You don't believe that Adriana killed Serafina, do you.' He made it more of a statement than a question.

'No,' she said instantly. 'I know you think Serafina was responsible for Lazar Drogovic's death, but even if she was – and I don't know that you're right – Adriana wouldn't have murdered her. It would be stupid, apart from anything else. Serafina was dying anyway, and in some distress. If you hate someone as deeply as that, you want them to suffer, not to be let off lightly.'

'Revenge is usually stupid,' he said quietly. 'For an instant it feels wonderful, then the fury dies away and you're left empty, and wondering why it didn't work, what it was you were expecting that didn't happen.'

She stared at him. 'When did you ever take revenge on anyone?'

'I've wanted to,' he replied, looking back with a sense of shame, not so much for the anger of it as for the futility. 'Some people I've arrested, people I didn't have the proof that they were guilty, or simply couldn't catch them at the crime. Even recently, people I just had to arrest calmly, but whom I would like to have beaten with my fists, and I couldn't because I wasn't alone with them. I don't know whether I would have if I'd been certain of getting away with it.'

She looked at him with amazement, and a degree of curiosity. 'You've never said that before.'

'I'm not proud of it.'

'Do you tell me only the things you're proud of?' she challenged.

'No, of course not.' He smiled ruefully, softening the moment. 'I would probably have told you if I'd actually done it.'

'Because I'd find out?'

'No, because it was a weakness I hadn't overcome.'

She gave a little laugh, but there was no edge to it, no criticism. 'What about Adriana? If she didn't kill Serafina, who did? And why did she then kill herself?' Her voice dropped. 'Or didn't she?'

Pitt avoided her question. 'You spent quite a lot of time with her. Do you think you learned to know her at all? I want your opinion of her, not in kindness, or decency because she's dead. Tell me the truth. A great deal may depend on it, even people's lives.'

'Whose?' she came back instantly. 'Blantyre's?'

'Among others, but I didn't mean principally his. Other people, most of whom you don't even know.' He made a slight, rueful gesture. 'But my job as well.'

The last vestige of amusement or defensiveness vanished from Charlotte's face. Her eyes were steady and serious. 'I don't think she was fragile at all. She had been hurt terribly, seeing her father beaten and then executed. But many people see very bad things. It's painful. One never forgets it, but it doesn't make you deranged. Nightmares, maybe? I've had a few. Sometimes if I sleep really badly, or I'm worried or frightened, I remember the dead people I've seen.'

She did not move her gaze from his, but he saw the sudden return of memory in her eyes. 'One of the worst was the skeleton of the woman on the swing, with the tiny bones of the baby inside her. I still see that sometimes, and it makes me want to weep and weep until I have no strength left. But I don't. I didn't know her, I just feel as if in some way she's every woman: happy, believing, looking forward to life in the future, trying to protect what is precious and vulnerable inside her.'

Pitt started to reach across to touch her, then changed his mind. This was not the moment. 'Adriana?' he said again.

'She wasn't hysterical,' she said with conviction. 'And I don't believe she would ever have killed herself. Who did kill her, Thomas? Why then? Wouldn't it have been the same person who betrayed her father? Did Serafina know who that was? She would have. That was why she was killed too. That's the only thing that makes sense.'

'I imagine so.' Should he tell her? Did she have to know, for her own safety? Or would knowing endanger her instead? Except even if he did not tell her, Blantyre would assume he had.

'It was him, wasn't it?' her voice interrupted his thoughts.

'Him?'

'Blantyre!' she said sharply. 'He was the only one who could have betrayed Adriana's father, killed Serafina and then killed her.' She made it sound so simple. 'Thomas, I don't care what secrets he knows, or what kind of office he holds, you can't let him get away with that! It's . . . monstrous! If we let that happen when we don't have to, then what makes us any better?'

'You want revenge?' he said.

'Maybe! Yes. I want revenge for Adriana. And for Serafina. She deserved better than to die like that! But call it justice, if you like. It is – and you'll feel better.'

'Everybody calls it justice,' Pitt pointed out.

'Then call it necessity. You can't have someone like that in high office in the government. Such a man could do anything!'

'Oh, indeed. And probably will. Some of it we will praise him for, and some we will be glad enough not to know about.'

Charlotte said nothing. He looked across at her and could not read what she was thinking.

First thing in the morning, Pitt went to see Vespasia. It was far too early to call, but he disregarded courtesy and told the maid that it was urgent. Vespasia's maid had become used to him, his polished boots and crooked ties, and above all, the fact that Vespasia was always willing to receive him.

He found her in the yellow breakfast room, sitting at the cherrywood table with tea, toast and marmalade. The maid set up another place for Pitt and went to fetch fresh tea and more toast.

'Good morning, Thomas,' Vespasia said gravely. 'It must be serious to bring you at this hour. Please sit down. I hate to sound like Victor, but you give me a crick in my neck staring up at you.'

He smiled bleakly and accepted the invitation to sit opposite her. He loved this room, in which the light made it seem as if the sun were always shining.

'It is serious. Serafina Montserrat knew who betrayed Lazar Dragovic.'

Vespasia inclined her head very slightly. 'I thought she might. She was seldom fooled, and she loved him enough not to rest easily until she knew. Does it still matter? Don't tell me she told Adriana . . . unless it was accidentally? Was it? That would make perfect sense of her fear. If she had not told her already, then it was because she did not wish her to know.'

'You are right,' he agreed.

The maid returned with fresh tea, a second cup and more toast. She left without speaking and closed the door behind her.

'Which must mean it was Evan Blantyre,' Vespasia concluded. 'If it were anyone else, Serafina would not have protected them.'

'Did she care about him?' he asked.

Vespasia raised her eyes in exasperation. 'Don't be absurd, Thomas! She must have found out after Adriana was committed to marry him. That would make it impossible for her to do anything then. She would stifle her own feelings and keep silent for Adriana's sake.'

'In the end it served neither of them,' Pitt said unhappily. 'Poor Serafina. She paid a very high price for nothing.'

'Not for nothing,' she corrected him simply. 'Adriana had many happy years. She grew to be a strong, beautiful woman, and I think she always knew that Serafina cared for her.'

'And Blantyre?' he said bitterly.

'Perhaps in his own way he did also. But not as he cared for his ideals and his beliefs in Austria.'

'I'll prove it, one way or another,' he said grimly, as if he were making an oath.

'I dare say you will.' She poured a cup of tea for him and passed it over.

'Thank you.' He took it and then a piece of toast, buttering it absent-mindedly.

'That is hardly your most urgent concern,' she observed.

He looked up at her.

'My dear, if Evan Blantyre spent long enough at Dorchester Terrace to realise that Serafina knew he was the one who betrayed Lazar Dragovic, then he must have listened to a great deal that she said. What else was there, do you suppose? Most of it may be irrelevant now, but what about that which is not? Who does it concern?'

It was what he had feared.

'I don't know,' he admitted. 'That same thought had occurred to me. I could find out all the places he served, but it wouldn't tell me much, except the extent of the possibilities, and I can already guess that.'

She spread more butter on the last edge of her piece of toast.

'All kinds of people have served in the embassies of Europe, at some time or another, especially that of Vienna. And apart from government positions, most of the aristocracy travels for pleasure.'

She passed him the marmalade. 'Men go to hunt in the forest, to drink beer, to exchange ideas – philosophy and now emerging sciences. To climb mountains in the Tyrol, or to visit the lakes. Even braver souls go to sail. We go to visit Venice and the Adriatic, especially the coast of Croatia with its islands. And always we go to the glory and the ruin of Rome, and imagine ourselves heirs to the days of its empire. Some of us go to Naples to gaze at Vesuvius and imagine the eruption that burned Pompeii. We see the sunlight on the water and dream for a little while that it always shines.'

'Has that much to do with Austrian survival as an empire?' he asked.

'Very little,' she replied. 'But a great deal to do with indiscretions, with secrets that people still wish to keep, even forty years later.'

The crisp toast and sharp marmalade lost its taste. Pitt could have been eating cardboard.

'You mean Serafina was in these places and would have known all sorts of things?'

'She was very observant. It was part of her skill.'

'Austrians she could blackmail,' he concluded.

'Certainly. Or, of rather more moment to us, British as well.'

Now he was cold inside himself, in spite of the warmth of the yellow room.

'She was neither spiteful nor irresponsible,' Vespasia said gently, 'but she understood the weaknesses of people. And now Blantyre may know a great many things he can piece together, even from Serafina's confused mind, and he may well have no moral boundaries to his crusade to preserve the power of the Austro-Hungarian Empire, and all that he believes depends upon it.'

Pitt leaned forward slowly, his hands pressed hard against his face, as if he could hide from this possibility, gather his strength before facing it. It was a nightmare.

'It is time for some very difficult decisions, my dear,' Vespasia said after a moment or two. 'When you have made sure that Duke Alois is safe, you are going to have to deal with Evan Blantyre. You have the heart of a policeman, but you must have the brain of the Head of Special Branch. Don't forget that, Thomas. Too many people are relying on you.'

Chapter Twelve

❧

Pitt sat in the housekeeper's room at Dorchester Terrace waiting for Nerissa Freemarsh to come. He expected her deliberately to keep him waiting, and he was not disappointed. It gave him time to think very carefully what he intended to say, how much of the truth to tell her, and how much pressure to exert. To begin with he had felt a certain compassion towards her. At one time or another during his career in the police he had seen many single young women who were dependent upon a relative who made full use of them as unpaid servants. Occasionally, a parent had intentionally kept one daughter at home for precisely that purpose; most often the relative was a mother who had failed to marry off her daughter successfully.

It was wretched for anyone being a dependant, an onlooker at life and never a participant, even if many of those they believed to be fully involved were actually far less happy than they professed to be. Nerissa had been one of those with very little choice. She had not the charm or the daring to have set out on her own to create adventure, as Serafina had done, and perhaps Serafina had secretly despised her for that.

Nerissa would know, even if she could not have put a name to it.

Was Nerissa flattered that another woman's husband had made advances to her, professed a kind of love? Or had she genuinely cared for him, probably far more than he had for her? Was Pitt insulting her in assuming that Blantyre's interest was solely in Serafina, and Nerissa was merely the excuse to visit? He felt a certain anger for a man who could use her obvious vulnerability. Now Pitt had to prepare to expose a pain it was going to be pathetic and disturbing to see. No matter how essentially selfish Nerissa was, that pain was still born of a kind of despair.

The door opened, without a knock, and Nerissa came in, closing it behind her. She stood facing him as he rose to his feet. Today she had a jet and crystal brooch at her throat and matching earrings giving light to her face. They were beautiful. Pitt wondered briefly if they had been Serafina's.

'Good morning, Miss Freemarsh,' he said quietly. 'I'm sorry to disturb you again, but several new facts have come to light, and I need to ask you some further questions.'

She seemed calmer today. There was no sign of anxiety in her face as she heard this news.

'Indeed? I am aware of Mrs Blantyre's suicide,' she answered coolly, standing facing him with her hands folded in front of her. 'A tragedy, and yet it appears to have been inevitable. I gather that she held my aunt responsible for her father's death, or at least for his being caught by the Austrians and executed for insurrection. I was aware that she was –' she looked for the right word, cutting and yet not overtly cruel – 'fragile. I was not aware that it was so very serious. I'm sorry. I know that suicide is a sin, but in the circumstances, perhaps it is better that she should have taken her own life rather than face arrest and trial, and the shame of all that.' Her face tightened.

'And they might have locked her away in an asylum, or even hanged her, I suppose. Yes, I . . . I have to respect her for that. Poor creature.'

Pitt looked at her with a well of pity, disgust and revulsion building up inside him. Did she know that it was Blantyre who had betrayed Lazar Dragovic, killed Serafina, and then Adriana also? Had she overheard the conversation? Was she even party to it, or ignorant of everything but falling in love with another woman's husband? Now that he was faced with it, he did not know.

'Please sit down, Miss Freemarsh. I'm afraid the situation is not as simple as that.'

She sat obediently, hands folded in her lap, and he returned to the housekeeper's chair as before.

'You're not going to make the case public, are you?' she said in dismay. 'Surely that is not in the government's interest? It is simply the tragedy of a woman who suffered as a child, and did not recover from it.' Her face tightened. 'You would drag her husband through a mire of shame and embarrassment he does not deserve, and to what purpose? Please do not say that it is justice. That is complete nonsense, and would be the utmost hypocrisy on your part. My aunt caused the death of Mrs Blantyre's father, politically justified or not. Mrs Blantyre's mind was unhinged as a child because of it. I believe she was actually there and witnessed the whole appalling thing. She never knew who betrayed him, until Aunt Serafina's own mind began to wander, and somehow in her ramblings she gave herself away. In a hysteria of revenge, Mrs Blantyre killed her, and then, realising what she had done, she took her own life. Justice has already been more than served.'

He looked at her and wondered how much of that she truly believed, and how much she had convinced herself, because it was the justification she needed.

'Are you sure?' he asked, as if he were seeking proof himself.

'Quite sure,' she replied. 'And if you consider it, you will see that it makes perfect sense.' There was no doubt visible in her, no unease. He could see no sign of real pity either. She could not, or did not, wish to imagine herself in Adriana's place.

'When did your aunt tell you about Lazar Dragovic's death?' he asked, affecting only mild interest. 'And when did you realise that Dragovic was Adriana's father?'

Nerissa looked startled. 'I beg your pardon?'

She was playing for time, trying to understand what he was looking for, and how to answer him.

'You know about Dragovic, and that Adriana witnessed his death herself, as an eight-year-old child,' he explained. 'Someone told you. It is not recorded in any written history, obviously, or Adriana would have known it all the time. Only those present knew the truth.'

Nerissa swallowed. He could see her throat convulse with the effort of it.

'Oh. Yes, I see.' Her hands were knotted in her lap now, knuckles white.

'So when did your aunt tell you this?' he persisted. 'And why? She cannot have wished you to tell anyone, least of all Adriana Blantyre.'

'I . . . I can't recall.' She took a deep breath. 'I must have pieced it together from her ramblings. She was very incoherent at times. Lady Vespasia would tell you that. Bits and pieces, jumbled, not knowing who was with her, and could hear.'

'And you realised from all those bits and pieces that Adriana Blantyre was actually Lazar Dragovic's daughter, and that Serafina Montserrat had betrayed him to the Austrians, and she and Adriana had witnessed his execution, which had turned Adriana's mind, although she did not know who was behind the betrayal.' He kept the disbelief from his tone, but barely. 'And then Adriana later pieced together the truth, also from Mrs Montserrat's ramblings, and lost her mind so completely that she murdered her, using the laudanum whose whereabouts she happened to know. But you did not think to mention this to anyone when Mrs Montserrat was killed. You are a brilliant, complex and quite extraordinary woman, Miss Freemarsh.' Now he did not even attempt to keep the sarcasm out of his voice.

Again she stared at him. What little colour there was in her face was draining away leaving her almost grey.

'I don't . . . I don't know what you mean,' she stammered.

'Yes you do, Miss Freemarsh. You know a great deal about Mrs Blantyre and her past, which you did not learn from her, because she did not know it herself. The whole motive for her killing Mrs Montserrat was that she had just discovered this apparent betrayal. Mrs Montserrat was quite unaware that she had revealed it, or she would have taken precautions to protect herself. Miss Tucker, at least, would have been aware. And naturally Mrs Blantyre would have been immediately suspect in Mrs Montserrat's death. Which also follows that Mrs Blantyre told no one. So how did you know?'

'I . . .' She gulped again, as if starving for air. 'I told you. I . . . learned it from Aunt Serafina's rambling, the same way Mrs Blantyre learned. If she did, why is it difficult for you to understand that I did also?'

'Because you would have me believe that she acted on it, and yet you did nothing, even after Mrs Montserrat was murdered.'

She was rigid now, her muscles locked so tight her shoulders strained against the fabric of her dress. She started to speak, and then stopped, staring at him defiantly.

Pitt waited.

'It is pointless for you to say that you don't understand,' she said at last, angry now. 'Mrs Blantyre did learn it from my aunt. As you have made very clear, she was the only person who knew about Lazar Dragovic's execution, and it was she who betrayed him to the Austrians. You also pointed out that I could not have known. I was barely even born at the time.' Now there was a ring of triumph in her voice. Her eyes were brighter, the blood returning to her cheeks.

'You assume that Mrs Blantyre learned from your aunt's disjointed ramblings, and was certain enough of what she pieced together to kill Mrs Montserrat, without making any attempt to check the truth of it with anyone,' he said.

Nerissa's eyebrows rose.

'Check the truth of it? What on earth are you suggesting? With whom?' she demanded. 'Where would she even find anyone? Are you saying she should have taken a trip to Croatia and started searching for survivors from the rebels and insurgents of thirty years ago? That's absurd!' She gave a little snarl of laughter. 'And even if she succeeded, Aunt Serafina could have been dead by the time she returned,' she added.

'Exactly,' he agreed. 'No satisfaction in killing someone who is dying anyway. In fact really very little purpose.'

Her eyes were like pinpoints. 'Then why are we having this ridiculous conversation?'

'That was your suggestion, Miss Freemarsh. I was not thinking of her going to Croatia, or anywhere else, simply going home.'

Now she was sarcastic. 'I beg your pardon?'

'I was supposing she would have asked her husband,' he explained. 'After all, he was involved with the insurgents at that time. He was one of them. Or pretending to be. I think actually he was always loyal to Austrian unity and dominance in all the regions of its Empire.'

She said nothing.

'I would simply have gone home and asked him, wouldn't you?' he pressed.

She stared at him in angry silence, as if his question did not merit an answer.

'Unless, of course, Serafina did let something slip,' he went on relentlessly now. 'But it was not she that was the betrayer. Why would she be? She was always an insurgent, a fighter for freedom – if not for Croatia, then for that part of northern Italy that was under Austrian rule.'

'What are you saying?' Nerissa's voice was hoarse.

'That the betrayer was not Serafina but Evan Blantyre, and that was what Adriana discovered,' he answered.

She was struggling now, pushing away the truth. 'That makes no sense!' she said sharply. 'How dare you say such a thing? If Aunt Serafina knew that, or even believed it, why didn't she say so long ago? Why did she ever let Adriana Dragovic marry him?'

'I wondered that myself,' Pitt admitted. 'Then I realised that Adriana was beautiful, but poor, the orphan daughter of a man who had been executed by the Austrians. She was in ill health. She might very likely not bear children. What were her opportunities? She had met Evan Blantyre, he was in love with her and could offer her a very good life. Serafina could probably not prove anything against him. He had acted according to his own loyalties to Austria because he believed passionately that the Empire was for the good of Europe – a conviction he still holds. Serafina loved Adriana enough to let her be safe, and happy. Accidentally revealing the truth and giving her a burden she could not live with was the thing she was most afraid of when she knew her control was slipping away and she might forget where she was, or to whom she was speaking.'

Nerissa breathed out slowly. 'Then it seems she was right to fear it, since that was exactly what happened.'

'Really?' he said with a disbelief she could not miss. 'And when it did, Adriana killed her, then went home and killed herself? Why, for God's sake?'

Nerissa started to shake her head.

Pitt leaned forward a little, his voice urgent now. 'It was her husband who betrayed her father, not Serafina. Surely if she were going to kill anyone, it would have been him? Except she didn't know, Miss Freemarsh. Serafina kept her secrets and died with them, before she could tell anyone else – except perhaps Mr Blantyre. He spent time with her, didn't he? When he came here telling you it was to see you, as your lover, but he sat with her, so it would look respectable. Isn't that what he said? Only it was really the other way round. He came to see Serafina, to find out how far her mind had disintegrated, and what of the past she might betray to Adriana.'

'No!' she cried out. 'No! That's horrible!' She made a swift movement with her hand, as if to sweep the suggestion away.

'Yes, it is,' he agreed. 'But we are speaking of a man who believes in the value of the Austrian Empire above all else. He betrayed his friend Lazar Dragovic, to his torture and death. He married Dragovic's daughter, perhaps from guilt, perhaps because she was beautiful and vulnerable. Maybe he felt safer if he knew where she was. And it would give him a standing in the community of those who still seek to throw off the Austrian yoke. Heaven knows, the whole Balkan Peninsula is teeming with them.'

'That's . . .' she began, but could not finish the sentence.

'Logical,' he said. 'Yes, it is. And you are just one more victim, both emotionally and morally.'

She stiffened but the tears were sliding down her face. 'I have done nothing . . .' She stopped again.

'I am prepared to accept that you did not know beforehand that Blantyre would kill Serafina, and perhaps not immediately after,' he said more gently. 'You may have wilfully refused to think about Adriana's death, or work out for yourself what the truth had to be. At the moment I can see no purpose in charging you as an accessory. But if you do not now co-operate, that could change.'

'Co . . . co-operate? How?' She started to deny her complicity, even her knowledge, but the words died on her tongue. She had known – at least, she had guessed – but refused to allow the thoughts to complete themselves in her mind. She knew now that Pitt could see it in her eyes.

'Tell me who was in the house the day Serafina Montserrat was killed, and the day before as well.'

'The . . . day before?' Her hands twisted around each other in her lap.

'Yes. And please don't make any mistakes or omissions. If you do, and we discover them afterwards, it will point very powerfully to guilt, at least on your part – and probably on theirs as well, or why would you conceal it?'

She was trembling now. He could imagine he heard her teeth jittering together.

'You have no choice, Miss Freemarsh, if you wish to save yourself. And I will, naturally, be speaking to at least some of the staff again.'

It was several seconds before she spoke, as if she were still looking for some way to avoid committing herself.

He waited for her in silence.

'Mr Blantyre was here the day Aunt Serafina died,' she said at last. 'He came often. I don't remember all the days. Two or three a week. He spent some time with me . . . and some with her. For the look of it.'

'And he was definitely here the day she died?' he insisted.

346

'Yes.'

'Did he see her alone, before Mrs Blantyre was here?'

'Yes.' Her voice was barely audible.

'What reason did he give?' he pressed her.

'What you said. For the . . . the look of it!'

'Anyone else?' He was not even certain why he asked, except that he sensed a reluctance in her, a preparation to defend something further. 'I would prefer to have it from you than from the staff. Allow yourself that dignity, Miss Freemarsh. You have little enough left. And by the way, I would not let your staff go, if I were you. Employed here, they have an interest in maintaining some discretion. If they leave, it will make a great many people wonder why, and they will most certainly talk, no matter what threats you make. You are not in a good position to do anything other than maintain a silence yourself. If you are not prosecuted for anything, you will be in a comfortable financial situation, and free to conduct yourself as you please.'

Her eyes widened a little.

'Who else was here?' he repeated.

'Lord Tregarron.' It was little more than a whisper.

'Why?'

'I beg your pardon?'

'Why was Lord Tregarron here? To see you, or to see Mrs Montserrat? I assume it was both, or you would not have been so reluctant to say so.'

She cleared her throat. 'Yes.'

'Why did he wish to see Mrs Montserrat? Were they friends?'

She hesitated.

He did not ask again.

'No,' she said at last, speaking in gasps as if it caused her an almost physical pain. 'His calling on her was . . . an excuse. I'm not certain if he was interested in me – he pretended to

347

be – or in Aunt Serafina and her recollections about . . . all sorts of things.'

'He spent time talking to her?'

'Not . . . much. I . . .' She breathed in and out several times, struggling to control her emotions. 'I had the feeling that he did not like her, but that he wished to hide it, not merely from good manners, or to spare my feelings because she was my aunt.'

'Thank you,' he said sincerely. 'Did he express any interest in Mr or Mrs Blantyre?'

'Not . . . more than I would expect considering . . .' She tailed off, again unwilling to complete the sentence.

'I understand. Thank you, Miss Freemarsh. I think that is all, at least for the time being. I would now like to speak to Miss Tucker.'

Tucker confirmed all that Nerissa had said, including several visits from Tregarron, over the period of the last four or five weeks.

Pitt thanked her and left. He walked back to Lisson Grove with his mind in turmoil. The heart of this case was no longer anything to do with Serafina's death, or Adriana, but two other matters.

The first and most urgent was the question of Evan Blantyre's loyalties. Had he given Pitt the information regarding Duke Alois out of loyalty to the Austrian Empire, which it seemed he had never lost, in spite of working for the British Government? If that were so, and his betrayal of Lazar Dragovic, and the later murder of Serafina, and then of Adriana, were to preserve the unity at the heart of Europe, then it would be as safe as anything was for Pitt to rely on it. He could deal with the prosecution and conviction of Blantyre after Duke Alois had been and gone.

If, on the other hand, Blantyre had some other purpose,

his information about Duke Alois was very far from reliable.

And then the other obvious question arose: after Duke Alois left, what was Pitt going to do about Blantyre? What could he do? What evidence was there? He had no doubt now that Blantyre had killed Serafina and Adriana, but he doubted that there was sufficient proof to convict a man of such prominence and high reputation as Blantyre now had.

But that would have to wait. It was two days until the duke crossed the Channel and landed in England. Individual murder, however tragic, would pale beside the effects of a political assassination in London; moreover, one of which Special Branch had been personally warned, and yet had still failed to prevent.

Pitt checked with Stoker at Lisson Grove. Then, after one or two items of urgent business, he left again and took a hansom to Blantyre's office. In spite of his bereavement, Blantyre had chosen to continue working. Duke Alois's visit could not be put off. There were arrangements to make, details to be attended to, and Evan Blantyre, with his intimate and affectionate knowledge of Austria, was the best man for it. Many who had at one time or another also lost someone they loved found his continuing to work both understandable and admirable.

Pitt had telephoned in advance, and found Blantyre in his office waiting for him.

'Anything further?' Blantyre asked as he sat down in his large chair close to the fire. He poured whisky for both of them without bothering to ask. In spite of being the middle of March, it was a bitter day outside, and they were both tired and cold.

'Yes,' Pitt answered, accepting the exquisite glass, but putting it down on the small table to his right without drinking from it. 'I know now who killed Serafina, and why. But then so do you.' He watched Blantyre's sensitive, haggard face and saw not a flicker in it, not even a change in his eyes.

'And who killed Mrs Blantyre,' Pitt continued. 'Again, so do you.'

This time there was a shift of pain, which Pitt believed was perfectly real. Blantyre must have hated killing her, but known that if he himself were to survive then he had no alternative. Adriana would never forgive him for her father's death, and maybe not for Serafina's either. Even if she told no one, he would never be able to sleep again if she were in the house; perhaps not eat or drink. He would always be aware of her watching him. His mind would run riot imagining what she felt for him now and when she would lose control and erupt into action.

Pitt went on levelly. 'I also know who betrayed Lazar Dragovic to the Austrians, so he was beaten and shot to death, which of course was the beginning of all this.'

'It was necessary,' Blantyre said almost conversationally. They could have been discussing some regrettable financial error, or the dismissal of an old but ineffectual servant.

'Perhaps you don't understand that,' he went on. 'You are a man of reason and deduction who comes to conclusions, and leaves it for others to do something about it. My father was like that. Clever, and he cared, but never enough to do anything that risked his own moral comfort.' A passion of bitterness filled his face and all but choked his voice. 'Whoever else lived or died, he must always be able to sleep at night!'

Pitt did not answer.

Blantyre leaned forward in his chair, still holding the whisky glass in his hand. He looked steadily at Pitt. 'The Austrian Empire lies at the heart of Europe. We have discussed this before. I tried to explain to you then how complex it is, but it seems you are a "little Englander" at heart. I like you, but God help me, you have no vision. You are a provincial little man. Britain's Empire covers most of the globe, in patches here and there: Britain itself, Gibraltar, Malta, Egypt, Sudan, most of Africa all the way to the Cape, territories in the Middle East, the entire continent of India, Burma, Hong Kong, Shanghai, Borneo, the whole sub-continent of Australia, New Zealand, Canada, and islands in every ocean on Earth. The sun never sets on it, in the sense that it's always daylight somewhere that's British.'

Pitt stirred.

Temper flared in Blantyre's eyes. 'Austria is completely different! Apart from the Austrian Netherlands, it stretches in one continuous land mass from parts of Germany in the north-west to Ukraine in the east, south to most of Romania, north again as far down the Adriatic Coast as Ragusa, then west through Croatia, northern Italy into Switzerland. There are eleven main languages and the richest, most creative and original culture, and science in every field of human endeavour. But it is fragile!'

His hands jerked up, and apart, as if he were encompassing some kind of explosion with his strong fingers.

'Its genius means that it is also liable to be torn apart by the very nature of the ideas it creates, the individuality of its people. The new nations of Italy and Germany, born in turmoil and still testing their strength, are tearing at the fabric of order. Italy is chaotic; it always has been.'

Pitt smiled in spite of himself.

'Germany is altogether a different matter,' Blantyre went on with intense seriousness. 'It is sleek and dangerous. Its government is not chaotic, anything but. It is highly organised and militarily brilliant. They will not be contained against their will for long.'

'Germany is not part of the Austrian Empire,' Pitt pointed out. 'They have a language in common, and a certain culture, but not an identity. Austria will never swallow them; they will not allow it.'

'For God's sake, Pitt, wake up!' Blantyre was nearly shouting now. 'If Austria fractures, loses control of its possessions, or there is an uprising in the east that is sufficiently successful to be dangerous, Vienna will have to take reprisals, or lose everything. If there is trouble in northern Italy it hardly matters, but if it is in one of the Slavic possessions, like Croatia or Serbia, then they will turn to Russia for help. They are blood brothers, and Russia will not need more than an excuse. Teutonic Germany will have found the justification it needs to take German Austria.'

His voice was growing harsher, as if the nightmare were already happening. 'Hungary will secede, and before you know how to stop any of it, you will have a war that will spread like fire until it embroils most of the world. Don't imagine England will escape. It won't. There will be war from Ireland to the Middle East, and from Moscow to North Africa, maybe further. Perhaps all of Africa, because it is British, and then Australia will follow, and New Zealand. Even Canada. Perhaps eventually the United States as well.'

Pitt was stunned by the enormity of it, and both the horror and the absurdity of the view.

'No one would let that sort of thing happen,' he said soberly. 'You are suggesting that one act of violence in the Balkans would end in a conflagration that would consume the world. That's ridiculous.'

Blantyre took a deep breath and let it out slowly.

'Pitt, Austria is the linchpin, the glue that holds together the political body of Europe.' He was staring intently at Pitt now. 'It wouldn't be overnight, but you'd be appalled how quickly it would happen, if Vienna loses control and the constituent parts of the Empire turn on each other. Picture a street riot. You must have had to deal with them, in your days on the beat. How many men does it take before the crowd joins in, and every idiot with a grudge, or too much to drink, starts swinging his fists? All the old enmities under the surface smoulder and then break out.'

Pitt's memory brought back violently exactly what Blantyre had said: rage, hysteria, violence spreading outwards until it took hold, simply for its own sake, screaming and lashing out beyond thought of any kind. Too late to regret it afterwards when the houses were in ruins, broken glass everywhere, fire-blackened walls, blood, even deaths.

Blantyre was watching him. He could see the understanding in Pitt's eyes. It was too late to hide it.

'There will be a vacuum at the heart,' Blantyre went on. 'And however much you like to imagine Britain is the centre of Europe, it isn't. Our power lies in pieces, all over the globe. We have no army and no presence at the core of Europe. There will be chaos. The Austrian and German part of Europe will be at the throats of the Slavic, northern and eastern part, which will call on its old ally in both race and faith, Russia. There will be a pan-European war, economic ruin, and in the end possibly a new and dominant Germany. Is the peaceful death, in her sleep, of one old woman so important to you that you will solve that, at the expense of guarding an Austrian duke so he is not assassinated on English soil, in the capital of the only other truly great empire in the world?'

'That is not the point,' Pitt said quietly, facing Blantyre across the two untouched glasses of whisky. 'I have no intention of pursuing that now, probably not at all. What concerns me is the validity of the information you have given Special

Branch regarding Duke Alois, and the apparent threat of his assassination.'

Blantyre raised his eyebrows. 'Why should you doubt it? Surely you can see that I, of all people, do not want an Austrian duke assassinated. Why the hell do you think I turned Dragovic over to the Austrians? He was planning the assassination of a particularly brutal local governor, a pig of a man, but the vengeance for his death would have been terrible.' He leaned forward, his face twisted with passion. 'Think, damn it! Use whatever brain you have. Of course I don't want Alois assassinated.'

Pitt smiled. 'Unless, of course, he is another dissident. Then it would be very convenient if he were killed while he was here in London. Not the Austrians' fault – it's all down to the incompetent British, with their Special Branch led by a new man, who'll swallow any story at all.'

Blantyre sighed wearily. 'Is this all about your promotion, and the fact that you don't think you are fit for the job?'

Pitt clenched his jaw to keep his temper. 'It's about the fact that most of the information we have on the assassination here came from you, and that you are a murderer and a liar, whose principal loyalty is to the Habsburg Crown, and not the British,' he replied, carefully keeping his voice level. 'If Duke Alois were your enemy rather than your friend, you would be perfectly capable of having him murdered wherever it was most convenient to you. Come to that, even if he were your friend, if he stood in the way of your beliefs.'

Blantyre winced, but he did not speak.

'Or alternatively, there is no plot at all,' Pitt continued. 'You wanted to keep Special Branch busy, and the police out of any part in investigating the murder of Serafina Montserrat, and then most regrettably, of your wife. You had to kill Serafina, once you knew she was losing grip over her mind, and might betray you to Adriana, because she would never excuse you for betraying her father. That forced your hand. And you need to survive, or how can you be of service in helping Austria keep control of its rapidly crumbling empire, after the suicide of the Crown Prince, and his replacement by Franz Ferdinand, whom the old Emperor despises.'

Blantyre's jaw was tight, his eyes hard, as if Pitt had changed without warning from something agreeable into something hideous.

'A fair estimate,' he said between his teeth. 'But you will not know if I am telling the truth or not, will you? You have checked all the information I gave you, or you should have. If you haven't, then you are a lot greater fool than I took you to be. Dare you trust it?' He smiled thinly. 'You damned well daren't ignore it!'

Pitt felt as if the ground were sinking beneath him. Yet the fire still burned gently in the hearth, the flames warming the whisky glasses, which shone a luminous amber in the soft liquid.

'Be careful, Pitt,' Blantyre warned. 'Consider deeply what you do, after Alois has been and gone. Assuming you manage to keep him alive, don't entertain any ideas of arresting me, or bringing me to any kind of trial.' He smiled very slightly. 'I visited Serafina quite often, and I listened to her. A good deal of that time she had no idea who I was. But then you know that already. You will have heard it from Lady Vespasia, if nothing else.'

'Of course I know that,' Pitt said tartly. 'If you were not afraid of her talking candidly again, to others, you would not have taken the risk of killing her.'

'Quite. I regretted doing it.' Blantyre gave a slight shrug. 'She was a magnificent woman, in her time. She knew more secrets of both personal and political indiscretions than anyone else within my knowledge.'

Pitt was aware of a change in the atmosphere: a warmth in Blantyre, a chill in himself.

Blantyre nodded his head fractionally. 'I see that you understand. I listened with acute interest. She rambled on about all manner of things, of people. Some I had already guessed, but much of it was new to me. I had no idea that her circle was so wide: Austrian, Hungarian, Croatian, Italian were all what I might have imagined. But the others: the French, for example; the German; and of course the British. Now there were some considerable surprises.' He looked very steadily at Pitt, as if to make certain that he had grasped the weight of what he was saying.

Pitt thought of Tregarron, also using Nerissa Freemarsh to disguise his visits to Serafina. What did he fear that could be so much worse than being thought to have an affair with a plain, single woman of no significance, and almost on his own doorstep? It was a despicable use of a vulnerable person whose reputation it would permanently ruin. If it ever became known, it would take from her the last chance of any respectable marriage.

'The British Special Branch, and various other diplomatic and intelligence sources, have a record of some very dubious actions,' Blantyre continued. His voice dropped a little. 'Some have made them vulnerable to blackmail, with all its shabby consequences. And of course there are also the idealists who set certain values above the narrow love of country. Serafina was another little Englander like you. She kept silent.' He left the further suggestion hanging in the air. It was not necessary to spell it out.

Pitt stared at him. He had no doubt whatsoever that he meant it. There was a confidence in him, an arrogance that filled the room.

Blantyre was smiling broadly. 'Victor Narraway would have

killed me,' he said with almost a kind of relish. 'You won't. You haven't the courage. You may think of it, but in the end you will not bring yourself to do it. The guilt would cripple you.'

A look of contempt filled his eyes, and at the same time an extraordinary pain, as if the words meant far more to him than the time or circumstances explained.

'I like you, Pitt,' he said with intense sincerity, his voice thick with emotion. 'You are an intelligent, imaginative and compassionate man. You have quite a nice sense of humour. But in the end you haven't the steel in your soul to act outside what is predictable, and comfortable to you. You are too much for the conventions that furnish the inner safety of your mind. You are essentially bourgeois, just like my father.'

He took a deep breath. 'Now you had better go and make sure you save Duke Alois. You can't afford to have him shot in England.'

Pitt rose to his feet and left without speaking. There was no answer to offer that had any meaning between them.

Outside he walked along the windy street. He was chilled and shivering in spite of the sun, which sat low in the sky, giving a clean-edged, late winter light. Was Blantyre right, that Narraway would have shot him, but Pitt did not have the courage when it came to the moment? Would he stand with a pistol in his hand, unable to fire in cold blood at a man he knew, and had liked?

He did not know the answer. He was not even certain what he wanted the truth to be. If he could do such a thing, what would he gain, other than the right to hold the position he did? But he must also have the intelligence, the judgement, and all the other skills.

And what would he lose? His children might never know

anything about it, but it would still be a barrier between them, because he knew himself.

And what ruthlessness would Charlotte see in him that she had not seen before, and had not wanted to? Or Vespasia? Or anyone? Above all these, what would he know of himself? How would it change him from who he was now? Was Blantyre right, and his inner comfort was what he cared about most, in the end?

He was walking rapidly, not certain where he was going. He was less than half a mile from the part of the Foreign Office where Jack worked. There were no secrets left about Blantyre. Pitt knew the worst. The resolution as to what to do lay in the turmoil of his own mind. It was brutally obvious what Blantyre was doing and why.

Vespasia knew from the moment Victor Narraway came into her sitting room that he had serious news. His face was pinched with anxiety, and he looked cold, even though it was a comparatively mild evening.

Without realising she was doing it, she rose to greet him.

'What is it, Victor? What has happened?'

His hands were chill when he took hers, briefly, but she did not pull away.

'I have learned something further of Serafina, which I am afraid may be more serious than I had supposed. Tregarron visited Dorchester Terrace several times. I thought at first it was primarily to see Nerissa . . .'

'Nerissa?' For an instant she wanted to laugh at the idea, then the impulse died. 'Really? It seems an eccentric idea. Are you sure?'

'No, I'm not sure. Men do sometimes have the oddest tastes in affairs, with women as different from their wives as possible. And perhaps the element of danger, even absurdity, is part of the appeal. But now I believe that Nerissa was the excuse and Serafina the reason.'

'She was at least a generation older than he, and there is no proof, in fact not even a suggestion, that they knew each other,' she pointed out.

'But his father did,' Narraway said grimly, watching her face. 'Very well.'

'Oh. Oh dear. Yes, I see. And you are assuming that perhaps Serafina was indiscreet about that also. Or perhaps others were able to deduce that the present Lord Tregarron was visiting for fear of her saying something unfortunate. Who is he protecting? His father's reputation? Is his mother still alive?'

'Yes. She is very old, but apparently quite clear in her mind.' His expression was sad and gentle. 'What a devil of a burden it is to know so many secrets, however you learned them. How much safer it would be to understand nothing, to see all manner of things before you, and never add it up so you perceive the meaning.'

It was not necessary for either of them to say more. Each carried his or her own burden of knowledge, differently gained but perhaps equally heavy.

They sat by the fire for a few more moments, then he rose and wished her good night.

But when he left, going out into the dark and the mild, blustery wind, Vespasia remained sitting beside the last of the fire, thinking about what he had said. Of course Tregarron would rather his mother never heard of her husband's affair with Serafina, on the assumption that she did not have a perfectly good idea anyway. But it did not seem sufficient now to cause Tregarron to make so many visits to see Serafina, all these years afterwards. Surely there was something else, possibly something about that affair uglier and more dangerous than unfaithfulness, which was regrettably not as uncommon as one would have wished?

She must make her own enquiries. The day after tomorrow Duke Alois Habsburg would land in Dover. There was no time to spare for subtlety. It was not a thought she wished to face, but she knew whom she must ask for this possibly dangerous piece of knowledge. She had reached the point where the price of evasion would be greater than that of asking.

The morning was bright and full of the promise of spring. Vespasia called her carriage and alighted in Cavendish Square at a quarter to ten. It was a long time – over two decades – since she had last seen Bishop Magnus Collier. He was a little older than she, and had retired several years ago. It was a fortunate chance that she knew from a mutual acquaintance exactly where he lived. As she crossed the pavement and mounted the steps, she had a momentary feeling that she wished she did not, or had forgotten. It was a cowardice she was ashamed of, but very real.

The footman who answered the door had no idea who she was. She offered her card, telling him that she was an old acquaintance and the matter was of extreme urgency.

He looked doubtful.

'His lordship would not be amused should you leave me standing on the step in the street,' she said coldly.

He invited her in and, in a manner no more than civil, showed her to a morning room where the fire was not yet lit. It was fifteen very cool minutes before he returned, pink-faced, and conducted her into the bishop's study. There, the fire was burning well, and the warmth in the air wrapped around her with instant comfort.

She accepted the offer of tea, and occupied herself looking at the rows of bookshelves. Many of the titles she was familiar with from long ago, though they were works she would never have read herself. She found most of the very early Church fathers 'much encumbered with small things', and more than a trifle pompous.

She heard the door open and close and turned to find Bishop Collier standing just inside, a curious smile on his lean face. He was very thin, and far greyer than when they had last met, but the warmth in his eyes had not changed, nor the quick intelligence.

'All my life it has been a pleasure to see you,' he said quietly. 'But I am concerned that you say it is a matter of such urgency. It must be, to bring you here, after our last parting. What can I do to help?'

'I'm sorry,' she said softly, and she meant it. The impossible feelings were no longer here, but it had still been a wise decision not to meet again. There were other people's perceptions to consider as well.

He gestured towards the chairs near the fire and they both sat. She arranged her skirts with a practised hand, in a single, graceful movement.

'Perhaps you read that Serafina Montserrat died recently?' she began.

'Time is catching up with us rather more rapidly than I expected,' he said ruefully. 'But perhaps that is its nature, and ours to be taken by surprise by what was utterly predictable. But I'm sure you did not come to discuss the nature of time and its peculiar elastic qualities. I hope her passing was easy. She was a remarkable woman. She would have faced even death with courage. I would be surprised if it had the temerity to inconvenience her over-much.'

Vespasia smiled in spite of herself. She had forgotten, temporarily, what it had been in him that she had liked so much.

'I think it was simply a matter of going to sleep and not

waking again,' she replied. 'The part of it that brings me here is that the sleep was the result of having been given a massive overdose of laudanum.'

All the light vanished from his face. He leaned forward a little. 'Are you saying that it was given to her without her knowledge, or that she took it herself, intending to die? I find the latter very difficult to believe. If that is true, then she changed beyond all recognition.'

'No, I am not. She rambled in her mind, sometimes forgot what year it was, or to whom she was speaking, which caused her profound anxiety, in case she would accidentally let slip a confidence that would do much damage.' She recalled the terror in Serafina's face with acute pain. 'She did make such slips, and she was murdered.'

He shook his head. 'Are you certain beyond doubt?'

'Yes. But that is not why I have come. My concern is with one of the secrets she let slip, and the damage it could cause now.'

'What can I do to help?' He looked puzzled and very much aware of the widening circle of damage such things can create.

'The secret concerns an affair she had very many years ago, with the late Lord Tregarron.' She stopped, seeing the change in his face, the sudden darkness. It would be impossible now for him to deny that he was bitterly aware of what it was she was going to ask.

'I cannot repeat to you things that were told to me in confidence,' he said. 'Surely you know better than to ask?'

'There is a very slight deviousness in you, Magnus,' she said with a curve of her lips that was almost a smile. 'Anything Tregarron might have told you may be confidential, although the man has been dead for years. What Serafina told you might have been in the nature of a confession, but I doubt it. Is an old affair, which neither you nor I will repeat, really so very important that we can allow it to cost a man's life now? And if the worst comes to pass, it may be more than one.'

'Surely you are exaggerating?' he demurred, but there was no conviction in his eyes.

This time she did smile. 'You are not built for deceit, Magnus. Are you now going to pretend that there was nothing more to it than an indiscretion – one that is long ago over, and both people involved are dead? Even the elder Lady Tregarron is not likely to care a great deal. I doubt she was as innocent as her son seems to believe.'

'What is it you imagine I am hiding, Vespasia?' he asked.

'A truth that is a great deal uglier,' she replied.

'He was married,' he pointed out reasonably. 'It was a betrayal of his vows to his wife.'

'Would you excommunicate him for it?' She raised her silver eyebrows curiously.

'Of course not! And I dare say he repented. I do not have the right, or the wish, to assume that he did not.'

'Of course you don't,' she agreed. 'So we may dispense with the fiction that it had anything to do with that.'

'But it did, I assure you,' he said immediately.

'A sophistry, Magnus. I gather it sprang from that. By having an affair with Serafina he had laid himself open to blackmail. He may have wished profoundly at the time to keep the matter secret. He was in a senior diplomatic position in Vienna. It would have made his discretion severely suspect.'

His gaze wavered for an instant. 'I cannot tell you, Vespasia.'

'You do not need to, my dear. I can deduce it for myself. Now that I know where to look, I can inform the appropriate people.'

'I believe Victor Narraway is no longer in office,' he observed, this time meeting her gaze squarely.

'That is true. His place has been taken by Thomas Pitt, who is married to my grand-niece. I have known Thomas for years. His brother-in-law is Jack Radley, who is assistant to the present Lord Tregarron.'

'Vespasia! Please . . .' he began, then stopped.

'I assume it was treason of which his father was guilty?' she said so quietly it was almost a whisper.

'I cannot say,' he answered, but his face showed she was right. His lack of denial was an admission.

She stood up slowly. 'I'm sorry. You deserved better from me than this. Were it not now treason, and more murder yet to come, I should not have asked.'

He rose also. 'You always had the better of me, in the end.'

'It was not a battle, Magnus. I understood you more than you did me, because your beliefs were never hidden. It is a good way to be. I am glad you have not changed. That is a victory; don't regard it as anything else.'

He smiled, like sudden sunlight on a landscape, but his eyes were still grave. 'Be careful, Vespasia. Although I suppose that is a foolish thing to say. You haven't changed either.'

Vespasia had no doubt now what she must do. She would like to have seen Jack at his rooms in the Foreign Office, but she could not go there without Tregarron being aware of it. Instead she would have to speak to Emily, and hope to impress on her the desperate urgency of what she had to say.

As it transpired, Emily was not at home. Vespasia had either to wait for her, or to leave and return again in the late afternoon. She went home and used her telephone – an instrument of which she was becoming increasingly fond. However, on this most urgent occasion it did not help her. She failed to contact Victor Narraway, or Charlotte, and she did not dare to spark curiosity and possibly alarm by trying to reach Jack.

So, in the end, she returned to Emily's home at five o'clock. She had only half an hour to wait before Emily herself arrived.

'Aunt Vespasia!' She was instantly concerned. 'The butler tells me you called this morning as well. Is everything all right? What has happened? It . . . it isn't Jack, is it?' Now she was afraid.

'No, not at all. As far as I know Jack is perfectly well, at least so far,' Vespasia replied. 'But there is a situation he is unaware of, which may endanger him very badly, unless he acts now. It will not be easy, and he might have wished to wait, but I am afraid circumstances may not allow him that luxury.'

'What?' Emily demanded. 'What is it?'

'When do you expect him home?'

Emily glanced at the ormolu clock on the mantelpiece. 'In half an hour, maybe a little more. Can you not tell me what it is?'

'Not yet. Perhaps you would care for a cup of tea while we wait?' Vespasia suggested.

Emily apologised for her oversight in hospitality and rang the bell for the maid. When she had requested the tea, she paced the floor, unable to relax. Vespasia thought of asking her to desist, and then changed her mind. In the same circumstances, she might have been unable to rest either.

When Jack Radley arrived home, the butler informed him of the situation. He stopped long enough only to hand his overcoat to the footman before he went to the withdrawing room.

He saw Emily at the window. She swung around to face him as soon as she heard the door. Vespasia was sitting on the sofa before the fire. The remnants of tea and biscuits were on the tray, Emily's undrunk.

365

'Is it something serious?' Jack said, as soon as he had greeted Vespasia appropriately.

'I am afraid it is,' she replied. 'If Emily is to remain, then she will have to give her word that she will repeat no part of this to anyone at all, not even Charlotte or Thomas. It would be better if you did not know.'

'I'm staying,' Emily said firmly.

'You are not,' Jack responded. 'If I think it is wise, I shall tell you afterwards. Thank you for keeping Aunt Vespasia company until I arrived.'

Emily drew in her breath to argue. Then she looked again at his face, and obediently left the room. On the way out, she instructed the footman to see that no one intruded into the withdrawing room, even to collect the tray, or to offer Mr Radley anything.

Briefly, and with as few explanations as she could manage without risking his doubt, Vespasia told Jack what she had learned.

He stood by the fire, his mind racing, his whole body feeling tight and bruised. He wanted to cry out that it was impossible: only a collection of circumstances that did not fit together and, in the end, meaning nothing at all.

And even as the words formed in his mouth, he knew that it was not so. There were other things that Vespasia did not know but which his imagination filled in hideously well, like the last pieces of a jigsaw. Mostly they concerned the way Tregarron had dismissed Pitt, but there were other small things as well: contradictions Jack had tried not to see. There had been small items of information that had turned up with people who should not have known them.

'I'm sorry,' Vespasia said quietly. 'I know that you believed Tregarron to be a good man, and that it was a considerable promotion for you to assist him as closely as you did. But he will be brought down, Jack, sooner or later. You must see to it that you do not go down with him. Treason is not a forgivable offence.'

But Jack's mind was already elsewhere. Tomorrow Alois Habsburg was due to arrive in Dover. Pitt would go there tonight to be on the train with him when he came up to London. Tregarron had left the office at midday. There was no decision to be made. Of course Tregarron had denied there was any attempt to be made on Alois's life! He was the one who was going to make it!

'I'm going to warn Thomas,' he said, his voice shaking. 'I must go immediately. We'll leave for Dover tonight. Please tell Emily.' He turned and strode towards the door.

'Jack!' Vespasia called after him.

'I have no time to stay. I'm sorry!'

'I know you haven't,' she replied. 'My carriage is at the door. Take it.'

'Thank you,' he said over his shoulder. He ran out onto the footpath and looked for the carriage. It was only a few yards away. He ran to it, calling out to the coachman, and gave Pitt's home address. Or should he go to Lisson Grove? He stopped.

'Sir?'

'No – right! Keppel Street.' Jack scrambled into the carriage and it pulled away from the kerb. He sat white-knuckled while they raced through the streets. It was not far, but it seemed as if they crossed half London.

They skated to a stop. He flung the door open and strode over the pavement. He knocked on the door, which was opened by the new maid, Minnie Maude.

'Yes, sir?'

'Is Commander Pitt at home?'

'No, sir. I'm afraid yer just missed 'im.'

'Has he gone to Lisson Grove?'

'No, sir. 'E's gone ter the railway station.'

'How long ago? Quickly!'

'Quarter of an hour, sir. Mrs Pitt's at 'ome.'

'No . . . thank you.' He swung round and went back to the carriage. He was too late. There was nothing he could do now but go home and get money, and perhaps a swordstick from the library, and go down to Dover himself.

Chapter Thirteen

Pitt woke up in the morning with a jolt, taking a moment to stare at his strange surroundings and remember where he was. It should not have been difficult. He had spent enough of the night lying awake staring at the unfamiliar streetlamp patterns on the ceiling of his hotel room in Dover. This was the day Alois Habsburg was to land and take the London train. From the moment he set foot on English soil he was Pitt's responsibility.

He had gone over the plans in his mind, trying to think of anything more he could do to foresee the attack, exactly where it would come, and how, even if it would come at all. Had they been carefully misdirected here, to Dover and Duke Alois, and in reality the crime would be something entirely different? In the small hours of the night he thought of the Bank of England, the Tower of London and the Crown Jewels, even the Houses of Parliament.

Pitt had fallen asleep still without any answers, and knowing that it was pointless even to ask the questions now, but still the anxiety remained.

Now he rose quickly, washed, shaved and dressed. There was

time for a quick breakfast and it would be stupid not to eat. The best decisions were seldom made on an empty stomach.

He found Stoker in the dining room but they sat separately, to draw less attention to themselves. They left a few moments apart also. It was probably completely unnecessary, but the observation of it was better than beginning a habit of carelessness.

They were close to the docks anyway. It took them only ten minutes to be at the pier where the cross-Channel ferry was already approaching. Pitt stood with his hands in his pockets watching the outlines of the boat as it came closer across the choppy grey water. He hunched his shoulders and turned his collar up against the chill of the wind. He liked the smell of salt, even the tar and oil and fish odours, but somehow sea wind was colder. It crept through every crevice in clothing, no matter how carefully one dressed.

He knew where Stoker was, and the other three men he had brought, but never once did he look at them. He had not asked assistance from the Dover police. They were there as a courtesy, knowing from the Austrian Embassy of Duke Alois's visit, but he had weighed the issues and decided it was better not to let them think there was particular danger.

He was standing in the wind, part of the crowd, when he felt a nudge next to him and half-turned. Jack was standing beside him, pale-faced, cold, his coat collar turned up.

'You were right,' Jack said before Pitt could speak. 'It's Tregarron. I'm sorry. Serafina seduced his father into an affair, then because of it, he was blackmailed into treason. It was all a long time ago, and obviously he's dead now, but the present Lord Tregarron was desperate to conceal it, for his own protection, and his mother's too, I imagine. It . . . it explains a few other things he was doing. I should have seen it earlier. I didn't want to.'

Pitt looked at him with surprise and a sudden warmth of affection. 'You came down here to tell me?'

'Of course.'

'Thank you.'

'Be careful . . .' Jack warned urgently.

Pitt smiled. 'I will. Then get back home, before you're missed.'

'Can't I help?'

'You just did. Go back home. We may need you there yet, if Tregarron's at the party this evening.'

Jack smiled, and moved off into the crowd.

The ferry was nosing in gently; in a few minutes the gangway would be lowered. The Port Authority had told Pitt Duke Alois would be disembarking first. It would have been better had he come amidst the other passengers. It would have been less conspicuous, but it would have been contrary to protocol, and thereby signalled that they felt unable to protect him in normal circumstances. It was a debate Pitt had had with himself, and was still not sure if he had come to the right answer.

He watched as the docking procedure took place. It seemed infinitely slow, and yet when a slender elegant figure appeared at the top of the gangway, his dark hair blowing in the wind, he felt a leap of alarm. His mind raced to think of anything he might have missed, failed to do, not thought of, and Reibnitz, if he were really here, would have prepared for.

Alois came down the steps, slowly, giving a slight salute and smiling at the dignitaries waiting at the bottom to welcome him. He was followed by four casually dressed, very fashionable men around his own age. None of them were in any kind of uniform. Pitt was seized with a sudden conviction that they had not the faintest idea that there would be any danger. They were on a foreign holiday to a country where they had no enemies, no rivals, and no one who could be anything but delighted to see them.

The Mayor of Dover stepped forward and the welcome began. It was a long, highly formal affair.

Pitt watched the small crowd of people gathered to observe an event, or to meet their own friends, trying to appear as if he were looking for some family member himself. He saw Stoker, and the others of his men, coming a little closer now as Duke Alois moved away with the Mayor and his officials.

'Looks as if he has no idea of danger,' Stoker said quietly as they walked side by side from the dock along the street towards the railway station. 'I suppose somebody did tell him?'

Pitt did not reply, because he did not know the answer. Perhaps the Austrians had thought it wiser only to tell the four men with the duke. There must be somebody assigned to care for his safety.

Stoker grunted, and increased his pace.

Pitt was tense as Duke Alois and his men stepped up into the carriage and it moved off at a walk, the general traffic held back to allow them passage. Pitt looked from side to side of the street but he saw no dust carts, no sweepers. Where was Staum?

He and Stoker followed after the carriage on foot, watching every movement, occasionally glancing up at higher windows above shops and offices. The wind was gusty with a light spatter of rain, and as far as he could see, none of them was open. Still he was nervous. Why was it so easy?

He glanced at Stoker, and saw the same anxiety in his face, in the stiff, tight-muscled way he walked.

If there was no attack in Dover, did that mean it was going to be on the train after all? A diversion? A crash?

The station was in sight. Two hundred yards to go.

A dust cart trundled away, wheels bouncing on uneven stones.

Fifty yards, then they were there. Duke Alois and his men alighted. The Mayor of Dover conducted them inside. Pitt and Stoker gave a last look around, saw nothing suspicious, and followed them in.

The railway station was large and busy. A porter pushed a trolley weighed down with trunks and cases, its wheels rumbling over the slightly uneven platform. A few yards away a family were arguing excitedly, children jumping up and down. A small boy wailed with frustration. A man waved his arms and shouted a greeting. Half a dozen carriage doors slammed in the nearest train and ahead of them the engine blew out great clouds of steam and smuts. Pitt brushed them off his face, unintentionally smearing the dirt across his cheek, to Stoker's amusement. For an instant the tension was broken.

Pitt wiped away the smuts and they pushed their way past other passengers. They reached the train at which the Mayor was already bidding Duke Alois goodbye. His escort were looking far more attentive, standing on the platform looking first one direction then the other, eyes searching.

As Pitt drew closer, he saw that one of them had his hand out of sight under his coat. Pitt knew it rested on the grip of his revolver. Pitt stopped and looked straight at the man's face.

'Commander Pitt, Special Branch,' he introduced himself. 'If you will allow me, I shall show you my identification.'

Before the man could reply, Alois turned from the Mayor and stepped towards Pitt, smiling. He had a pleasant face, although it was a trifle too individual to be handsome: ascetic and filled with a kind of lop-sided amusement.

He held out his hand. 'How good of you to come,' he said.

cheerfully. 'Quite unnecessary, I'm sure, but a damned decent gesture.' He spoke English without any trace of an accent.

Pitt offered his hand and met a firm, surprisingly strong grasp.

'How do you do, sir?' he replied. 'It probably is unnecessary, but it might still be a good idea to get into the carriage anyway, if you don't mind.'

'Certainly. Cold out here. Always damned cold, railway platforms, don't you think?' With alacrity, Duke Alois gave the Mayor a small salute, and disappeared into the very handsomely decorated first-class carriage. Pitt was a step behind him.

Duke Alois looked around approvingly. 'Oh, very comfortable,' he said with satisfaction. 'Plenty of room.' He looked at his own escort, standing to attention waiting for his orders. 'You chaps can busy yourselves doing whatever you do, looking out of carriage windows, or watching doors, or whatever. The Commander here will have a cup of tea.' He looked at Pitt. 'Won't you?' It was a question, but the look in his light blue eyes was level and unflinching. In its own discreet way it was an order.

'I'd prefer to make sure of the rest of the carriage, sir, if you don't mind,' Pitt answered.

Duke Alois laughed. 'For heaven's sake, man, have your fellow here do it.' He gestured towards Stoker. 'I'm sure he's excellent. If you brought only him, you can't really imagine there's anything to worry about.'

'There are others,' Pitt told him.

'Very good. Then we shall have a cup of tea, and leave them to it. Come.' He opened the compartment door, and – short of an outright refusal, which really would be only for the sake of asserting his own authority – Pitt was obliged to accept.

The duke closed the door, sat down in one of the very

comfortable seats and crossed his legs, indicating the seat opposite for Pitt. This looked like being a long and very tedious ride. Narraway might have been versed in the art of conversation to entertain an Austrian duke, but Pitt was very definitely not. They could not have had less in common. Even the long-distant childhood memories of growing up on a country estate in England's gentle Home Counties, where his father had been gamekeeper, would be totally different from the duke's upbringing in the palaces of Austria.

Pitt had no interest whatever in philosophy, and none in the more abstract sciences he had been told Duke Alois devoted his time to.

'This is very good,' Duke Alois repeated with a smile, leaning back in his seat and stretching his long legs. 'Now we can talk.'

Pitt swallowed. This was the one nightmare he had not foreseen, and he had no idea how to deal with it. What possible excuse could he make to escape?

'I was hoping you would come,' Alois continued. 'Rather beefed up the bit about Staum,' he went on. 'Nasty little swine, but actually he's one of ours. Reibnitz too. Have to use them, now and then. I expect you have them yourself.'

'I beg your p-pardon, sir?' Pitt stammered.

Duke Alois looked amused. His face radiated a pleasure that made him look more relaxed, less studious and far more like a man on a holiday. Was it possible he was even in some way enjoying this? Had he no conception of danger, of blood, pain, even death?

Pitt drew in his breath and tried to speak levelly, courteously. For all Duke Alois's divorce from reality – and heaven knew, the Habsburgs had bred more than their fair share of imbeciles – he was still a royal duke.

'Sir, we cannot afford to take the threats lightly,' he began.

375

'I don't,' Alois assured him. 'I am quite aware that it is serious, which is why we should have our conversation immediately, just in case we should be disturbed.'

'Sir—' Pitt began.

Duke Alois held up his hand. 'Please don't interrupt,' he requested. 'It is the whole purpose of my journey.' He saw Pitt's bewilderment. A brief, wry smile lit his face for a moment, then disappeared. 'You find that absurd? Good. That means at least so far, I am succeeding.'

Pitt gritted his teeth. This was assuming the proportions of a nightmare.

The duke leaned forward. Now his face was totally earnest. 'You have a traitor in your government, Commander Pitt. In your Foreign Office, to be precise. I am happy to give you all the details I have, which are considerable.'

Pitt swallowed. He was out of his depth, but he did not wish Alois to know it.

'And why would you do this, sir?' he asked with what he hoped was an expression of polite interest.

'Because I wish to establish a good working relationship with British Special Branch,' Alois replied. 'I believe we may turn this particular gentleman into a double agent, to both our advantages.'

A wild idea occurred to Pitt. He looked at Alois's face, at his level, intense stare. It was suddenly very apparent the man had a depth of intelligence he usually chose to mask. Pitt took a deep breath and plunged in. 'You are speaking of Lord Tregarron, I presume?' His heart pounded so hard it almost choked him.

Slowly Alois smiled, ruefully, like a child whose game has been spoiled. He let out a sigh. 'Damn! I thought I had something worth trading. Have I tipped my hand for nothing?'

More wild ideas chased across Pitt's imagination. 'Not

necessarily,' he replied. 'I have only just realised Tregarron's treason. I assume it has to do with his father, and Serafina Montserrat, at least to begin with?'

'Indeed. Rather before my time. Even before my predecessor's,' Alois replied.

'Your predecessor?' Pitt questioned.

'As Victor Narraway was yours,' Alois answered. 'The difference between your position and mine is only that I prefer to allow everyone to presume that my only interests are science and philosophy, intellectual hobbies rather than of any practical use. It allows me a much greater freedom. Everyone of importance to your position knows exactly who you are. That also must have its advantages, but then our systems are different. We, alas, are an empire very much in decline. And our emperor is less checked by any parliament than your queen is – perhaps I should say empress, since she is Empress of India, I believe.'

'For what purpose might Tregarron be turned to both our advantages?' Pitt asked. He had no idea whether Duke Alois knew anything about Blantyre or not, but he had no intention of telling him.

Alois gave a slight shrug. 'I am head of my country's "Special Branch", as you are of yours. I do what I think is best in our interest. It is not always exactly what my government would do. But then I have knowledge that they do not, and perhaps I can see a little further ahead. I am sure you will find yourself occasionally in the same position. It would be to my advantage if Tregarron's information came to me.'

'Doesn't it anyway?' Pitt asked drily.

'Unfortunately not. It is dictated by Mr Blantyre, the one who is aware of his late father's treason, and his adultery with Mrs Montserrat, which was the cause of it in the first place. The present Lord Tregarron is particularly concerned that his mother, who is still very much alive, should not learn of it.'

'I think she was probably perfectly aware of it at the time,' Pitt observed.

'Of the affair, probably,' Alois conceded. 'The treason is an entirely different matter. How did you know of it, by the way?'

'I deduced it,' Pitt replied.

Duke Alois waited, his clear blue eyes steady, searching Pitt's face.

'It was the only answer that fitted certain other information,' Pitt told him. Then he smiled back to indicate that that was all he was going to say on the subject.

'I see. A pity. But I had no opportunity to tell you sooner. It is not something I would like known any more widely. It would destroy its possible usefulness.' Alois made a slight gesture of regret, but he did not evade Pitt's gaze, leaving the question open.

Pitt wanted to weigh every possibility, to discuss it with Narraway, and knew that was impossible. He tried to think of any comparable arrangement in the past, and could remember none. If it had ever happened it was not recorded. But then if he accepted Duke Alois's offer now, he would make no written record of it, at least not for general Special Branch availability. He must decide within the next few minutes. Was he giving Alois a weapon to use against him? Making an agreement perhaps useful to both of them? Earning a favour that might be reclaimed at some future and inconvenient time? Were favours repaid?

Duke Alois was waiting.

It was up to Pitt what false information to feed Tregarron. Was he foolhardy to accept? Or cowardly not to?

'We can begin,' he said. 'Tregarron is a man in an extremely awkward position, but he is not a fool.'

Duke Alois smiled with wry regret, and perhaps a touch of pity. 'Yes, he is. But I know in what sense you mean, and of course you are right. Excellent. We shall both prosper from it, if we are careful.'

Pitt was far less certain, but he did not want Alois to know that; it would make him appear indecisive. He tried to keep the doubt from his face. 'And how will you know if the information I give him is true or false?' he asked.

'A gentleman's agreement,' Duke Alois said wryly, meeting Pitt's eyes.

'You are a gentleman,' Pitt responded. 'I'm not.'

'You are a gamekeeper's son,' Alois said, still lightly, still leaning back in the carriage seat. 'Which means you have a good servant's sense of honour. I am a prince, which means I have very little sense of honour at all, only such as I choose.'

Pitt was startled that Alois knew so much about him, then realised that he should have expected it. He also appreciated that Alois's comments were at least half ironic.

'I imagine that after the affair at Buckingham Palace you are little inclined to trust princes,' Alois went on. 'Whereas I am much inclined to trust a good gamekeeper. A man who nurtures the earth and the creatures on it may lie to other men, but he knows his job. Nature forgives no mistakes.'

'Nor does Special Branch, yours or mine,' Pitt told him.

'Precisely. One might say the same of the tides of history.' Alois was very serious now. There was no amusement in his eyes, only an intense emotion. Pitt could not look away from him. 'Social change is coming in all Europe, whether the House of Habsburg wants it or not,' Alois went on. 'If we release our grip voluntarily it may come without bloodshed. If we try to prevent change by oppression then the end will be bloody, and the hate will remain. Maybe Britain will find the same one day, in half a century's time.'

'Emperor Franz Josef does not agree with you,' Pitt said grimly.

'I know.' A flash of bitter humour crossed Alois's face again, and impatience for stupidity. 'There is little I can do. But what I can, I will, which is why I would find it very useful to be more aware of Tregarron's information, and perhaps have a little . . .' he hesitated, '. . . more managed details going in both directions.'

Pitt understood very well, even if he was possibly not as certain of Alois's motives as he would like. But there was no question in his mind any longer that he should accept the offer. The risk in refusing was greater that that of agreeing.

'Yes,' he said with a very slight relaxing of his expression, an easing of the tight muscles in his shoulders. 'We might think of a few ideas that would be profitable to one or the other of us, some even to both.'

Duke Alois held out his hand. Without hesitation Pitt leaned forward and took it. Then he excused himself and went to check with Stoker.

Fifteen minutes later, he was outside the compartment, standing at the window watching the wooded countryside slip by, very slightly blurred by the spatters of rain on the glass. Suddenly the train slowed abruptly, as if the driver had jammed on the brakes.

Pitt stiffened, then turned and sprinted back the dozen yards to Duke Alois's compartment. 'Stoker!' he shouted above the screech of the wheels on the iron track.

The connecting door to the next carriage flew open and Stoker was there, immediately followed by one of the duke's men.

The compartment door opened and Alois looked out. 'What is it?' he asked, his voice steady but his face tight and pale.

'Farm cart on the rails,' Stoker answered. 'Looks like its load of hay fell off and it got stuck.' He looked from Pitt to Duke Alois. 'Sir. It's probably nothing, but—'

'Get back in and keep your head down!' Pitt finished for him. He made it sharp, an order.

'Farm cart?' Duke Alois questioned.

Stoker took a step towards him. 'Maybe just an accident, sir, but maybe not.' He stopped so close to Alois it was almost as if he had touched him to push him back inside the compartment.

The duke glanced at Pitt.

The train jerked to a halt.

One of Duke Alois's men, tall, thin, dark-haired, like the duke himself, came down the corridor.

'What the devil is—' he began.

A shot smashed the glass of the window. The man staggered backwards and fell against the compartment wall, then slumped to the floor, a slow, red stain spreading across his chest.

Stoker lunged towards Duke Alois and forced him down onto the floor. One of the other men kneeled beside the fallen man, but Pitt knew without bothering to look again that he was beyond help. He turned and ran along the corridor towards the end of the carriage and the connection with the rest. Throwing open the door on the opposite side, he leaped down onto the track, his hand already on his gun. If he had gone onto the same side as the marksman he would have been a perfect target, even an expected one. This gave him the cover of the train, but it also meant he had the length of at least one carriage before he could get anywhere near the man.

Would the assassin want to take another shot? Or was he certain he had hit Duke Alois, and so would make his escape immediately? There was no time now for Pitt to curse himself for not having foreseen such an attempt, but he knew he would later. Who was it? Tregarron? Or one of the Austrian factions he had believed in from the beginning? If it was

Tregarron then he would be alone. But if it were a socialist assassination attempt simply to draw attention, or any of the other minor nations rebelling against Habsburg rule by shooting a member of the ruling family, then there could be half a dozen. Was Stoker staying to guard Duke Alois? He hoped so. He was still a prime target. But Pitt hoped profoundly that he was not also out here, creeping along in the temporary shelter of the carriages.

He reached the end connection, and dropped to his hands and knees. He peered beneath and saw nothing but a narrow strip of wooded verge on the other side. Was the marksman waiting just out of sight, ready to pick off anyone who appeared? There had been no second shot. Would he wait to see what happened, or make his escape, certain that someone would come after him?

He probably knew he had hit someone, but he could not be certain it was Duke Alois. Who? He would surely know that someone either British or Austrian, or both, would come after him. Would the marksman retreat a little to a point from which he would see the train, but not easily be seen himself? Whoever he was, he had chosen a farm cart to stop the train, and a wooded area from which to attack. Perhaps he was a countryman, not one who had lived all his life in a city. He was an excellent shot, possibly a hunter.

Pitt had grown up in the country as well. He had followed Sir Arthur Desmond on pheasant shoots, even deer hunts once or twice. He knew how to stalk, to keep low, to stay downwind, to move silently. He had only a handgun to the other man's rifle, which perhaps even had a telescopic sight on it, judging from the shot that had killed Duke Alois's man. Pitt must take very great care, but not be too cautious to succeed.

He went the length of the next carriage as well, then dropped to his hands and knees again and peered under. No one in sight. He scrambled through the gaps quickly and stayed low, rolling down the embankment into the underbrush and then up onto his feet again as soon as he was within the copse of trees.

Which way would the man go after making the shot? Probably to the high ground where he would have a chance of still seeing the train, and also of seeing anyone who might come after him. A slight hollow would hide him better, but also place him at a disadvantage to see, or to climb out of it, putting any adversary above him. It was instinctive.

But how long would he watch the train to make sure he had killed the right man?

Pitt wished he had told Stoker to make it appear they were flustered, and in some way indicate that it was Alois who was dead. It was too late now. Perhaps he would think of it anyway.

Pitt moved forward through the thickest part of the trees. The ground was damp. He was leaving footprints. That meant the other man would be also. If Pitt could cross his track he could follow him. But he would know that as well. Would he stay on the high ground then?

Pitt moved as quickly as he could towards where he judged the shot had come from, trying to move silently, looking down where he trod to avoid snapping further sticks or getting tangled in the long, winding branches of bramble. Every now and then he glanced up, but all he could see was underbrush, tree trunks with glistening wet bark, a lot of it birch, hazel, black poplar, and here and there a few alder.

He looked backwards once. The train was out of sight, except for the engine, which was stopped a few yards short of the huge hay wagon still splayed across the track, its load now largely moved onto the embankment. From the way the whole thing listed, one of the wheels had broken, or come off. But if it were off, somebody would have found a way to put it back on again. There were half a dozen men working to clear the track. When they did, surely they would go, whether Pitt had returned or not? Stoker would see to that? Or the duke?

Pitt stopped and stood still. He strained to hear movement anywhere ahead of him. How long would the marksman wait? Surely he would take it for granted that someone would come after him? Even if he had not seen Pitt through his scope, he would assume his presence? Why had he not shot at him, at least on the embankment? Had he been concentrating on what was going on inside the train?

Pitt could hear nothing except the steady drip of water off the branches onto the wet leaves, which by this point in March almost mouldered down into the earth.

Was there any water here? Yes, a stream along the lower ground. That would be the place to hide tracks. What would a clever man do? Go to the stream leaving footprints easy enough to follow, then walk along the bed of the stream, leaving no trace at all, and then step wherever he would leave least mark. Perhaps he would even create a false trail, and go back into the water again upstream or downstream from his entry, or possibly even on the same side as he went in.

How did he get here? How would he leave? Not by train, perhaps not by road – at least for the nearest few miles. Horseback. It was the obvious way, perhaps the only one in this part of the countryside. Faster and easier than walking all the way himself.

Then where was his horse? He would have left it tied somewhere. The last thing he needed was to come back and find it wandered off, so he would have to start looking for it. If Pitt could find the horse, then the man would come to him. Where was the main road from London?

He turned and started to make for the high ground himself. Perhaps it would even be a good idea to climb a sturdy tree and see if he could see it? The horse would be at some point close to the road. He increased his pace, even at the risk of breaking a stick here and there, or startling a bird.

At the top of the next rise he selected a strong, well-grown alder. Putting his revolver in his pocket, he began to climb. It was awkward. It must have been at least twenty years since he last climbed a tree.

It took a few moments to reach a satisfactory height where he could see at least a couple of miles in all directions. As he twisted his body the trunk swayed. Better not to risk going any higher. If it broke, it would not only send him crashing down, possibly injuring himself, it would also make a considerable noise and tell the marksman exactly where he was.

Holding the trunk hard with his left arm, he looked around as widely as he could, searching for the road in the distance. It was not hard to see. After a moment or two he could trace it from south to north, swinging away to the west eventually. Surely the marksman would have left his horse at the nearest point to it. Once he reached the road again, he would have escaped any pursuit. No one on the train had a horse, or any way of communicating with the outside world in order to call for help.

Pitt climbed down carefully and set off as rapidly as he could, without making noise, in the direction of the road. If he was wrong, he would lose his quarry completely, but he had no way of knowing where the marksman was anyhow. To follow his tracks on the ground would be far too slow, and they were too easily disguised.

Every now and then he stopped to listen, but he heard nothing more than bird calls, the whirr of wings now and then, and a couple of times a dog barking somewhere far in the distance.

He came out on the road a hundred yards or so ahead of where he judged to be the easiest way towards the railway. It was about a mile away from the train, perhaps a little more. He kept to the trees at the side. When he had made certain of his bearings, he went back into the wood again and started moving very carefully, looking for a clearing where someone could leave a horse unseen. He had to be quick. Once the marksman had made certain of his kill, and was back here and mounted, it would be impossible for Pitt to stop him, except by shooting him. Pitt was good with a gun; he had learned from his father. But a handgun is very different from a rifle or a shotgun. He knew his chances of hitting a man astride a fast-moving horse, probably riding straight at him, would be pretty poor. There would be no time even to make sure he had the right person. It could be some innocent rider at the wrong place at the wrong time.

And the marksman would know all this too.

Pitt moved as rapidly as he could, sprinting in the few open patches he passed. He was deeper into the wood now. He realised it, and swerved back towards the road. The marksman would not have left the horse where he had to walk it through trees; only far enough in to be hidden from passers-by.

He almost stumbled on it: a beautiful creature, moving quietly, cropping the grass in as wide a circle as its long tethering rope allowed it. It heard him at the same moment as he saw it. It raised its head and looked at him curiously.

Pitt drew breath to speak, then realised the man could be close, so he stepped silently back into the shadow of the trees. The horse lowered its head again.

Pitt had not long to wait. Less than four minutes later, he heard the faint crack of a twig. A man dressed in browns and greens stepped out of the shadows and walked towards the horse, which lifted its head again and blew through its nostrils, taking a step towards him.

The man had a rifle with telescopic sights fixed to it. But Pitt did not need the gun to identify him as the assassin. It was Lord Tregarron.

Pitt stepped forward, his revolver raised high, pointing at Tregarron.

'If you move any closer to the horse I will shoot you,' Pitt said very clearly. 'Not to kill, but enough to hurt very much indeed.'

Tregarron froze, surprise in his face more than fear.

Pitt moved further out of the shadow of the trees. Tregarron had killed a man. He would inevitably learn that he had not hit Duke Alois. Could he be charged with attempted assassination? There would have to be a trial. It would inevitably expose the duke's secret position.

Was the bargain Duke Alois had proposed still useful? It was a risk, but then it always had been.

Pitt came further forward again, angling closer to the horse so Tregarron could not get in between them and spoil his clean shot. The revolver was pointed at Tregarron's chest.

Tregarron smiled. Pitt knew its cruel twist was out of fear.

'Failed, didn't you?' he said with malice edging his voice. 'You let Duke Alois be killed. Not likely to remain in your position much longer, especially when the Austrians tell London who he really was. You didn't know, did you?'

'Alois?' Pitt raised his eyebrows. 'Is that who you were aiming at?' He saw a moment's doubt in Tregarron's eyes. 'I'd like to let you think you succeeded, but you'll know soon enough that you didn't.'

Tregarron blinked, not sure if he was being lied to or not, or even why.

'But you did kill someone,' Pitt went on. 'Poor chap was one of Alois's men. Resembled him, certainly.'

Tregarron was standing stiffly, the rifle still in his hands.

'Put it down,' Pitt told him.

'Or what? You'll shoot me? How would you explain that? I'm out for a ride in the country. Thought I'd shoot a few rabbits. You're a fool!'

'Good idea, shooting rabbits,' Pitt lifted the barrel of the revolver an inch higher. 'Might shoot a few myself.'

'Don't be so damn stupid!' Tregarron snapped. 'You're supposed to be on a train guarding the head of the Austrian Special Branch, not strolling through the woods shooting at small animals!'

'You're right,' Pitt agreed. 'I wasn't shooting at small animals, I was shooting at the man who killed one of Alois's companions. Didn't see his face. Never realised it was one of our own Foreign Office staff.'

A little of the colour drained from Tregarron's skin. 'You can't try me in court, even if you imagine you could find any proof. You'd create a scandal.' But his voice was hollow. 'It'll still look like an accident: tragic, but no one's fault.'

'Not even mine, for incompetence?' Pitt said sarcastically. 'Shouldn't I have foreseen that we would have one of our aristocratic ministers wandering around the woods shooting at rabbits – at head height? Roosting in the trees, were they?'

The blood surged up Tregarron's face and his grip tightened on his rifle till his knuckles were white.

'But as it happens,' Pitt went on, 'I don't wish to try you. I have a much better idea. You will pass me your rifle, then I will take your horse and ride to the nearest public transport back to London. You will walk to wherever you wish. I will say that I did not find the man who murdered our unfortunate Austrian visitor, and in return for that favour, at whatever time I wish in the future, you will pass on certain information which I will give you to your connections in the Austrian Government.'

Tregarron stared at him as if he could not believe what he had heard. Then, as he studied Pitt's face, it came to him with paralysing horror that he meant it exactly.

'And if I should hear – and I would hear – that you have passed it incorrectly, then you will be exposed as the traitor you are,' Pitt continued. 'And what I believe concerns you even more, your father's treason would become equally public. And of course the reason would come to light also. I refer to his regrettable affair with Serafina Montserrat.'

'You filthy bastard!' Tregarron spat. 'You—'

'Because I would rather use a traitor than shoot him in cold blood and create a scandal I could not control?' Pitt asked, the sarcasm back in his voice. 'It's a matter of opinion. Mine is that you have betrayed your country rather than allow your father's treason to be exposed, or your mother's possible embarrassment that he betrayed her also. This last she may well have known anyway, but that is a side issue now. You had better make your choice quickly. I am not going to wait.'

'And what is to force me to keep it?' Tregarron asked.

'Exposure,' Pitt replied succinctly. 'Pass me the rifle.'

Slowly, as if his limbs hurt him to move, Tregarron obeyed.

Pitt took the rifle, still keeping his revolver pointed at Tregarron. Then he moved very carefully to untie the horse and walk it beyond Tregarron's line of sight before he mounted it. Slinging the rifle over his shoulder, he urged the horse into a trot along the road.

At home at Keppel Street, Charlotte awaited Pitt with intense nervousness. She kept telling herself that there would be no attack in Dover, the train journey to London would pass

389

without incident. She would busy herself with some household task, then halfway through it stop off, pace around, then forget what she had been doing and start something else.

''Ave yer lost summink?' Minnie Maude asked anxiously.

Charlotte swung around. 'Oh, no, thank you. I'm just wondering if everything is all right. Which is quite stupid, because I can't help, even if it isn't.'

The telephone rang, and she was so startled she flinched and let out her breath in a gasp. Instead of allowing Minnie Maude to pick it up, she dashed into the hall and picked it off its rest herself.

'Yes? I mean, good afternoon?'

There was a pause while the exchange made the connection. Then: 'Charlotte . . .'

It was Pitt's voice and she was overwhelmed with relief. 'Where are you? Are you all right? When will you be home?' she demanded.

'I'm still in Kent. I am fine and I shall be late home,' he replied. 'Please go to the reception with Aunt Vespasia, or with Jack and Emily. I shall come when I can.'

'Why are you still in Kent?' she demanded. 'Are you sure you're all right? Is the Duke Alois all right? And Stoker?'

'We are perfectly fine. And you will like the duke when you meet him. And I'll explain later. Please, just go with Aunt Vespasia, or Emily. I am not hurt in the slightest, really.'

'Oh . . . thank heaven for that. Yes, I'll go with Emily and Jack.' Already she knew what she meant to do. It was the opportunity she needed. 'I'll see you there.' She replaced the receiver with a smile.

Then immediately she picked it up again and asked to be connected to Emily's number. She had only a few moments to wait before Emily herself was at the other end.

'Emily? It's me. Thomas has been held up and cannot

accompany me to the reception at Kensington Palace. May I come with you, please? I . . . I would like to.' She said it gently; it mattered very much.

There was a moment's silence, then Emily's voice came back over the wire, filled with relief.

'Of course. That would be excellent. It will be like it was years ago, going together . . .' She stopped, not sure how to finish.

'What are you going to wear?' Charlotte filled in the silence. 'I want to wear black and white. It's the only new really grand gown I have.'

Emily laughed. 'Oh, that's wonderful. I shall wear the palest possible green.'

'That was always your best colour,' Charlotte said sincerely.

'Then we shall take them by storm,' Emily agreed. 'We shall call for you at half-past seven.' She laughed; it was a light, happy sound. 'Goodbye.'

'Goodbye.' Charlotte replaced the receiver and went upstairs overwhelmed with relief, smiling all the way. 'Minnie Maude! I think perhaps it is time I prepared for the evening,' she called from the landing. Jemima's door opened up on the next floor; she would want to help too, offer advice and dream of the day when she too could attend such events.

Charlotte arrived at Kensington Palace with Emily and Jack. It was a trifle crushed inside their carriage. Both sisters looked superb. Emily's gown was huge in the crown of the sleeve, the Nile-green silk gleamed like sunlight on still water, and the huge skirts, when swept around, revealed a silver lining underneath. It was slender-waisted, and low at the neck. Diamonds shone at her neck and ears, and in a bracelet over her elbow-length white kid gloves. Her hair, with its natural curl, was a pale crown under her tiara.

Charlotte's choice was entirely different. For once – as she had told Emily – she could afford to have a new gown that was designed specifically for her. Indeed, with Pitt's present position, she could not afford to do less. It was a fine, sheer silk, black overdress with a gleaming white gown beneath. The effect was all light and shadow, and when she moved it had a most extraordinary grace. The ribbon of black satin around the waist accentuated the natural curves of her body, and she wore pearl and jet jewellery with crystals that also caught the light in momentary fire. She knew that as she followed Emily in she drew more eyes, and she held her head a little higher, feeling the warmth in her cheeks. She did not normally consider herself beautiful, but perhaps for this occasion she could make an exception.

The Queen herself was not attending. She came to very little these days, only those functions where her absence would have been a serious dereliction of her duty as monarch. The Prince and Princess of Wales were travelling abroad, so – fortunately for Pitt, considering the affair at Buckingham Palace – they were not here either. It was all a somewhat relaxed atmosphere with plenty of laughter amid the clink of glasses. Somewhere just out of sight a small orchestra was playing lush, lilting Viennese music so that one could not help but wish to dance.

Vespasia arrived, escorted by Victor Narraway. She was always beautiful, but it seemed on this occasion as if she had paid even more attention to her appearance than usual. She wore a gown of soft violet. Its skirt was not as large as many, and the narrowness of it was very flattering, especially to someone of her height and who walked as if she could have balanced a pile of books on her head without losing any of them. She too wore a tiara. It was not primarily of diamonds but a very slender thing, a mere suggestion of amethysts and pearls.

Watching her, Charlotte found herself smiling, and knew that Jack, who was beside her with Emily on his other arm, was wondering why.

They moved on, smiling, talking politely, making conversation about anything and nothing. She missed Pitt. It was odd to be here alone. In spite of the magnificence of the palace, with its great high-ceilinged rooms and its sweeping shallow marble staircases, there was a kind of vacuum. There was wit, glamour, ceremony – and emptiness. Charlotte thought of Adriana Blantyre, and for a moment she felt the tears prick her eyes. Would his love of Austria be enough to bring Evan Blantyre here, in spite of all that had happened? She scanned the room to see if she could find his familiar figure. He had a grace, a way of standing that would mark him out immediately. Twice she thought she saw him, but when she looked more closely it was someone else. She was not sure if she was disappointed or relieved.

She had been in the palace over half an hour when she was introduced to Duke Alois Habsburg. He was tall and a trifle thin, with dark hair and an agreeable, slightly absent-minded expression. But the moment his attention focused on her she saw the bright intelligence in his eyes.

'How do you do, Mrs Pitt?' he said with a smile.

'How do you do, Your Highness?' she replied with a very slight curtsey. She would not have wished him harm, but she wondered why Pitt had to risk his life to defend a man who played at academic pursuits for pleasure, and served no actively useful purpose.

Someone made a joke and Duke Alois laughed, but he did not move from standing almost in front of her. A young woman in pink was staring at them both, clearly waiting for Alois to notice her; at least that was clear to Charlotte. The duke appeared not to have realised it.

'I imagine your husband will arrive soon,' he said to Charlotte.

'Yes, sir,' she replied, forcing herself to smile back at him. 'He has been held up. I don't know why. I apologise.'

'Don't you?' Alois raised his eyebrows. His expression was agreeably interested. 'They stopped our train. Put a hay wagon across the track.' He said it as if he were commenting on something as trivial as the weather. She barely saw the shadow of grief in his eyes. 'Unfortunately they shot my friend Hans. Your husband went straight after the marksman, without hesitation. I am informed he caught him.'

Charlotte was stunned. Suddenly the hubbub of laughter and music drifting from the other room seemed pointless, a chatter of noise without meaning.

'I'm so sorry. How is your friend?' she said quietly.

'I am afraid he is dead,' he replied. Only his voice changed, not the bland look on his face. 'I think he may not have suffered. It was a perfect shot, through the heart.'

She could not think of anything to say. She felt foolish, inadequate to the sudden, complete loss.

'He looked like me,' he said. There was a catch in his voice that he could not hide. 'Your husband is a good man. I look forward to knowing him better. Perhaps you will come to Vienna one day? You would enjoy it. It is a beautiful city, full of music, ideas, history.'

She took a deep breath. 'I look forward to it. Thank you, sir.'

He smiled, then turned away to make polite and meaningless conversation with the young woman in pink.

At the further side of the room, Emily was standing beside Jack. They also finished a courteous discussion and drifted from one group to another.

'Where is Thomas?' Jack said very quietly to Emily. 'Why isn't he here?'

'I don't know,' Emily replied. 'But wherever he is, Charlotte isn't worried about him.'

'Are you sure?' he said anxiously. 'She wouldn't show it if she were.'

'Of course I'm sure,' Emily said with an elegant shrug of exasperation. 'She's my sister. I'd know if she were pretending.'

He looked at her with a raised eyebrow. 'You haven't read her very well over the last few weeks.'

She flushed. 'I know, and I'm sorry about it. I thought she was being very self-important.' She took a deep breath. 'So was I.' She did not add that she had been afraid that Jack was out of his depth with his promotion to Tregarron's assistant. That was something he might guess, but she would a great deal rather that he did not know it for certain. 'We understand each other better now,' she added. She knew he was still looking at her, so she flashed a quick, confident smile, and saw him relax. Now she wondered how worried he had been, and decided she would prefer not to know either. It would be a good thing for them both to have the chance to deny things, and for each to be able to pretend to believe the other.

She tucked her arm in his. 'Let's go and be polite to the Duchess of whatever it is. She's a fearful bore. It will take some concentration.'

'All you need to do is listen,' he replied. He placed his hand momentarily over hers in a quick, gentle gesture, then removed it again instantly and walked forward with her beside him.

'That's not enough,' she whispered, leaning closer. 'You have to smile, and nod in all the right places, and try not to fidget, or let your eyes wander to other people . . .'

*   *   *

Almost under the great chandelier Narraway was standing next to Vespasia. For a moment or two they were not engaged in conversation with anyone else.

'Where is Pitt?' he said quietly. 'Charlotte doesn't look worried, but he should be here with Duke Alois. I've seen Stoker, looking like a footman, but that isn't enough.'

She looked at him closely. 'You think something could happen here, in the palace?'

'It's unlikely,' he replied, almost under his breath. 'But it isn't impossible.'

She was alarmed. She turned to face him, studying his eyes, his mouth, trying to read whether it was fear or merely caution that moved him. His eyes were shadowed, nearly black, the lines around his mouth scored deep.

'An outrage, here?' she whispered.

He put his hand on hers, his fingers warm and strong. 'Oh, nothing so melodramatic, my dear. Far more likely to be a quick scuffle in the shadows of a corridor, and then a body behind the curtains to be found in the morning.'

She searched his eyes and saw no laughter at all, nothing beyond the wry, gentle irony that softened his words.

'I don't know where Thomas is,' she answered his first question. 'I think there may be something quite important that we are not yet aware of. Duke Alois looks as if he is mastering his emotions with some difficulty, and I have not seen Lord Tregarron. Have you?'

'No. Please don't . . . enquire for him . . .' He stopped, uncertain how to continue.

'I won't,' she promised. 'At least not yet.'

This time he did laugh, so quietly it was almost soundless. 'Of course you will,' he said ruefully. 'But please be careful. I have an awful feeling that this threat is not over yet.'

'My dear Victor, our concern with threats will never be

over, I hope. And so do you. You would rather go out in a blaze of glory than die of boredom. As would I.'

'I am not ready to do so yet!' He took a deep breath. 'And I am not ready for you to either.'

She felt a distinct warmth of pleasure. 'Then I shall endeavour to see that my next blaze of glory is not an exit line.' She said it with a lightness that all but choked in her throat. She was also very much not ready to end yet.

Pitt arrived at Kensington Palace just under two hours after the reception had begun. He had been home to Keppel Street and washed, shaved and changed into his evening suit. Leaving Tregarron's rifle locked in the wardrobe, he had then eaten a cold beef sandwich and drunk a cup of tea. Then, with his revolver in his pocket, which felt lumpy and conspicuous, he had caught a hansom cab, paying extra to the driver to take him with the greatest speed possible.

He remembered the jolt of the train stopping, and then the shot, the splintered glass, and the blood as Hans fell, and died within seconds. The devil's luck, or a brilliant shot? He thought the latter. Had Hans been chosen to accompany Duke Alois because he looked so much like him? Had he known that, and still been prepared to take that risk?

Had Pitt made the right decision in turning Tregarron rather than arresting him for the murder of Hans? He might never have proved it. Even if he had, what would have been the result? A major scandal, a foreign policy embarrassment of considerable proportions, possibly the loss of his own position, for political clumsiness, even stupidity.

Or alternatively, it would never have come to court anyway. That would have left an impossible situation.

Yet it galled Pitt that the man had attempted to murder Duke Alois, and instead murdered his friend, and he would walk away from it with neither injury nor blame. Had Pitt made the right decision to try to use him? Would refusal have been prudent, or cowardice?

He entered the glittering reception hall feeling absurdly out of place. And yet, he did not look outwardly different from the scores of men standing around talking to each other and to the gorgeously gowned women in their brilliant colours like blown flower petals, their jewels sparking fire in the light of the huge chandeliers pendent from elaborate ceilings.

His eyes searched the crowd for Charlotte. He saw Emily. He recognised her fair hair with its diamond tiara, and the pale, liquid shade of green that suited her so well. She looked happy.

He also saw Vespasia, but then she was usually easy to see in any crowd. She was beside Narraway and they were talking to each other, heads bent a little.

What could Charlotte be wearing? Blue, burgundy, some warmer colour that flattered the rich tones of her skin and hair. Lots of women were wearing such shades. All the skirts were enormous, the sleeves high and almost winged at the shoulder – it was the fashion.

He saw Duke Alois briefly, laughing at some joke or other and smiling at a duchess. He looked exactly the pleasant, absent-minded sort of academic he affected to be. The serious and idealistic man who was willing to risk his life, to carry a dangerous burden of secret office, the man who had seen his friend shot to death only this afternoon, seemed like something Pitt had dreamed, and now on waking, it had disappeared.

The duke had known about Tregarron's treason, and his father's before him, which had been the knife twisting inside the man that had forced him to sell his country as well. Would Pitt be able to use the threat of his own knowledge to force

Tregarron to continue, and the skill to trick him into giving false information to Vienna – or at least misleading?

No wonder Tregarron had tried to kill Duke Alois. What man would not want to rid himself of such mastery by another, such power to manipulate, or destroy? And it had been to protect his father's name, and his mother's feelings. Not a bad motive. Most people would understand it.

Pitt still could not see Charlotte; he gave up trying from this vantage. He went down the steps slowly and into the crowd. Hardly anyone knew him, so he had no need to stop and acknowledge people.

How had Alois known of Tregarron's vulnerability? That was something that could not have come from Serafina Montserrat. She had been active long before Duke Alois's time, and he had not been to London before.

Yet Pitt could not rid himself of the belief that it was Serafina's crumbling memory that had fired this whole complex series of manipulations. It was Serafina's memory of Lazar Dragovic's death that had driven Blantyre to kill her, and then to kill Adriana. Pitt still burned with anger and a kind of shame that Blantyre could taunt him so completely.

Blantyre also knew of Tregarron. He had said as much. Had Blantyre told Duke Alois of it?

That made no sense at all. Blantyre might have co-operated with Duke Alois, within limits, but he would never have given him, or anyone else, control of his own means of power, the secret knowledge that enabled him to manipulate Tregarron.

Then like sun rising on a hideous landscape, the whole picture became clear in his mind. Blantyre would want Duke Alois dead. As long as he was alive, it was he more than Blantyre who controlled Tregarron's knowledge. With Duke Alois dead, there was no one else but Pitt who knew the secrets, and Blantyre discounted Pitt's courage to act.

Perhaps he also believed that if Duke Alois were murdered under Pitt's protection in London, Pitt too might be disposed of. Surely it would not be too difficult a task. Pitt was now the Head of Special Branch, but he had not proved himself yet. He was still something of an experiment: a man risen from the ranks of the police rather than a gentleman from the military or diplomatic services. Kill Alois and blame Pitt's incompetence, and Blantyre would be the only man left with the power to manipulate Tregarron into telling Vienna whatever Blantyre wished, and learning whatever he wished in return. He needed both Duke Alois and Pitt dead for Tregarron to be of use to him.

It had to have been Blantyre who had sent Tregarron to kill Duke Alois today. It would have worked perfectly. Pitt would like to have seen Blantyre's face when the duke arrived this evening, very clearly alive and well!

Where was Blantyre? Was he here? He started to look more earnestly. He would have to find Charlotte later. He pushed through the gaps in the crowds, excusing himself, brushing past, turning from right to left, searching for Blantyre. He ought to be able to spot him. He was a little taller than average, he stood and moved with a unique kind of elegance, a trifle stiff. He carried his head in a characteristic way.

Pitt glanced over to where Duke Alois had been talking to a duchess, or whoever she was. She was still there, but it was a large, middle-aged man she was speaking with now.

Pitt turned round slowly, taking a deep breath and letting it out between his teeth. He could not see the duke. One of his men was standing over near the wall, but there was a slight frown on his face, and he too was looking from side to side. Clearly he had also lost him.

Pitt started to look for Emily. Her fair head and the pale

green of her gown might stand out. Yes, there she was, and Jack was still beside her.

'Excuse me,' Pitt said hastily, brushing his way past a woman in a mulberry-coloured silk gown. She glared at him, but he barely noticed. He walked right between two elderly gentlemen, excusing himself again. He must not lose sight of Jack.

'Here! I say!' a young man protested as Pitt bumped him. He in turn trod on a woman's skirt, which was a fraction too long for her.

'I'm sorry,' Pitt said over his shoulder, and kept going.

'Jack!' he called just as Jack appeared about to begin a conversation with a young man wearing lush side whiskers. 'Jack.'

Jack turned, startled. 'Thomas! What's wrong?'

'Excuse me,' Pitt said to the young man. 'Something of an emergency.' He took Jack's arm and pulled him to the side, several steps away from the nearest group. 'There was an incident on the train this afternoon. One of Duke Alois's men was shot – killed outright.'

Jack looked appalled. The blood drained from his face. His eyes swept down Pitt to reassure himself he was unhurt, then a flash of relief filled his eyes. 'I'm sorry. The duke himself is putting a hell of a good face on it. Or is he too stupid in his studies for physical reality to touch him? He does know, I presume?'

'Yes. And he's anything but out-of-touch, I promise you.'

'Do you know who it was?'

'Yes, but this is not the time to explain. The duke was here a few minutes ago, but I can't see him now. Blantyre was behind the shooting, and I can't see him either. I think he'll try to finish the job . . .'

'Here? For God's sake, Thomas, the place is full of women and—'

'Where better?' Pitt cut across him. 'No one will be

expecting it. Duke Alois and his men will think he's safe. I nearly did, until I realised exactly why Blantyre has to kill him. He can't afford to let him get back to Vienna.'

Jack gulped. 'What do you want me to do?'

'Find the duke, tell him you're my brother-in-law, and keep him in the middle of a crowd, any crowd.'

'What about you?'

'I'm going to find Blantyre.'

'And do what, for God's sake?'

'Arrest him, but if he forces me to, I'll shoot him.' As soon as he said it, Pitt was not certain if he would do it – if he could. He was not even certain if he could prove Blantyre had murdered Serafina.

Jack stood motionless for an instant, then he gave a very slight nod, and turned on his heel, disappearing into the crowd immediately.

Where would Blantyre have gone? One of two places. He could hide in the crowd, where he would be concealed among hundreds of other men dressed exactly the same. However, his face was known, so people would stop to speak to him, to express condolences. Anyone watching carefully would see him sooner or later. A few polite questions and someone would point him out.

The alternative would be to stay out of sight almost altogether, in the darker, narrower passages, any place where he would not be expected. Change his attitude, his grace of stance or movement, and – from the back at least – he would appear like anyone else, even a servant. The footmen were in livery, but there were always others: a butler, a valet, even a messenger of some sort.

And if he really meant to kill Duke Alois, he would have to do that when he had privacy. He would not intend to be caught.

Pitt went back up the stairs, taking them rapidly. They were too wide and shallow to take two at a time, unless he drew attention to himself by doing it at a run. At the top he stopped, looking for more private rooms, corridors, anterooms, galleries – anything away from the crowd. If he could find Stoker he would ask his help, but he had no time now to look for him. He too could be anywhere.

There was a door to his left. It was as good a place as any to begin. He had opened it and gone inside when he realised how much better it would be to get some order into his search. Blantyre need not be in wait for Duke Alois. He might wait for ever. He would stalk him, go where he knew the duke would be, sooner or later, and alone.

Where? The room where the orchestra was playing? A gallery beyond that? A corridor from one to the other? A lavatory – the one place where a man could spend a few minutes, and expect quite reasonably to be alone. Blantyre could close a door and be there indefinitely, unseen.

Pitt walked away from the room and towards one of the footmen standing at the bottom of the stairs.

'Excuse me,' he said calmly. 'Can you direct me to the gentlemen's lavatory, please? The most convenient, if there is more than one.'

'Just the one available to guests, sir,' the footman replied. 'If you go along there to your right.' He gestured discreetly, so no onlooker would have been aware of where he was pointing. 'It is the third door along that passage, sir.'

'Thank you,' Pitt accepted, and walked quickly in the direction the man had indicated. He came to the door, hesitated a moment, then turned the handle and went inside. It was beautifully appointed, as one might have foreseen, with half a dozen conveniences each with its own door. There was only one occupied. Was Blantyre in there, waiting until Duke Alois should come? Surely in the course of the evening it was certain that sooner or later he would?

Pitt stood silently with his back against the wall, his heart pounding. Seconds ticked by. There was no sound from the occupied cubicle. Perhaps Alois was already there, already dead? Or unconscious and dying while Pitt stood out here like a fool? Or maybe his whole guess was completely wrong!

There was a noise outside: footsteps, men's voices.

Pitt turned his back to the room and pretended to be drying his hands on a towel.

Behind him two men came in. He glanced around. Neither of them was Alois. He went to the basin and washed his hands again, slowly, as if he had something under a fingernail. After several minutes first one man left, and then the other. The door at the far end remained locked. There was no sound from within. Was it someone ill? Someone dead? If it was Blantyre waiting for Alois, why had he not even looked out to see who had come in? He had not looked at Pitt, nor at the second or third man to enter. Why not?

More minutes went by. Another man came in, and several moments later left again.

Was Pitt standing here incessantly pretending to wash his hands while outside, Blantyre was stalking Alois, and perhaps catching him? Was the duke's body already stabbed and bleeding to death behind some curtain?

He went to the outside door and, pulling it open abruptly, slipped out. He closed it, then waited. How had Alois walked? Uprightly, but not like a soldier. With grace, a sort of lanky elegance, as if nothing troubled him. He tried to picture it exactly. A slight swagger – a very slight limp, as if his left leg were just a little stiff.

He walked away a few steps, turned and walked back, trying to imitate Alois. He put his hand on the door and opened it, then went in walking casually, dragging his left foot so slightly he was not even certain it was enough. He swallowed, gulping air.

The last door opened and he was looking at Evan Blantyre, a long, curve-bladed knife in his hand. For a silent, burning second they stared at each other. Pitt could see Blantyre's eyes as if there were nothing else in the room. His fingers closed around the revolver in his pocket and he lifted it out slowly.

Blantyre smiled. 'You haven't the courage,' he said slowly.

Pitt did not take his eyes from Blantyre's. 'You killed Serafina, and Adriana . . .'

'And Lazar Dragovic,' Blantyre added. 'He was a traitor to Austria. But you can't prove any of it.'

'Austria is not my territory,' Pitt told him. 'London is.'

'Austria is the heart of Europe, you provincial fool!' Blantyre said between his teeth. 'Get out of my way.'

'And London is the heart of England,' Pitt replied. 'Which is irrelevant, except that it is my responsibility. You blackmailed Tregarron into trying to kill Duke Alois, and only killed his friend instead. But one dead man is as important as another.'

'You can't prove that either, without exposing Tregarron, and his father, and the whole sordid treason of both of them. And Duke Alois as well, of course,' Blantyre agreed. 'So there isn't a damn thing you can do. Now get out of my way, and don't oblige me to hurt you.'

Pitt stood still, his heart beating so violently he felt certain he must be shaking, even swaying where he was. His hand ached, gripping the revolver.

Blantyre moved the knife a little so the light caught on its blade.

'What are you going to do, stab Alois?' Pitt asked, his voice rough-edged.

Blantyre paled a little.

'Because you can't afford to leave him alive,' Pitt went on. 'As long as he pulls the strings on Tregarron, and you don't.'

There was a flash of understanding in Blantyre's eyes, perhaps of the knowledge that he couldn't afford to leave Pitt in office either. For an instant he moved the knife a fraction, then let it fall again.

'You can't arrest me, you'd only make a fool of yourself. And you haven't the nerve,' he said very softly. 'I'm walking out of here and I'll find Duke Alois another time. Perhaps I'll follow him back to Vienna. No reason why I shouldn't. You're out of your depth, Pitt. Pity, because I liked you.' He gave a slight shrug and took a step forward.

Everything that Blantyre said was true.

Pitt raised the revolver, his fingers tightened on the trigger. 'God forgive me,' he said to himself, and fired.

The sound was deafening.

For an instant Blantyre's eyes were wide with amazement, then he staggered backwards against the cubicle door and it crashed open behind him. He fell backwards, his chest soaked in red, arterial blood. He slithered to the floor, and lay still.

Pitt forced himself to walk over to the cubicle and look down. Blantyre's eyes were still open, and sightless. Pitt felt a physical pain of regret. There seemed to be a chasm of silence before he heard shouts and footsteps along the corridor. He put the revolver back in his pocket and took out his identification. He had it in his hand when two men in dinner suits flung the door open and stopped abruptly. Narraway was immediately behind them, and Jack Radley on his heels.

'God Almighty!' the first man exclaimed, his face ashen, staring first at Pitt, then past him to the open door, and Blantyre covered in blood on the tiled marble floor.

Narraway pushed past him, then stopped.

Pitt started to speak, cleared his throat, and started again.

'I am Thomas Pitt, Head of Special Branch. I regret to say there has been an unpleasant incident, but there is no danger now. You might be civil enough to inform Duke Alois Habsburg that the immediate danger to his life is over.'

The first man gaped, then turned very slowly to Narraway.

Narraway looked at him, his eyebrows slightly raised.

'Quite right, Ponsonby,' he said. 'He is precisely who he says he is, and the facts are as he states. Be a good chap and get everyone out of here while we have someone clear this up, will you?'

When they were gone, too numb with shock to argue, Narraway closed the door.

'Well done, Pitt,' he said quietly. 'It'll hurt like hell. You'll dream about it as long as you live, but that's the price of leadership, making the grey decisions. Black and white ones are easy; any fool can deal with those. You'll have to live with it, but you would have had to live with the failure to make it as well, and every grief that followed because of that.' He smiled very slightly. 'I always knew you'd do it.'

'No, you didn't,' Pitt replied, his voice hoarse.

Narraway shrugged. 'I believed it more than you did. That's good enough.' Then he smiled and held out his hand.

Pitt took it, and held it, hard.

'Thank you.' Simple words, but he had never meant them more.

Anne Perry is a *New York Times* bestselling author noted for her memorable characters, historical accuracy and exploration of social and ethical issues. Her two series, one featuring Inspector Thomas Pitt and one featuring Inspector William Monk, have been published in multiple languages. Anne Perry was selected by *The Times* as one of the twentieth century's '100 Masters of Crime' and now lives in Scotland.

Praise for Anne Perry:

'Brilliant . . . that rare breed of novel that's a page-turning thriller yet literary'
Jeffery Deaver

'A beauty: brilliantly presented, ingeniously developed and packed with political implications that reverberate on every level of British society . . . delivers Perry's most harrowing insights into the secret lives of the elegant Victorians who have long enchanted and repelled her'
New York Times Book Review

'The novel has a totally contemporary feel and is admirably well-written'
Guardian

'Her Victorian England pulsates with life and is peopled with wonderfully memorable characters'
Faye Kellerman

'Anne Perry, mistress of the Victorian murder mystery, has taken over where Dickens left off . . . A murder mystery made to make you think'
Lancashire Evening Post

'Perry stirs your conscience as well as your soul'
Northern Echo

'Perry's characters are richly drawn and the plot satisfyingly serpentine'
Booklist

'A complex plot supported by superb storytelling'
Scotland on Sunday

'A surpassingly excellent historical and psychologically intricate mystery'
Publishers Weekly